LIFE BEGAN WITH:
MOMENTS BETWEEN

RA'JEAN KING

Inquiries and Book Orders should be addressed to:

Great Writers Media
Email: info@greatwritersmedia.com
Phone: 877-600-5469

ISBN: 978-1-960939-86-9 (sc)
ISBN: 978-1-960939-87-6 (ebk)

CHAPTER 1

A beautiful morning, everything green and fresh with flowers blooming and a crisp feel in the air. The horses were enjoying the fresh green grass of Spring for their breakfast and the blackbirds were singing happy tunes as they perched in the Oak trees. The chickens had been released from their coup and were playfully running around the barnyard. Baylee, the ranch's rescued dog, was playing tag with the young hens. Ralynn, wrapped in a soft, green shawl, sat in the wooden rocker on the front porch, cup of coffee in hand, thinking about what she planned for the day. The chickens squawked, catching her attention. "Baylee! Come here! You, leave the girls alone, now." Baylee came and lay down by her feet. "A good day for working the garden, don't you think?" She glanced toward her shadow lying by your feet, as if expecting an answer. Baylee looked up then laid his head back down and closed his eyes. Ralynn recalled the day Baylee showed up at the ranch, such a little thing, covered in mud, that had dried on his coat. He was sitting on the steps, at the back door, looking so afraid, hungry, and out of sorts. There were no neighbors within 10 miles, it was no telling where he came from. She took him inside, fed him, gave him a bath, discovering he was a beautiful Golden Retriever, with a shiny coat of gold. She found an old blanket, laid it in front of the fireplace, placed him on it to get warm, and he slept. That was 6 months ago, no one ever came for him. So, she claimed him as hers and Baylee did the same, rarely leaving her side. She reached down, patted his head, then stood and headed inside, Baylee followed.

Martha, the family's cook and housekeeper was at the cook stove preparing breakfast and glanced in her direction. "Nice outside, isn't it?" "Yes, just right for working the garden before it's too hot." "Where did you stop yesterday?" Martha looked up, "You might check the tomatoes again and pick the beans today. I'll be doing laundry if you need me." "Oh, I think I can manage, I'll put Matt to work, he needs to do something to stay out of trouble," they both laughed. "Breakfast is ready, go wake up your brother, he sleeps too much as it is," Martha stated. Ralynn laughed as she headed for the stairs. She was in no hurry to have to wake her little brother, he could be a bear, at times. She walked past the double oak doors, gathered and raised her skirt and slowly went up the stairs. She knew Martha wanted her to hurry, but she just couldn't make herself rush to fight with her brother. She recalled the story her mother had told her about how Martha came to be with them.

Martha had been with the family since before the Parker's children were born. The Parker's had taken her in and given her a job as a cook and housekeeper at her tender age of twenty, when her father had sent her West as a mail-order bride. Ralynn's mother had told her the story several times in her nineteen years. Martha came from a family that worked hard to survive day to day. Her mother was a seamstress that took in mending and laundry for those who were well off. She had not been able to sew the new gowns that was trending, since her arthritis took over her hands, so she did the best she could. Her father worked in the coal mine and brought home what money he could. They weren't starving, but life was hard. Her father and mother had a loving relationship between them and with their daughter. They were a happy family. Then, one day her mother came down sick and the doctor said there was nothing he could do for her. Her father struggled to keep his job and to be there for his wife. He could hardly stand to watch her suffer. Then, one morning, she drew her last breath, and he became devastated and withdrew from everyone, even his own daughter. Martha tried to please her father, but he kept pushing her away. He never talked to her or acknowledged she was around. On the days he did make it to work, he'd come home and go straight to his room with a bottle of cheap whiskey. If he did make it to the kitchen for a meal, he usually criticized the food and threw it at her or the wall.

He would send her to her room or just flat out told her to disappear and go away. He said he could never love another person, except his wife, and she was nothing to him, he wished she were dead. A few weeks after her mother had passed from a heart attack, her father wanted her gone for good. He told her she looked too much like her Ma and he couldn't look at her, couldn't stand the sight of her, so, he had sold her to a rancher, a Mr. Houser, from Archer, Wyoming, as a mail-order bride, and that she was to pack her belongings and be on the train first thing the next morning. Not caring what this man was like, he sent his daughter away. When she arrived in Archer, Wyoming, no one was there to meet her. She sat on a bench and waited, after an hour, still nothing. She walked over to the ticket window and asked the clerk if he knew Mr. Abel Houser. The clerk looked up at her with a concerned look on his face. For a moment she wasn't sure he would answer, then he said, "Are you family lady? "She answered "Not yet, I was to marry him today, but he hasn't shown up." "Lady, you haven't heard, Mr. Houser was killed in an Indian raid last week." "I thought all Indians were on reservations now," she said, shocked to hear the news. "Is that what they are reporting back East these days? Well, it's not true. There are a few tribes left that are peaceful that are not on reservations, but these were renegades, and they are raiding all over the place taking livestock and anything else they want. The Sheriff buried him on his ranch, so you should talk to him. He can probably help you." Martha, still in shock, asked for directions to the Sheriff's office, picked up her bag and left. In search of the Sheriff's office, she pulled her cloak tighter and began her walk into town.

John Parker, a big stocky man, was sitting with a cup of coffee in his hands, chatting with the Sheriff about the Indian raids and more cattle missing. "It's not the Indians that are solely responsible for the missing cattle, Tobe. From what I can tell they're rustlers, meaning white men involved," John said. "How can you tell, John?" the sheriff said looking puzzled. "Well, a couple hands of mine and I found a campsite in the area where my cattle disappeared. It wasn't made by Indians. Most Indians make their camps in neat and precise ways, whereas white men are careless and leave their trash around. That's what we found." "Geez! Not what I wanted to hear." the sheriff said, shaking his head. "Now, we have to start over, looking for white men. Is this day going to get any better?" he said, speaking more to himself. "More coffee?" he asked John and turned to refill their cups.

Martha had been walking about five minutes when she saw the sheriff sign above the door of an old, but sturdy building. She realized on her walk, she would need to buy warmer clothing, it was quite cold here, but she had no money. All she had with her was a couple of cotton dresses for daily wear, the woolen dress she had on, and her sleeping gown. She only had her shawl that she wore and needed warmer clothing, a coat, and some boots for this weather. Her father had kept all the money the rancher had sent, telling her the rancher would provide all she needed. Well, the rancher was dead, she was unmarried with no answers and no place to go. Maybe the Sheriff can help her. She crossed the street, straightened her clothes and knocked on the door. The sheriff opened the door surprised to find a woman standing on the other side. "Hello Miss, may I help you?" Martha sweetly smiled. "I hope so Sir, I'm in a slight predicament at the moment."

"Come on in and take a seat please, tell me how I can help. Would you like some coffee? You look almost frozen." She nodded her head, yes, and pulled her cloak tight. She wasn't sure where to start or how when the sheriff sat a mug of coffee in front of her and introduced himself. " I'm Tobe Mason, the town's Sheriff, and this is John Parker, he owns one of the largest ranges around here. Martha glanced towards John and said, "Hello Sir." John nodded. He looked at Tobe, "I'll be going Sheriff, remember what I said." Martha stood up. "Please stay Sir, I really need all the help I can get," her voice quivering. She sat back down wringing her hands together. The room was quiet, so John decided to start the conversation, "How may we be of assistance? I'm sorry I didn't catch your name." She blinked her eyes as if needing to focus. "I apologize, my name is Martha Simms. I came here on the train to marry a Mr. Abel Houser, only to find out from the ticket clerk that he was killed last week. I have no money, no place to stay, and I was wondering if Mr. Houser had mentioned me. My father sold me to him and kept the money, sending me here with nothing but a few clothes, which are not warm enough for this weather. I'm not sure what else to say or what I should do." Martha took a deep breath and sat there waiting for some kind of advice. Sheriff Mason looked at John making eye contact, neither knowing what to say. "Well, we need to find you a place to stay for the night. We will pay a visit to George's office tomorrow to see if Abel left any will or provisions for you. Let's get you settled over at the hotel, where you can freshen up and rest. They have a dining room so you can get something to eat as well." "I can't pay for that," she burst into tears. "Don't worry about that, the town will pay for it out of their emergency fund. Let's get you registered, and we will work on the rest tomorrow." He led her out the door and across the street to the hotel. a sign above the doorway read, JENNY'S PLACE. They entered the lobby heading towards a desk in the left corner of the room. A handsome woman, close to thirty years old, Martha guessed, looked up and smiled. She had dark hair that shined when the light hit it, was trim in the waist, and about 5'7" or so. Her blue eyes sparkled as she asked if she could help them. The Sheriff introduced Martha to Jenny Pram and explained her situation. Jenny smiled and said "No problem, I have just the room. "She took Martha by the arm and led her away.

CHAPTER 2

Tobe entered his office, surprised that John was still there. "Oh, glad you stayed. Not sure what to do about that situation," he said. "Well, that's why I stayed, thought you may need help with it. Coffee's fresh, want some? "The Sheriff nodded, and John poured himself and the Sheriff a cup each. They sat at the wooden table, both deep in thought. Silence.

The sheriff stood and went over to the stove, he stoked it and added more logs. John looked around, as if, noticing the decor for the first time. The room showed no personalization. It was one big room with a few rifles and shotguns hanging on the wall by the desk to the right as you enter from the front door. The table sat in the center, the wood stove was to the right in the corner, and a cot set against the back wall next to the back door. There was a door to the right of the desk that opened to the two jail cells. John snapped back to the present when Tobe sat back down. "Any ideas?" he asked John. "I guess you had the best idea about talking to the attorney. If Able had a Will, he may know about it or any record of paying for a bride. I don't think he had any children; I do know, his first wife died in childbirth years ago. He worked his ranch along with his few hands. It was doing good when I spoke to Able a few weeks back. He did mention that things were going to change some but didn't go into detail. Maybe this Miss. Simms was what he was talking about. I don't know." "You'll know more tomorrow hopefully," John said, rising from his chair. "I'm heading to the house. Susan may start wondering where I am." he collected his hat placing it on his head and walked out the door. The sheriff sat there, sipping on his coffee, thinking about how he and John had met, all those years ago. They had been rodeo bums, going from one rodeo to another, kicking up dust and trouble as much as they could. They each had won their share of buckles and prize money, but John had been the smart one and saved his to build his ranch, whereas, he had spent his on pretty ladies and whiskey. He, once, thought he'd buy his own ranch, but he never did. He took the sheriff's job here in Archer and had been here for the past ten years. He and John reconnected and have been best friends ever since. John was a broad-shouldered man with a trim waist at around six foot, three inches tall and dressed like the gentleman he was. It's no wonder that when he met Susan at their last rodeo together that she fell for him as much as he did for her. They married six years later and are as much in love all those years ago as they are now. At times, he felt a bit jealous, because he saw Susan first, but seeing how happy they are, he knows he has no right to be. He shook his head to clear his thoughts, got up, poured himself another cup of coffee, and sat down at his desk to look at the new Wanted posters that had come in the mail.

Martha woke refreshed the next morning, but it took a while for her to remember where she was. She recalled the sheriff walking her to the hotel, meeting Jenny, and taking a nice hot bath after dinner. She climbed in bed and slept. Remembering everything now, she recalled the sheriff mentioning a meeting with a Mr. George or someone about Mr. Houser's estate. She threw off the blankets and grabbed her robe to make her way to the privy.

John had come in late, and Susan had already retired. He went to bed deciding he would talk to her in the morning. He awoke to the smell of coffee and bacon and in no time his mouth was watering, and his stomach growled. He quickly dressed and made his way to the kitchen.

Stepping quietly, he approached his wife, reaching from behind, he placed his hands on his wife's waist and bent down placing slight kisses along her neck and jawline. "Stop that!" she said laughing. "I'll burn you bacon." "Can't have that," he said as he released her. He poured himself a cup of coffee and sat down at the table. He smiled to himself as he watched his wife. Married only two years, she was beautiful as ever. Her dark hair pulled up in a messy bun, her cheeks were rose-colored, her green eyes were the color of spring grass, and her waist was slightly round. He recalled the day she sprang the news on him, that she hoped her garden did well, due to more mouths to feed. He didn't get it right away, but when he did, he gave a yell that most of the town could probably hear. "John, John!" His wife was trying to get his attention. He jumped realizing he'd been off in his own world again. "What?" "Your breakfast is getting cold," she replied. "Oh!" Susan sat down picking up her fork, "What happened last night? I finally gave up on you." He had just taken a bite and finished chewing before taking a sip of coffee. He told her of the young girl that came into the Sheriff's office and of her situation. He took another bite and sat there watching her, his mind racing with new thoughts. "What are you thinking about? I know that look." "I was just thinking you could use some help around here." He said thoughtfully. "What do you mean I'm doing okay?" "Well, before long you won't be able to do things you're doing now, so I was thinking about that young girl with no place to go. What if, I hired her to help you out, then after the baby's born you can decide if you want her to stay. At least, she'll be able to save some money and plan ahead. It's more than she has now." Susan smiled, "I'd love to have the company. Yes, go into town and see what has transpired. Then, decide whether to ask her." John stood and bent down to kiss his wife. "I'll go after lunch, that will give them time to speak to that attorney." He grabbed his old worn Stetson and out the door he went.

Martha dressed and brushed her hair pulling it up into a ponytail. She pinched her cheeks to add a little color to her face and examined herself in the mirror. She considered herself pretty with big brown eyes, a perky nose and pouty full lips. She wore a white blouse with a green skirt that emphasized her trim and slender waist. Acknowledging, she had done her best with what she had, she decided it was time to head to the Sheriff's office and get this over with. A few minutes later, she was standing outside the Sheriff's office, hand raised when the door opened. "Oh, Miss Simms, I was on my way to the hotel. Are you ready to go see the attorney?" "Yes, Sheriff Mason,

I don't want to take up your time, but I need to figure out what I'm going to do." Sheriff Mason placed his hand on her elbow and led her across the street. They passed the hotel, a general store, and a harness shop before reaching the attorney's office. The sign above the door read: George Murphy, Attorney at Law. Sheriff Mason opened the door and motioned for her to go in first and he followed.

CHAPTER 3

Martha stepped inside a small room where four chairs were sitting against the wall. Across the room sat a desk and chair close to another door. She and Sheriff Mason took a seat and waited. Shortly the door by the desk opened and a lady, with brown hair, piled on top of her head, rosy cheeks and ruby red lips, dressed in a light blue blouse and dark blue skirt, entered the room, seeing them she asked if she could help them. The Sheriff's introduced Martha and himself and explained the reason they were there. "Well, Sheriff, Mr. Murphy is with a client, but it shouldn't be much longer. My name is Kate Parsons. I'll let Mr. Murphy know you are here," she stated with a smile. She left the room, for only a moment, then returned, seated herself at the desk, putting on a pair of glasses, and made herself busy reading some papers.

Not a word passed between Martha and the Sheriff. Martha was nervous, her hands cold and clammy and her mind racing with all kinds of thoughts, some she had no idea where they came from. She feared the attorney wouldn't be able to help her and she wasn't sure what she'd do then. The door opened; a man crossed the room and exited the office. "Kate, please send in the sheriff and the young lady," A deep voice bellowed from inside the office. Kate stood, smiling and said, "Sheriff, Miss Simms, please follow me." They both stood and followed her into the next room. "Sheriff Mason, Miss Simms, please have a seat and tell me how I can help.

Something about Able Houser," he said. Martha looked over at the Sheriff with her big brown eyes shining with unshed tears.

"It's like this, Mr. Murphy, Miss Simms was sent here by her father to marry Mr. Houser. Mr. Houser sent money to Mr. Simms for a mail-order bride. Her father kept the money expecting Mr. Houser to provide for her, but as you know he was killed last week in the raid at his ranch. So, what we are trying to find out is whether Mr. Houser left a Will or whether he made any provisions for her." Mr. Murphy sat down at his desk, propped his elbows on it and placed his chin in his hands, his mind pondering away. He leaned back in his chair and placed his hands on his rotund belly then said, "Sheriff, Mr. Houser was by here a few weeks back. He did say he had a few changes he wanted to make because he planned to marry soon, but that's all he said. He had his Will at the ranch, said he would make the changes and stop by next time he was in town. I do believe he has a nephew in Colorado, Utah, or somewhere. We need to look for his Will at the ranch and look for any information about the name and whereabouts of his nephew and try to locate him. When we find it, I will check to see if the Miss is listed to receive anything, you understand, Miss?" Martha sighed, "I understand sir," she stood straightening her skirt, she put her hand out toward Mr. Murphy and they shook hands. "Thank you for your help." She turned toward Sheriff Mason, extended her hand again and said, "I really appreciate your trying to help me Sheriff, I won't bother you anymore." She composed herself, turned and walked out the door. She entered the hotel and went straight to her room, mentally thanking Jenny for allowing her to stay a few days. Once in her room, she shut the door and fell onto the bed. Then, the tears came, along with sobs she could not control. She slept.

John Parker was waiting in the sheriff's office when Tobe came in. "Hey John, what are you doing back in town?" he said. "I was waiting to see how things went at the attorney's office." "Not well. It seems Able has a nephew somewhere and he must be found, plus the Will is at the ranch and I need to find that and any other papers that may be changes to his Will. Able did mention to Murphy that he planned to marry soon, but gave no details, so until this is all found and sorted out, there's not much help for Miss Simm's. Why were you wanting to know?"

"Susan and I were talking and with her being this far along with child, we were hoping Martha would come stay with us and earn her keep by helping Susan in the house, garden, and other things. What do you think Tobe, will she be interested?" John waited while Tobe pondered on his answer. "I think you have something there, John. Let's go see."

John and Tobe entered the hotel and found Jenny at the front desk. "Hello Jenny," John said. "John, Sheriff, how can I help?" "Is Miss Simms in her room?" The sheriff asked. "I believe so, I haven't seen her since she came back earlier. I assumed things didn't go well, she seemed upset, so I haven't bothered her." "Would you please go up and check on her and ask her to meet John and I in the dining room? Do let her know that John must get back to the ranch, but he would like to talk to her first. We'll be in the dining room waiting," he said as he and John headed in that direction. They found an empty table, sat down and motioned for the server to bring coffee. "I hope she's interested; Susan gets lonely being the only female out there. I know she'd enjoy the companionship more than anything," said John.

About that time, Martha entered the dining room, saw them, and began walking towards them, hoping they couldn't tell she'd been crying. She probably looked a mess but didn't want to keep them waiting. She tried to smile, but it was hard. As she approached their table, both men stood and greeted her. "Hello Sheriff, Mr. Parker. Jenny said ``you wanted to see me?" John pulled out a chair for her and she sat down, and they did the same. Martha looked at each of them, both seemed a bit uneasy. Finally, the Sheriff spoke, "Miss Simms, what are you going to do now?" Martha really had no idea what to do or say. She was looking at her hands around her cup of coffee when John spoke up. "Miss Simms, my wife and I are expecting our first child and so far, Susan, my wife, has done well, but she is exhausted. She could use some help. We thought if you wanted to stay here in Wyoming, we'd hired you to be our cook and housekeeper and whatever Susan needs. Would that be something that might interest you?" John watched her reaction but couldn't read her thoughts. Martha sat there, as if in shock, staring at the table. John decided to ease the tension and said, "How about thinking about it and let the sheriff know your answer. If you decide you want the job, have the Sheriff bring you out to the ranch. is there anything you would like to ask me?" Martha looked up. "I appreciate the offer Mr. Parker, but I need to get a job and find a place to live." John, confused, was watching her and wondering if she understood what all he had said. He cleared his throat and said, "Martha, did you understand what I said?" Martha looked at him, a bit nervous, "I think so." "Well, you said you needed a job and a place to live, I was offering that to you. You'll come live on our ranch, and you will be paid for your work. I realize you are young, but if you need help, Susan will be right there with you. Your main job will be watching Susan and helping her, but not letting her over work herself. She needs rest and she would definitely love some female companionship. I need to get back to the ranch, so think on it and let Tobe here know." Martha said, "Okay, Mr. Parker." Then John stood, picked up his black Stetson and said his goodbyes.

Martha wasn't sure what to think. Sheriff Mason went over to his desk leaving her to her thoughts. She watched the sheriff as he shuffled through some papers. He was a tall man, thin, and graying just a bit at his temples. She figured he was about the same age as John Parker, yet, looked older, somehow. She assumed it was because of his job and probably, why he wasn't married, something Jenny, at the hotel, had told her. She could tell that Jenny really liked him but couldn't tell if the feeling was mutual. Maybe one day they will be together. She hoped so for Jenny's sake. She stood up, walked over to the desk, and stood in front of it, waiting for the sheriff to finish reading. Tobe looked up with a curious look on his face. "Did you need something, Miss Simms?" he said. Martha smiled, "Well, I was wondering if you could tell me about Mr. and Mrs. Parker." "Sure thing, what would you like to know?" "He seems nice. What is his wife like?" "Well, I can tell you that they both are well liked and respected by pretty much the whole town. They have the biggest branch within 20 miles, and he raises cattle and horses. They've only been married a couple of years and are now expecting their first child. Susan is the only woman on the ranch, and I think John, Mr. Parker, was hoping to help you out, as well, by having you help his wife. I know he worries when he's going on a drive or when he's away for a few days. I believe you'll like them. This offer will help you if you want to stay in Wyoming. If you are worried about clothing, I'm certain they will work something out with you. So, what do you think?" "I'll have to think about it, right now it's the best offer I got."

Martha sat in the rocker in her room, letting today's conversations play over and over again in her head. She did know that she would like to stay in Archer, everyone was really nice and helpful, and she had no concern of returning home to a father that didn't want her. She'd make a new life here. The more she thought about the Parker's offer and the Sheriff's praise of them, she figured it wouldn't hurt to go out to the ranch and meet with them. If she liked what she saw, she'd take the job, save some money and plan ahead.

CHAPTER 4

S he walked into the Sheriff's office, with a smile on her face, and stood in front of the desk. "It's nice to see a smile on your face," the sheriff said. "Did you make a decision concerning the Parkers?" "Yes, but I would like for you to take me out there, so I may talk to them and have a look see. If I like it, then I'll stay. Would you be able to take me when you have a moment to spare?" She waited for his reply, wondering if he had changed his thoughts about her taking the job. "Miss Simms, I'd be glad to take you out to the P3 Ranch, if you can wait until tomorrow. Can you be ready by 9 in the morning?" Martha smiled, "Yes, I can and will be ready by nine. I have a good feeling that this is going to work out," she said. "See you in the morning, Sheriff." were her last words as she walked out the door. Martha felt lighter than she had since her mother passed away. She was almost happy. When she returned to her room, she pulled a piece of paper out of her bag, sat at the small table, and began writing a letter to her father. She told him about the death of Mr. Houser and that she was not returning home. She would make her own way and be happy and hoped he'd have a happy life too. She signed it, Sincerely, Martha. She placed it in an envelope and went downstairs to find Jenny to ask if she could mail it for her. Jenny was busy, but said she'd take care of it. Martha decided that she needed something to eat, so she headed for the dining room, seated herself and waited for the server to take your order.

The next morning, Martha rushed around getting dressed and packed up, so she could eat something before going out to the P3

Ranch. She collected everything, picked up her bag and left the room. Martha walked over to the desk and laid down the key to her room. "Leaving us, are you?" Jenny said. "Maybe," Martha replied. "I'm hoping I'll have a job at the P3 Ranch today." "Wonderful!" Jenny smiled. "How did that come about? "Well, Mr. and Mrs. Parker are expecting, and Mr. Parker feels his wife could use some help and companionship and asked me if I'd be interested in the job. The Sheriff will be taking me out there in a bit, so I wanted to return the key just in case I don't return." "Thank you, Martha, I appreciate that," Jenny said. Jenny's eyes moved to the door. "Hello, Sheriff." Her smile reaching her eyes. Martha turned as the Sheriff approached the desk. "Hello, Jenny, Martha," he said tipping his hat. "Nice day for a ride. Are you ready Miss Simms?" "Yes, Sheriff, I am ready whenever you are." "Here let me take your bag and we'll go. We'll get there before it starts to get warm." The Sheriff picked up her bag and headed for the door. Martha turned towards Jenny and said, "Thank you Jenny, for everything." "You come back and see me sometime, okay?" "I will, goodbye." Martha waved and exited the hotel. Outside, she saw the Sheriff climbing in a wagon. He saw her approaching and jumped down so he could assist her up. He held out his hand, she placed hers in his and he helped her up then, climbed up himself. Once seated, he took the reins, slapped the horses, and hollered, "Get Up!" and they were off.

They rode in silence for about an hour, Martha was fixated on the scenery. Spring was almost here, yet the chill in the air told her that winter was not quite over. She pulled her cloak tighter trying to get a little warmer. Sheriff Mason saw her, "Why didn't you say you were cold? Reach behind the seat and there's a couple of blankets. I'm sorry I didn't think about them sooner, most folks know the weather around here." Martha turned in the seat and reached down and found a blanket, wrapped it around her and instantly felt a bit warmer. "Thank you for this, the blanket, and for taking me to the Parker's." "No problem. John and I have been friends forever, we help each other, when it's needed." He smiled at her, then focused on the horses and the road again. "How much longer?" "Oh, I say just about 7 to 8 miles. We'll be there before lunchtime." She was getting excited and nervous now, hoping this job will be what she needs and is looking for. Susan was on her knees, scrubbing the floor, when John walked in. He watched her for a moment, sweat on her forehead and looking exhausted. "What do you think you are doing, Honey?" He said forcefully. Susan stopped and looked up. "My job, sir," she replied. "Not much longer." He leaned down, placing his hands under her arms and pulled her up to stand. "What do you mean by that? Are you going to do it?" she laughed, making him laugh as well. "No, I'll have one of the hands do it." "Oh, no you won't. It will remain dirty until after the baby's born before I allow one of your hands in here to clean. They don't even know how to clean their own boots, unless there's a dance or something where a woman is involved." She took a deep breath and placed her hands on her hips staring at him. He just laughed and walked over pulling her close and kissed her. The noise of an approaching wagon got John's attention. He walked over to the window and peered out. A smile came across his face. "It's Tobe and Miss Simms. Maybe she's going to take the job. Come on Susan, let's go greet them." He took her hand as they walked out onto the front porch.

Martha took in the view of the P3 Ranch. There were two barns with a corral behind each one and several outbuildings, one being the bunkhouse with wooden tables and benches sitting in front of it under a small grove of Oak trees. There was a beautiful flower and vegetable garden next to the house. The house was two stories with one large and too small windows on the front of the first level and two windows on the second level. A covered porch ran across the full length of the house with four wooden pillars supporting the overhang with decorative railing. In front of the porch, in the center, were four steps that led up to the porch. The Sheriff pulled the horses to a stop, jumped down, turned, and reached for Martha to help her down. He took her by the elbow and led her up the steps and onto the porch. "Martha, you know John, and this is his beautiful wife, Susan," he said. "Welcome, Miss Simms," John said. Martha acknowledged them with a nod and smiled. "I assume your trip here is due to a decision you have made, Miss Simms?" Martha smiled feeling nervous, all the sudden, playing with a strand of her hair.

"I'm not 100% sure of my decision yet. I asked the sheriff to bring me out, because I wanted to meet your wife and have her tell me what she would expect of me, because you said she would be my boss. Also, I wanted to get a look at where I'd be working and what the arrangements would be for me living here on the ranch, before I make a final decision," she trembled as she took a deep breath. "That's understandable, Miss Simms. How about you ladies go on in and do whatever you women need to do, while Tobe and I check out the livestock." He gave Susan a kiss on the cheek, then the men walked down the steps and out towards the barn.

CHAPTER 5

The women entered the house; Susan led her into the kitchen and told her to have a seat at the table while she got them some refreshment. Martha looked around the kitchen. It was the largest kitchen she had ever seen in a house, kitchens like this were only found in restaurants, she thought. Upon entering the room, there was a large table with eight chairs to the right, past that were double doors, she assumed, led to the dry goods pantry, there were more cabinets above a counter and several lower cabinets, next to that was a door, probably the room for the broom and cleaning supplies. The next wall was the door that opened to an outside screened room and another door that opened to the garden. The fourth wall was the work area with a six-burner wood cooking stove, a farmer's sink, and lower cabinets that ran along the whole wall. There was a double window above the sink that looked out over the flower garden. The cabinets were all white and the floor was covered with a soft green color tile. Apparently, most of it had just been cleaned since there was a bucket filled with water and a scrub brush next to it on the floor. Susan must have noticed her looking at the bucket, she broke the silence by clearing her throat and said, "Oh, sorry for my mess. John interrupted me and I forgot it was there," she set down the two glasses of tea on the table and walked over to move the bucket out of the way. "Don't mind me, that would be my job, if I decided to stay, right?" Martha asked. Susan stopped, turned around and sat down at the table. She took a sip from her glass and then said, "Yes, you are correct. The floor cleaning would be one of your tasks along with others. Would you like to discuss things about the job first and then take the grand tour or the other way around." "I'd like to discuss the job duties first, then I can finalize my decision." Susan smiled, "Alright, let's get started.

Susan stood up, went over to the work area counter, pulled open a drawer taking out pen and paper, and returned to the table. "I meant to write down your duties sooner, but since I wasn't sure if you would accept our offer, I just hadn't done it." She grinned. "So, we'll do it now, that way you'll have it to go by, if you need to." Martha smiled, "Where do we start?" She took a sip of her tea and concentrated on Susan. "I guess, I should ask if you cook?" "Yes, I can cook. It was just me and Pa after Mama passed. Just basic meals, nothing fancy, but I'm a quick learner," Martha said proudly. "That's fine, I'll teach you what you don't know, and we can learn the other stuff together." They talked about the things Susan was finding it difficult to do now, then, they went on to the chores she could still do. Next, was the chores that were not daily tasks, like the wash, the floors, and the garden and flower beds. After an hour or so, Susan said, "Well, that takes care of the household chores. You can work with me for now, then, when the time comes and I'm not able to do much, you can work out your own schedule. John thinks I need to rest more, so I'll probably start taking a nap sometime after lunch. You can work on whatever you need to then. Oh, I forgot to tell you that John likes his breakfast at 5 am, lunch at noon, and supper at 6-7 pm. He's used to late meals, and I often eat without him, but you and I can eat together if you wish." "That would be nice," Martha said. I believe I'll take you up on your offer. It will really help me out and you as well." Susan stood up, wrapped her arms around Martha's neck and hugged her tight. She giggled; she was so happy. "That's great! Let's go find the men and tell them the news."

They stepped outside, the air warm with a feel of heaviness about it, making it a bit hard to breathe and beads of perspiration appeared almost instantly on their skin. They found the men in the barn looking at the newborn calves. Both men looked towards the women as they entered the barn. The smell caught Martha off guard, hitting her all at once. It was a mixture of dust, hay, straw, musty grain, and urine. She sucked in her breath and started coughing. Her vision was off focus due to the darkness inside and the dust swirling around. "Are you alright, Martha?" Susan asked, patting her on the back. She coughed a few more times, then said, "Yes, I'm fine now. I've never been in an actual barn before, not used to the strong smell." "I guess it would be for a person from the city," John said. "Oh, John, they're beautiful," Susan said. "They're just a few hours old and twins, at that." "Aren't twins unusual for cows?" Martha asked. "Not really, but it doesn't happen often. This is, actually, our first set of twins here at the P3," John replied proudly. "First set I've heard of around here," Tobe said. They watched, in silence, while the babies suckled their mama for their dinner. John spoke up, "Have you made your decision, Miss Simms?" Martha was smiling ear to ear, "Yes, I have made my decision," "She's staying, John, isn't that wonderful!" Susan said with a big smile on her face. "I'm so excited, it's going to be great." "Yes, I've decided to stay. As I told Susan, it will benefit us all." He watched his wife, all smiles and a little giddy with her eyes all cheery and bright. "Do you need to go back into town to gather your things or do you need a few days before starting?" Martha looked at Sheriff Mason, then at John, she smiled just a little. "I have all my belongings with me in the wagon, besides I've already given Jenny back the key to my room, just in case I didn't return. To be honest, I pretty much already had planned to stay, I just wanted to meet Susan and talk with her to see if we would get along and what she wanted me to do. I didn't want to accept the offer without knowing, for certain, if I'd be happy here. I believe I will." "That's understandable. Just remember, if you need anything, please ask us. We are not shy and will help you as much as possible. One thing more, next time we go into town, we are going shopping for some clothes for you or material, if you want to make them yourself. I'm guessing you sew?" Her nervousness subsided, and she just spoke up without thinking, "Can we work out a payment schedule first, then go shopping?" "That's fine with me." John said. "Okay, let's get your things out of the wagon and Susan will help you get settled." They walked out of the barn and towards the house. Sheriff Mason stopped at the wagon, reached in the back and got Martha's bag. "Do you need me to carry this in for you?" "No, Sheriff, I can handle it from here. Thank you, for bringing me out, and for everything," she said. "You're welcome, Miss." He said his goodbyes and climbed in the wagon and headed back to town.

Sam, the foreman of P3 Ranch, a man of average height, blue eyes, short brown hair, and muscular build, was sitting at one of the tables, in front of the bunkhouse, watching the group as they crossed the barnyard. He knew the sheriff, but he had never seen the young lady before.

His eyes became fixated on her. She was about his height, nice build, curves in all the right places, long black hair, and ruby lips. He couldn't take his eyes off her, she was the most beautiful woman he'd ever seen. He couldn't wait to meet her; he was already in love.

CHAPTER 6

Ralynn was at Matt's door, reminiscing, when Martha shouted. "Ralynn, have you got that boy up yet?" Ralynn, jumped, returning to the present, knocked on the door. No, answer. "Well, that's not unusual." she said in a whisper to herself. She knocked again, harder this time, still no answer. She, really, hated going in to wake him up, because he could be a real bear at times, but if she didn't, Martha would have her hide. She walked over to the bed, "Matt, wake up, breakfast is ready." She watched him, as he turned away and ignored her. "Matt, get up!" He pulled the blankets up over his head. She reached over and pulled the blankets off of him. "Stop that! Let me sleep," he groaned. She began tickling him and he roared with laughter. "That's not fair, Sis. Let me sleep," annoyed at his sister's pesturing. "Okay." She threw the blankets over him and started walking away. "Matthew, get up or Martha will be up here next." "Okay! Okay! I'm awake, now get out! I'll be right down," he moaned. He sat up in bed glaring at her with an angry stare. "Better hurry up!" she said, as she made her way to the door, she ducked just in time before a pillow whizzed by her hitting the wall. "Missed me!" she laughed and shut the door.

She hurried down the stairs, catching her foot in the hem of her skirt, lost her footing and landed on her butt, then tumbled down the remaining six stairs. She didn't scream, instead, she laughed. Picking herself up, then, rubbing her behind and straightening her skirt, she made her way into the kitchen giggling. She went right over to Martha and gave her a huge hug. "What was that for?" Martha asked. "Just don't know what I'd do without you. You know that you are loved very much, right?" she said, not expecting an answer. "Well, what brought that on?" "Oh, I was remembering the story Ma told me about when you first came here. I just realized how lucky Matt and I are, not only to have Ma and Pa, but to have you too. You're a lot like a second mother to us and we both love you so much, only Matt's scared of you," she giggled. Martha looked at her with a glistening of tears in her eyes. "I love you both as if you two were my own children. Thank you, now, please put the flapjacks on the table. Is your brother awake? That boy is late for everything. What do you mean, he's scared of me?" "I'm right here, Martha, I do need my beauty sleep, you know." He laughed, then sat down at the table. "And I'm not scared of you, Martha, Ralynn's just trying to cause trouble." "You are too! You said she's mean and makes you work too much." He didn't like the way his sister was making him look bad; he wanted to punch her, but instead he pulled her hair. She squealed, loudly. Martha, already tired of their bickering, nixed the argument in the butt before it could get started. "You two stop it right now, before I get the broom out and wallup you both on the behind." The three of them ate in silence, then Matt asked to be excused. "Not so fast, young man. I need the wash tubs filled with water for the laundry and the eggs gathered, before you run off with the men." "That's woman's work." Matt moaned. "We, women, have our own chores to do, now do as your told," Martha ordered. Matt turned, shuffling his feet in the dirt, as he picked up buckets and headed towards the well. "Ralynn, go on upstairs and gather all the bedding first. We'll do the clothes after lunch. I'll work on the dishes, by then, Matt should have the tubs filled." Ralynn headed for the stairs, then suddenly stopped. "Martha, do you think Matt will remember to light the fire?" she asked with a curious tone in her voice. "Oh my, I'd better check. That boy will forget it and run off to be with that mare. Go on with your chores, child, and I'll take care of the fire," she said, as she hurried out the door. Just as she thought, Matt was nowhere near the wash tubs and the fire had not been lit. "Matt! Where are you?" she yelled. "I was gathering the eggs like I was told." He was carrying a bucket with about a dozen or so eggs in it. "Thank you, but you didn't light the fire." "You didn't tell me to light it." "Matthew, why would I have you to fill the wash tubs, if I didn't need the fire lit to heat the water?" "Well, I didn't think of it. I'll put these in the kitchen, then I'll get it started." "Thank you." They both went into the house; Martha began washing the dishes and Matt placed the bucket on the counter and went out to start the fire, grumbling all the way.

* * * * *

Matt was looking over the stall gate watching his mare, Darby, as she paced back and forth in her stall. She was to foal any day now and Matt couldn't wait. This would be Darby's first foal, as well as Matt's. "It's okay, Darby, just a while longer and you'll have your baby right at your side. It will be a happy day on the ranch," he said. Matt crossed his fingers, wishing everything goes well. Dr. Braeden, the veterinary, told them, yesterday, that it shouldn't be long now, and everything looked good. He'd be back by tomorrow to check on her, if any problems arise, come and get him, he'll leave word with Jenny at the hotel if he was called away. "Well, so far so good, Darby, I'll check on you later, girl," he said, as he tossed her a flake of hay. Walking out of the barn, he ran straight into Sam, the foreman, mild mannered man, who never raises his voice in frustration or anger. "Whoa, there young man! What's the situation this morning with Darby?" "She's pacing back and forth, but she's still eating, so it may be a while," Matt said. "You do remember that mares usually foal at night, so her labor may just be getting uncomfortable. We'll check on her after lunch and see if she's progressing. You may want to stay close to the barn and not go out with the hands today. She may need a little help later." "Sure, Sam, I don't want to be too far away from her now," Matt replied. "Why don't you help me clean up the bunkhouse while the hands are out with the herd? It'll keep us busy and close to your girl, so we can keep an eye on her." "Do you expect problems, Sam?" Matt looked worried. "Nah, just being cautious, first-time mama's just need a bit of special attention, in case they get scared themselves. It's all new to them, too." Sam smiled and slapped Matt on the back of his shoulder as they headed toward the bunkhouse. Matt opened the door to the bunkhouse and their nostrils were assaulted with the smells of cowboys, sweat, dust, dirt, and leather. He looked around, wiped the tears forming in his eyes and said, "It definitely needs a good airing and sweeping out." "Let's open the windows and leave the door open to air this place out, while we work. You sweep while I tend to the kitchen," Sam said, rubbing his itching nose. Matt collected the broom from the corner of the room and began sweeping. Dust and dirt flew everywhere making Sam start coughing. "Matthew, stop! I'll be outside until you get the kitchen area swept out. I can't handle all that dust in my lungs." He left the kitchen and sat at one of the tables outside, trying to stop coughing. He coughed so hard and long that his chest hurt. When the coughing stopped, he laid his arms on the table and rested his head on them.

Dust and dirt were rolling out of the bunkhouse door and windows as Matt continued sweeping; the dirty air getting to him as well. He exited the bunkhouse coughing and waving his hands in front of his face as to remove the dust out of his path. He sat down across from Sam. "Are you alright, Sam?' Raising his head he answered, "Yes, just couldn't handle all that dust. Seems I let it go too long between cleanings." "Not your fault, Sam, the other cowboys should help out more; this is where they live," he said. "Besides, I was behind the broom and it still got to me." "Did you finish?" "No, just have the bunk area to go, but I had to catch my breath." "Let's try it again, I'll be in the kitchen." Sam said, as he stood, tied his bandana over his nose and mouth, and headed back in; Matt doing the same. Time went by fast and both were relieved when it was done.

* * * * *

Hidden by the trees, just outside the property line of the P3 Ranch's Northeast corner, a man dressed in a black overcoat and Stetson, sat on his horse on top of the ridge, watching the cowboys drive the herd below him. He'd been watching the herd a couple of days now, but had seen no signs of the rustlers that were thought to be stealing from the P3 Ranch's herd. The Sheriff, Seth Stevens from

Archer, had wired the Governor about the situation, believing that Indians, renegades that had escaped the reservation, were the ones stealing the cattle, So, the Governor called in Luke Conrad, took him off his current case, and sent him undercover to Archer, Wyoming to investigate. Since he was half Indian, he and the Governor believed he could float between the whites and the reservation without drawing too much unwanted attention. It would be easier for him, than others, because his mother was a Commanche, and his father was a white trapper that had come to their village to trade, all those thirty-one years ago.

The Chief traded his only daughter for all the hides his father had with him. A year later, Lucus Bear Claw Conrad was born. He grew up in a white community and learned his father's and the white man's ways, but his mother took him, twice a year, back to her village to see his grandfather, *Dithit Go'she',* (Black Dog), to learn the ways of her people. He learned them both well and has benefited from knowing the ways of both worlds. He became an investigator for the purpose of helping people when the local lawman couldn't find the answers to a dilemma they were facing. The job has been a good fit for him. The Governor thought that he would be able to find out more information than just any white man. Luke agreed with him on that, but he was leaning more to the rustling being done by white men and not the Indians. The Indians were always making complaints about not getting their promised beef, but in his gut, it just didn't feel that this was the work of the Indians. In the two weeks he'd been in the area, he'd found no trace of Indians, anywhere, even Indians were not that careful that they didn't leave any trace at all.

Usually, he'd found something by this time. He's missed something, somewhere, but where? What was he not seeing? He was frustrated. He lifted his Stetson and ran his fingers through his thick dark hair, as he watched the activity below. He wanted to go farther up north, just to satisfy his frustrated mind and make sure that the rustling was happening closer to the P3 Ranch than what was first believed. He would, eventually, try to get closer to the ranch to see if anything suspicious catches his attention, otherwise, he would stick to the plan and try to hire on as a ranch hand. "Okay, boy, let's ride awhile," he said as he reined his big white faced, black headed Paint horse in the north direction.

* * * * *

Matt and Sam worked all morning in the bunkhouse and were satisfied with their accomplishment. Sam put the broom in the corner and said, "Ready for lunch, Matt?" Just at that moment, Matt's stomach growled, "I'm starving, let's go!" He replied. "Well, we finished a little earlier than expected, hopefully, the ladies won't be too mad at us for coming in early." Sam laughed. "Martha will probably yell at you, Sam," Matt joked, running out the door. "She'd better not," Sam replied with a smile on his face.

CHAPTER 7

"I'm glad that's done," Ralynn said, rubbing the back of her neck, as she set the basket down by the door. "By the time we get lunch over with, the bedding will all be dry, you know that. Then, we'll start again. Let's get lunch ready, you know Sam has a habit of showing up early, when the hands are out with the herd," Martha said. Just then, the back door opened, and Matt and Sam walked in. "I told you we would be early," he told Matt. Matt just laughed and made his way to the table and sat down, Sam did the same. Ralynn walked over and placed a glass of sweet tea in front of each of them. "Thanks Miss Rae, this will really soothe our throats, as well as our thirsts," Sam said. "You're welcome, Sam," she said, smiling at the name that only Sam has ever called her. "Something wrong with your throats?" "Just a bit dry and scratchy from coughing so much. I let cleaning the bunkhouse get away from me and Matt and I just about choked on all that dirt and dust. This will help," he said, lifting his glass in the air. "I told him the other cowboys should help out more," Matt added. She nodded and stepped over to the counter to continue helping with lunch.

"So, what have you ladies been up to this beautiful morning," Sam asked, jokingly. Martha looked at Ralynn, winked, and with a twinkle in her eyes, stated, "As a matter of fact, we, ladies, went into town, shopped all morning, and spent all our money. We haven't been back long, but boy, are we exhausted. We may just need a nap after lunch." Ralynn slapped her hand over her mouth to keep from laughing out loud. "Yes, we are quite tired. By the way, Matt, we found your stash and spent it all as well. "You, what! How could you?" Matt yelled with hurt and anger in his voice. They both burst out laughing as Matt ran from the room and up the stairs. "That was cruel," Sam conveyed, beginning to laugh as well. "Why do you torment him so?" "Have to get him excited about something, he's always so serious lately," Ralynn said. "He's worried about that mare. She's due anytime now, but she's really acting more uncomfortable than most mares. I just hope all goes well with her delivery. When Matt comes down, we'll go out and check on her. I've never seen a mare just pace back and forth during labor, I hope Doc Braeden gets here before she goes to deliver. My gut is telling me something is not quite right." The ladies walked over and placed lunch on the table. "Have you told Matt how you feel Sam?" Ralynn questioned. "Not yet. I'll decide if it's necessary, when I check on her again." "What's necessary?" Matt asked, walking into the room with an expression of relief on his face.. "Just talking about if we need to feed Darby while she's in labor," Sam said, looking at Martha and Ralynn with eyes that were telling them not to say anything. "Oh, okay," Matt said. "You, two, lied about taking my money, it's still where I hid it." "I was just joking you, Little Brother.

Wanted to see your reaction. I wondered if you could move fast or not," she laughed. "Not funny, Sister," he replied. "Bout ready to check on your girl? See if there are any changes since we last checked on her," Sam asked him. Matt, serious again, said, "Yès, I'll be ready after we eat." As soon as he finished, he was out the door.

Matt entered the barn, his eyes adjusting to the dim light. He walked over to the stall and watched Darby, still pacing around. He entered her stall, walked up to her and ran his hand along her neck. "What's wrong, girl, uncomfortable are ya?" He continued rubbing her and talking softly to her. Darby made a moaning sound and started pacing again. Matt went to get some fresh straw for her bedding, so she could lay down on it when the time comes. When he returned, Darby was standing in the corner of the stall. He watched her for a few minutes, noticing that something was not right, by the way she was acting. Her breathing was becoming erratic, and she stood as if frozen to that particular spot. He went into her stall and spread out the fresh straw and then tried to move her out of the corner, but she wouldn't budge. He wasn't sure what he should do; so, he ran out of the barn toward the house, yelling for Sam, frantic and breathing hard. Sam came out the door. "What is it, boy? Whoa! Take a breath and slow down." Matt, still breathing hard, tried to catch his breath, calming down a bit, then said, "Sam, I need your help, something is wrong with Darby. She's breathing funny and won't come out of the corner of her stall."

* * * * *

Luke was passing the P3 Ranch; his ears fixated on the slightest sounds, heard a boy yelling. He heard the fear in the boy's voice and heard a man trying to calm him down, so he could explain the problem. He caught the words, horse and trouble, and knew he could help, if they'd accept it. One thing Luke knew was horses. He rode up to the gate of the P3 Ranch and entered the barnyard, heading towards the barn, where he'd seen two people enter. He tied his horse to the rail, in front of the barn, and entered carefully, so as not to startle the horse. Once he saw the horse was in trouble, he spoke out loud with confidence, "I can help if you would allow me." Matt and Sam, both startled, turned to face the stranger standing outside the stall's gate. Sam looked at the stranger for a moment and then asked, "Who are you and what do you want?" "I'm Lucus Conrad, most call me Luke. I was passing by, when I heard the boy yelling about a horse in trouble. I'm good with horses, I can help," Luke replied. "We could use some help. We're not sure what's wrong. I've been around horses all my life and I've never seen this kind of behavior in a laboring mare," Sam said. "May I have a look at her?" Matt looked at Sam with questioning eyes, as if, begging him to allow this stranger to help. "Sure, of course," Sam said.

Luke walked up to the side of Darby, laying hands on her underside and moving them around and repeated the same on her other side. He, then, placed his hand on her nose, whispering to her and backed her out to the corner and made her lay down. Matt and Sam were awestruck. Once he got her calmed down, he turned to

33

Sam and said he'd need several pieces of cloth, a fire for the hot water, and a knife. The knife would need to be placed in the fire to sterilize and the fire needed to be close enough to the barn to get to it in a hurry. "If I am correct in my thinking, the foal is backwards, and I'll need to try to turn it around. If that doesn't work, we'll have to cut it out. "But Darby will die," Matt said in an irate voice. "She'll die if we don't. "I'll do my best to save them both, I'll need a place to wash up and then we'll need to be quiet, this won't be easy or fast. Matt, I'll need you to stay at her head and talk to her calmly and quietly to keep her as calm as possible. She will be in a lot of pain, so do your best. Sam, I'll need you with me." Matt stayed with Darby, talking calmly, as Sam and Luke got a fire started and Sam gathered the supplies needed. Luke took off his shirt and washed his arms clear up to his shoulders, then he placed the blade of the knife, Sam brought him, into the fire to sterilize it. As he stood, he noticed a movement to his left, he turned for a better look and saw a young woman working in the garden. He couldn't see her face clearly, but he could imagine it; thick auburn hair with hazel eyes, a small upturned nose, luscious lips to kiss, and a pretty sprinkle of freckles. Darby moaned loudly, he put his thoughts of the woman to the back of his mind; there were more pressing things to tend to at the moment. Sam returned with the rags and found Matt at Darby's head, talking to her, and Luke was, what looked like, rubbing her belly. "What are you doing?" Sam asked. "Calming her before the storm hits her. Let me explain what I am about to do. Sam, I'll need you here to the side of her and hold her tail up across her back and hand me whatever I need. Right now, just have the rags close by for me." Luke took a deep breath, then told Matt that his job was very important and not to pay any attention to what was happening. He needed his complete attention on Darby to keep her calm and do his best to keep her head down, so she doesn't try to get up, unless he says otherwise. He explained to Sam how he was going to reach inside the birth canal and try to put the foal in the right position. Luke hoped it would work because he didn't want to have to perform surgery, knowing he wouldn't be able to save the mare. He wanted to save them both.

Luke took a deep breath, laid his left hand on the mare's hip and with his right hand, he carefully inserted it into the birth canal, continuing to push forward until he could feel the foal. When he found the foal, he could tell it was in the wrong position, just as he suspected. Darby moaned in loud cries and a tear ran down her face. He tried to be as careful as he could, but he knew it hurt her. He moved his hand around then he found the two back legs, the foal was backwards and had to be turned. He stopped and concentrated on how best to proceed. He could surely use another hand, but that was impossible, he thought. He raised his eyes towards the Heavens and said a silent prayer, then proceeded to turn the foal around, so that the front feet would exit the birth canal first. It seemed to take forever, but Luke was moving as quickly as possible. Matt, becoming anxious, continued talking to Darby and rubbing her neck, they all knew time was running out. Luke knew he had to hurry but was trying his best not to hurt them more than he had to. He, finally, got the foal in the correct position and pulled his arm out of the birth canal.

Sam handed him a couple rags to clean his arm. He looked at Matt and told him to move away slowly and come stand by Sam. "I believe she'll do okay now, the foal was backwards, but I got it turned around," he said. Matt stood and backed away to stand beside Sam. He watched Darby as she raised her head and began to push almost instantly. She moaned, then stood up, circled and then laid back down. She pushed again. All the sudden, there they were, the two front feet appeared and then the nose. She pushed again and there was the head. Luke motioned for Matt to get a rag and instructed him on how to clear the birth bag and mucus from the baby's mouth and nose so it could breathe. Just as Matt finished, Darby moaned again, and the body came and finally the back feet. It laid still for only a moment, then began to move. Darby stood and turned towards her baby, sniffed it then began to clean it. A few moments later, the foal struggled to stand. It took three tries and then it was on its feet searching for Mama's teat. Matt walked up to Darby and congratulated her on becoming a mom. Darby nuzzled Matt and then walked over to the hay manger and began to eat, the foal following. Matt was mesmerized by the new foal. He watched as it struggled to stay up on all fours, then it found what it was looking for and began sucking to take in his first meal. "Hungry little fella," Sam said. They all laughed. Luke and Sam congratulated Matt on a job well done and on having his first colt. Matt's smile was like sunshine, he was so proud. He watched the little fella and was trying to come up with a name.

The colt was an odd color, so he was a bit slow at what to call him. Matt studied his colt, big, soft brown eyes, a white star on his forehead, a coat the color of silver, and four white stockings. The colt was so unique that he couldn't think of a name, so he decided to think on it awhile. "Got a name, yet?" Sam asked him. "No, I have to have the perfect name for him, so I'll think on it for a bit." Matt replied. At that moment, he noticed the stranger in their midst. "I want to thank you for your help, but who, exactly, are you and why are you here?" He looked towards Sam and Sam said, "I was about to ask the same thing."

CHAPTER 8

Ralynn and Baylee were out in the garden. She was hoeing around the pole beans while Baylee slept under the shade of the corn stalks. Movement over by the barn caught her attention. She couldn't see clearly due to the sun in her eyes, but she knew it was a person, but not her brother or Sam. She continued her work, but her curiosity was getting the better of her. Though she kept working, she couldn't get the nagging feeling out of her head, who this person might be. No one had come out of the barn, and she knew Matt and Sam were still inside. She had heard Matt's mare moaning a while ago, but it was quiet now. She set her hoe up against the house and walked towards the barn, curious to see if the stranger was still inside and whether Darby had foaled yet. It was dark, as she entered and it took a minute for her eyes to adjust, before she proceeded further. Once she could see better, she quietly walked towards Darby's stall. There, she saw Darby standing with her new colt. She approached the stall, "Oh, Matt, He's a beauty.

What are you going to call him?" Matt looked her way, "I had to think on it, but I have the perfect name, Silver Bullet. His color will probably change some, so Bullet for short." "I do believe that suits him," Sam said. "I agree," she said. Looking away from the colt, there he was, the stranger, leaning against the wall, watching the mare and colt. Sam saw the look of curiosity in her eyes, "Rae, this is Lucus Conrad. We were just talking to him about his reason for being here." "Well, who are you? And why are you here?" she asked. Luke turned his head, looking at her for the first time.

Luke shuffled his feet in the straw and put his hands in his pockets. "I'm Lucus Conrad, most call me Luke, I'm from Sedona, Arizona and I came up here with a herd and decided to stay awhile. I was looking for work. I just happened to be passing the ranch, when I heard the boy say a horse was in trouble. I know horses, so I stopped to offer my assistance. "Thank God, he did. Darby was having some real issues and I had no idea how to help her. He sure knew what to do," Sam said, nodding in Luke's direction. "How did you know what to do?" Matt asked, looking at Luke for answers. "I've been around horses, and I've learned to read them pretty well. Growing up, taking care of them was my job, especially when my mother took me to her people's village. I've had incidents like this before. When she was in the corner, she was in tremendous pain and afraid to move. I could see her tensing up and I knew the foal may be in the wrong position or tangled in the cord. When a mare acts like that, you need to go inside her and get the foal in the right position, before the mare gives up, otherwise, you'll lose them both," Luke replied. "I'm glad you were here, then," Ralynn said, smiling at him. Luke returned the smile, and she felt her face become warm from his attention. What was wrong with her? She'd never had that kind of reaction before from a man's smile. She looked away from him and watched the colt as it was standing, trying to get strength in his legs. She, then, excused herself, told Baylee to "Come", and went back to the garden to finish up her hoeing.

Sam and Luke left the stall, leaving Matt to watch his mare and colt in awe. Sam broke the silence between them, "Are you really looking for work or is there another reason you are in the area?" Luke looked at him and knew he needed to talk to someone he could trust, and he had a good feeling about Sam. "Yes, I'm here for work, but I'm, also, here at the request of the Governor." "I knew there was another reason, I just had a feeling in my gut," said Sam. "Is there a place where we can talk?" Luke asked. "Let's go to the bunkhouse, all the hands are out with the herds right now." As they walked, Luke began telling Sam why he was sent to the P3 Ranch by the Governor. He told him that he was part Apache and he and the Governor agreed that he was the right choice to send because he could mingle with the whites and Indians both hoping to find the rustlers that were causing a ruckus in the area. He continued telling Sam that he had been in the area for the past two weeks and had found nothing so far, but his gut was telling him that rustling was being done closer to the ranch property. They reached the bunkhouse and Sam opened the door entering a room full of bunk beds with a couple of tables over to one corner, a wood stove in another corner, and a kitchen in the back of the room. The room smelled of horse and leather from all the tack hanging on the walls. Sam led the way over to a table and told Luke to have a seat, he would get them some coffee. Sam returned and set two cups of coffee on the table, then sat down. "So, Luke, you're telling me that someone from the P3 is involved in the rustling around here as well as the other ranches?" "I'm not saying anyone from here is involved, what I am saying is that whoever it is, knows the lay of the ranch and covers their tracks exceedingly well." Luke removed his Stetson from his head and ran his fingers through his thick, dark hair and sighed. "Sam, what can you tell me about the rustling and how many cattle have you lost?" "I only know we're missing twenty-five to thirty head according to our last count two weeks ago. We do a headcount once a month, because we are getting ready to take several to market at the end of the month. The hands will be doing another count in a day or so to see if we are missing more or not. Now, we do suspect that we lost a few due to the winter weather, but it's never been this many. We've never found any signs of where they left the pasture. My fence riders have found no signs either. Luke stood, walked over to one of the bunks and rested his foot on the trunk at the end of the bunk and his hand on the top bunk. "I don't know what to think, Sam. I cannot find their camp area or any sign of fence cutting anywhere. Do you know how many your neighboring ranchers have lost?" "Not really. The Walker Ranch has lost 15–20 head of their Brahma herd. I'm not certain, but I recall Ben Cooper, of the Rocking R Ranch, said they have lost several head as of a month ago." So, this has been going on longer than the Governor and I thought." Sam shook his head, wiping his brow with the back of his hand. "I'll get the boys to round up the herd tomorrow, so we can do another count," Sam said. "I think that's a good idea. If you counted them a few weeks ago and more are missing, we'll know, for sure, whether they are still active or not." "It'll make for a long day, I'd better inform the ladies, they'll want to fix lunch for the boys," Sam added. Putting his hat on his head, Sam headed for the door. "You, coming, Luke?" He looked at Sam and nodded, "Sure thing," he replied.

Martha was finishing the last of the laundry; hanging the clothes on the line to dry. Sam motioned to Luke to remain silent as he quietly stepped behind her and grabbed her around the waist. Martha squealed, as Sam spun her around to face him. "Sam! What are you doing? Let me go!" "Oh, come now, Martha, you needed a good laugh," Sam laughed as Martha joined in. It was at that moment that Martha realized there was another person in their presence. "Who is that, Sam?" "I forgot. Martha, this is Lucus Conrad, our new hand. He stopped by just in time to help with Matt's mare; she was having a difficult time with her delivery. Matt, now has a beautiful colt." That's wonderful! Is she doing okay, now?" "She's doing just fine, the colt was backwards and Luke, here, repositioned it, then the birth came pretty easy. A beautiful silver colt," Sam said. "Has he named him, yet?" "He did, but I'll let him tell you and Rae at the same time. I'm sure he'll be taking you out there to see it as soon as he gets over that Aww feeling. I believe he is still in the barn," "I'm glad that's over, now, maybe I can get some work out of that boy," she said laughing. Sam and Luke joined in.

* * * * *

Ralynn, just having finished making up the beds upstairs, came down the stairs and into the kitchen, surprised to hear the laughter coming from outside the back door. She walked over to the door, opened it, seeing first, Sam, with his arm around Martha's waist and, then the stranger, laughing right along with them. "What is going on out here," she asked. Martha smiled, "Nothing, sweetie, Sam just grabbed me and scared the silliness right out of me." "Really?

Something I should know about?" she asked sheepishly. "No, Rae, just wanted to catch her off guard, is all," Sam said, smiling as he looked at Martha. "Are you sure about that? Then, why is your arm still around her?" Sam quickly removed his arm and moved over towards Luke.

Martha, blushing, said, "Sam, were you needing something?" "Oh, yes, I need to talk to you ladies about some changes in tomorrow's activities. By the way, Rae, Luke here is our new hand. Let's get something to drink and we'll sit and chat a bit." "Sounds fine, how about on the front porch, Ralynn and I will bring out some lemonade in a moment," Martha said.

Once the ladies, with the lemonade, arrived on the front porch, Sam began explaining the next day's plans. "I'm going to have the boys bring up the herd, tomorrow for a new headcount. Luke heard in town about more rustling happening and I want to make sure how many we have before we drive them to market." "How many are you bringing up?" Ralynn asked, in her business-like tone. "As many as we can find." "Well, if you are going to do that, then why don't we go ahead and sort off the culls and the ones for market and vaccinate the herd while we have them up here? The drive is only a few weeks away, so we do it now and won't have to be rushed so much when time comes." "Yes, we can do that, like killing two birds with one stone," Sam replied. Just then, Matt came out of the barn, full of smiles and energy, and headed towards them. He reached the house and climbed the steps to the porch. "Why are you doing that?" "Doing what?" Sam asked. "Killing birds?" "Oh, that's just an old saying, meaning doing two things at once. How's Darby and the colt doing?" "They're doing fine. Darby, finally laid down and the colt is sleeping beside her." "They've had a rough day and need the rest," Sam said, standing to put his arm around Matt's shoulders. "So, what two things are we doing tomorrow?" he asked. Sam sat back down and began telling Matt the plan. Ralynn had stepped inside and came back with a glass of lemonade for her brother. "Thanks, Sis, I was getting thirsty." "Little brother, did you know that Mr. Conrad is our new hired hand?" "Glad to have you." Matt put his hand out and shook Luke's hand. "Glad to be here," Luke responded. Martha left for a moment and returned with a plate full of sugar cookies and a pitcher of lemonade and offered some to everyone, before seating herself. There was complete silence, as they ate their cookies and sipped their drinks. Matt broke the silence, "So, why are we doing this so early this year?" "Just to see if we can get a day's work out of you, little brother," Ralynn stated, as she reached over and ruffled his hair. Everyone but Matt laughed.

"I decided, after talking to Luke, we need to bring up the whole herd from the North and South pastures first and then, we'll get the East pasture last. It will take at least two days to get them all. After the cattle are up and counted in the corrals, we can sort out the culls and those for market and put them in the large corral. We'll keep the heifers separate and vaccinate them and notch their ears. Once that is done, we'll turn the cattle we are keeping out to the South pasture. The market cattle, we'll feed grain and hay and, hopefully, fatten them up, some, before the drive," Sam stated. "Pa said, last year, that I could go this year, so can I go?" he asked, eagerly, changing the subject. Ralynn looked up from mending a shirt and saw the look in Matt's eyes, pleading with her to let him go. She knew if she didn't answer him, he'd be begging before long. "What happens if Ma and Pa get home and you're not here?" "You know Pa said I could go," he stated firmly, while his hands turned into fists, as though he wanted to his something if she denied him. Ralynn quietly replied, seeing his reaction, "I'll tell you what, if you get all your chores done with no complaints, and Martha and I don't have to keep reminding you, then I'll give it some serious thought. But, if Ma and Pa get home before the drive, it will be Pa's decision, no matter what I decide. Do you understand little brother?" "Yes, I understand, thanks Sis," he replied. "Well, I haven't decided yet," she laughed. "When is Ma and Pa supposed to get back, anyway?" Matt asked, with sincerity. "They've been gone for a while now." Martha looked away from her basket of laundry, "I'm really not sure, I thought they would have been back by now," she answered, trying not to show her concern too much. "Maybe, they decided at the last minute to do some sightseeing or visit some friends they ran into." "I don't think they know anyone in Emery, except the sheriff and the banker," Ralynn said. "I'm sure they'll be home soon, "Sam added. "You're right, we should not be worried for nothing, and get back to our chores, if this meeting is over," Martha said. On that note, everyone got up, left the porch, and went about their business.

* * * * *

Sam, Luke, and Matt left the porch. Matt headed straight towards the barn. "I should look in on Darby and Bullet to make sure all is going well," Luke said. "Okay, when you get done, come on over to the bunkhouse and we'll get you settled." "Sure thing," Luke said. Sam turned toward the bunkhouse as Luke headed in the direction of the barn. He found Matt, seemingly in deep thought, at the gate of Darby's stall watching her and her colt. Matt jumped when Luke's hand touched his shoulder. "I didn't mean to scare you," he apologized. "You didn't, just startled me a bit." "How are they doing? Any issues I can help you with?" "No, I believe we are good. Bullet has been up playing and eating, and Darby seems much better too." "Good, let me know if you need anything, I'll be over at the bunkhouse with Sam," Luke informed him. "Okay, thanks Luke," Matt said, turning back to watch his new family. Luke stepped back and watched Matt for a moment, seeing how proud he was of his mare and colt and watching Matt's eyes glistening over, he then headed for the bunkhouse.

CHAPTER 9

Martha and Ralynn had finished the dishes and Martha returned to folding laundry, while Ralynn took to sweeping the floor. Martha was humming her favorite gospel hymn and then just broke out singing and Ralynn joined in. *"Amazing Grace, how sweet the sound, that saved a wretch like me, I once was lost, but now I'm found, was blind, but now I see."* There was silence, then Martha said, "How about singing this one with me?" *"When I'm low in spirit, I cry Lord lift me up, I want to go higher with thee, But the Lord says I can't live on a mountain, so He picked out a valley for me. He leads me beside still waters, somewhere in the valley below, then He draws me aside to be tested and tried, but in the valley, He restoreth my soul. It is dark as a dungeon, and the sun seldom shines, and I question, Lord, why must this be? Then, the Lord says there's strength in my sorrow, and there's victory in trials for me.* They repeated the chorus and ended the song, both were smiling, as they finished their chore. Ralynn put away the broom and grabbed the feather duster heading for her father's office.

Leaving the big oak doors to the office open, she first went to her Pa's desk and sat in his chair remembering all the times she used to sit on her father's lap, as a young girl, while he worked the books and taught her the business along the way. She always joked with her Pa about running the ranch with him one day, and they both would laugh. Her Ma and Pa had raised her as a lady and wanted her to be able to explore new avenues, instead of just marrying a rancher and settling for that. But Ralynn had never wanted anything more than running the ranch with her Pa. She loved the ranch and that's where she wanted to be. She really didn't care about exploring the world. She became a bit emotional, thinking about her parents since she knew they were to be home a week ago. Sam and Martha were worried too, she was certain, but didn't want to worry Matt. She said a small prayer that they'd be home soon. Taking a deep breath, she got up, began dusting and straightened the office. It was a huge room for an office, but her parents both shared in the joy of reading. Over the years they acquired a huge collection of books of several genres. Ralynn had inherited their passion for reading, Matt, not so much. She often came to what she called the library, although she'd never been in one, to get a book to read in bed before she slept. Reading books always seemed to calm her racing thoughts, after a day's work. The hard part about it all, was there were so many books, it was difficult to choose which one to read. As she dusted the shelves of books, she recalled how reading about different things made her feel when she discovered something new, like her discovery of a new style of dresses, with patterns, that she could make herself, or a recipe she was excited to try, or even new seeds to sow in her flower and vegetable gardens. There were so many things to learn, like new places to go and stories of all kinds, about history and fun things. She liked this room of knowledge that her parents provided for her and Matthew. She could learn all she needed to know right here on the ranch, there was no need to go elsewhere. Hopefully, her parents would understand. She finished up her dusting and headed to the kitchen. She picked several items from the garden this morning and she knew it would be time for dinner before long, so she went right to work putting them where they belonged in the pantry, leaving out two large pans full of beans to break.

She sat down at the table and began breaking beans, when she heard the backdoor open. She was startled to see Luke come in, carrying a basket of laundry. "I see, Martha put you to work." "It would seem she did," Luke said, smiling. "Sam, not have anything for you to do?" "Not today. He said to familiarize myself with everything and I should be ready to work tomorrow." "Well, that's good. What do you think of the place? Think you'll be happy working here?" "I believe I will. Do you ride much?" "Not as much as I'd like, but, yes, I ride." "Maybe, you could show me around sometime." "Matt could easily do that for you, in your spare time," she commented sternly; she shut him down quickly. She didn't understand the attraction that she was having. where he was concerned. She wanted away from him, so she could feel herself again. "I best be back outside; it was nice talking to you." He turned and walked out the door, he just came through.

She just sat there, concentrating on breaking the beans for dinner. She couldn't understand her reactions towards him, or why she was acting so mean to him. She felt so different when he was around, all nervous with butterflies in her stomach. She's been around cowhands, all her life, and she never felt this way around a man. She was excited to see him, but when he was near her, she became all mush. She tried to focus on her task; finishing one pan of beans and starting on the other. Martha came in with the last of the laundry. "Need help, there? I'll be done in just a few minutes." "I sure can use some," Martha replied, in a tired tone. "Take the laundry and put it away and I'll start dinner. Ralynn finished the beans and set them on the counter. "I'll be back in a few minutes to help with supper," she said, and left the kitchen with the basket of laundry.

Matt was getting excited about the roundup; Ralynn said he could go this year. He, really, didn't know what to expect, only that he would be riding with the cook, Raymond (Raydog) Hamilton. Such an odd nickname, he'll have to ask him about it. Sam told him that he was to help the cook for now, and after a few days on the trail, he'll be able to ride with the cowboys and drive the herd. He couldn't wait! He enjoyed working the cattle, from the top of a horse, but he wasn't so keen about the old bull, Chester, that was included on this drive. Chester, the oldest bull on the ranch, was being sold to make room for the younger bulls. He was a mean one, when left alone, so Sam and the cowhands were trying to figure out a way to keep him confined until the drive.

When left alone, he became a terror and would charge at anything that moved, and would try to jump any fence to get back with his ladies. It had been suggested, from the cowhands, to wait and sell him separately, roast him over a fire, BBQ style, put him in a wagon and haul him, or somehow, put hobbles on him to slow him down and keep him confined. It was a unanimous vote to figure a way to hobble him. They would need something tough enough so he wouldn't break out of it. The ball and chain method was mentioned, but how would they get it on him?

They didn't want to hurt him or break a leg, so Sonny, one of the youngest cowhands, suggested using hobbles, like they used on the horses. "We could do that, but I don't think they would be strong enough," Sam said. "What if we made something similar, with stronger leather?" one cowhand said. "George, you're a blacksmith, do you think you could make something strong enough to hold Chester for three weeks?" "Well, I've never done anything like that before, but I can try." George replied. "Good, see what you can come up with. You, boys, help him out.

He'll need some super strong leather and hardware for this." Sam ordered.

Matt was still in the barn, feeding the horses, when Sam and Luke walked in. "Hey, son, you about done for the day?" "Yep, just about, wanna check on Darby and Bullet once more, before I go in," he said, as he walked towards Darby's stall. As Sam and Luke started to leave the barn, he grabbed an armful of hay and dropped it in the manger, so she and the colt would have something to eat for the night. He then headed out to meet up with them. "It should be about dinner time, how about we wash up and go see," Sam said. They headed for the back of the house, where a wash station was set up. Each one rolled up their sleeves, washed their faces and arms and dried off with the towel that hung on a hook. They were about to enter the house, when Matt started laughing. "What's so funny?" Luke asked. "Oh, I was just thinking about a joke I read," he replied. "Well, are you going to tell us?" Sam asked. "Yeah, ok. What do you get when you cross a Golden Retriever with a Wiener dog?" "I don't know," Sam said. "A Golden Wiener," Matt said, laughing. Sam and Luke began laughing as well. "You better not tell that to the women, you may get your mouth washed out with soap," Luke added.

They entered the kitchen, laughing. Martha and Ralynn looked up from preparing the meal and Martha asked, "What is all the ruckus about?" "Oh, nothing, just guy talk." "Oh, well, dinner will be ready in twenty minutes. Have a seat at the table and I'll bring you some iced tea." "How is the ice holding up, do you need me to get some from the ice house?" Sam asked. "No, we're good till tomorrow. Thanks for asking." Martha replied. Ralynn took the glasses to the table and Martha filled them. Right after she filled Sam's glass, Sam gave her a love pat on her behind, looking around hoping no one saw what he did. Martha smiled as she walked away, unaware of the pair eyes that had been watching them. She enjoyed the attention that Sam gave her, although she had told no one how she felt, not even Sam. She has loved him secretly for twenty years. She wanted to tell him, but was afraid he would laugh at her. She thought he was just messing with her, playfully, and it meant nothing more. She put it out of her mind and went back to fixing dinner.

CHAPTER 10

Luke, trying to stay in the conversation with Sam and Matt, couldn't take his eyes off the beautiful lady, who was standing at the kitchen counter. He has traveled across the country and had never seen a more exquisite example of a woman. He looked at her, lush pink lips, a cute upturned nose, eyes green, like the spring grass, with flecks of brown, and long auburn hair that fell to her waist and splayed across her shoulders. He figured she was about five feet, six and she had curves in all the right places. To him, she was the most beautiful woman he'd ever seen. He wondered why she was here on the ranch and not married. If only she would let him get to know her. She already had part of his heart and it wouldn't take much for him to lose it all to her, if she'd accept it. He'd have to find a way to talk to her before the time came for him to leave. He should be focusing on the investigation, but he didn't expect to fall in love. He was falling hard. He sat there listening to Sam and Matt discussing the round up, but he couldn't stop looking at Ralynn. He assumed she was eighteen or nineteen and probably had all the single men wanting to court her. When she moved, she carried herself gracefully in every way. He noticed her looking his way, but when he tried to make eye contact, she quickly turned away. He was becoming more curious by the second. What would it be like to kiss those luscious lips and hold her in his arms, he wondered? He knew he shouldn't think like that. He would be heading back to Arizona when the investigation was resolved. He would have to admire her from afar, until he could talk to her Pa and ask permission to court her.

At that moment, he realized that Mr. And Mrs. Parker still had not returned home. According to his information, the Parker's should have been back a week ago from their trip to Emery. In his gut, he knew something was amiss. He met Mr. Parker, in Emery, a few weeks back, along with two other prominent ranchers, Skye Walker of the SW Ranch and Gerard Michaels of the GM Ranch, at the sheriff's office to discuss the rustling in the area. They knew he'd be arriving in the area to go undercover and secretly investigate the rustling, via the Governor's orders, they just didn't know when. Now he's here, but Mr. Parker isn't. Maybe, he should ride out tomorrow and do some tracking; see if he could find any signs of the Parkers or signs of foul play on their way back from Emery. The more he thought about it the stronger his gut feeling was telling him something was wrong. From what he sensed about Mr. Parker, he knew he wasn't the kind of person to delay getting where he was going and definitely not when he was coming home. He made his decision and was going to tell Sam he would be leaving to track the Parkers down in the morning. He felt the need to find out and give the family the answers they were looking for.

* * * * *

Emery, WY

In a saloon on the west side of town, early in the hot and humid afternoon, sat five men around a table, playing poker. A couple of tables over, sat three men in a hushed conversation. The man doing the talking was a big man, wearing a dark blue suit, the newest style in men's wear. He had a full head of thick dark brown hair, graying at his temples, a full beard, black beady eyes, a hawk-like nose and thin lips. The men sitting with him were his top hands at his ranch, the GM Ranch, in other words, his flunkies. One was tall and thin and the other was short and balding; they both wore six-shooters and acted like they knew how to use them. They were talking amongst themselves, voices low with grim expressions on their faces. Gerard raised his hand trying to get the bartender's attention. "Bill! Bill, bring us another round of White Lightning," he said, in a demanding tone. He continued his conversation while waiting. "Alex, Jake, I have a project I want you to carry out. It will be easy as pie as long as long as you follow my instructions. I intercepted a telegram, yesterday, that was to go to the P3 Ranch. It was from the sheriff here in Emery." The conversation stopped, abruptly, when Bill arrived at the table with the three glasses of whiskey. Once Bill left the table, Gerard began promptly. "The telegram was bad news for the P3, apparently Mr. and Mrs. Parker has had an accident and both have died. Now, the others at P3 have no idea about this, which makes my plan that much easier. Tonight, I want you both to gather some men and ride out to the P3's North pasture. It should be easy enough to take a few hundred head of cattle, get them hidden in the canyon holding pen, and be back here before daybreak." "What about the men night hawking? Are we to kill them?" Alex asked. "Well, I have another plan for that. While you and your men are on your way there, I'm going to have another one of my cowhands deliver this telegram to the P3 Ranch. They will be so distraught, that they will not be as efficient and possibly forget to send the men out. This way you'll have time to get the herd rounded up and moved before anyone notices. Now, I don't want you using torches or having any fires, tonight, the moon will be full, so you will have plenty of light." "Sure thing, Boss," Alex said and Jake nodded his head in agreement.. They gulped down their whiskey and stood to leave. "Boys, I want this done quickly and quietly, you understand?" the Boss said in a whispered tone. "Yes, Sir." They both acknowledged in unison as they left the saloon; little did they know that the round-up at P3 Ranch had already begun.

* * * * *

"Here comes the first herd, Martha," Ralynn hollered excitedly. She had already changed into her man clothes and hurriedly put on her boots. She loved working cattle with Sam and the cowhands, sorting, giving vaccines, and notching their ears. She knew this drive included Chester, the old bull. He had given all he could to the ranch and now it was time to make room for the younger bulls. They had three other bulls ready to step up and fill Chester's spot with the ladies. Once back from the drive, the cows that were kept would be sorted into three separate herds, each herd with one bull and hopefully, by Spring, the ranch will have a great herd of calves.

Carrying a clipboard, with all the necessary paperwork she needed to record the day's events, she walked out the door towards the largest corral and holding pen. As she walked, she looked at the corral, taking in the three-rail fencing her Pa and Sam had built years ago. It was safe and sturdy, and showed some wear and tear but was still in good shape. It still had a few good years left before it would need replacing. The holding pen had been separated into smaller pens to hold the heifers in one, the cows in the other, culls in another and one for those that needed treatment and one for the steers. A special, sturdy, pen had been built for Chester, alone, so he couldn't break through or jump out of it. She heard the cowhands shouting and walked faster. When she reached the corral, she stepped up on the bottom rail, threw her left leg over the top rail, and positioned herself to prepare for the count. Luke and Matt had been assigned the job of doing the first and second headcount and she would do the third, that way they could compare their counts to make sure all cows were accounted for. Chester would be brought in last. While waiting for the cattle to arrive, she looked over her papers to make sure she had what she needed. The papers consisted of the headcount of cows, heifers and steers, vaccinations, tick and flea dips, and any wounds that needed to be tended, plus those that needed the P3 ear notches.

Satisfied that she had all she needed, she got comfortable and waited.

The cattle were getting close enough that she could hear the bawling and mooing of the cattle. A cowhand rode up and opened the gate, then returned to help with the herd. Sam was the first one through the gate and rode up to Ralynn. "Rae, keep your eyes open and stay on the fence. This is the North pasture and Chester is in this first group. We couldn't get him separated to bring him last, so watch yourself. If he gets too close to you, jump out, understand? I don't want him knocking you off the fence." "Yes, Sam, I understand," she replied. "Luke and Matt will be up at the gate shortly to do the first and second count and you'll do a third when they walk through this gate." He turned to ride back to the herd. "Yell, at first count, please," she hollered. Sam rode off with a wave of his hand, letting her know he heard her. Luke and Matt rode up as Sam approached the gate. They spoke for a moment, then climbed off their mounts and helped Sam adjust the gates. They remounted, waiting just inside the gate, as the cattle started through. Sam yelled, "Here we go, Rae." "One, two, three...," she counted, watching closely, as more came through, and then, there was Chester, all big and bossy. He was alert and aware of everything around him and his ladies. He was making his way around his ladies, keeping them all together, as Sam closed the gate. Luke and Matt rode over to Ralynn to give their count. "Two hundred, forty-seven and one bull." Matt said. Luke looked at her and said, "I agree, I got the same." "That's cool, we all agree then." Ralynn added. Sam rode up, looking over the first herd. "We would get Chester's herd first. This should be fun," he said sarcastically. "Where do we start?" Luke asked, as he watched Chester and the herd. Sam, wiping his brow, said, "Let's get the boys together and figure out our next step with what to do with Chester. We'll meet at the bunkhouse." He rode off to gather the cowhands.

* * * * *

Martha sat on the front porch enjoying the afternoon breeze. Everyone was working the round-up, so she had the day to herself. She had finished her daily chores and decided to take a much-needed break before dinner time. She did, however, bring out some mending with her to keep her hands busy, not one to be idle for long periods of time. She was worried about the Parker's. They were, now, two weeks late arriving home. It was not like them not to send word if plans had changed. Her mind was conjuring up all kinds of thoughts and images she didn't like. She wanted to talk to Sam and get his thoughts on the issue. Was he as worried as she was? she wondered. She would try to get him alone later, after dinner, to talk to him. She heard the pounding of hooves on the hard ground and knew the crew was on its way. So soon? She thought, how long had she been out here? She, hurriedly, put her mending in the basket and headed inside to finish preparing dinner. All the prepping had been done earlier and now she just needed to cook it. She went to the wood box to get some kindling to build up the fire in the cook stove. Once that was accomplished, she began cooking. She was humming, The Rock of Ages, when Ralynn came bouncing in, like she was on cloud nine, hugged her, and headed up the stairs to clean up. "I'll be back shortly to help," she hollered and proceeded up to her room. Martha looked out the window and saw Sam speaking to the cowhands. She wondered what was going on, but knew she'd find out later at the dinner table. She felt her cheeks grow warm when she thought of Sam. She didn't know why she was so shy around him. She wanted to tell him how she felt, but she didn't know how; someday, maybe. She has loved him for twenty years, it was time; she wasn't getting any younger.

* * * * *

It was almost dusk; Alex and Jake were in Gerard's office discussing their plan to rustle some cows from the P3 Ranch. "We're ready to go, Boss. We have three other guys going with us. I don't assume there will be any problems since that is the farthest grazing ground from the ranch,' Alex said. "I've made it easier for you by sending that telegram out to the P3 Ranch a couple hours ago. They should have it by now." Gerard said, laughing. "Thanks Boss," Jake said, as he and Alex headed out the door. Gerard was full of himself, feeling giddy; he just knew his plan would work. He would hit the Parkers hard and make them pay for John Parker's actions against him.

CHAPTER 11

Sam, Martha, Ralynn, and Matt were sitting at the dinner table discussing the day's events. Martha had prepared chicken and noodles, mashed potatoes, and salad for the evening meal, along with fresh bread and blackberry pie for dessert. "This is delicious, Martha. How do you make things taste so good?" "Oh, I just boil a whole chicken, remove the skin, debone it, shred it and put it back into broth to simmer. Then, I take a bowl, add 2 eggs, flour, and salt, mix it together and then drop by spoonfuls into the broth. Cook until done. It's not complicated. I'll teach you if you want to learn." she said laughing. "I don't think so, I have enough to do besides cook." They all began laughing. There was a knock at the front door. Matt pushed his chair back and hurried to answer the door. He opened it to find an unknown cowboy standing there; Sam saw him too, a rugged and mean looking fella. He had a telegram in his hand and handed it to Matt, not saying a word. Matt brought the telegram to the table and handed it to Sam. He sat back down to finish his meal.

Ralynn was watching Sam's face as he read the message; all at once, his face paled. He tried to compose himself the best he could and handed it to Martha. Her reaction to the message was similar; she looked at Sam with questioning eyes. "Okay. You two are scaring me. Is it from Pa?" She questioned, with a wavering voice. Sam, his head bent, resting in his hands, sat up and cleared his throat. "Rae, Matt, I have some bad news." Taking a deep breath, he continued. "The telegram is from Seth Stevens, the sheriff in Emery. There's been an accident, your Ma and Pa were killed when their rig went off the road around that sharp bend after leaving Emery.

Apparently, something spooked their horse right before that turn and it broke free from the rig. The rig ran off the road. That's all it says." No one spoke. Martha and Sam were watching Ralynn and Matt's reaction. Matt had his elbows on the table and his head in his hands. Ralynn just sat there, tears streaming down her cheeks. Both were in shock. Sam stood up, went over to the kids and laid his hands on their shoulders. "I'm so sorry," he said. He then walked over to Martha and whispered in her ear. "I need to find Luke; I'll be right back." Martha stood and began clearing the table. She wouldn't cry, not in front of the children, she told herself. She kept working, then she heard chairs scooting across the floor. She looked over at the kids, with concern, and saw Ralynn going up the stairs and Matt went outside. She knew they needed to grieve in their own way, so she let them be, for now. She would check on them at bedtime.

Sam found Luke in the barn, saddling Comanche. "I'm glad I caught you before you left on your search." "What's up? I saw a guy stop by earlier," Luke said. "Yeah, he delivered this telegram." Sam reached in his pocket and pulled out the telegram and handed it to Luke.

Luke took the paper and read the sender's name. "I know Seth Stevens, he's a good man." Seconds past, Luke looked at Sam. "Damn, this is not good. How are those two taking it?" Sam shook his head. "They're in shock, I'd say. They were sitting at the table when I came to find you. I knew I had to catch you before you left on your search." Luke was studying the telegram. "Sam, did you notice the date on this? It's over two weeks ago. Did you see the guy who delivered it?" "I did see the guy, wasn't anyone I knew; he was a mean looking man. I wasn't paying any attention to the date on it." Sam remarked. "Well, it seems odd to me that it took over two weeks to get here. Emery is only one hundred fifteen miles away. This should have been here ten days ago, at the latest, especially when it was sent from the sheriff. Someone intercepted this and held it before sending it now. Sam, have you had any other problems besides the rustling?" "No, nothing out of the ordinary." "What about financial issues? Any problems there?" Sam hesitated, then said, "John, Mr. Parker, took care of all that, but Ralynn always helped him with the books. She could probably tell you if anything is going on there, but we'd have to tell her the truth about you, otherwise, she won't help you." "I think we'll have to take a chance, if we're going to find out the truth about her parent's deaths." "I understand," Sam said. "I don't see any other way around it, Sam, there's something not right with this. If the sheriff couldn't bring this himself, he would have sent one of his deputies. I need to talk to Sheriff Stevens and find out what took so long for you to get this." "Sounds like a plan, Luke," Sam said, sounding heartbroken.

Ralynn, lying across her bed, hugging her tear drenched pillow, was in a state of shock. Her parents were dead, she would never see them again. She just couldn't believe it. She would never again work next to her Pa repairing fences or counting cattle, or even playing a silly game of tag with him and Matt. She would never, again, work in the garden with Mama, or sew things together, check out new patterns or cook together; her heart was broken and the tears flowed.

She lay there a while longer and just cried. A few minutes later, she sat up, then walked over to her wash stand, poured water in the basin and washed her face. She looked at herself in the mirror, her eyes were red and swollen from all her crying and her cheeks were a bright pink. She took the washcloth, wet it again, and just held it against her face, hoping it would help her look normal, it didn't. She put the wet cloth on the towel rack to dry, straightened her dress, and left her room. She needed to check on Matt; knowing this would be harder on him. It was also time to talk to Sam and Martha and discuss what was ahead for her and Matt.

She found Martha, Sam, and Luke in the kitchen, sitting at the table, deep in conversation. She stood at the doorway, for a moment, no one noticed her. She felt oddly confused as she looked at this stranger, Luke, that just suddenly appeared in their lives a few days ago. She felt butterflies in her stomach, as she looked closely at him for the first time. He was a handsome man, probably the most handsome she'd ever seen. His hair was black and long, tied back with a strip of rawhide, his skin was the color of dark caramel, eyes the color of liquid brown, his nose was straight, and his lips were full. He was a tall man, six feet or so, and he was dressed in jeans, boots, and a fringed shirt. His voice was deep toned yet soothing as he spoke to Sam and Martha. She was drawn to him and it confused her. Never before had a man ever made her feel so many emotions at once, especially when they have never really spoken to each other. When she entered the room, three pairs of eyes turned towards her, all speaking sympathy for her. The men stood and Sam pulled out a chair for her to sit in. As she took a seat, Martha stood and went over to the stove, returning a minute later, with a cup of tea and sat it in front of her. She leaned down and hugged her before returning to her own seat. There was silence, with a kind of eerie feeling in the air around them.

Ralynn broke the silence. "Where's Matt?" she asked, almost in a whisper. Sam spoke up, "He ran out the door and hasn't come back in. I figured he was out with Darby and Bullet and just needed space right now. He'll come in when he's ready." "How are you feeling, Sweetie?" Martha asked, concerned. "I'm okay, after the shock wore off. I've cried all I can cry; I don't think I have a tear left in me. I knew, deep down, that something was wrong, I just didn't want to think about it." She took a sip of her tea and with shaky hands set it back down. "I know this has been a shock for all of us, but we have to move forward. I need to know what to expect next. Where's my parent's bodies and can we bring them home and bury them in the family plot?

What about the ranch, the round-up and the drive? Where do we go from here?" She asked, her words coming quickly. "I understand your concern, Rae, but we don't have to solve them all tonight. We do, however, have some things to figure out. That's what we were talking about when you walked in. Luke has something important to talk to us about and we need to listen to what he has to say." She stood up so quickly, her chair fell backwards onto the floor. Her eyes filled with anger and she slammed her fists on the table so hard that it rattled the cups sitting on it. "What does he have to do with our affairs and why is he here with us at this table in our time of mourning?" she asked, abruptly, almost screaming, "Rae, calm down, please! There is a reason and I'll let him explain in just a moment," Sam assured her. Luke, feeling like the outsider he was, picked up her chair and placed it behind her; he stood there until she sat down, then walked over by Sam. "Go ahead, Luke." Sam took his seat to listen and back Luke up if he needed it. He was curious to see Rae's reaction to the news.

Luke removed his Stetson and ran his long fingers through his dark hair. His eyes spoke volumes as he looked at her, not understanding why this particular tragedy had him tied in knots. He knew it was important to his case, because his gut was telling him that the deaths were somehow connected with the rustling. It was a strong feeling that he could not ignore and it was rarely wrong. He would keep that information to himself, for now, he wanted to talk to the sheriff first. Now, he just had to tell her and Martha the truth about himself and why he was here. He wanted to see their reactions before he divulged too much to them. Becoming nervous, which he never was, he began. "My name is Lucus Conrad, as I mentioned before. I'm from Sedona, AZ, but I work for the Governor of Wyoming. I'm an undercover investigator looking into the cattle rustling that has been going on in this area. I'm here by request of the Governor. I'm here to find out who the rustlers are, but mostly to find out who is behind it and why. We both, the Governor and I, feel that it is not Indians behind this like everyone thinks. We feel that it's white men doing all this, all I have to do is prove it. I met with your Pa, Miss Parker, a little over three weeks ago in Emery, at the sheriff's office. We were there with other ranchers that have had cattle missing in the past few months. Your Pa invited me to stay here while I investigated. I was to leave Emery before your parents left and come here as a drifter looking for work. Then they would arrive a few days later. When I realized that they weren't here at their designated time, I knew something was wrong, but I couldn't just up and leave without blowing my cover. I was getting ready to go search for them when Sam caught me and showed me the telegram. Now, we know why." He stopped when he saw Ralynn lay her head down on her arms on the table. A few minutes passed before she raised her head. "Please continue Mr. Conrad," she said wearily. "That's about it. I just have to figure this out; I'm just having no luck right now." Luke took his seat as the door opened and Matt came rushing in straight into Ralynn's arms, sobbing his heart out. "We'll continue this later this evening. My brother and I need some time alone right now," she said, tears streaming down her face. "That's fine, Miss Parker, you two take all the time you need, I'm not going anywhere," he said. Sam, Martha and Luke left the table and went about their business, leaving the kids to themselves. Baylee, who had been laying in his bed by the door, came over and laid his head on Ralynn's feet, as if, knowing that something was terribly wrong and that they needed comfort and love.

An hour later, Baylee looked up and whined, needing attention, wanting them to know he understood that they were in pain. Matt reached down and patted him on the head and Ralynn did the same. "Thanks, my friend, I know you understand in your own way." Baylee stood up shaking his tail, as if to say, I'm always here for you.

* * * * *

Gerard was pacing back and forth in his office, hands clenched at his sides, thinking about Alex and Jake. "Where the hell are they?" he said through clenched teeth. "They should have reported to me by now." He walked over to his solid oak desk, sat down, pulled out a bottle of whiskey, and poured himself a shot. Waiting. He was becoming furious when Alex and Jake returned with the bad news; there were no cattle in the P3's North pasture. Gerard was fuming, his eyes bulging, then slammed his hands on his desk; he was seeing red like a bull in an arena.. "What do you mean, no cattle?" He yelled. "Round-up is weeks away." "Sorry Boss, but the pasture was empty, we searched it twice," Alex replied, shaking and worried what the Boss would do to them. "I had it all planned out, it was the perfect plan. How could it all go wrong?" He said with frustration and anger in his voice, then threw his glass into the fireplace . "Well, I have to come up with another plan, the Parker's owe me and I'm going to collect, however I can." "So, what are you thinking, Boss?" Jake asked. "I don't know just yet, come back in the morning. I have to think on this." Alex and Jake left and Gerard's mind was busy conjuring up all kinds of evil plans. He'd make them pay what he was owed: cattle or money, he didn't care. He sat at his desk and poured himself another drink. A plan started to form and an evil smile crossed his lips. "This is good," he said.

The next morning, bright and early, Alex and Jake were at the GM Ranch like they were told. They stood in the office, nervously, waiting for him to say something about their failure last evening, but, instead, he said, "I have a new plan, boys. We are going to take out the drovers of the cattle drive, one by one, and infiltrate our guys into the herd." "How will we do that, Boss," Alex asked. "Well, it won't be easy, but my drovers and cattle will already be in the drive and they sure won't expect this. You and your boys will distract the other ranch's drovers, one at a time, and get them to a place where they are drawn far enough from the herd so you can grab them and then take their gear and their places in the drive." "What are we supposed to do to get their attention?" "Jake, there are always strays along the drive, catch them and pull them close to where you can lure the drovers to you, then knock them off their horses and knock them out, then send one of your boys out to take their place. When we get all your boys infiltrated in the herd, we'll stampede the herd and run it right into the canyon. Should take us about two days to start and then about four days to be completely infiltrated in the herd. Once our last man is in, we will start the stampede. Just make sure you tell the boys and for them to stay alert." Gerard explained. "Won't that trail boss know it's not his drovers?" Alex asked. "This is when the switch comes in. When you capture and knock out a drover, you'll change hats and coats with them and ride right back to his position, returning with the cow or calf that lured him away in the first place. If there is no animal to use, you make sure you get them one way or another." Gerard explained. "When do we do this?" "The drive is to start in a couple of weeks, so we'll prepare until then. Get your boys together and work out your plans." "Sure, Boss," Alex answered as he and Jake left the room. Gerard walked over to his desk, poured himself a drink, turned and looked out the window. It was early in the day for a drink, but he needed it. He smiled, thinking about his new plan. "Pretty genius, if I do say so myself," he said aloud. "But just in case they fail again, I need a back-up plan. They will pay!" he said as he slammed his fist into the wall.

CHAPTER 12

Three weeks later:

With the round-up finished, Ralynn returned to her regular chores. She was working in the garden, when she caught movement to the right of her. Looking in that direction she saw Matt turning Darby and Bullet out into the corral for the first time since Bullet's birth. Darby headed straight for the fresh green grass, but Bullet was a little leery of the unknown. He stood proud, for such a little thing and didn't move. Darby whinnied and Bullet ran right to his mama's side. He wasn't sure of the lush grass under his tiny hooves, so he decided to explore a little. He walked around his mama a few times, then all at once, he kicked up his hind feet and took off in a trot. Ralynn stood mesmerized, watching the little beauty. She giggled a little, then all the sudden, she was laughing so hard, tears formed in her eyes. Bullet was running and bucking in the air and running again.

Baylee started barking and ran over to the fence, where Matt stood, to get a closer look. Matt reached down and patted his head. "He's a happy boy, isn't he Baylee?" Baylee barked as if to answer him. Raylnn calmed herself and watched them for a moment longer. She was thinking how much she loved her brother and Baylee, she had to include Darby and Bullet as well. She thought of her parents with sad emotion, then looked back at Matt and Baylee. If she ever lost them, she'd lose her soul, she thought. Tears ran down her cheeks.

"Ralynn, are you done in that garden, yet" Martha hollered. "It's time to start lunch and I can use some help." "I'll be right in," she replied, drying her eyes with her apron. She looked over the garden and decided she had done enough for today. She walked over to the shed to put her tools away, stopped at the wash station, and washed her hands. Once inside, she saw Martha's need for her assistance. Martha had bread in the oven, two apple pies on the counter waiting their turn in the oven, vegetable soup cooking on the stove, and material and patterns laying all over the table. "What do I need to do first," she asked. "Oh, stir the soup and see if it's about done, the bread is ready to come out and put the pies in, please." She did as Martha said. The soup was done, so she moved it from the stove and set it on the butcher block, she removed the bread from the oven and, also, set it on the butcher block, and put the pies in the oven. She, then, walked over to the cabinets, took out the plates, glasses and utensils, setting them on the counter. Suddenly, she had a thought; Luke. Was he eating with them or in the bunkhouse? She really had not seen or talked to him since the round-up was over, three weeks ago. It seemed, as if, they were avoiding each other. "Why would they be doing that? She thought. He did not join them for dinner.

After dinner was finished and dishes done, Martha assumed Ralynn and Matt had retired to their rooms, she stepped outside, closing the door quietly and proceeded through the garden to the bench behind the grape arbor. She sat down, taking in the crisp breeze, and relaxing her muscles. Out of the shadows, Sam appeared with a big smile on his face and wild flowers in his hand. He knew Martha came out here to unwind when she could after the kids went to bed. He had seen her do it often, since the weather had been nice in the evening. "Hello, beautiful lady," Sam said, handing her a bouquet of wildflowers. She looked up at him sporting a shy smile. "Why hello, Sam. I thought you had retired for the evening." "No, I was watching for you," he replied; his gut in knots and he was slightly shaking. "For me?" she asked, surprised. "Yes, for you. You surely know that I'm crazy about you. I've tried to give you all kinds of clues over the years," he stated boldly. "I assumed as much, but I wasn't sure. I was afraid to make any forward moves, besides, I'm not one to put my personal life out there for all the world to see." she explained, trying to stay composed after his declaration. "What personal life, woman? As far as I know, you've never had a personal life, you have always cared for and looked after the Parkers and always here at home." Sam pointed out to her. "Never had a reason to go anywhere, when everything I want and need is here," she expressed as she twirled the flowers in her hand. "What do you mean, everything you want and need is here?" he asked demandingly. She looked up at him with a sincere expression on her face. "Okay, I'll be honest with you. You, Sam, I have loved you ever since the day we met twenty years ago." "How did I not know that?" Sam sat down beside her, wiping his brow with the back of his hand. She answered him with certainty, "Because, like me, we were busy raising the Parkers and making this ranch work, that's why. We had no time for personal things or feelings, especially after Ralynn was born, then Matthew came along, and the herd kept growing and the ranch grew. We were just too busy for much else." Sam shook his head, "Yes, you are right, I see what you mean. We were definitely busy, but I noticed you as well, that first day." He smiled.

The full moon was shining brightly and a breeze sent a chill through Martha, as she pulled her shawl around her shoulders. Sam, seeing this, placed his arm around her shoulders and pulled her close; she laid her head on his shoulder, sitting there in silence. Time passed and time was forgotten. A lone coyote howled in the distance and brought them alert. She quivered at the sound "A little too close for comfort, there. I'll have to get the boys to check the stock carefully tomorrow and keep a watch out. Don't need to lose any of our herd. Allow me to walk you to the door, My Lady." He stood up, she placed her hand in his, she stood, and he escorted her to the door. "May I kiss you goodnight, Martha?" She nodded yes. Their lips met, warm and wet, emotions grew, and they both wished it wouldn't end, but it did. "I'll see you, in the morning, for breakfast." He walked towards the bunkhouse, whistling a tune full of joy. She entered the house, picked up the oil lamp from the counter, and made her way to her room. Once in her room and the door closed, she leaned against it, her heart fluttering. She felt like a schoolgirl, all giddy and excited. At forty years old, she finally received her very first kiss. It was magical and amazing. She now knew what love was like between two people. She climbed up in bed but could not sleep; Sam and that kiss was on her mind. Her last thought before falling asleep was, what's next?

A pair of eyes had watched the secret courtship from a distance. "Interesting turn of events," a voice whispered. Sneaking into the bunkhouse, Sam closed the door quietly and went into his room, separate from the main bunkroom. It was a small room with a bed, table, a couple of chairs, and an old desk, where he did his paperwork for the ranch. This has been home to him for over twenty years. He was comfortable here, but now, his dreams were becoming a bit different with Martha in mind. Now that he knows she feels the same way, he wants her to share her life with him. He wants to marry her. The question on his mind, as he drifted off to sleep; will she say yes?

* * * * *

Sam quietly left the bunkhouse, leaving Luke, who was still awake, watching him. Being an investigator, his curiosity got the best of him, so he followed. When he realized Sam had a romantic reason for sneaking out, he returned to the bunkhouse but never entered, instead, he sat at one of the tables, taking in the cool night air, since he wasn't, at all, sleepy. When he realized Sam was coming back, he rushed inside and climbed in bed. He was lying there quietly, on his cot, watching Sam as he slipped into his room. He wondered how long this secret romance had been going on. He smiled as he watched their encounter take place in the garden. He liked this pairing, as a couple, and wondered if wedding bells may soon be ringing.

His mind, automatically, switched to Ralynn, the beautiful, auburn-haired, green-eyed woman, with the luscious pink lips. She was often on his mind these days, especially since the round-up and he realized how unique she really was. What other woman could be a lady one minute and a "Ranch Boss" the next? It was like she was two different people, all wrapped up in one. He'd asked Sam why there was such a change in her? Sam replied, "It's not so surprising to us here, as it would be to a newcomer like yourself. Rae has always been interested in running the ranch with John, her Pa. She would sit with him for hours, in his office, going over plans for building up the ranch to working the books. But, I'm certain, doing it alone had not been in her plans.

She knows all the ropes to running this place and that it needs a leader to run it and she has assumed the position. She'll be a good "Boss," I'm certain." Sam informed him. Luke continued thinking about the change that had taken place in her. Remarkable! He thought. He wanted to get to know her better, on a personal level, but how should he approach her, now that she was his Boss? That complicates things even more. They've barely spoken or acknowledged each other in the past three weeks. "Why is that?" he said aloud, questioning himself. He instantly looked around, hoping he didn't wake anyone, days were hard, on the range, and the boys needed their sleep.

He'd been thinking, a lot, lately, about his future with the government, especially since meeting Ralynn. Was he ready to quit and settle somewhere?" Where she was concerned, yes, he was, but it really depended on how she felt about him, if she had any feelings for him at all. He could see a future with her, in his mind's eye, a practice learned while with the Apache tribe, with a beautiful house, children everywhere, and cattle all around them on their own ranch. It was a wonderful thought. Now, he would just have to convince her. That may take some doing, he smiled.

CHAPTER 13

Ralynn spent what free time she had, to prepare for the drive. This was her first event acting as 'Boss' and her nerves were on pins and needles; trying hard to keep herself calm. She wanted to appear confident in what she was doing so she practiced in front of the mirror, daily. As time passed, quickly, and neared the 'Big Day', she felt prepared and ready to step in her Pa's shoes. She would make her Pa proud, but in reality, she only had to prove it to herself.

Two weeks later:

Ralynn had called a meeting and Sam got everyone going on the drive to meet at the bunkhouse. It was time to get started so she stepped up on a platform and cleared her throat, loudly, to get everyone's attention. "Here goes nothing," she told herself; as she dried her sweaty hands on her jeans. "Okay, everyone, it's two days until we set off on the drive. I want everyone prepared and ready to move out with the other ranchers early Wednesday morning. Double check our herd, get them road branded, and have plenty of hay available in case of the unexpected.

Raydog, you, go into town and get the supplies we need, stop by the house and I'll have a list prepared for the supplies and I'll have cash for you to get what you need for cooking as well. This will be a short drive, compared to others, but being prepared is most important. Let's get to work then. Juan and Matt, I want to see you both in the library this afternoon, Sam, I want to see you and the trail boss in a half an hour," she ordered. She climbed down from the platform and headed toward the house.

She was going through all the forms she needed to take on the drive to present to the buyer in order to get paid. She heard Martha tell Sam for them to go on in. Sam knocked on the door. "Come on in, Sam," she said. Sam and Luke entered the room, and all at once, her butterflies returned and her palms became sweaty, her cheeks felt warm, and her spine tingled clear down to her tailbone. What was wrong with her, she thought. "Rae, Luke, here, knows this country so I have appointed him trail boss of the drive. We, both, know he's trustworthy and he'll help keep an eye on Matt." "Okay, if you think that's best, Sam, although, you won't have to watch Matt so closely, because I'm going along as well." She said smiling. "You're what? They both spoke at the same time. "I'm coming along. I'll be riding with Raydog in the chuckwagon and Matt will be helping Juan with the remuda. That way I can keep an eye on Matt and deal with the buyer when we get to the stockyard." Sam could see the confidence in her posture and in her eyes. "Are you sure that's a good idea, Rae?" "No, it's not a good idea," Luke interrupted. "Why not?" she asked in a raised voice. "Because I'll have two kids to keep track of, that's why." "Well, for your information, I'm not inexperienced and I'm not a kid. I can do everything any of these cowhands can do on this ranch and besides, I'm the Boss. So, I decide who can and cannot go on this drive. Is that understood, Mr. Conrad?" She stared directly into his eyes with her hands on her hips, waiting for an answer. "I've never heard of a woman going on a drive, but if that's what you want, then fine. Just remember one thing, young lady, I'm the trail boss and you will follow my rules and do as you are told, with no arguments, do you understand me, Miss Parker?" He asked seriously. "Yes, Mr. Conrad, I understand," she replied. Just at that moment, Martha yelled, "Lunch is ready." "Let's eat," Sam said, wanting to stop the discussion from becoming something more. As they entered the kitchen, Matt and Baylee came running in the back door. "Did you wash up, young man?" Martha asked him. "Yes, we both did," he said looking at Baylee as the dog went to his bed by the door and laid down. Everyone sat down, Sam said Grace, then they all enjoyed their meal.

After lunch, Ralynn was drying the last of the dishes when Matt came in with Juan in tow. "Have a seat at the table guys, I just need a few minutes of your time, then you can go back to work." She dried the last dish, put it away, and hung up the towel on a hook. She walked over to the table and sat down. "I wanted to talk to you both, because there have been some changes made. Matt, you won't be riding the chuckwagon, I will." Matt jumped up from his chair, anger and disappointment in his eyes. "You said I could go, why are you changing your mind and why are you going?" He demanded with a raised voice as his hands turned into fists at his side.

"Matt, sit down and listen. I apologize, I guess I started out wrong and didn't explain that well. Juan, you have been our wrangler for years and I was wondering if you would take Matt and teach him the ropes of breaking broncs?" "It's been a while since I've actually trained anyone, but I'll do my best," he replied. "Great. Matt, you'll be working the drive with Juan training and breaking the horses in the remuda. Will that work for you?" "It's fine with me." "The answer to your other question about why I'm going is because now that I'm in charge, I need to learn the ropes as well in order to run this ranch correctly. I need to watch when Luke deals with the buyer and introduce myself, so I know what to do next time, understand?" "Yes, Sis, I understand now." "Okay, back to work." She ordered.

The day of the drive arrived quickly. Excitement was everywhere around the ranch. All the surrounding ranches, The SW, The Rocking R, The GM and a few smaller ones, would be arriving with their herds to meet at P3 to combine into one large herd. The P3 cowhands/drovers had already begun branding the road brand on their cattle, a herd of three thousand, then they would start on the other herds as they arrived. Skye Walker, from the SW ranch, arrived first with twenty-five hundred head and announced that she would be going on the drive as well.

Luke shook his head and muttered, "Another woman, I give up," and walked away; no one else seemed to mind. Two of the smaller ranches showed up next, then the GM Ranch arrived with thirty-five hundred head. Gerard was just as smug, as usual, telling everyone that his herd was better than all the others, as well as portraying himself as King of the Ranchers. Luke disliked him instantly. He looked at Ralynn with questioning eyes. "What do you know about him?" He asked. "Not much, really. My Pa rarely dealt with him. He's not well liked in the area. I've heard he's only been in the area around two years or so." "He sure has acquired a lot of cattle in such a short time." "Yes, I know, and no one seems to know where they have all come from. It's as though the ranch grew overnight," she told him. "I'll have to keep an eye on him. Let me know if you hear anything about him. Be careful and I'll check on you later," he told her, smiling, as he rode away. Ralynn smiled and went back to helping Raydog load the chuckwagon with the drover's bedrolls and the last of the supplies. Martha brought out the tin plates, tin cups, coffee pot and the utensils to the chuckwagon and wished them all a safe trip, before heading back into the house. Sam was loading the last of the hay in the feed wagon for the horses. Juan was explaining to Matt what he expected of him on the first day and Luke was overseeing the branding. Skye Walker rode up next to the chuckwagon and stepped down off her horse. Skye was a looker. She had blond hair, tied up in a messy bun, wore faded jeans showing her amazing figure, and a western shirt unbuttoned to where a bit of cleavage was showing. Raydog noticed her right away. She was the flirty type, but sweet and honest for a woman ranch owner. "Need any help here?" She asked. "Nope, we're all good here," Raydog spoke up. "Well, if you do, I'll be close by, and I'll be glad to help out during meal time," she said. "That will be fine, Ms.

Walker," Raydog replied with a smile as she rode off. "My, my, Mr. Hamilton, I'd say you're smitten with Ms. Walker," Ralynn teased. "Nah," he replied, wondering if his feelings really showed that much; he'd secretly had a thing for her for a while now.. He went back to work.

She laughed when she saw him blush, but said nothing more and went about her business. Raydog's real name is Raymond, but he picked up the nickname when he was in the calvary, a few years back. He was a tall man about thirty-five in age, short light brown hair, blue eyes, and rough features. On his left cheek was a scar that ran from his temple to his chin, but it took nothing away from his handsome face. He had told Ralynn earlier that he loved to cook, anywhere and anytime. His mother taught him as a young boy and he has done it ever since. He said he'd rather cook on a drive instead of driving cattle, and most everyone liked his cooking.

Martha returned to the chuckwagon with the last of the utensils and handed them to Ralynn, with sadness in her eyes. "Oh, Martha, don't look so sad. We'll only be gone for two weeks, three at the most, and will be back before you know it," she told her. "I know, Sweetie, but you guys are all I have in the world. It's sure going to be lonely here without you all. I've never known a time when not one Parker was here on the ranch. It saddens me to my core," Martha explained with tears in her eyes. "No tears now. You know, if I'm going to run this ranch, I have to do this. I have to make the people at the stock-yard know that I'm no pushover, besides, Skye Walker is going on the drive, as well, so I won't be the only woman on the drive and I'll be well looked after; Matt too. We'll be careful." "I understand, just please take care of yourself and Matthew," she said and hurried away. "What's wrong with Martha?" Sam asked when he stopped the team of horses and the feed wagon next to the chuckwagon. "She's just worried, that's all. You take good care of her, Sam," Ralynn ordered. "Oh, I will," he said with a smile. "Ready to go then?" "Just as soon as the branding is finished. How far along are they?" "I don't know, but I'll check right away." He climbed off the wagon and walked away. Sam returned to tell her that they were finishing up with the Rocking R herd and that should take a couple of hours. "Thanks, Sam," she said and went about her business, checking things off her list.

A little over a couple of hours, two shots rang out bringing a hush over the crowd. Ralynn went looking for the source and found Luke standing on a platform trying to get everyone's attention. He put his colt away and began his speech. She stood in silence, listening. "Well, everyone, today is the big day. We've branded 15,600 head and now we are ready to move on. I'm going to tell you the time-line, so those with families will know about when to expect our return. There are 250 miles between us and Emery stockyard. If we travel 18 miles per day, that should get us into Emery in 14 days (about 2 weeks), depending on good weather and no unforeseen problems.

There should be plenty of water along the way, even though rain has been scarce so far this Spring. So, fill up your water supply, it will be two days until we reach the first watering hole.

Families, you can expect us back in approximately three weeks, so say your goodbyes now, and let's get started. Oh, by the way, we'll have two wagons with us, the chuckwagon and the feed wagon. They will be traveling mid-herd during the drive. We eat, only after the cattle are calmed for the night. Drovers, check with me for night-hawk duty, mount up and get into position, I'll give the signal to move out in about ten minutes. Minutes passed and all eyes were on Luke, waiting for the signal to move out. Luke held his position in the middle of a herd of 15,600, took off his old Stetson, waved it in the air and yelled, "Ho!" All at once the dust kicked up and the drive was in full swing.

* * * * *

Gerard waved as they left and laughed under his breath, as he mounted his horse and rode off with Alex and Jake trailing behind him. Boy, were they going to be surprised in a couple of days? He thought. "I can't wait," he said, aloud. He just knew everything was going to go his way. "I'll teach them all who's the best around here, and the richest. Everyone will be afraid to go against me," talking to himself. "You, say something Boss?" Jake asked. "No, nothing at all." His evil grin appeared as he answered. Alex and Jake knew that this time could mean their lives if they failed. It could be their heads hanging on Gerard's wall instead of an animal. "Do you think we can pull this off, Alex?" "It's not a matter of if we can, it's a matter of we must," Alex answered. "Do you know what will happen to us if we don't, he'll kill us," Jake said in a low voice. "I believe that, for sure. I just hope it all goes as planned, we have no other choice," Alex replied. Not a praying man, he shot a glance towards the Heavens and whispered a prayer; he wasn't ready to die.

CHAPTER 14

The Drive:

Day 1

With half the day gone, Luke decided to only travel 12 miles the first day. The herd stretched for miles and miles, and to get them all together for the night took a few hours. The day had been hard, long, hot and tiring for everyone. While Luke and the drovers were getting the cattle calmed for the evening, it gave the crew, at the chuckwagon, time to set up and prepare the meal for the forty-five mouths to feed. The drovers came riding in a little after dusk to eat and sleep. Luke called out Frank and Glen of the P3, Joe and Tom of the GM, Ted and Jim of the SW, and Mike and Dave of the RR for night hawking the first night. He figured eight drovers would be sufficient to keep the herd calm and the wild animals away. He informed them to eat and get a few hours' sleep. He'd wake them at midnight so they could relieve the other drovers to come in to eat and rest.

Ralynn and Skye served the meal of beans, beef, and biscuits, while Raydog kept the fire going and the coffee perked. The drovers ate and then came back for Raydog's famous apple pie.

After all was served, the girls sat down to eat, taking a break, while waiting for the remainder of the drovers to come in at midnight. "Wow, what a day." Ralynn said. "This is an easy day, don't think it will be this way all through the drive," Skye said. "I don't want to think of what a bad day is." "We should be just fine. I just wish it hadn't got so hot so soon this Spring. That's the most we have to worry about, the weather, I mean. At least, that's what I think." "We better get to washing up these dishes. Morning will come too soon," Ralynn said. While they were busy with the dishes, Raydog walked up and said, "Why don't you ladies finish up there and then get some sleep. I'll wait up for the others and finish the clean-up. I don't need much sleep." "I'll help," Skye said. "I'm not sleepy at all yet." Ralynn giggled. "I'm not going to pass up this opportunity for sleep. I'm going to get some shut-eye." She said her goodnites, climbed under the wagon and into her blankets.

* * * * *

Day 2:

"Up before dawn, yuk," Ralynn said, still half asleep. "You'll get used to it about the time we get home," Skye said. "Really?" "Of course not, but it sounded good, didn't it?" They laughed as they picked up and put away their bedrolls. "Are you ladies helping this morning or not?" Raydog asked. "We're coming Sugar," Skye replied, pulling her boots on. Just then, Ralynn heard Luke talking loudly. "Get up boys, we're burning daylight!" Everyone was scrambling around, putting on their boots, putting away their bedrolls, and started forming a line to get their food, before Luke ordered them to mount and ride out. Mornings on a drive are all chaos, no time to be lazy. The evenings, however, were not rushed. The drovers were non-stop with jokes, singing, and playing cards until they ate and relaxed a bit before going to sleep.

The day went well, and they reached the water hole just before dusk. Luke had told Raydog to cross Cottonwood Creek and then go a couple or three miles before setting up for the night. Raydog crossed and then traveled about three miles then stopped. He and the women began setting up for the evening meal. Matt came riding in after the horses were calmed for the night. "Well, little brother, how do you like it so far? You learning anything out there? Aren't you tired at all?" She asked as she watched her brother bounce around pulling out the drover's bedrolls and setting them down in a pile, several feet away from the chuckwagon. "I love it, Sis. Juan is teaching me all kinds of things about horses. I even got to break one this morning, well, Juan did the hardest part, and I am a bit tired but it's a good kind of tired." "That's good, but don't expect me to not worry about you." "Well, what about you, how are you handling everything?" "She's doing fine from what I can tell," a voice came from behind them. They both turned around to find Luke leaning against the chuckwagon wheel with a cup of coffee in his hand. "Where did you come from so quiet like?" Matt asked him. "I was down by the bank helping get the remainder of the cattle across. The men will start coming in soon. Is dinner about ready, I'm starving." "When I say it's ready, that's when." Raydog replied in a loud tone. "Yes Sir!" Luke said curtly. They all started laughing out loud. Luke put his cup on the make-shift table and walked off waving his arm in the air. "Did I upset him?" Raydog asked. "No, I think we did by laughing at him. He's a might touchy today. I hope he's not going to get worse, it's only been two days," Skye remarked. "Oh, he'll get over it. Tomorrow will be something else." Raydog said, and he was right.

Day 3:

The day began just like the previous one and at dawn the drive was in full motion, heading West towards Emery. The ladies left Raydog driving the chuckwagon and hitched a ride on the back of the feed wagon to keep the dust out of their eyes and mouths. They watched as they passed the herd. "It's much better back here," Ralynn spoke loudly. "Yes, it is." Skye remarked. "By the way, my young friend, you and Luke have something going on?" Ralynn looked over at Skye with a shocked look on her face, then said, "No, why would you even ask me that?" "Well, my female instincts tell me that there should be something going on." She giggled. "What do you mean?" "It's the way he looks and watches you all the time. You may not be interested in him, but he's sure into you." "Oh, you're joking." "I don't think so, I know what I'm seeing." Skye told her. All at once the wagon bounced hard sending Ralynn right out of the wagon onto the hard ground. "Ouch!" she yelled, trying to get up before she got trampled. Luke saw it happen and laughed out loud, but quickly recovered. He kicked Comanche into high gear, leaned down, grabbed her by the waist, and hoisted her up into the saddle in front of him, seating her sideways. "You alright?" He asked her. "I think so, I'm sure I'll be sore tomorrow." What happened, anyway?" "I wasn't holding on tight enough, I guess." They both broke out laughing. Once the laughing stopped, something magical happened. He tightened his arm that held her. It felt so warm and right around her, a perfect fit. It felt natural and comfortable for her to be in his arms. She felt her heart beating so hard, she thought her chest would explode. She looked up into his eyes and felt as though she was drowning in a pool of brown liquid. She was being drawn to him, closer and closer. His lips were so close. Her stomach fluttered as she anticipated the kiss that was sure to come. Her arm moved up around his neck, on its own, and she could feel the heat of his breath on her face. Her eyes shut as she waited for his lips to touch hers, for him to take her to a magical place, only they could go. His breath was hot, she waited. "Ralynn, you alright?" Raydog yelled. "Let me down, now, Luke," she whispered, embarrassed to be seen in such a compromising position. "You know I really don't want to, but I will." He told her in a soft, seductive tone only she could hear. A moment between them.

* * * * *

The day was winding down so Raydog pulled out of line and drove his team to a place under the shade trees. The feed wagon followed. The ladies jumped down and headed over to help with the evening meal. "I pulled over so I could get some pies baked today. We won't have to rush this way." "That sounds great. I'll get started with the apples," Skye said. Ralynn looked around and asked, "What do you need me to do?" "How about peeling the potatoes and getting them started," Raydog said. At that moment, Matt rode up all dusty and serious. "Hey, Sonny, we need you over at the remuda, Juan wants to feed some hay to the horses tonight," he hollered. "No problem, get right on it," Sonny hollered back. He jumped up in the wagon seat and headed the horses west. "Hey, Sis, Raydog keeping you busy?" "Sure is," she said while continuing to peel the potatoes. "It takes a lot of food to feed forty-five people. Do you see what Skye is doing?" Matt looked over at Skye and saw the apples. "Yeah, so?" "Think, little brother, yummy apple pie," she teased him. "That's great! I'm going back to the remuda to see if Juan needs any help. See you at dinner." He mounted his horse and headed west.

The day winds down, dinner is served and now it's sleep and clean-up time. After the chores were done, Skye and Ralynn decided to walk down to the water hole, next to the camp, and take a swim. The days were hot and dirty and a bath was much desired by the ladies. Eyes followed them as they disappeared into the bushes. "That water looks so good, I can't wait to get in and wash my hair and body, this three-day layer of dirt off my skin will feel like heaven." Ralynn pointed out an inlet surrounded by brush. "Okay, let's go." Skye said. They ran over to the inlet, checked to see if anyone was watching, stripped their clothes and jumped in the cool water calling to them. The moon was full and shining brightly, so the ladies had plenty of light to see each other. They began splashing each other and laughing like little girls. Then they submerged themselves and began washing the dirt and grime from their skin and hair. They were laughing and splashing at each other when a noise came from the brush. Ralynn saw the branches of a bush move. "Oh, it's probably just an animal. A cow, probably, had a calf and hid it like they do the first few days." Skye reassured her. "I know my herd has a few cows that we suspect are pregnant, so it's probably one of them." "Let's get out before someone catches us without our clothes on." "Okay, that would be embarrassing with all these men around." They got out, dried off with the towels, and quickly dressed. They sat on a large rock and put on their boots. On their way back, they were surprised to find Luke sitting alongside the creek. "What are you doing here?" Ralynn asked sharply. Luke took off his Stetson, ran his fingers through his hair, then said, "I saw you two leave but you never came back, so I came to check on you but when I heard you two laughing and the splashing water, I knew you had gone for a swim. So, I sat here and waited.

"Really? You waited here?" she questioned and pointed to the rock he was sitting on. "You never ventured over to where we were to take a peek at us?" "What are you talking about?" Luke questioned. "Oh, you know what I mean. The rustling of the bushes trying to scare us." "It wasn't me. If I find out it was one of the drovers, I'll whip the curiosity right out of them. They should have better respect than to do something like that." Luke said through clenched teeth. Skye spoke up, "We don't know who or what it was, Luke." "But there was something in those bushes." Ralynn said, a bit concerned that someone may have been watching them. "Show me where you two were swimming and where you saw the movement at. I'll check it out." Luke told them. "It is possible that it's a calf. If so, we'll need to find a place in the wagon until we find the mother so it can eat." He looked towards the area where they saw the movement and told them to get back to camp. He watched as they headed back to camp. He sat on a rock listening and watching for anything out of the ordinary. He only heard the crickets and bullfrogs, but he still wanted to check it out, his gut was talking to him again, telling him something was off. He already knew it wasn't a calf, otherwise the mama wouldn't be far away. He pulled out his colt and walked quietly through the brush and then came to the place the ladies pointed out. Sure enough, someone or something had been there. The branches of the bush had been broken and smashed down, as if someone or something had been laying there for some time. The trail of broken branches led off to the East so he followed it to a tree where there were hoof prints all around. Apparently, a horse had been tethered there but was gone now; the trail led off to the East as well. It would be pitch black in the trees and brush so he knew he couldn't follow the tracks. Someone had, definitely, been watching the ladies, but who and why? He'd have to keep a sharper eye on things in order to solve this mystery. He thought of Ralynn and how he'd feel if anything happened to her. He was captivated by her; she had his heart and didn't even know it. "How did that happen so soon?" He asked himself. He holstered his gun and headed back to camp. He wasn't going to tell the ladies that they were being watched, especially since he had no proof, so he'd just tell them it was some animal.

It was midnight when he finally reached the campsite. The fire was low so he added some wood to it and looked around. Everyone was sleeping and accounted for. He picked up his bedroll and laid it out, close to the chuckwagon where the ladies slept. He shook his head and mumbled to himself, "I knew having women along would be a mistake and a distraction, but I'm glad she's here." He didn't know if he could have stood being away from her that long. He pulled his blanket over his shoulder and slept.

* * * * *

Just east of the campsite, the herd was calm and quiet. The midnight drovers had taken their positions, and all seemed well, until it wasn't. Alex and Jake had men tucked away in the brush along the trail and tonight was the beginning of their boss's evil plan. They were to take out two drovers farthest from the campsite, make the switch, and start implanting their men into the drover's positions. The third man with them would take the kidnapped man to an old, abandoned line shack, Gerard had told them about, and tie him up, then get back to help the men. Alex and Jake were ecstatic, everything went perfect. They were confident now; they could pull this off and Gerard would be thrilled with them. They mounted their horses and headed West to their camp.

* * * * *

Day 4:

Before dawn, they were moving again. Breakfast was served, consisting of beef steak, sourdough bullets, and cowboy coffee. The drovers and crew ate quickly and shortly after Luke gave the order to move out. Ralynn and Skye were driving the team of horses, while Raydog walked alongside gathering cow chips, used for starting the campfire, and putting them in the catch-all that was tied under the belly of the chuckwagon. Luke rode up beside them.

"Goodmorning." "Good Morning to you, Luke." The ladies said to him. "I see you put Raydog to work." "We had to do something. He was getting lazy." Ralynn and Skye burst out laughing. "He told us to drive because he wanted to walk a while and gather some cow chips." "Oh.

Sounds like fun work. Well, I gotta get back to the herd." He rode away. As he was riding alongside the herd, his thoughts turned to Ralynn. He purposely rode up to the wagon just to see her, as least once in the daylight. She kept him grounded. She was so beautiful, but looked worn down. He had hoped she would make this trip without becoming too exhausted. Cattle drives were rough and took its toll on everyone and the cattle. He rode up to the first drover and said a few words to him. He didn't know all these men, so he had no idea that this was one of Gerard's men, who had infiltrated the drive. He rode to the head of the herd and spoke to his scout, Fred. "Have you made a run today?" "No, just getting ready to." Fred answered. "Can you ride ahead about twenty miles and find the next watering hole?" "No problem, Boss, I'll head out right now." Fred turned his horse around and headed towards Emery.

* * * * *

Alex had been trailing alongside the herd, out of sight from the drovers. The trail boss was a few miles ahead, so he gathered his men to get ready for another switch. "Alright boys pick your drover and take them out." "Sure Boss," one of the men said. "Okay, let's do it." The three men huddled together to choose which drover was next. "I'll take the closest one, wish me luck." He rode out of the thick brush and up behind the drover. He could tell everyone was concentrating on the herd, so he got up close to the drover and hit him in the back of the head with his gun, knocking him out cold. He grabbed the horse's reins and headed back into the brush. Once in the clear, he stepped off his horse and pulled the drover off his. He put him on the ground, switched coat and hat, mounted his horse, and rode out of the brush to take the drover's place.

The fourth man was tying the drover's hands and feet together. He put the drover in a wagon, but not before he put a rag in his mouth, then climbed up into the wagon and took off, heading to the line shack.

A few miles back, another group of three men were ready to do the same switch. An hour later, Alex rode up to check on the progress of both groups. Success. Alex was thrilled. Now that the drive was infiltrated with Gerard's men, they were going after the remuda. There were only two men, an old Mexican and a boy. Easy pickins, or so they thought.

Day 5:

Alex was sitting in a saloon called Eliza Jones, telling Gerard that everything went as planned. The drive was infiltrated with eight imposters and tomorrow they were grabbing the horses and starting the stampede of the herd towards the canyon. It was expected to be an easy, yet sneaky way of doing things, but Gerard was all about sneaky and stealing. He told Alex to be ready early and to make sure his men were prepared.

Luke was riding with the herd thinking about the evening before. Something was gnawing at his gut, but he didn't know what the cause was. Several of the men seemed to have pulled away from the group in the evening and had started their own group, not mingling with the other drovers and whispering amongst themselves. He asked the cook if he noticed or heard of anything taking place, such as an argument but Raydog said no. He spoke to Fred and Sonny and a few other hands but no one had a clue as to what was going on, so he told them to keep their eyes and ears open. It just didn't sit well with him. He decided to let it go and keep his eyes open that much more. He walked over to the campfire and poured himself a cup of cowboy coffee. He took a sip, it was hot, and slightly burnt his tongue. "You should know better than to drink that so soon, especially when it's sitting on the fire," Raydog laughed. "Yeah, I know. Wasn't thinking, I guess." He sat down on his bedroll and watched the group of eight men as they prepared their bedrolls and then retired for the evening. Come morning it was the same, eight men separated themselves from the others, mounted up and headed out to the herd. That nagging feeling came back, so he decided to watch them closely today. He gave Comanche a command and decided to ride around the herd.

The chuckwagon was moving along at its usual pace; Ralynn and Skye were driving the team and Raydog was gathering cow chips again. "Clouds rolling in, must be going to rain," Raydog said. "Rain sounds good, just don't want to be in it," Skye commented. "Oh, Skye, what else are we going to do? "Find a place with a lot of trees for cover," she said. "I guess, you'll just have to suffer with the rest of us. I doubt Luke will stop just because of rain." Ralynn stated, "What if a storm blows up, like lightning and all? Won't he stop then?" directing her question towards Raydog. "Depends on how bad it is. Trail bosses don't usually stop during the day." "Nothing is happening right now, so don't worry about it." Ralynn said, trying to calm her.

An hour or so passed and then it came; howling winds, thunder, and lightning. The cattle were uneasy and the rain poured hard. Luke and Fred were trying to figure out where to stop the herd for the night. "There's a place with a grove of trees over the ridge; good place to camp for the night," Fred said. "Okay, let's start shutting the herd down for the night. I'll inform Raydog so he can go on ahead," Luke said. "Sure thing, Boss." Fred rode ahead to get the drovers to help get the herd stopped. Luke turned back to inform the others and the crew. As he passed the first drover, he stopped him to tell him the plan. The drover just acknowledged him with a nod of his head and rode on. The next drover, he recognized but the following one did the same as the first, just a nod. Strange, Luke thought. Now, they weren't speaking to him. What was going on? He met the chuckwagon, Raydog, in the driver's seat, and told him the plan to shut down early.

Raydog slapped the reins and headed for the grove Luke told him about. The ladies were in the back of the wagon being bounced around here and there. "Wow! He must be in a hurry to get somewhere." Skye remarked. The wind was howling and whipped the canvas on the wagon so hard that they did not hear when Luke had stopped by with new instructions, so they just needed to hang on until they got wherever Raydog was going. Luke kept going until he reached the remuda and informed Juan and Matt to start slowing the horses and find a place to stop them for the night. He told them to settle them and then come up and eat at the grove of trees a few miles up. He also informed them of his uneasy feeling and that he thought they both should be on watch tonight. "Matt, I've never asked you, but how are you with a gun?" "I can shoot if that's what you mean." "Yes, that's what I mean. Keep a rifle or shotgun with you at all times tonight, and you too, Juan. Tonight would be a good night to start a stampede, so be careful and keep safe." He said. "Will do," Matt replied. Luke turned and kept riding, informing all the drovers of the plan. He met up with Fred about mid-way of the herd. "Get everyone told?" He asked. "Yep. Got them slowing down as we speak." "Good, let's see if the chuckwagon got set up. I'm hungry.?" They turned around and headed for the campsite.

By the time Luke and Fred reached the campsite the rain was pretty much over. It was just drizzling a bit now. Ralynn was busy setting up the wagon so they could begin cooking, Raydog was starting the fire, and Skye was peeling potatoes. The ground was too wet to lay out the bedrolls, so he and Fred stacked them on a fallen tree trunk to keep them dry, so the crew could get the chuckwagon set up. Ralynn was trying her best to set up the make-shift table, but the ground was slippery and wouldn't let the legs take hold. Fred saw her struggling so he headed for the wagon. Fred took a shovel out of the wagon and dug two small holes, set the legs in them and packed some mud around them so they wouldn't move. "Thanks Fred," she said. "You're welcome, Ma'am." Fred replied and walked away. "Having trouble setting up?" Luke asked. "Not anymore." "That's good. I'm sure getting hungry. Wouldn't want to starve." "Like you're going to starve any time soon. You can wait just like the others, Mr. Conrad," she said curtly. "When are you going to talk to me like we were normal people, instead of always biting at me?" "I guess when I think there's something important to talk about. What else is there to talk about?" "Well, I'm curious about you. Why did you really want to come on the drive?" "It's not that I particularly wanted to come, more of I needed to come." "What do you mean?" "My Pa is dead and it's up to me to take over. I felt that I needed to learn the ropes about the drive and selling of the herd. I can do, pretty much, everything on the ranch and run it too, but I have no experience with the drive or the actual selling. I know the market, but being a woman, I'm certain the buyers will try to take advantage of me. So, I assumed I could watch you and at the same time introduce myself as the new Boss of P3. You think I'm a bit loco, don't you?" "No, I don't think that. I do, however, understand it now. I guess I'm a fool for assuming the wrong reason. I figured you were just asserting your new position as boss. I didn't even think that you were coming for the ranch business. I apologize Miss Parker." "I will accept your apology on one condition." "And that is what?" "That when we get to Emery, you will treat me as the owner and boss of the ranch and teach me what I need to know." "I can do that, but will you allow me to call you, Miss Ralynn?" "Yes, of course, if I can call you Luke?" "Sure can," he replied. "Now, that wasn't so bad, was it?" "What?" "Talking. We seem to have the hang of it now, don't you think?" "Oh, yes, I guess, we have. I need to help get dinner, please excuse me." She turned to the table, making sure it was sturdy enough, and went to help Raydog prepare the meal.

CHAPTER 15

Day 6:

Luke woke up with a gnawing feeling in his gut, again. Something was off, but what? He had to figure this out: his gut usually steered him in the right direction, no reason to think it wasn't this time. He rolled up his bedroll and tossed it in the chuckwagon. Raydog was tending the fire and the ladies were still asleep. He walked over and asked Raydog if he noticed anything last evening. Raydog shook his head, no, but said, "I do see what you meant about those eight men. What is funny to me, is why all of a sudden. The drovers all seemed to get along, well enough, up until a few days ago, then they just split off from everyone else. They don't even eat with the others or associate with them or me. Strange." "Yes, that it is. Let me know right away if something happens." "No problem." Raydog replied. He didn't say anything to Luke, but he had that same gnawing feeling in his gut. He was going to keep a sharp eye out, for sure. He had noticed, lately, that Luke had been keeping a close eye on them too. He wasn't sure why, but ever since the ladies went swimming, a few nights back, he always knew where they were.

Something happened, he was sure of that. Maybe, he should ask them in case there is a problem ahead of them.

Luke walked over to the remuda and found Juan and Matt working a Paint mare. She was a pretty thing, he thought. "Mr. Boss, what brings you out here?" Juan said. "Well, I was thinking I'd pick out a horse and let Comanche rest for a few days." "What are you looking for? We have several kinds to choose from, but the ones over there are broke and ready to ride. Matt, here, has really got a knack with the horses. He's broken two by himself now, the one he has now will be his third." "That's great. I'm glad he has a passion for the job. Let me look at those and I'll choose one." He walked over to the horses that had already been broke to ride, and found a Paint, about seventeen hands high with beautiful markings of black and brown on white. He was gelded and gentle. That was good, because with Comanche being a stud, he didn't need another one. He patted the Paint on the neck and walked around him taking in his build and width. He should ride smoothly, and his legs look strong, he thought. He walked back over to Juan and told him which horse he wanted. Juan asked, "Where's Comanche, Boss?" "Oh, he's at the . I had things on my mind and didn't even think to bring him over. I'll go get him and be right back." Luke left the remuda and headed back to the camp. When he arrived, the ladies were up and breakfast was ready. He got his plate, filled with steak, two eggs, and a fresh slice of bread, along with his cowboy coffee. He sat down, on the tree trunk, and ate. After a second cup of coffee, he took his utensils and handed them to Ralynn, winked at her, and walked over to Comanche. Ralynn was watching him as he picked up his saddle, threw it over his shoulder, untied his horse, and led him towards the remuda. She figured he was getting a fresh horse, so she hollered at him. Hey, Luke, tell Matt and Juan to come eat before it's gone." He turned and looked at her to acknowledge her and to tell her he heard what she said. Ralynn smiled and went back to work.

Luke reached the remuda and told Juan and Matt to go eat. He would turn Comanche in with the other horses and would stay until one of them got back, but they needed to hurry a bit. He walked over to the Paint and rubbed his hands all over him, let him smell his scent and talked softly to him in his ear. He put the saddle blanket on first to see how he reacted. He stood calm and still. Next, was the saddle and then the bridle and bit. The Paint wasn't too keen on having something on his back, but he accepted it. The bit, however, did not go over as well. The Paint stuck his tongue out, pushing at the bit to get it out of his mouth. Luke looked at it and realized it didn't fit his mouth. He looked around and found one that would fit, but he needed to find out if there was another one like it, apparently, it was one Juan used in introducing the bit to the horse when breaking it. He removed the bridle, bit from the horse's head, and tethered him back to the temporary fence rail. He took his bridle and removed the bit he had on it. He was checking out the different bits, ten of them, when Juan and Matt came back. "Having a problem, Luke?" Matt asked. "No. Well, kind of. The Paint won't take my bit, so I was checking out what you have here. I found this one I think will work, but I can't find another one like this. I didn't want to take one if you needed it for your job." "Oh, that is fine, Boss. I have another in my saddle bags. That is a popular bit, so I do bring a couple of extras with me when I'm working. Go ahead and take that one, I used that one on him, he'll be used to it." "Okay, then, I'll get saddled up and get to work." He thanked Juan and went to finish getting the Paint ready to ride. He got the bridle and bit on, tightened the cinch, and stepped up into the saddle. He had not gone twenty-five feet when the saddle loosened. "Oh, mister, we are not playing that game," he said sternly. He stepped off and tightened the cinch again, this time tighter. "Now, you won't be losing me or the saddle." he told the horse. He stepped back up and the Paint moved as commanded. He rode back to the campsite and the crew was packing up. Some of the drovers were just standing around. "Hey, we're burning daylight! Get mounted and take your positions, now." The men went to their horses, at their own pace, irritating Luke that much more. He watched them until the last one was mounted and back with the herd. He rode over to Ralynn, smiled at her and asked, "Everything alright this morning?" "Yes, fine. You have a good day, Luke." She smiled back and climbed up in the wagon seat.

Luke rode ahead, on the north side of the herd. He passed the first drover and said good morning, like he does every day, and expected a response like always, but got nothing. He didn't know all the drovers from the other ranches, but he had never been disrespected from any of them until today. "Somethings up. I know it. Better stop and prepare before it happens," he told himself. He passed four more drovers and another one of the drovers acted with the same disrespect. By the time he reached the front of the herd, four of the drovers did the same.

Curiosity was strong. He found Fred and told him of his suspicions. Fred agreed that he found that strange. "Do me a favor, Fred. Ride around the herd and inform only the drovers you know and trust, that something is brewing with those eight men and to be prepared for anything. Tell them to keep their guns at the ready. I don't know what or when, but something is going to happen." Fred took off to spread the word and Luke rode back towards the chuckwagon. He had a feeling that a stampede was going to take place and he needed to get the wagons and Ralynn out of harm's way. He reached them about twenty minutes later and explained the situation to Raydog and Sonny, then he rode on. They did as he ordered and drove the teams over to the North side of the herd and into a wooded area; they waited. The ladies started asking what they were doing. All Raydog and Sonny would say was that it was ordered we find a safe place away from the herd and wait and we would know when to move ahead. Frustration hit Ralynn like a ton of bricks. She needed to know what was going on. She started to get out of the wagon and Raydog stopped her. She stomped her foot and sat down. Luke had better have an explanation for not informing her of what was going on.

Matt was working one of the horses and had been hard at it since before breakfast. He was getting thirsty, so he circled the horse once more and stopped. He led the horse along with him to his saddled horse and retrieved the canteen hanging on the saddle horn. Juan was about five hundred feet away trying to catch one of the wild mustangs. He figured Juan would get a drink when he was ready, so he went back to his training area and began circling the Bay horse and teaching him to stop on command at different places, only by the command of the rope. He circled the horse a couple more times. He looked towards the East and saw three men approaching with their guns pulled. He released the horse and ran to his and jumped in the saddle. He rode over to Juan and yelled, "Juan, men are coming with guns pulled. I'm going to warn the others and find Luke."

He dug his heels into the sides of his horse and took off towards the herd at high speed. He didn't see any drovers, so he kept going.

He was closing in on the herd when he felt fire light up his back and legs. He fell from his horse, screaming and crying at the same time. The pain was excruciating, and he couldn't move. He tried to sit up with no success, nothing worked. What was wrong with him? He tried every way possible to move and then he just gave up. He laid his head down and cried; thinking that he let Luke and Ralynn down because he couldn't warn them. He knew the cattle were moving fast and could hear them coming towards him. He was going to die today were his last thoughts.

Luke was riding alongside the herd, heading towards the end of the herd, when he heard a shot and then someone scream. It wasn't the ladies; they were safe up the trail and out of sight. He stood up in his stirrups and looked around, seeing nothing. There it was again, another scream. He headed in that direction, keeping a sharp eye in front of him. There was a break in the herd and he started to cross over towards the remuda. He could hear the thundering of hooves getting close and knew the stampede was happening. He yelled, "Stampede!" He searched the surroundings for any sign of an injured person. He heard it again, but not as loud this time. He rode on; searching. He looked East and saw the horses, from the remuda, had been spooked as well and were headed his way. He kept searching the area, and then he saw a body lying on the ground right in the path of the oncoming horses. He knew he had to hurry, in order, to reach the person and get him out of there, but time was not on his side. He jumped off his horse and ran over to the person. It was Matt. He looked towards the oncoming horses and knew there was no time left. He laid on top of Matt's body to protect him and waited for the horses to trample him. He was ready to die protecting Matt. He put his arms over Matt's head, said a prayer, and closed his eyes.

In the distance, Luke heard yelling and gunfire, but the pounding of the hooves was close. He kept his head down and felt Matt go limp underneath him. He could do nothing. Just then he was stepped on and kicked by the hooves that were passing over him. It seemed to last a long time, but all at once, it was over. He raised his head to look around; all was clear. He moved off Matt's body and tried to wake him. He got no response. He turned him over to find him lying in a pool of blood. He opened Matt's coat and searched for the cause. He found a hole; he'd been shot. On a closer look, he found another hole on the opposite side, apparently the bullet went through; in the left and out the right. He tore off his shirt and tore it into pieces, then stuffed what he could into the wounds to stop the bleeding. He needed help and no one was around. He knew if he tried to move him, by himself, he could cause more damage, so he waited.

Ralynn and the crew watched the cattle run by and then the horses at high speed. She became worried when she hadn't seen Matt, Juan, or Luke pass by. In her gut, she knew something more had happened. She convinced Raydog to go back to where the camp was last evening to see if Matt had gone there looking for her. He agreed to take her and told Sonny and Skye to take the chuckwagon on ahead and find a place to camp for the night. She and Raydog headed east in the feed wagon towards the previous campsite. Once there, they saw no one around, so they headed for the area where the remuda was. It was taking forever to reach their destination; she prayed, silently. She told Raydog to go faster; he whipped the reins, and the team began to run.

* * * * *

Alex was mortified. They had failed again. Jake was a nervous wreck. Somehow the other drovers were expecting them and disrupted their plans. His men had either been killed or taken by the drovers, and the cattle and horses were still intact under the other rancher's control. "How did they know? Everything was going as planned," Jake said. "I don't know, but I'm not waiting around to see the Boss's reaction. I'm heading to Mexico. You coming along, Jake?" "You bet I'm coming! I don't want to be anywhere around here, now." he said. They mounted their horses and rode off.

Gerard was fuming when he got the news, even more so when Alex and Jake had not returned. He sent two of his men to find them and told them to bring them back, Dead or Alive. He didn't care which. He went into his office and slammed the door shut, pulled open the top drawer of his desk and took out a fresh, unopened bottle of expensive whiskey. He opened it, poured himself a shot and then threw the glass at the wall, shattering as it fell to the floor. He sat in his chair and looked out the window. "They will pay! They will pay!" He kept saying. Then, in a slurred voice, he muttered, "Alex and Jake will pay as well." He took two, three more shots of whiskey and started writing something down on a notepad. The angrier he became, the faster he wrote.

Another plan was formed in his evil mind and this time he'll take care of it himself.

* * * * *

Back home at the P3: Martha was cooking lunch for her and Sam while he had taken out the kitchen trash and was in the process of lighting the match when he heard something shatter and Martha wailed in a loud and terrified voice. He ran up the steps and entered the kitchen. He stopped in his tracks when he saw Martha, on the floor, with broken glass all around her. "Stay still, honey, let me clean up the glass first before we get you up." She just sat there crying, tears running down her face. Sam swept up the glass, put away the broom and dustpan, and went to Martha's side and sat down on the floor. "What is it, honey? Why are you so upset?" Martha leaned into him, soaking his shirt with her tears, she was sobbing so hard she couldn't even speak. "Whatever it is, we can handle it together, my Love. Please, tell me what's wrong." Sam pleaded. She raised her head and wiped the tears from her face with her apron. "Oh, Sam, something terrible has happened to the kids, I can feel it. I was carrying the plates and cups to the table, when I was struck with such a feeling, a bad feeling. My hands shook and I dropped them. I couldn't help it. It came in a wave, like a wild wind, churned me around, and knocked me to the floor. I've never felt anything like it and it won't let me go. It's right here in my heart, pounding, and burning. Sam, I know it's the kids. What do we do?" She cried some more. Sam held her close. They stayed that way for a long time, holding each other. Sam moved his arm and she jumped. "Oh, my, I forgot all about lunch, help me up, Sam," she ordered. Sam stood, putting his arms out in front of himself, taking her hands, and pulled her to her feet. She was a bit unsteady, for only a moment, then regained her composure. I'll have lunch for you in a few minutes," she told him and kissed him gently on his cheek. "No rush, Love. Did you get cut anywhere?" "I don't think so," she answered. "Go about your cooking. I'll be right back. Sure, you're okay, Love?" "Yes, Dear, I'm fine." He gave her a quick, gentle hug and went out the door. Sam found Dusty, one of the top hands, and told him to ride into Archer and send a telegram to the Sheriff of Emery, stating that they wanted someone from the P3 Drive to return a telegram stating they had arrived safely. Dusty nodded and mounted his big Bay and rode towards town. That was all Sam could think to do. He had no idea how far or where they were with the herd and it would take days to reach them. He headed back towards the house to have lunch with Martha. "How are you feeling now?" He asked when he was, once again, in the kitchen. Martha was putting the last bowl of stew on the table and answered, "I'm fine. I just know that something is wrong, Sam." "I just sent Dusty to town to send a telegram to Sheriff Stevens in Emery. I asked him to have someone from the drive let us know that they had arrived safely. That's all we can do for now." "Thank you, Sam," she said as they sat down to eat.

They ate in silence, then Sam placed a hand over hers. "Martha, I realize we only just discovered our feelings for each other, but something has been weighing on my mind." "What is it, Sam? You know you can talk to me about anything." "Well, I was wondering, and I have given this a lot of thought, will you marry me, Martha and become my wife?" he said in such a sweet manner. She looked into his pale blue eyes, lifted his hand to her mouth, and kissed it softly, not once taking her eyes off his. She laid their hands on the table and said, "That's the sweetest thing anyone ever said to me. Yes, Sam, I'll marry you." He stood up, pulled out her chair, and twirled her around. They were laughing and crying at the same time.

* * * * *

Raydog and Ralynn saw Luke on the ground struggling with something. They drove the team faster towards him. As soon as they stopped, she was off the wagon running to him, calling his name. "Luke! Luke! Are you hurt? Are you okay?" When she reached him, she wrapped him in her arms, thanking God he was okay. She held him tight, while she looked him over. "Ralynn?" he said trying to get her attention, "It's okay. We'll get you to the...." her voice trailed off. At that moment, she saw Matt lying there, unmoving. She reached to touch him and Luke grabbed her arm. "He's breathing, but not well, I can't get him to wake up. He's been shot, Ralynn." She gasped, loudly, and her hands flew up to her mouth to muffle her cry. "Tell Raydog to come help me up. I don't think anything is broken; I'll just be sore for a few days. Tell him to bring a wide piece of lumber, so we can lift Matt out of this hole." She got up, still looking at her brother, then ran to the wagon to tell Raydog what Luke had said. He jumped up into the wagon, followed by Ralynn, slapped the team, and headed to Luke and Matt. They pulled the wagon as close as they could and jumped down. First, they got Luke up and moving, making sure he had no serious injuries, then Raydog went to the back of the wagon and returned with a wide board. "Let's put him on this and tie him down, so he can't move around and I can look at those wounds," he said. "I don't think he can move," Luke commented. They, carefully, lifted him up and placed him on the board; she was holding the rope to tie him down. Raydog went to the back of the wagon and returned with some clean strips of cloth. He cleaned Matt's wounds, packed them with clean strips of cloth, wrapped larger strips around him, then they lifted him into the wagon. "We are closer to Archer than Emery and Matt needs a doctor. I must get this herd to Emery, Ralynn, so I can't take you back, but I'll send Sonny back to drive you to Archer and straight to the Doc's office. You then can send someone out to the ranch to tell Sam and Martha what has happened. I'll get another drover to go with you, you'll need help when Matt comes to. Is there anyone of the drovers you prefer?" "Tom or Charlie, either one will do," she said. She looked up into his eyes, "Thank you for protecting my brother." "Let's go get Sonny. I'll need the papers on the cattle for the buyer." "Yes, they're in the chuckwagon. I'll get them for you when we reach Sonny and Skye." Raydog spoke up, "I sent them ahead when the girl and I came looking for Matt and Juan, and found you. Has anyone seen Juan?" "Not since this morning," Luke said. I'll send some drovers back to find him. Let's get these two on their way, first. "I'll ride ahead and send someone to find Sonny and have him head back here. The quicker we get them on their way; the sooner Matt will see the doctor."

Luke mounted the Paint and took off in search of the herd and the men. He came upon them miles farther West than they were before. He sent Cash to find Sonny and Jim and Dave to double back and find Juan. He stepped down from the Paint and pain shot through his right hip and up his back. He couldn't stop now; he'd see a doctor in Emery after everything was taken care of with the drive and cattle. He was sure it was just badly bruised and pulled muscles.

Thirty minutes later, Sonny pulled up, he explained the situation and the urgency and headed him East to meet up with Ralynn and Raydog. He took his canteen off his saddle, took a long drink, hooked it back over the saddle horn, then remounted, slowly, and headed back East.

She was collecting her and Matt's things and loading them into the feed wagon, while Raydog was transferring the feed and hay into the chuckwagon. Luke arrived, just a few minutes after Sonny and stepped off his horse. He went over to look in on Matt. No change. It looked like the bleeding had slowed some. He walked over to Ralynn. "Do you have those papers I need?" "Yes, right here." She reached in her bag, pulled them out and handed them to him. "Listen, Luke, I'm counting on you to get this herd through and get top dollar for P3's cattle. I'm trusting you with all I have. Please, don't disappoint me." she told him. He took her by her shoulders and looked into her eyes. "I promise to do my absolute best for you. I'll be pushing the herd hard the rest of the way. I want to get back to P3 as soon as I can. You make sure to take care of yourself. Matt's going to need all of you when he wakes up: make sure you take care of you. I'll be back before you know it." He placed his calloused hands, one on each side of her face, leaned down and kissed her on the lips. She wrapped her arms around his neck and kissed him back.

Their lips connected, as if they belonged there. It was hot, wet, and thrilling. She felt it all the way to her toes. The kiss lingered as Luke pulled her closer and placed his hand at the small of her back. It deepened as they were drawn closer. It was only when Sonny hollered, asking if she was ready, that they pulled apart. She looked at him, saying nothing, and climbed up into the back of the wagon with Matt. Sonny gave the team the command to move forward. Luke had asked Tom to ride along with them and watch over them. Tom accepted the task and was riding alongside. She watched Matt closely; was he breathing, has the bleeding subsided, is he bleeding inside? So many questions. She said a quiet prayer, asking God to let her brother be okay.

Matt still hadn't come to by the end of the second day on the way back. Sonny drove the team as hard as he could without jostling Matt too much. They were stopping for the night to let the horses rest and to let Matt be still and rest as well. She never left her brother's side except to get fresh water and relieve herself. Matt hadn't moved once. She cleaned his wounds, and repacked them like Raydog showed her. She was putting a cold cloth on his forehead and removed the warm one. "Miss Ralynn?" Sonny said as he opened the canvas at the back of the wagon. "Yes, Sonny, what is it?" She replied in a worn and tired voice. "We should be in Archer tomorrow afternoon if we leave at sun-up. Any objections?" "No, that will be fine." "How's the boy?" "No change, except he's running a fever now and that tells me there is infection somewhere. The sooner we get to Docs the better," she said. "I drove the horses pretty hard today. Okay to let them rest one more hour?" "Yes, that's fine, as long as we hurry and no stops till we get to Archer and the Doc's office." she said in a demanding voice. "Yes, ma'am." Sonny said and left the wagon. He knew the stress she was under, so he just let her attitude go by the wayside. She was sitting on the floor of the wagon beside her brother, exchanging the cloths on his forehead and wiping him down with a cool cloth. When she checked the bandages, they were saturated with fresh blood. She climbed out of the wagon and went over to the campfire Sonny and Tom had started. She bent down, picked up a tin cup and the coffee pot and poured herself a cup of Cowboy coffee. She took a sip and burnt the tip of her tongue. "Ouch!" she exclaimed. "You should know better than to do that," Tom commented. "I know, don't know what I was thinking." She sat down and sipped on her coffee in silence. In the distance a coyote howled giving her chills; she shivered. "You okay, Miss Ralynn?" Tom asked. "Just a bit chilled. I came over here for a reason, but the coffee smelled so good. The bandages on Matt need to be changed; they have become saturated and I need some help lifting him while I rebandage him." "Oh, I forgot to mention, we have run out of clean bandages," Sonny said. She sat there for a moment and then stood up and began pacing back and forth in front of them. "Got it! I can use my petticoat," she said. "Miss Ralynn, are you alright?" Tom asked. "Of course, why do you ask?" "Well, you're not at home and you are not wearing a petticoat. You're in jeans and a shirt." "Oh. I'm sorry. I brought a dress with me to wear once we got to Emery. I can make bandages out of the undergarments." she explained. "I'll help you with the boy, whenever you are ready," Tom said. "Thanks, give me a few minutes to make some bandages, then I'll be ready," she told him. She headed back to the wagon and climbed in. Locating her tapestry bag, she pulled out the petticoat and began ripping it into strips for the bandages.

Tom appeared at the back of the wagon, "Are you ready, Miss?" "Yes, let's do this. Come on in, Tom," she said. Tom lifted Matt so that she could change the soiled bandages and replace them with clean ones. When she was done, he laid him back down. "I'll take those to the fire and get you some fresh water from the stream. Matt feels pretty warm." "Yes, I'm afraid he's running a fever. I was just looking at his wounds for any signs of infection, but I didn't see anything. He could still have one inside." She handed him the soiled bandages rolled up in a strip of her petticoat. "Thank you, Tom," she said in a whisper. He tipped his hat, picked up the water bucket, and left the wagon.

CHAPTER 16

Fourteen hours later, the wagon pulled into Archer and headed straight to Doc's office. There was no change in Matt. Before the wagon stopped, she jumped out of the back of the wagon and ran into the office. "Doc! Doc!" she yelled, loudly. Within seconds, she was back with Doc in tow. When he saw Matt, he said they needed to move him into the exam room very carefully.

Tom and Sonny lifted Matt out of the wagon, on the board, and into the exam room as the doctor had instructed. After they moved him onto the exam table, the doctor turned to her and asked what she had done to care for him. She told him that she cleaned the wounds and changed the bandages when they became soiled and that she kept cold compresses on his forehead for the fever. "You did an excellent job." He told her, then asked her to wait in the waiting area. "Please, send in my nurse when you go out. I'll be out to talk to you after my examination." He then turned back to Matt. She took one last look at her little brother, then left the room. Sonny and Tom were waiting for her. "Thanks for getting us here, so quickly," she said. "I hate to ask more of you, but I must. Sonny, please take the team home and take care of them. Tom, ride out with him and inform Sam and Martha what has happened. Have one of the other men bring them to town and you both get some rest. It's been a rough few days." "Don't like leaving you here alone, Miss," Tom said. "I'm not alone, Doc and the nurse are just in the other room. Just get the news to Sam and Martha, I really need them here when Doc comes out to talk to me."

"Okay, Miss, we'll get it done," They left and she sat down on the worn sofa to wait. She thought to herself how good it felt instead of that wagon seat. She leaned her head back and silently said a prayer for her brother, then the lids of her eyes became heavy; she slept.

Tom returned with Sam and Martha. They rushed in the waiting area, only to find Ralynn sound asleep. "Should we wake her?" Sam asked Martha. Tom broke in saying, "She hasn't slept for over three days watching over Matt." "Let her sleep. We'll wake her when the doctor comes out to talk to us," Martha said. Sam gently picked up her feet and laid them on the sofa so she would be lying down and resting more comfortably. They all took a seat and waited. Martha looked around the room. It was a dreary place with four chairs and a sofa. There were two doors to adjoining rooms: one to the exam room and one to the Doc's office. Above the door was a sign that read, Dr. John Tapwater; he had been the town's doctor for over twenty years. Everyone loved and admired him. Families would take turns inviting him to their homes to have a meal or to happy events. P3 had invited him several times over the years. He had brought both Parker children into the world all those years ago. She was becoming restless and stood up and began pacing back and forth across the room. Tom was twirling his hat in his hands and Sam was twiddling his thumbs. All at once the outside door opened and Sonny came in letting it close loudly. "Any news yet?" He asked. Ralynn jumped up, rubbing her eyes, and letting them focus. "Sam! Martha!" She arose from the sofa and went right into Martha's arms and the tears and sobs came. Sam walked over to them and wrapped his arms around both of them. Sam moved away from them and motioned for Tom and Sonny to come close to him. I didn't want to talk while she was sleeping, but what, in the world, happened?" Tom answered, "Really don't know, Sam. Luke came to us and asked us to take those two home. All we know is that the boy had been shot." "Shot!" Martha screamed. "Yes, Ma'am. The bullet went clean through and the cook and Ralynn bandaged him up and Luke sent us on our way." "So, Luke is taking the herd on into Emery, then?" "Yes, Ralynn gave him the papers for the buyers and if anyone has a problem with him, all the boys will vouch for him." "That's fine, then," Sam said. Martha had Ralynn sit back down on the sofa. She held her against her bosom and let her cry. "When we get you home and out of those men's clothes, we'll get you in a warm bath, then you can sleep in your own bed," she whispered to her. Ralynn nodded and wiped her eyes. "Only after we hear what Doc says about Matt." "Of course," Martha replied.

It had been over three hours before Doc came out of the exam room. Everyone stood up, at once, and four pairs of eyes were focused on him. "I have good and bad news. The good news is that he is stable now, his heart is strong, and he is breathing normally. The bad news is that he has lost so much blood and needs a transfusion. I believe Ralynn is the best candidate for that job." He looked at her for some sort of reaction, then continued. "The other news is that he came to, for only a moment, long enough to tell me he couldn't move his legs. So, I did some tests and from what I can tell, he is paralyzed from the waist down. His wounds will heal fine, but he's going to need a lot of help from here on out. He'll need to learn how to get around, all over again." "Ralynn, are you up to doing this?" "Of course, I am." "Okay, then, go into the exam room and the nurse will get you ready." He turned to go into his office. "Doc, I want to hear the rest," she said. "I've told you all I know, for now. Matt's a strong young man, and I believe he'll be fine. He'll just have to learn new ways of doing things. I won't know if this is permanent until Matt wakes up and we can do some more tests. Only he can tell me what his body can and cannot do." He took a deep breath and continued. "I will say this to you all, if this is permanent, it will be a long and rough road ahead, but we'll discuss that when we know more. We'll do the transfusion, then I want you to take that young lady home, feed and bathe her and put her on bedrest for, at least, three days to give her body time to rest and regenerate her blood supply.

She's going to need all her strength when her brother comes home. I'll be keeping Matt here for at least a week to watch for any infections and get his fever down. Right now, take care of her."

Looking at Ralynn he said, "Now, run along, we need to get this done." "Thanks, Doc, we'll do that," Sam said.

Nurse Watkins explained to Ralynn what to expect, and then went to the door and asked Tom and Sonny if they would lend a hand. Both men stood, then walked into the exam room. "I need to elevate this bed, please. Grab some of those books over in the corner, then put stacks of them under the bed's legs. It needs to be higher than the bed Matt's in," she explained. Tom and Sonny walked over to the corner and picked up several books. They put three big books in a stack and placed them under each leg of the bed. Nurse Watkins stood by the bed and looked over at Matt. Can you add one more book to each leg? We need it high enough for the blood to flow easily from Miss Ralynn to Matt." When the task was completed, she thanked them and they left the room. "Miss Ralynn, let's get you into the bed now and I'll get the needle and tube to get you started, I already have Matt ready." She climbed up in the bed using a step stool, laid down, and pulled up her sleeve. The nurse came back with the needle and tube and laid them beside her. Nurse Watkins cleansed her arm with whiskey and proceeded to place the needle in her left arm, close to her elbow. Next, she connected the tube to the other end of the syringe, somehow. Ralynn saw her blood run through the tube to her brother and she felt like she was giving Matt renewed life. All of a sudden, she began to feel weak and tired; her stomach churned. She turned her head away and that's all she remembered before she passed out.

Two hours passed before Ralynn came out of the exam room, steadied by Nurse Watkins, at her side. Martha stood up and took Ralynn by the arm. "She's weak and exhausted and needs rest as soon as you get her home. She won't be wanting to eat much, if any, and everything else can wait till tomorrow. Just get her to bed tonight," she said. Sam spoke up, "We've got that covered, Ms. Watkins, Tom, we brought that stack of covers and blankets for taking Matt home, they are in the wagon under the seat. You and Sonny make a bed with them in the back of the wagon for Rae to lay on while we head home." "Sure thing, Boss," Tom replied. Sam turned to Martha, "How's she doing?" "She'll be fine after she gets some rest," she said. "And a bath but it will wait until tomorrow ." Tom and Sonny came back inside and sat down. "Sam, I want to see if we can see Matt before we go. I'll go ask Doc," she said, and knocked on Doc's office door. "Come in," Doc said. Martha stepped inside, still holding onto the door.

"Sam and I were wondering if we could see Matthew before we left?" "Yes, certainly, go right on in, but make it brief, please." "Thanks, Doc," she smiled and closed the door. "Tom, you, and Sonny watch over her while we go in to see Matt for a few minutes, then, we'll head for home." "No problem, we'll take care of her." Martha came out of Doc's office and motioned for Sam to come in.with her. They stood at the side of his bed and just watched him breathe. Martha leaned over, kissed his forehead, she told him she loved him and to fight with all he had. She turned to Sam and said, "Let's get our girl home." Sam and Martha came out of the exam room. "Let's head home boys," he said. Tom stood up from where he was sitting, walked over to Ralynn, picked her up off the sofa, and carried her to the wagon. Once they got her situated, Sam helped Martha up in the back of the wagon to sit with Ralynn. Sonny mounted his Bay and Tom drove the team.

Sam rode up front with Tom. "Here we go." Tom flicked the reins and headed towards home. An hour later, they were pulling up to the house on the P3 Ranch. Tom stopped the wagon and applied the wagon's break. He jumped down and hurried to the back. Sam was helping Martha down and as soon as she was out of the way, he reached in, picked up Ralynn, and carried her into the house; Martha and Sam followed. "Where should I lay her down, Miss Martha?" "Upstairs, second door on the right," Martha said. Martha led the way up the stairs and into Ralynn's room. She pulled back the bed covers and Tom laid her down gently. "Thanks, Tom, I'll take it from here." "Welcome, Ma'am," he said and left the room. Martha took off her boots and clothes, washed her face and arms and put on her nightgown. Then, she covered her with blankets, blew out the lamp, and left the room. Downstairs, Sam was sitting in the kitchen waiting on the coffee to finish cooking. Martha came into the room and went over to the cabinet and took out two cups, set them on the counter, and then checked the coffee. "Our lives have changed in an instant, Sam. What do we do now?" She was looking at the cup as she poured the coffee. "Of course, it has changed, but we haven't. Our plans will stay the same, we will just have to adjust things, that's all." "I'm so worried about Matthew. He will be devastated when he comes to and realizes he can't use his legs. I can just imagine the look on his face. And Ralynn, she'll blame herself for letting him go on that drive, I know her." "Dear, quit fretting. We'll rest tonight and face everything in a new light tomorrow. I don't have the answers to all the questions running through our minds. All I do know is that we will be here for them when they need us and that's the most important thing." Martha laid her hand on his and they sipped their coffee.

CHAPTER 17

Six Weeks Later:

Luke, the crew, and the drovers came riding in late in the afternoon. The men were tired, worn, and dirty, and couldn't wait to get to the creek, strip down, and jump in to wash away all the dirt and grime from the past two months on the drive. Skye rode on ahead to her own ranch, as well as the drovers from the other ranches. Luke wanted to stop and check on Matt's progress, but really wanted to see Ralynn. He wanted to get his horse, Twisted Mister, the name he gave the Paint, settled in the barn, and get himself cleaned up first. He rode up to the barn, stepped off Mister, he called him for short, and led him into the barn. He unsaddled his horse, curried, and brushed him down, put him in a stall, and fed him some grain and hay. He walked out of the barn and towards the bunkhouse, gathered some clean clothes and headed to the creek.

Ralynn was exhausted. She took over the care of Matt ever since she recovered and he was brought home, which wasn't an easy task. He was so angry; he permanently lost the use of his legs and he blamed her for allowing him to go on the drive. She blamed herself. She should have taken better care of him. He yelled at her, constantly demanding her attention, when he wanted something; it was to be now, not a few moments later. He demanded her there when he woke up and when he went to sleep. She had to bathe him and help him with the catheters he had to use to pee. He was embarrassed, as well, and that made things worse. At first, she was so guilt ridden that she did everything for him, every time he needed or wanted something she was right there. It was wearing heavy on her and she was just hindering herself. Martha talked to her several times about Matt needing to learn to do things on his own, but she wouldn't listen. She was waiting for Ralynn to come into the kitchen. She was going to talk to her again; she had to take care of herself. It was taking its toll on everyone. Maybe, she and Sam should, both, sit down and talk to her; that might get her to see what she was doing to herself, and Matt. Something had to give. Martha caught Sam that afternoon and mentioned to him about him and her talking to Ralynn together. Sam walked her over to the garden bench and sat down with her. "Love, we're going to have to try to understand them the best we can and give the situation a lot of patience. Neither one of us can know what is in their minds. That's just something they will have to work out. I will, however, sit down with you to talk to Rae, she is pushing herself too much; doing her chores, taking care of Matt, and even doing his chores. She must learn that she isn't in this alone. We are all here to help." "Thanks, Dear. Oh, I don't think we should mention anything about the wedding, just yet. I think we should postpone it for now." Sam stood up and sharply said, "Postpone it? For how long? Weeks, months, years?" He was floored that she would even mention such a thing. "Don't be upset. I just think we have enough on our plates right now," she said. "No! I won't have it. We'll keep our plans just as they are. If Matt wants to be angry and sulk in his room and Rae wants to be at his beck and call, then so be it. We are not putting our lives on hold any longer. We will be married on June 1st as planned, and if you cannot do that, then you had better let me know. You think on that now!" Sam walked away leaving her without another word or a kiss. He never did that. Thinking about it; she couldn't really blame him for getting upset. They deserved their happiness too. She would apologize to him before dinner; she knew she hurt him; her heart ached.

At the dinner table, Ralynn sat there listening to Sam and Martha. She knew they were right. She had let Matt run her ragged; all because she felt guilty about his situation. She knew it wasn't her fault that he had gotten hurt, but she still felt responsible. Sam was talking, "Rae, do you understand what we are telling you?" "Yes, I understand. It's just hard because I said he could go. If I hadn't this would not have happened." "Rae, it could have happened here just as well, falling off a horse or being run over by cattle, working a ranch is dangerous and you can't always prevent accidents or tragedies; they happen all the time. "Matthew loves you so much, and you know that. He is angry at the world right now, but since you are the closest to him, it is you he will blame. You, both were on that drive, what if the situation was turned around and it was you lying up there in that bed? Do you think he'd feel guilty for you? Probably not. You chose to be there the same as he did and it was neither one's fault; it was those men that did this to him. The sooner you both realize that, the better you both will be," Sam explained. "I know that. I just don't know what to do. I'm so tired and I feel so weak." "You've overdone yourself, especially so soon after giving all that blood. You haven't gained back all your strength, yet. Why don't you go take a hot bath and go to bed? Sam and I can take care of Matthew tonight." "Are you both sure?" "Yes, now git!" Sam told her.

Ralynn shut her door and went over to the tub and just looked at it for a moment. A bath sounds so good, she thought, but I'm just too tired; her body ached and her head pounded. She changed into her nightgown and went over to her bed and climbed in. Pulling up the covers, she thought about what Sam and Martha had said. She knew she was going to have to get hard with little brother, and use tough love with him. She had to give in and let others help. She just couldn't keep caring for Matt and keep doing both of their chores. There are plenty of men on the ranch to take care of Matt's chores, besides, they will have to get used to doing them, now that he can't right now. He does, however, need to get out of that room. She'll just have to figure out a way.

The way things are going, twenty-four hours isn't enough hours in a day for her to get everything done and have any time to herself. She needs to make some changes. On that thought, she fell asleep. Martha was bringing up hot water for her bath and knocked on her door. After a minute and no answer, she opened the door and found Ralynn sound asleep. She went over and tucked the blankets in around her then walked out of the room and shut the door.

Luke approached the house as Sam, in a mood, ran right into him. "Woe there, Sam! What's going on?" "Get out of my way!" Sam demanded as he tried to push Luke aside. "Sam, are you alright? It's me, Luke." Sam paused and looked up, as if seeing him for the first time. "Oh, my word, Luke, your back!" "I'm frustrated with this whole situation, I apologize, Luke." "No apology necessary, Sam. Yes, I just returned about an hour or so ago. I wanted to clean up before coming up to the house. What has you all worked up, anyway, is it Matt, is he worse?" "Oh no, Matt is being his selfish self. He's running his sister ragged, so much so that she's exhausted, grumpy, and doesn't have a minute to herself. She hasn't slept since we brought him home. "What happened? Matt adores his sister." "Not anymore, at least not on the surface of things. He blames her for him being on the drive, for his injury, and for not being his shadow." "Seriously? She wasn't even there. I had her and the crew hidden away from the drive when all hell broke loose." "No one has been able to tell me what really happened. Fill me in please." Sam said. "Sure will, but can it wait? I want to check on Matt before he goes to sleep for the night." "Okay, I'll get my chores done and be available, anytime, later. I wish you luck, you may need it." Sam said and headed towards the barn.

Luke proceeded towards the house. He stepped up to the back door and knocked. He was about to head back to the bunkhouse when Martha, teary eyed, opened the door. "Martha, good to see you." He picked her up and spun her around. She giggled. "Now, that's my girl. I've missed that laugh and smile." He let her down and kissed her on the cheek. "Feeling better now?" She smiled, "Yes, much better." "I wanted to see Matt. I hear that he's being a holy terror to his sister." "You could call it that. No one but her is allowed to do anything for him; it's as if he's trying to punish her for his situation. She's not the sweet girl we all knew just a few weeks ago, Luke. She's exhausted and I don't know how much longer she can keep this up." "Let me see what I can do, maybe nothing, but I'll try," he said. She told him which room was Matts and to be sure to duck when he opened the door. Luke tipped his hat and headed up the stairs.

Once he found Matt's room, he prepared himself for the worst. He knocked and when there was no answer, he opened the door. He found Matt sleeping and Ralynn was occupied with something, he didn't know what, across the room. "Ralynn?" he said, in a whisper.. She turned around and he was stunned. Standing before him was a woman he did not know. She looked nothing like the woman he was in love with. Her expression was hard and she was pale, no smile to see him, or any sort of reaction. He, at least, thought she would be happy to see him, but there was nothing.

"What's happened to you, Honey?" "Nothing has happened to me and don't call me Honey!" she yelled. He took a step back. Martha wasn't joking, he thought. He looked over at Matt moving around; waking up. "Now, see what you did." "Ralynn, I just got back and I wanted to see you and check on Matt." "You don't need to see me, but there is Matt, if you must disturb him!" She turned her back on him and went back to what she was doing. "Luke, you're back! It's good to see you. How was the drive? Did you get what we wanted for the cattle? Any more surprises pop up? This one was a doozy," he said, pointing to his legs and then to the wheelchair in the corner of the room. "Grab that chair and sit down and tell me all about it." "Have you used that yet?" Luke asked as he nodded towards the wheelchair. "No. No one lets me do anything, especially her." He gave his sister a, if looks could kill look. "You can leave us men to talk, Ralynn. I don't need you here now," he said bitterly. She looked at him, turned, walked out, slamming the door. "Hey, Matt, that's no way to talk to your sister. She's only trying to help you." Luke scolded him. "She deserves it. I wouldn't be here in this mess if she had been looking out for me like Pa told her." "Oh, is that how it is?" Luke remarked. "So, tell me how the drive went." Matt said, changing the subject. Luke looked at the wheelchair. "I'll tell you what. I'll make a deal with you." "What kind of deal?" "You let me take you outside, using your wheelchair and I'll answer all your questions. It's dark outside now and all the boys will be in the bunkhouse, so no one will see you." He looked at the chair; how he hated that thing, but he wanted to talk with Luke, so he agreed.

Luke took the chair and moved it to the bottom of the staircase. He returned to Matt's room and picked him up. Matt grabbed his quilt off his bed then let Luke carry him downstairs. He set Matt in his chair and wheeled him outside onto the front porch. He helped Matt get comfortable and then sat in the chair across from him. Just then the door opened and Martha came out with two glasses of lemonade. "Thanks, Martha," Matt said. She almost lost her balance; she was so shocked to hear any response from him. "You're welcome." She went back inside, leaving them alone. "Now, tell me everything." Luke told him that once the cattle had calmed down, a couple of days later, they continued the drive. They made it into Emery a week later and he got a decent price for the cattle. They were glad it was over and the boys were exhausted, that the first night they slept in beds and on the second night they had to live it up some, after searching for the missing drovers all day. "Missing drovers, what happened? Last I remember was a sharp pain in my back and legs and the ground pounding." Luke filled him in and continued. "We searched for two more days before they came upon an old-line shack and found them tied up inside. They were in pretty bad shape, so they took them into Archer before coming home. He told him of how he found him during the raid and asked him if he remembered anything? Matt told him he only remembered seeing the three strangers with guns pulled and heading their way. He jumped on his horse and warned Juan, then he was headed to tell him and the others. All at once, his back and legs felt like they had caught fire and exploded, knocking off his horse. He tried to get up but his legs would not move. His body fell face first and he didn't remember anything after that, except he did feel heavy with some kind of pressure on him and he heard the pounding of hooves; that's it. "Didn't your sister tell you she found us and that I was lying on top of you to protect you from the horse's hooves after they'd been stampeded? Did she tell you that she didn't sleep one bit until she got you to Doc's office? Do you know she hasn't had a moment of peace or time to herself since you came home? What's going on with you, Matt? It is not her fault in any of this. If you recall, you pretty much begged to go on the drive. She said you could go on the drive; she didn't say you had to go. It was your choice and you made it. You wanted to be treated like a man and you were. You, also, knew it could be dangerous before you went, so why are you placing all this guilt on your sister?" Matt looked down, his cheerful smile faded as tears formed in his eyes. "Wow, I didn't know all that. She's not said anything, except to tell me what to do and stuff. Have I really been that bad?" "She loves you, Matt, you should think about what I've told you while I'm gone." "You're leaving, already?" "I'll be back. I just have some things to take care of that I couldn't do while on the drive." "Let's get you inside. Wonder if Martha has any of those cookies left?" "I bet she does, but if she says, no, I know where to find them." "Okay, milk and cookies, here we come." Luke laughed as he pushed Matt inside. He stopped before going into the kitchen, where Sam and Martha were sitting at the table. "There's one thing I want you to do for me while I'm gone, Matt." "What's that, Luke?" "I want you to let your sister off the hook. Let Sam and Martha help you sometimes and be part of the family again. Stop tearing your family apart and get it back together. Can you do that?" "I'll try, but it's hard, Luke." "I understand, but if you don't you might lose those you love the most. Think on that." Luke continued pushing him towards the kitchen. "Luke, thanks for saving and protecting me. I guess I could have died out there." "Yes, you could have died out there, but when I make a promise to do something, I do it, and I promised to take care of you and you're welcome." Matt kept letting Luke's words run over and over in his head and as he neared the kitchen, he smiled. Entering the kitchen they were greeted with two of the biggest smiles and lots of cookies and milk.

CHAPTER 18

An hour later, Luke carried Matt up to his room, leaving his wheelchair downstairs. "We need to see about fixing you a room downstairs, it would be a lot easier for you to get around using your chair. "I hate that chair!" Matt exclaimed, pouting. "Well, it's the only way for you to get around so you may as well get used to it. Don't you want to be able to see Darby and Bullet; have you even been out there since you've been home?" "No," he said, hanging his head. "Matt, have you done anything, for yourself, since being home?" "Been right here in bed." "So, you've just left everything for your sister to do, then? No wonder she's like she is. Worn down, so much so, she looks like death. No one else has had time for them since we've all been on the drive. Sam and Martha do all they can, and your sister does her chores, your chores and takes care of you. I'd be ashamed of myself, if I did that to my sister, if I had one. I understand you're angry due to you not being able to use your legs, but you need to get it together, kid. "What makes you so special that you have the right to make everyone miserable? You need to think on all I've told you or no one will want to help you. Think about where that will leave you." "I don't know, '' he replied; guilt in his voice. "Not in a good place, that's for sure. Well, goodnight, kid, I'll see you when I get back." Luke left the room and closed the door. Matt leaned back against his pillows; "I ain't been that bad," he said to himself in a cocky tone and closed his eyes. Ralynn came in a few minutes later and gave him his meds and readied him for bed. "Thanks, Sis," he said, in a whisper. She stopped in her tracks and turned around, but he was already asleep. She thought she had dreamed it, but it sounded real. She left his room, entered hers and fell onto her bed and slept.

Luke entered the kitchen and found Sam nursing a cup of coffee and Martha was working on something at the counter. "Can I have one of those?" he asked Martha, nodding towards Sam. "Sure thing. Have a seat and I'll bring one over for you." He sat down and she placed a cup in front of him. "It smells good." He took a sip. "It tastes good, too." "Thank you," she replied and went back to the counter. "Now, can we talk?" Sam asked. "Tell me what happened." Luke took off his Stetson and laid it rim up on the table; cowboys think it's bad luck to lay their hats rim down. He ran his long fingers through his hair and got comfortable. "Sam, things were going good, no problems with the cattle or even Chester was on his best behavior." "Did you have to hobble him?" "No, believe it or not, we never did. He did just fine. At the stockyards, though, was another story, but it wasn't our problem, anymore. I heard he caused quite a ruckus." Sam laughed so hard; he almost fell out of his chair. "I knew it would happen somewhere. That bull can be cantankerous at times; he was a good sire; gave us some prime stock over the years." Luke continued, "I really thought that after five days on the trail we would make it to Emery and back within two weeks, but that wasn't the case. On the sixth day, I woke up with a gut feeling that something was off, but had no evidence, except that I had eight drovers acting strangely. Raydog later told me he had the same feeling that morning, but like me, nothing else. I decided to give Comanche a rest and went to the remuda to get another horse, the Paint in the barn, and I told Juan and Matt to keep their rifles close by. I was riding up the North side of the herd and noticed some of the drovers not acknowledging my greetings, whereas they had every day before. I caught up with Fred and Charlie and told them to be prepared for anything and to pass the word to only the drovers they knew and trusted. I had Raydog and Sonny find a place to pull away from the herd and find a safe place for them and the ladies to hide, and stay hidden. They would know when they could move again. I rode down the South side and found a few more drovers that flat out ignored me. It was at that moment that I realized something was about to happen. I was riding back up the North side to check on Raydog and the ladies when I heard a shot and then a scream. It was so loud, I could hear it over the cattle, as they were getting restless. It was coming from the rear of the herd, so I knew it wasn't the girls. I rode hard to find the source. The cattle were beginning to run and I knew I had to hurry. I kept going and that's when I saw someone on the ground smack dab in the middle of the stampeding horses' path. When I got closer, I realized it was Matt; I didn't have time to get him out of the way of the horses, so I jumped off my horse and threw myself on top of him so he wouldn't be trampled. I didn't know at that time that he had been shot. Once the horses passed, I tried to wake him but he was out cold. I thought I just knocked the breath out of him. When I turned him over, that's when I saw all the blood pooled under him. I checked him over and found two bullet holes; the bullet went clean through from the left side and out the right side. I tore off his shirt and stuffed the wounds. A little while ago, Matt told me what he remembered. He said he recalled three men coming towards the remuda with their guns pulled. He jumped on his horse and warned Juan, then was coming to warn me. That's when he said it felt like his back and legs caught fire and he fell from his horse and couldn't get up, then he must have blacked out. Raydog and Ralynn found us and we got the wagons ready and loaded Matt and sent them to Archer. Then, our drovers and I finally got the herd stopped. There were eight drovers, we know of, not any from the drive, that were responsible for starting the stampede and were trying to take them. We got six of them; two dead and four captured. We tried to get them to talk to find out where our drovers were being held that had been kidnapped, but no luck. It took us a couple of days to find them in an abandoned line shack. They were in pretty bad shape. We left them at Doc's when we came through Archer. The sheriff, nor I, could get a name from any of them, so we know there's someone else running the show, so to speak. He must have lots of money with all the fire power he has hired. I don't think he's done, yet. I'm not certain, but I believe it's P3 that was the target. I need to have Ralynn look at those books, there's a reason P3 is being targeted. I'm pretty certain that they are only messing with the other ranches to throw off the author-ities and keep them from not knowing the real target. "Which you believe is us?" Sam asked. "Yes, I do. It sure looks that way. They have only been keeping the rustling going, but now they have paralyzed a young boy and Juan, who was shot in the arm, under their belts, but, so far, they have not been very successful. I remember the Governor said somewhere around three thousand five hundred cattle have been rustled so far." "Everyone around here has lost cattle, so they must be strangers to the area or are very clever," Sam said. "I'd say very clever, Sam." Sam scratched his head, "No one stands out to me, did you not hear anything on the drive?" "Nothing at all. Even the ones we captured were unknown to all our drovers. Not one of them was recognized. The "Boss Man" is here in Archer and hiring out of town outlaws, from far away, so no one knows them. That's the best I can figure." Luke explained. "Sure, is a mystery. One I hope we can figure out soon," Sam commented, with frustration in his voice.

A knock at the front door drew their attention immediately. "It's late, who could this be?" Sam said, as he walked to the door. Luke heard him open the door, but he couldn't hear what was being said. The door closed and Sam returned with a telegram. "It's for you, Luke." Luke reached out and took the telegram from Sam. He, already, knew who it was from: the Governor himself. He opened the telegram and read it. The Governor was calling him in; new infor-mation had come to light and the Governor wanted him to report immediately. He put the paper in his pocket and told Sam the news. He'd have to leave early in the morning and wasn't sure when he'd return. He told both, Sam, and Martha, that he had spoken to Matt and hoped he heard what he had said. He, also, told them about Ralynn's reaction to him and he never had the chance to let her know he would be gone for a while. He went on to say, "She may not even care, but let her know that I enjoyed that moment between us." Luke and Sam said their goodnights to Martha and left through the kitchen door. Sam hesitated until he heard the door lock and then proceeded to the bunkhouse. Luke noticed this. Things must have progressed between them since he had been gone, he thought with a smile on his face.

The next morning, Luke lit out at dawn. It was a two day ride to the Governor's office, so he wanted to get there and back as soon as possible. He didn't like the way things were with Ralynn and hoped he would have a chance to change her mind about him. He realized she was under a lot of stress, confused, and felt guilty, no thanks to Matt, but had she really forgotten the moment they shared. It was brief, but it was real. He knew in his heart that she knew it as well. He had to believe that.

The Secret Meeting:

Luke arrives in Cheyenne, WY, late afternoon, two days later. The secretary takes him right into the Governor's office. "Lucus, you made excellent time. I have some new information that our investigators here picked up. It seems that the Indians that jumped the reservation have all been captured and locked up, so we now know that it is white men running this rustling ring. Have you had any more activity in your area there?" "As a matter of fact, Sir, we did have quite a ruckus a few weeks back." Luke replied. He told the Governor the story about the drive, kidnapping of drovers, Matt being shot and paralyzed, the stampede and rustling of cattle and, now horses, as well. He, also, explained how they foiled their plans again. "I'd bet whoever is behind this is fuming about now. I don't think this is over and I believe that these activities have all been to distract from the P3 Ranch, which is, actually the target." "What proof do you have, Lucus?" "None, really, but it's a strong gut feeling and the Parkers were killed before I got on at the P3, the small attacks on the smaller ranchers and then the drive. The one thing in common to all of this is the P3 Ranch. There must be something I've overlooked, something I've missed."

"Now, Lucus, don't be so hard on yourself. I trust that gut feeling of yours, so get back at it. We'll talk soon." The Governor said. Luke shook his hand and left the office. He went across the street to send a telegraph to Sam to let him know he'd be arriving back at P3 in a couple of days. Then he headed back to the Imperial Hotel to think and get some shut eye. He knew the leader of this crime wave had to be near Archer or Emery. What was he not seeing? Who was at that first meeting at the Sheriff's office in Emery? he asked himself. "Let's see, P3 rancher, John Parker, SW ranch, Skye Walker, the Running R rancher, GM rancher, Gerard Michaels and a few smaller ranch owners. The top four ranches had cattle rustled from their herds and they are all located around Archer. Wait! That's not right, the GM Ranch is from Emery. Maybe that's why I'm not finding any answers. Gerard's ranch is in Emery. That's why the drovers could not identify the eight outlaws, they definitely were not from the Archer area. I need to change my focus and investigate Gerard Michaels." He finally stopped talking to himself. He felt a bit lighter, like a weight had been lifted from his shoulders. He blew out the lamp and went to bed; his thoughts going straight to Ralynn.

CHAPTER 19

Ralynn had finally got some rest and was surprised at Matthew's turn around; he was, actually, being nice to her. She didn't know what happened to change him overnight. She'd have to talk to Martha and Sam. She checked on Matt, and he was still asleep, so she went downstairs to the kitchen and found them having coffee. She went over to the stove and poured herself a cup, then joined them at the table. She didn't notice when she first came into the kitchen, but there were homemade cinnamon rolls on the table. "Good morning, Sweetie, can I get you some breakfast," Martha asked. "No, I think a roll and coffee will do for me, but thanks anyway." "Now, Rae, you need your strength. You haven't been yourself lately," Sam said. "I've been exhausted, that's all." "Emotionally and physically," Martha added. "Did something happen last night?

Matt's attitude has sure changed overnight." "You don't remember?" Sam asked. "No. All I remember is Matt ordering me out of his room. I went to my room, and I guess, I fell asleep because I was still in my clothes when I woke up this morning. By the way, when is Luke and the boys getting home? It's been over five weeks now." Sam looked at Martha, shook his head secretly telling her to say nothing. "Rae, Luke, and the boys got home yesterday. Luke came by to see you, but you were pretty mean and rude to him." "I don't remember him coming by." "You slammed Matt's door and ran off to your room, so he spent his time with Matt. Did you even notice Matt's wheelchair at the bottom of the stairs? Luke took Matt outside last evening and then they sat here with us and had cookies and milk.

I don't know what he said to Matthew, but he did say something." "I guess he did, hopefully it will stick. He exhausts me and needs to learn to do things on his own, like bathe and use his catheters, and get dressed. I'll forever have nightmares if he doesn't," she said. Martha and Sam burst out laughing. It must have been loud enough to wake up Matt because he was hollering for Sam and not Ralynn. Sam made a curious face and went upstairs to Matt's room. Martha and Ralynn just looked at each other, then Martha said, "Let's get our chores done, so we can start getting lunch ready in a couple of hours." Ralynn nodded and they both cleared the table and went about their chores.

Sam entered Matt's room and found him sitting on the edge of his bed. "Morning Sam," he said. Sam acknowledged him. "What's up. Son?" Sam asked. "I was wondering if you would help me to the commode and help me with my catheter. I need to learn how to do these things."

"Yes, it is time you did." Sam agreed and lifted him off the bed and onto the commode. An hour or so later, Sam came downstairs carrying Matt, when he reached the bottom, he sat Matt in his chair. He pushed Matt into the kitchen and up to the table. "Would you like some breakfast, Matt?" Martha asked. "Yes, some eggs and bacon, if we have any, please." "Sure thing.

Coming right up," she replied, with a big smile. Ralynn entered the kitchen surprised to find her brother at the table. "Here's your pill and some milk; take them now before you eat." "Sure thing, Sis," he said and took his meds without any argument. Ralynn stared at him for a moment. Matt looked at her, "I'm sorry for being so mean to you, Sis. I'll try to do better." "Thanks, little brother," she said, then walked over to help Martha, feeling a big weight lift from her shoulders; she smiled. "What's the plan for the day? Luke mentioned, maybe, I could have a room downstairs and I wouldn't have to be carried all the time. It would be easier for me to get around on my own and easier on all of you. "Hey, Sam, do you think you could take me out to see Darby and Bullet? I sure have missed them." "I don't see why not; I'm sure they have missed you as well. About that room; how about after you've seen your mare and colt and I get my chores done; we try to figure out where we can make a room for you?" "Sounds great!" He answered, as Martha put a plate of two eggs and four strips of bacon in front of him, with a slice of homemade bread and a cinnamon roll. "Yum!" Matt said as he dug in. Sam watched him swallow up his meal and then a thought came to mind. He'd have to clear it with Ralynn and Martha to make it happen, but he was sure they would agree.

* * * * *

Gerard came up with another plan, but this one would be tricky. His men had found Alex and Jake and brought them back. Gerard was going to make them work for their continued failures. "Joe, bring those two failures in here," he yelled. Joe opened the door to Gerard's office and escorted Alex and Jake into the room. "Take a seat, boys," he said, boisterously. They took their seats at the same time, both nervous, scared, and shaky about their fates. Gerard turned from the window he was looking out of. "You two have failed me time and time again. I was seriously thinking about just killing you both, but I have decided to give you one more chance. You are going to kidnap the Parker boy. It should be an easy task for you since he cannot walk." "What do you mean, he can't walk?" Jake asked. "During your last failure, one of your men shot him, leaving him paralyzed. You just watch when no one is around and grab him. Make sure you gag him so he doesn't yell out. As soon as you have him, one of you reports to me and I'll take it from there. You, two, will stay with him while I carry out the rest of my plan." "Where are we supposed to keep him?" Alex questioned. "I don't care; just keep him out of sight and somewhere he can't be easily found!" He blared. "Now, get to it and do not mess this up!" Alex and Jake jumped out of their seats and almost ran out of the room. Gerard sat down and took a sip of whiskey. "Surely, they can't mess this up." He said aloud. He sat there thinking. They get the boy, then I'll send a ransom note to P3 Ranch. I'll get what's owed to me one way or the other. John Parker, dead or not, you will pay your debt to me. He picked up his glass and this time downed it in one swig, then slammed it down

118

on his desk. "Joe, come in here!" "Yes, Boss?" "You follow those two and if they fail, you kill them!" he ordered. "Yes, Sir," Joe replied as he left the room. He filled his glass, downed it, then threw the glass at the fireplace causing it to burst into pieces and scattered on the floor. Surely those two dimwits cannot mess up such an easy plan, he thought to himself, as he watched out the window seeing Alex and Jake saddle up and ride off.

* * * * *

Ralynn decided that she should take time and go over the financial records of the ranch. Luke had left the money with Sam from the cattle drive and he put it in the safe. Since the men were all back from the drive and were working the ranch again, it was time to get them paid. Taking care of Matt had taken all her time and energy, but now that he was doing more for himself, she was resting more and had a bit of time to get some things done. She sat down at her father's desk and opened the bank book. A tear ran down her cheek. Oh, how she wished her parents were with her and Matt. She could surely use their love, hugs, warmth, and strength right now. She wiped her eyes and tried to focus on the task in front of her. As she was going through the transactions, she found a couple of payments made to the GM Ranch, both for five hundred dollars. "Pa would never have purchased anything from Gerard Michaels, that I know of. What could it be for?" She said, talking to herself. She looked closer at the book's figures to see if she could find anything to tell her what was purchased for a thousand dollars. "Nothing," she said in frustration. "I need to talk to Sam." She closed the book, placed it in the drawer, and closed it with a bit more force than intended. A piece of paper fell to the floor; it must have been stuck on the bottom of the drawer. She bent down and picked it up, unfolded it, and began reading it. She gasped and fell back into her father's chair. She couldn't believe what she was holding in her hand. Tears ran down her face, as she tossed the paper on the desk and pressed her hands against her face. "This can't be!" she cried. A few minutes passed. Finally, she sat up straight, wiped her face again and reread the note out loud. "IOU to Gerard

Michaels for ten thousand dollars for gambling debt." "My father never gambled, something more is going on here and I'm going to find out." She thought about asking Sam if he knew anything, then she decided not to. The fewer people that know about this the better. She had to think on this. If her father really did this, they'd have to sell all the cattle and maybe the ranch. "NO!" she spoke aloud. "I'm not losing this ranch to Gerard Michaels or anyone else." She folded the paper and put it in her pocket. She left the room, leaving the big oak doors open. Martha noticed that Ralynn was preoccupied and said nothing, until she kept stirring the stew non-stop. "Hey, Sweetie, you alright?" "Hmmm?" Ralynn muttered. Martha laid her hand on her shoulder and she jumped, startled by Martha's touch. "Oh, Martha, you startled me." "I guess I did. Everything okay, Sweetie?" Ralynn hesitated, then said, "I don't know. I found some transactions in the ranch's financials that Pa made, but it doesn't show and I don't know what they were for. He always put the transactions and what they were for in the register, but those two times he didn't. "Maybe, Sam knows, I'll ask him later." "That sounds like a good thing to do." Martha said. They worked together and prepared the evening meal. Sam and Matt had been to the barn and when they came inside, Matt was all smiles. "It's good to see you smiling, Little Brother," she bent down and gave him a hug. "Love you, Brother." "Love you, too, Sis." They all sat down to eat, but Sam asked them to wait a minute. "Okay, Sam, what's up?" Matt questioned. "Well, while you two were gone, Martha and I spent some time together and we discovered that we had feelings for each other and have had for years. Well, I popped the question to Martha and she said yes." "Popped what question?" Matt asked. "If she would marry me," Sam said. "She said, yes!" "I'm so happy for you both," Ralynn squealed with excitement. "Then you both approve?" Sam waited for their reply, then he thought, maybe, they didn't. "Heck, yes, we approve!" Matt exclaimed. "I hoped you would," Sam remarked, happiness glistening in his eyes. "Well, when's the wedding? I can cook and help with your dress and the flowers and Matt can help Sam prepare." Ralynn said all excited. "I'm glad you said that, I'll need all the help I can get, for sure." "Good, then I'm your girl. So, when is the date for this wedding?"

Martha looked at Sam, then Sam said, proudly, "Originally, it was June 1st, but then we decided on May 1st, the first day we met, twenty years ago. So, it will be our wedding day, our anniversary, and our moment between moment twenty years ago. That day is special and it's also my anniversary of my first day here on the ranch," Martha said. "Let's see, that's just about six weeks away; I'd better get busy to get you and this place in order and ready," Ralynn laughed. "I can't wait to get started." "Martha, we need to make a trip to Emery. They have the best dress shop and places to shop." "When can we go?" Martha asked, looking at Sam. "I'm not going." Sam said outright. "I didn't expect you to go, Sam. We have shopping to do." Martha stated. "Good, then I'll get one of the boys to go with you." "Sonny or Tom will be fine." Ralynn said. She sat back and formed a plan in her head; if she worked it out right, Martha won't even miss her. She would go to Emery, leave Martha at the dress shop for a while, then she'd find Gerard Michaels and confront him about the IOU.

"While we are all together, I have something to ask you three. Matt needs a room downstairs, where he can take better care of himself and get around better. Instead of changing the guest room around, why don't we give Matt your parent's room. What do you think?" Everyone became quiet. They sat there thinking about how to answer. "Just think about it. Matt and I are building a ramp up to the back door tomorrow so he can go in and out by himself." "That's cool, Sam." Matt said, with a twinkle in his eyes. "As far as the room goes, Matt needs to be down here, so you three think it over and let me know what you decide. If you decide to do this, Martha and I can pack it up if that will make it easier for you two. Well, back to work. Matt, are you up to go outside again or would you rather rest?" "If you'll take me upstairs, Sam, I think I'll rest a while; I'm pretty worn out." Matt said, in a tired voice.

* * * * *

Sam and Martha sat at the kitchen table making plans for their wedding. "Who would you like to have at the wedding, beautiful Lady?" Martha smiled, "Since it's the only wedding I plan to have,

I'd like to invite our neighbors, a few friends from town, the ranch hands, and their families. I guess I'm hankering for a party. We have all been through so much lately." "How about we just have a small ceremony?" Sam asked. Martha frowned. "Oh," she said. "Don't be so disappointed, I haven't finished yet." "Okay." "Let's do a small ceremony on May 1st, since that is on a Friday; we can have the evening to ourselves. Then on Saturday, the 2nd, we can have a BBQ and invite everyone to the party. We can cook a side of beef over the pit and arrange for some music; the boys can build us a dance floor and everyone can bring a dish of whatever they like. We can make a weekend of it. Now, what do you think?" "Oh, Sam, that sounds wonderful, but that's just four weeks away. What happened to June 1st?" she asked with a puzzled look on her face. "That's as long as I can wait. I can't help it. Will that be enough time for you women to get done what's needed?" he asked, with a sheepish grin. "It will have to be if you're set on May 1st," she replied. "Great!" he exclaimed. Ralynn and I can plan some side dishes and the cake. You boys can make room for those that will be staying overnight and plans for getting the beef." "Sounds like a plan," he said. "I'll need to inform Ralynn and you inform the boys. I know Matt will want to help. Have the kids given you an answer on the room yet? We should take care of that first, so we won't have to worry about him all evening." "I'll ask at dinner tonight," Sam replied. "Okay, Love, I need to get some work done. I'll see you at dinner." He leaned over and gave her a quick kiss on the forehead and headed out the door.

Martha grabbed his arm, stood up, and said, "You don't get off that easy." She planted a kiss on his lips and he returned it with the utmost passion. When the kiss stopped, she patted his cheek and said, "Now you can go." "Yes, my dear," he said with a smile. A beautiful moment between them.

Martha sat back down and wrote out a list of things she needed from town and the kind of dress she wanted. Instead of her and Ralynn making one, she decided she would get a store bought one. She had saved her money all these years just for this particular day, wondering if this day would ever come and now it's coming true. It was going to be glorious. She was so excited and just bursting at the seams. She carried such a glow about her; that's the first thing Ralynn noticed when she walked into the room. "My, oh my, aren't we just overflowing with happiness and sunshine today?" she said, sarcastically. "Does it show that much?" "Yes, it does show that much, just all over." She sat her basket of eggs on the counter and went over to Martha and gave her the biggest hug. "I wish my parents could have been here to see you and Sam get married.

They would be so happy for the both of you." "I think they would have as well. I miss them, too, Sweetie." Martha said, hugging her back. "I know." They both sat down and began working on the wedding plans. Ralynn had grabbed some stock paper from the library and began making up the invitations. Martha told her of their plans; the party planning began.

Matt had been outside in the barn all morning. He spent time with Darby and Bullet, then went on a search for some leather strappings scraps. He wanted to give Sam a special wedding gift, so he thought he'd make him a lead rope or a whip. He'd made them before, for his Pa and himself, but Sam didn't have a fancy one and that's what he wanted to make for him. "I know, I'll make him a crop whip, made like a whip but shorter to use for riding, that's what I'll make." Matt said to himself. One of the boys came into the barn for something, but ended up helping Matt find all he needed, then helped him hide all the supplies in a secret place. Matt, then, headed for the house. He was sure glad the he and Sam had finished that ramp, it made it a lot easier to get in and out of the house. He heard laughing as he entered the kitchen. He rolled up to the table. "What's so funny?" "Oh, nothing, just girl talk is all." Martha answered. "I came in to get some rest; thought Sam was in here." "Nope, he's out doing whatever he does all day." "Well, that's good. Do you think it would be okay if I rest in Ma and Pa's room? I'm too big for you two to carry me upstairs." "I think that's fine." His sister said. "By the way, when are you two going into Emery? I wonder if you could pick up something for me?" he asked. "We could go Wednesday," Ralynn said. "Just write down what you need and give me the money for it." "Aww, Sis, I thought you would pay for it." he said laughing. "Not a chance, Little Brother." "Okay, I'll have it for you tonight. I'll probably be asleep when you leave." "Okay, no problem." Matt went into his parent's room and closed the door behind him.

Matt had not been in his parent's room since they left on their trip over three months ago. His eyes teared at the loss he was feeling; so empty. What he would give to have them here while he was going through all these changes and for the wedding. He was certain his sister felt the same way. He rolled over to their bed and transferred onto the bed. He laid down. All at once, tears poured from his eyes and deep sobs consumed him. The smell, their smell on the pillows, hit him hard. How he longed to be in his Ma's arms right now. Ralynn came to check on him but when she heard his sobs, she hesitated. She and Matt had always been close and she could imagine what was going on in his mind. She cried, herself, as she slid down the wall until she was sitting on the floor. They cried together. They were sharing this moment between them, even though a wall was separating them. He cried himself to sleep.

CHAPTER 20

The next morning, Ralynn and Martha were on their way to Emery; Sonny was driving the team. They were planning on spending two days, shopping and dining in Emery's fine restaurants. The plan was to get everything done and head back home. While on their way, they talked about the newest styles and what Martha wanted in her wedding gown. They, also, discussed the menu and how many guests to expect for the BBQ and dance. There was a brief silence, then Martha asked, "Ralynn, Sweetie, would you stand up with me?" Ralynn looked at her with tears of happiness rolling down her cheeks. "Of course, yes!" She replied with excitement. "I'd love to." "Thank you," Martha said, squeezing her hand. "Just a few more miles, ladies." Sonny informed them. They put their papers away and straightened their clothes. Their eyes were full of excitement as the town of Emery came into view.

* * * * *

Alex and Jake had been watching the P3 Ranch all morning. They had seen the boy go from the barn to the house and waited to see if he'd come out again. They didn't see anyone with him, so they figured he didn't need someone with him all the time. They figured they would grab him in the barn when feeding time came for that mare and colt, he came to see all the time. "This should be easy enough," Jake said. Alex replied, "We thought that about every plan, so far, and we failed. If we fail this and don't get this right, we know death will be haunting us." "You really think the Boss will kill us?" "Yes, I do. He doesn't care about us, only if we do what he says. When he doesn't need us, he'll kill us or have someone do it for him," Alex said. "Do you feel like we are being watched?" "I've felt that way since we left yesterday. It wouldn't surprise me as furious as Gerard was."

As they sat on their horses, movement was taking place on the ranch. Men carrying lumber, wagons and equipment were being moved to various places, and the picket fence that ran along in front of the house was being painted white. "They must be planning something with all that going on. It should be a simple job to slip in the barn and grab the boy. "Jake, do you have the chloroform with you?" "Yes, Alex, I have it." "Good, now all we have to do is to wait for the boy," Alex said.

An hour later, Matt came out of the house, and as expected, he went into the barn. Alex and Jake dismounted their horses and tethered them to a nearby tree. They slowly crept down the hill to the back of the barn. "The boy has already taken the mare and colt into the barn." Alex whispered, "Come on Jake, it's now or never." They slipped inside the barn, thanks to the open door, and hid in the shadows. Matt was in the stall with Darby and Bullet placing hay in their manger and talking to them the whole time. "Was it a good day for you and Bullet?" he asked Darby. She nodded her head, as if to answer him. He curried and brushed her down and then did the same to Bullet. Once done, he opened the stall gate, then closed it after he passed through and locked the stall door behind him. He headed towards the tack room with the curry comb and brush on his lap and two halters in his right hand. He was trying to hang up the halters, when from behind came a hand and was pressed against his mouth. He struggled. A cloth replaced the hand and he fought against it. The arms around him were tight and he tried to kick, but he couldn't. He tried to push against them. Darby started rearing and slamming her hooves on the stall fence. She began making noises, which sounded like a scream and caught the attention of a couple of cowboys out in front of the barn. Matt collapsed in Alex's arms and Jake grabbed his feet. They were almost out of the barn when the cowboys came in and saw the two men with Matt trying to get out of the barn. Darby was going crazy, still pounding her hooves on the stall fence and Bullet was running around in the stall. "Hey, there. What are you doing?" one of them yelled. The other one gave a shrill whistle, alerting the other boys. Alex and Jake were moving backwards as fast as they could, both knowing that they had failed again. They dropped Matt and ran. Sam and Tom got to Matt as quickly as they could while a few of the cowboys pursued the two kidnappers on foot. Alex and Jake reached their horses, mounted, and took off. The men returned to the barn. Matt was still out, so Sam and Tom took him to the house and just before they got there Charlie yelled, "Hey, Sam, it looks like they used chloroform, I found this by the tack room door," holding up a bottle. "Thanks, Charlie," and continued into the house.

They took him straight to his parent's room and laid him on the bed. Tom returned to the room with a wet, cool cloth and laid it upon his forehead, "I'll stay with him, Tom, you can go about your business." "Sure thing, Sam." He left the room, leaving Sam with Matt. Sam sat in a chair across the room, watching Matt. His breathing seemed normal. He hoped he didn't take in much of the chloroform and would wake up soon. Sam got comfortable, tilted his hat over his eyes and closed them.

Sam sat straight up in his chair, putting his hat in place, and thought he was dreaming. How long had he been there? He thought. He heard his name again and looked over to see Matt sitting up in bed. "You're awake," Sam said. "What happened? Why am I in here?" He looked around his parent's room. "You don't remember?" Sam asked. "I was trying to hang up the halters when a hand came from behind and covered my mouth, then a cloth replaced the hand. I fought and tried to kick them, but couldn't, then all went black. I don't remember anything else." "Well, if it hadn't been for Darby, you would have been carried off. She put up quite a fuss. "That's my girl," Matt replied with a smile. "Why would anyone want to kidnap me? I'm not worth anything to anybody except you guys here on the ranch." "I don't know, Matt, but you and your sister own this ranch now. Maybe Luke will have some answers when he gets back." "When would that be?" "I got a telegram yesterday, he said he'd be here in a couple of days." "Do we have to tell my sister and Martha about this? I don't want to worry them." "We will keep it quiet until Luke gets back. I'll tell the boys. Ready to go back outside?" "Yes. Sam?" "What is it, son?" If Ralynn doesn't mind or object, I'll take my parent's room. It will be so much easier on me and everyone else. I'll talk to her when she gets back." "That's great! Let's get moving." Sam and Matt returned outside and rejoined the cowboys. Everyone was happy to see Matt was okay. "You gave us quite a scare, little man." Tom said. "Just keeping you on your toes." Matt laughed and the others joined in. Charlie pulled Sam away from the men. "Sam, after you took the boy into the house, we heard a couple of gunshots. At first, we thought our men had caught up with those two, but we were all accounted for. We haven't gone to check it out yet." "Send a couple of men. Let's see if we know these men if you find anyone." "Sure Sam." He walked away and Sam went back to work.

* * * * *

Luke was a few hours away from the P3 Ranch. He'd let Comanche walk most of the morning; it had been a long and tough ride. Everything the Governor said kept running through his mind, yet still no solution to the rustling problem. His mind kept leading him to Gerard Michaels, but he could not figure out a motive as to why Gerard would need to rustle cattle. The man owned the largest ranch within two hundred miles, so it made no sense to him. Since the Indians had been captured, it did make sense that white men were behind it, so he went to the reservation to speak to the captives and see if he could learn anything more. As he assumed, using his Native name, Bear Claw, he was allowed on the reservation with no prob-lem. The guard allowed him to speak to the leader of the renegades. Speaking in their native Apache language, he found out that the ren-egades had seen some white men moving a bunch of cattle into a canyon, Northwest of the big P3 Ranch. He told them that there were many cattle there and ten men guarding them. He and his warriors had thought about taking the herd, but they were only a hunting party for food for their families. He said his people were starving on the reservation and that is why they escaped. They had planned all along to bring back food but got caught before they could find meat. Luke thanked the leader, Skylark, and his men, then left the reservation. Where in the world were their beef and food rations? He asked himself. He needed to talk to Sam and the Governor about that.

He was only about ten miles from the ranch and his mind automatically switched to Ralynn. He wondered how things were going with her and Matt. He hoped his talk with Matt had helped. If it didn't then he may never have a chance with her. He understood she was under a lot of stress, but the words she said to him still hurt. If the case was the same as when he left, he wouldn't be able to stay. Being around her would be too difficult; especially having to see her every day and having her as his Boss now. He'd move on and try to forget her, which he knew he never could do.

The time went quickly as he spurred Comanche into a gallop. He could see P3 in the distance and he could wait no longer. He urged his horse into a run and his sights were on the ranch ahead. Within minutes, it seemed, he was entering the ranch gates. As he slowed his pace, he noticed all the activity going on. There was a platform being built, the picket fence was freshly painted, a ramp had been built to the back door, wagons had been moved, and the tables in front of the bunkhouse were being washed down. Buckets of paint were sitting alongside the bunkhouse wall and Sam was working on something in the grape arbor. He stepped off his horse, loosened the cinch on the saddle, pulled it off and placed it on the fence. He took the bridle off and hung it on the saddle horn. He reached into his saddle bag and brought out Comanche's curry comb and brush and went to work combing and brushing him down. After a good brushing, he took Comanche into the barn, opened the stall gate to his own personal space and fed him some grain and hay. He stopped by Twisted Mister's stall, greeted him, and gave him a flake of hay as well. He went outside and got his saddle off the fence, brought it in the barn and stored it in the tack room. Satisfied that Comanche was settled, he walked back outside to find Sam, instead he ran right into Matt. "Luke, you're back." Matt said all excited. "Hey Matt, how are you doing? You look different, good," Luke said. "I'm doing good. I have good and bad days. Even though I cannot move my legs, there is still a lot of pain." "What's going on around here, anyway?" "That's right you don't know about the wedding." "Wedding? I didn't know Ralynn was courting anyone?" He said with sadness in his voice. "No, Luke, not Ralynn, it's Sam and Martha getting married." Matt laughed. Luke's spirit picked up. "Sam and Martha's getting married. Well, that's grand. I always thought there was something between them." "Yeah, we all could see it except them." Matt said. "Sam's over at the arbor. I'll meet you over there in a few minutes. I must give Darby and Bullet some carrots for saving me earlier today." He raised his hand showing Luke the carrots he just pulled from the garden. "Saving you?" Luke questioned. "Sam and I will explain when I get over there. See you in a few." Matt wheeled into the barn to feed his heroes. Luke headed to the arbor, getting slapped on the back and welcomed home by the boys as he passed by them. He reached the arbor and found Sam, hard at work, painting the bench where he had seen Sam and Martha a few weeks back. "Hello, Sam," he said. "Luke! You're back." "Got in about thirty minutes ago. Ran into Matt, he said his horse saved him?" "She sure did. It was something. If that horse doesn't love that boy; I don't know what you'd call it." Sam smiled. "Matt said you two would explain when he got over here," Luke said. "Why don't you catch up with Matt. Go on inside and I'll be there shortly. Need to slap a bit more paint on here, first." Just then, Matt came rolling up. "Sam said to go inside, and he would be in shortly." "Okay, we can do that." Matt headed for the door. "Sam, how's Ralynn?" "She's better. She doesn't remember seeing you at all that day. Besides, she and Martha went shopping in Emery. They left this morning and should be back in two days. Go on in, I'll be right there."

CHAPTER 21

The ladies had shopped for two days, going to every shop possible. The last stop in their shopping spree was the dressmaker's shop. Martha was looking at the wedding gowns and Ralynn was looking through the piles of material. She knew Martha would be ready to head home as soon as she decided on a gown. Martha told her she wanted it to be a surprise and hoped she understood. She knew this would be a good time to find Gerard Michaels and confront him. She had to do it now, otherwise she would not have another chance. Martha called her over, telling her she was going to try on some dresses. "Okay," she replied. Just then she remembered Matt's list of things he asked her to pick up for him. "Martha, I forgot to get Matt's stuff. I'll do that while you're trying on the dresses." "Sure, thing Sweetie, I'll be right here." She left the dress shop, found the store to get Matt's things and went in to buy what he needed then went in search of Gerard's office. She recalled seeing his office sign a few blocks away; she headed that way. When she found the office, she went right in. There were no windows in the entryway, and it was dark; her palms became sweaty and her stomach churned. All of the sudden she was scared and thought she should turn around and leave, but she took a deep breath and moved forward. She found the next door, opened it, and went inside. She heard voices coming from the next room. There was no one at the front desk, so she knocked on the door. A man with graying hair and beard, opened the door. "Can I help you?" He asked. "Yes, I'm looking for Gerard Michaels," she said. "What do you want with him?" He was doing a once over look at her, making her uncomfortable. "That's between Mr. Michaels and myself."

She answered curtly. "Well, little lady, I'm Gerard Michaels, and who might you be?" "I'm Ralynn Parker and I've come to talk to you about an IOU I found in my father's books. It says it's a gambling debt. My father never gambled and I want to know what this is all about." She held out the paper in her hand. "Why don't you ask your father, I don't remember every detail or transaction I've done," he said, as he turned toward his desk, stepped behind it and sat down.

She stood silent for a moment. "My Pa is dead." She tried to not cry, but a single tear ran down her face. "Oh, I'm sorry for your loss, dear. What happened?" trying not to smile, so he cleared his throat to cover it up. "It's hard to talk about, but both my parents died in an accident a few months ago." "Is that the IOU? If I see it, maybe I'll remember it." She unfolded the paper in her hand and handed it to him. He looked at it for a few minutes. An eerie silence filled the room. "Well, now I do seem to recall this. Let me find my file." He walked over to the file cabinet, opened it, and pulled out a file. He crossed the room and was standing beside her. "Here, Miss, have a seat." He stepped behind her and offered her the chair, then reached back and locked the door without her noticing. He walked back over to his desk and sat down. He opened the file and looked it over, acting as if he didn't remember. "Well, yes, I do remember this. Your father owes me a lot of money. Too bad he died, before he could pay me." "I know my Pa didn't gamble, so what exactly did he owe you for?" she demanded. "Your father cheated me out of ten thousand dollars. Now that he is dead, I guess you'll have to pay his debt." "What did he cheat you out of anyway? What do you mean I'll pay?" her temper rising. "Did you know about the bull, a full-blooded Longhorn, that he bought from me? He was registered and everything; I had all the paperwork on him. He bought him sight unseen, but the bull died during transit from Texas, for reasons unknown. He refused to pay me, so I told him that he'd either pay or I would ruin him, first, by spreading the word that he'd been gambling and owed me all that money." He stared at her with his beady black eyes. "It sure was a shame, your parents dying like they did. Your father should have been more careful and checked his rig before they left Emery." His smile became wicked and she became afraid. "What do you mean?" She asked, getting more nervous by the minute. "Well, sometimes those double trees come loose or break free with little or no pressure on them. You never know what might happen." He snickered.

She froze. In her mind, she could see Pa's rig with him and Ma going over the side of the cliff and falling into the ravine below. She could hear her mother screaming, and then the crash. All at once, she stood up staring him in the face, "You killed my parents!" she screamed. "I do not want to hear anymore until the sheriff arrests you. I'm going to get him now!" she turned and quickly walked to the door. "Oh, my dear, you can try, but I don't think so." He laughed. She reached the door, but it wouldn't budge. "Doesn't look like you are going anywhere, little one." She looked at him; an evil smile crossed his lips. "Let me out of here! I have friends waiting for me and they'll come looking for me," she exclaimed. "So do I, little one." He walked over to a door that led outside behind the building and yelled, "Joe, you and Casseus get in here and bring some rope." She became terrified. She had to get out of there, Martha and Sonny were waiting for her. She had to escape. She looked around and saw a key on the corner of the desk. Gerard was busy, talking to the two men outside, so she grabbed the key and ran to the door. She was trying to unlock it when a pair of big hands grabbed her by her shoulders and turned her around. "Looking for this key?" He laughed as he pulled a key from his pocket and dangled it in front of her. She was defeated and by the looks of the two men, now inside, she knew she had no chance of escaping. All her defenses left her, and she felt a heavy weight on her shoulders. He took her by her arm and led her over to Casseus. He told Casseus to tie her hands and feet, gag her, then take her to the out-of-the-way cabin. She knew that could only mean it was a place that couldn't be found.

Sonny and Martha were waiting by the rig. It had been two hours since Martha had left the dress shop. Sonny had walked up and down the street looking for Ralynn, but she wasn't to be found. "What has happened to that child? She wouldn't just disappear." Her voice was shaking with fear. "Tell me again where she was going?"

Sonny said. "She said she was going to pick up the things for Matt and she would be right back. That was almost four hours ago," her fear rising by the second. "I'll check the shops again." Sonny started to walk away but turned around and looked at Martha, "You stay here and don't disappear on me," he ordered. He walked up North Street and down South Street twice, and she was nowhere to be found. He remembered Martha said she was going to get Matt's things and that meant some kind of hardware. He stopped at the Tool Shop and inquired about her. He asked the owner if he had seen a young woman with auburn hair, hazel green eyes, wearing a green dress. The owner said no, but a young clerk walked up and said that he had seen a woman like that, he actually waited on her. He said that when she left, she headed East. "Are you sure she went East?" Sonny asked. "Yes, I watched her for a bit, she's a pretty lady. She went a couple blocks down, and then I had customers, so I don't know where she went." Sonny thanked them, walked out the door, and headed East. All he saw was the Doc's office, an attorney's office, and Gerard Michaels' office. He didn't figure she had any business with them so he went on. Two hours passed by the time he returned to the wagon and a teary-eyed Martha. He told Martha that they would stay the night and he would go talk to the sheriff, as soon as she was settled in a room.

Then he would send a telegram to Sam. He took Martha over to the Emery Hotel and got two rooms; a room with two beds for her and one for him. He took her up to her room, put the key in the lock, opened the door, and let her inside. He stood at the doorway and watched her for a moment. "Martha, here's the key, keep the door locked. I'll let you know when I get back." She took the key with a shaky hand. "Just find her, something is terribly wrong," she said with tears running down her cheeks. She closed the door and locked it.

Sonny walked out into the street and headed straight to the sheriff's office. He opened the door and walked in. Sheriff Stevens was sitting at his desk. "Hello, Sonny, I saw you and the ladies earlier, thought you all would be back at P3 by now." "Hey, Seth. We would have been, but Ralynn is missing. We waited for her for a couple of hours, thinking she was just taking her time getting things for her brother and the wedding." "Wedding?" "Oh, I guess you haven't heard.

Sam and Martha are tying the knot in a couple of weeks or so." "That's wonderful! It's about time," the sheriff said, as he slapped his leg. He then became serious. "So, back to Ralynn," he said. Sonny told him he had checked every shop and the guy at the Tool Shop said she left there after her purchase and went East. It was strange because she knew we were waiting for her west of the shop. I've walked both sides of the street and all that's down there is professional buildings, nothing that she would be interested in." The sheriff thought for a moment. "Well, they did just lose their parents and she's running the ranch now, I assume. Maybe she had some things she needed to talk to the attorney about?" "I never thought of that, but surely, she would have said something to Martha, if that were the case. She wouldn't have just gone off and said nothing." "Okay." "Martha said she went to pick up something for her brother and said she would be right back. She hasn't been seen since the Tool Shop. That was over six hours ago; that's not like Ralynn. She has always been very responsible and what she says she does." "Yes, I know she is. This is definitely a mystery. Have you sent word to the ranch yet?" "No, I was getting ready to do just that, but wanted to see who you would recommend and trusted enough to make the trip and deliver the message, especially at night," Sonny stated. "I'll get my deputy to take it and have him ride back with whoever P3 sends to help in the search." He walked to a door, opened it, and called for his deputy, Virgil. He came back and wrote a note to P3. It read:

> *Sam, Ralynn is missing. Send men to help with search.*
> *Sheriff Stevens.*

He gave the note to Virgil and sent him on his way. Sonny sat down and Seth offered him some coffee; he accepted. "Is there anything else you can remember?" He hesitated, "I've told you everything I know."

"Okay, then let's look at the town's map and see what businesses are east of here." He laid the map out on the table and he and Sonny studied it.

* * * * *

Casseus and Joe took Ralynn to the wagon, laid her in the back, and pulled away from Gerard's office. They blindfolded her and tied her hands and feet. She didn't know how long they had traveled or how far; even her sense of direction was off. She tried to get her hands free, but was only making them hurt even more. It seemed to take forever before they stopped. One of them picked her up and carried her inside; the whole time she was kicking and pounding the man's back. It didn't seem to faze the man at all. He threw her down on a bed, untied her and took the blindfold off. She bolted for the door, but Joe was right there in the doorway. There was no escape. She went over and sat in the chair by the window; it was already dark outside. The sky thundered in the distance and a bolt of lightning flashed, lighting up the night; she jumped. "May as well make yourself comfortable. Boss will be here shortly, so don't try anything, we'll be right outside the door." Casseus and Joe left the room and closed the door; she heard the key lock the door. She stood up and looked around the room for a way to escape. She checked the window, it wasn't locked, opened it and gasped; discovering that she was three stories up. "Where am I?" she asked herself. No secret walls or openings. She opened a door; it opened into a water closet, she sighed. The room, itself, was larger than her parent's room, one window, a wardrobe, and a vanity. She sat in the chair and looked into the mirror. She stared at herself and whispered, "What have I done?" She hoped someone had seen where she went, but they moved her, so how could anyone find her? She stood up, ran over to the bed, threw herself on it, buried her face in the pillow and cried.

CHAPTER 22

Luke and Matt were waiting for Sam in the kitchen. Martha and Ralynn had not returned from Emery, so they found some leftover ham and homemade bread and made themselves sandwiches. They put the ham away and cleaned up their mess, then went over to the table and sat down. "Wonder what is keeping Sam?" Matt asked. "I don't know, he said he was about done," Luke replied. "Well, he can't be doing much when it's dark outside." "Well, tell me, young man, how Darby saved you." Luke took a bite of his sandwich and waited. Matt swallowed, then began telling his story about the two men that chloroformed him and tried to take him, but failed, because Darby started stomping and pawing at the stall fence, and making these shrilling sounds, like she was screaming, and drew the attention of a couple of the cowboys, out in front of the barn. When they entered the barn and saw them with me, they dropped me and ran. Sam told me that I was out cold and he carried me into the house. Sam told me later that the men heard two gunshots a little later. A few of the men ran after them, but they got to their horses and got away. "Charlie sent some men to investigate; I don't know if they are back or not." Matt cleared his throat and took a bite of his sandwich. Luke sat there and ran Matt's story through his mind. He was thinking that makes two attempts on the P3 family. First, it was the drive and now the kidnap attempt on Matt; both failed. Whoever is behind this is becoming desperate; sending his men out in broad daylight to kidnap a young paralyzed boy.

Sam opened the door and yelled, "Luke, come out here, you need to see this." Luke grabbed his Stetson, off the table, and headed towards the door. Matt followed. Outside, by the barn, men were gathering around three men on horses. They walked over to the crowd to see what was going on. Sam and Luke made their way through the crowd and Matt was right behind them.

Sam was waiting for Charlie to step off his horse. When all three riders had dismounted; there were two dead bodies laying across two of the horse's backs. "Who are they?" "We don't know, never seen them before," Charlie told Sam. Sam looked at Luke. "Let's take a look." Sam and Luke raised the dead men's heads to have a look at their faces. "I don't know them. Do you Luke?" Sam asked. Luke looked at the first one, short and baldheaded, and did not recognize him. He then looked at the next one and stopped in his tracks. "Something wrong, Luke? Do you know him?" Luke looked around then told Sam to come closer. "I do know this one. He's an undercover agent working for the Governor, like me. I understand now, why their plans kept failing, makes sense to me now" He stepped away from the body and looked for Charlie. "Hey, Charlie, did either one of them speak before they died?" "Funny, you asked, because all he kept saying was, Boss Mike. I don't know if that helps, but maybe it will. "That's interesting. Are there any Mikes around here?" "I'm Michael Wright," one cowboy said. "Thanks, but I don't believe you are whom I'm looking for." "Let's make the area larger. Anyone with the name of Mike live in the area or in town?" Charlie spoke up, "No one within a twenty-mile radius is named Mike, that I know of." The others agreed. Matt spoke up, and said, "The only one I know of is Gerard Michaels of the GM Ranch. He has some land around Archer where he keeps cattle and on office in Emery. Not sure where he lives, though, but his last name is Michaels." "Boss Mike, that could be who he was talking about." Sam agreed. "He was pretty cocky the day of the road branding. That's it!" Luke stated. "What?" Sam asked. "Those two were there with Michaels that day." "That's right! I remember them now. They were acting funny that day.

Gerard and those two were more interested in watching the crew, than they were in their cattle getting road branded," Raydog stated.

Charlie commented, "Now that you mentioned that, I remember them as well. Couldn't quite put my finger on it; the way Gerard, with his beady eyes, was watching the crew. It was a bit creepy." The men took the bodies, wrapped them in blankets and buried the unknown man. They built a coffin for Alex, Jim Stone, in case the family would want to move the body, and bury him close to home..

When Luke got Sam alone, he told him that Alex was his undercover name and his real name was Jim Stone. He also told him that Jim was a good investigator and played his part well. "I'm sorry it had to end like this for him." "Luke, does he have a family that needs to be notified?" Sam asked. "I'll send a telegram to the Governor and he'll take care of it." Luke stated. They went into the house and Matt followed. "Sam, what's bothering you?" "I'm worried about Martha and Rae; they were due back today. Something must have gone wrong." "They went to Emery, right?" Luke asked. "Yes, but Martha and Rae aren't city folk and they would have contacted us if plans had changed and they intended to stay longer." Just at that moment, a horse and rider rode up to the house. A minute later, there was a knock on the front door. Matt went to answer the door, opened it to find a deputy standing there in front of him. "I have a message for Sam Frye. I'm Virgil Jones from the Emery Sheriff's Office." Matt invited him inside. Virgil walked over to Sam and Luke and asked for Sam Frye. Sam spoke up and introductions were made. Virgil took out the message from the sheriff and handed it to Sam. "It's urgent," the sheriff said and I was to hand deliver it personally." Sam took the note, read it, and then handed it to Luke. Sam's face turned as white as a sheet; Matt asked, "What was wrong?" Sam just stood there, as if in shock. Rae was like his own daughter and she was missing; that's all he could think of at the moment. Luke read the note and asked Virgil what plans the Sheriff had in mind. Virgil told Luke that he was to wait here and ride back with whoever they sent to help in the search. Matt was getting frustrated and asked again. "What happened?" "Your sister has gone missing for over two days now, Matt," Luke explained, "What about Martha?" "She's fine, just worried. Sonny put a note at the bottom saying that Ralynn just disappeared, no one has seen her." "Emery is where Gerard Michaels lives isn't it?" Luke asked, looking at Sam for an answer. "Sam! Sam!" Luke exclaimed, while shaking Sam's shoulders to get him to come back to the present. "What?" "Doesn't Gerard Michaels live in Emery?" "Yes, he has a ranch somewhere east of town, but it's well hidden back in the hills somewhere, people say." "Well, I'm going to Emery to find Ralynn." "I'm coming too, Martha must be beside herself; maybe I can calm her down and she may remember something else." "I want to go, but I'll stay here and run the ranch. You two, find my sister, please, If I lose her, I don't think I can handle much more right now." Matt said, with tears in his eyes. "Matt, I'm going to leave you with a skeleton crew. I'm going to take most of the boys with us. We'll need all the help we can get; it's a big country out there to search," Sam said. "That's fine, Sam. Take whoever you need. We'll manage just fine until you get back." I know you'll do fine. I'm going to tell Charlie to have a couple of the boys to stay close to the house, in case you need help with anything." Sam hugged him; Luke gave him a pat on the back, and they headed to the bunkhouse with Virgil following.

* * * * *

Ralynn was tired of all the games Gerard was playing. She realized that she was at his home, but where exactly was that? She had no idea. So far, he has wined and dined her, and brought her fancy dresses, which she was to wear at dinner. She was to wear a new one every day. She thought it was such a waste to have so many clothes. At home, she had her everyday clothes, her boy clothes, that she wore working the ranch, and her gowns that her ma had made for her. She had four of them; one for her coming out party when she turned sixteen and then one every year after that. This year she would be turning twenty, but Ma wasn't here to make her a dress this year. She shed tears, thinking of her; her heart breaking. She could always talk to her about everything, even boys. Now she only had Martha to talk to, and she was thankful. Would she ever see Martha or Matt again? She didn't know what was going to happen to her. She was watched closely whenever they let her out of her room. She was never alone, except in this room. She heard footsteps approaching her door, she

140

went over and grabbed a book that Gerard had given her to read and sat down in the chair by the window. She knew he'd ask her about the book at dinner, so she tried to read the last few chapters. She heard the key being put in the lock, then the door opened. It was the maid with a bunch of packages in her arms followed by Casseus with packages, as well. They laid them on her bed and left the room. She got up and opened the packages. More fancy dresses, undergarments, shoes, and ribbons. They were beautiful. She picked one for dinner tonight and hung the other three in the closet. She did the same with the other items. She then picked out the ribbons to match her dress, for when she put up her hair for dinner, and placed the rest in the top drawer of the vanity. The maid would return soon with hot water for her bath; she has never been so clean. It was the luxury of having money, she guessed. That didn't interest her, she was happy on the ranch. The ranch, would she ever see it again?

Will she be rescued? It was questions that ran through her mind constantly.

She bathed and dressed and waited for her escorts, Joe and Casseus. It was always both of them to escort her to the dining room, where Gerard would be waiting. As she entered the dining room, she noticed Gerard wasn't there. She looked at Joe. "Boss will be here in a few minutes. He said for you to be seated," Joe said. She took her seat and waited. A moment later, the side door opened and Gerard entered the room in a new coat and tie, carrying a small package. He set it in front of her and told her to open it. She unwrapped the package and was shocked at what she saw. In it contained the most beautiful diamond pendant she had ever seen. He took the pendant from the box, walked behind her and placed it around her neck. He stepped to the side of the table and looked at her. "Beautiful," he said. He turned, walked to the other end of the table and took his seat. He rang a tiny bell, and the maid and cook entered the room with their food. They placed their plates in front of them, lifted the lids, then left the room, leaving them to eat.

"How was your day, Miss Ralynn? Did you read the book I gave you?" "Yes, I read it. It was interesting." "Good, I'll get you another one from the library before you return to your room. Any subject you prefer?" "No. I enjoy reading so anything will be fine." She stared at her plate and pushed her fancy food around with her fork. She never knew exactly what she was eating and was afraid to ask. "Food not to your liking tonight?" "It's fine. I'm just not hungry this evening." "How about dessert? You have to have the dessert tonight, I had it made special." He called for the dessert to be brought in. The cook entered the room carrying a beautiful cake with red roses and green vines on top of the white icing. It was, at least, three tiers high with a small box covered in ribbons in the center. The cook set the cake in the center of the table and left the room, entering once more with the dessert plates and set them beside the cake. Gerard stood up, went to the side of the table, stopped, picked up the box, and set it in front of her. Her mind was confused. "Why the gifts tonight?" "Open it! He said excitedly. She opened the box. Inside the box was another diamond. This time it was a ring. He took the box from her, took out the ring, and placed it on her left ring finger. She looked at him with an expression of shock on her face. He bent on one knee and said, "Marry me, Miss Ralynn. I'll make you the happiest you have ever been. You'll have everything your heart desires." She took the ring off her finger and threw it across the room; she tore the necklace from her neck and threw it as well. "No! I will not marry you. You can give me what my heart desires now, but you won't." "And what would that be?" He asked in a rough and loud voice, becoming frustrated by the minute. "Let me go!"

She screamed at him. "That I won't do. If you won't marry me, then you can just stay in your room. I don't even want to look at you." She stood up, turned, and ran up the stairs to her room slamming the door. She threw herself on the bed and wept.

The next morning, she was woken up by someone knocking on her door. She put her robe on, walked to the door, and asked who it was. It was the maid. "I just wanted to be sure you were awake before I came in," she said. The maid unlocked the door and entered her room with several articles of clothing in her arms. "Mr. Michaels said to bring you these and to take away all your gowns, shoes, and anything else he has bought for you. He said to tell you that you will no longer share meals with him. You will be served in your room and you are never to leave this room. There will be a guard at your door at all hours and no more requests. You will only get what he allows you to have. I'm so sorry but those are his orders. The maid gathered the gowns and left the room, saying, "I'll be back shortly for the rest." She couldn't feel anything. She was lost and alone. She cried, "Somebody, please, find me and take me home."

CHAPTER 23

Luke, Sam and several of the P3 cowboys rode into Emery two days after Sam received the note from Sheriff Stevens. Sam told the boys to rest their horses and he and Luke were going to talk to the sheriff. They dismounted, walked across the street, and entered the sheriff's office. Seth Stevens was behind his desk. "Sam, Luke, I'm glad you're here. We have looked and searched for Ralynn and have found absolutely nothing. We don't have a lead or any evidence of foul play. Sonny has been searching until he was about to drop. I sent him over to the hotel to get some sleep. Sam, Martha's in the room next to his, I think it's room two thirty-seven." "How's she holding up?"Sam asked. "As well as to be expected," the sheriff answered. "Sam, go on over, she needs you. The boys and I will get started with the search, as soon as we get some coffee in us and I study the map of the area. No need for us to search, if we don't know what to expect out there in those hills," Luke told him. "I'll come back to help, as soon as I can, Rae's like my own daughter." "We have plenty of men for the search, Sam, stay with Martha for a while. If we need you, I'll come and get you myself,?" Luke told him. "Okay, just remember I'm available." "I will." Sam turned to the door, opened it, and left. "Now, Sheriff, who knows this area best?" "The best is Clay Johnson. He's the town's veterinary, but he's hiked these hills for years." "Well, we have a good idea of who we are looking for, but no one seems to know where he lives." "Okay, who is it?" "Gerard Michaels." "Of the GM Ranch?" "One in the same, Sheriff." "You're serious?" "Yes, I'm serious," Luke said sternly.

* * * * *

Matt was doing all he could around the ranch, but he was frustrated about all he couldn't do. He ran out of the hay he could reach, and the rest was in the loft. He couldn't climb the ladder to throw some down, so he had to rely on someone else to get it for him. That meant having to rely on other people a lot. He didn't like that. He wanted to pull his own weight on the ranch, but it sure wasn't easy. Sam had left him with a few men, so he knew he could depend on them, but every time he needed help, he was pulling them away from their work. He was beginning to feel like a burden to them. No one said anything, but he was sure they were frustrated with having to help him all the time. Today, he awoke with pain that just wouldn't subside. He took his medicine, ate a slice of homemade bread with fresh butter, and drank a cup of coffee. He headed out to the barn to feed Darby and Bullet. Darby was happy to see her Master and whinnied when he entered the barn. Bullet was growing so fast and was eager to get outside to run. As he was feeding them their grain, he remembered he forgot to ask for help getting more hay down from the loft. He left the barn in search of one of the boys to help him. As he rolled across the rough ground, his wheelchair hitting every stone and hole in his path, his pain increased so much that he had to stop. His legs felt like they were on fire, like the day he was shot; he bounced around in his chair trying to ease the pain. It was not going away. "Matt, boy, you all, right?" Charlie asked coming from the corral. He couldn't answer; the pain was too intense. "Let me get you inside so you can rest." "No. I want to do my part," he said through clenched teeth. "Boy, I can see you're in pain. I can see it all over your face. We don't need complications with your health with all else we have going on," Charlie said sternly. "We need you in top shape, son. Why don't you rest for an hour or so, and then you can come back out? You're going to have to learn your limitations." Matt agreed to rest a while and allowed Charlie to push him into the house. "I'll rest a couple of hours, then I'll be back out to feed. Hey, Charlie, would you have one of the boys throw down a couple of bales of hay from the loft so I can feed my mare and colt?" "Sure thing, Matt. I'll do it now and toss a couple of flakes in for them." "Thanks, Charlie." As soon as Charlie went out the door, he rolled into his parent's room, transferred onto the bed and tried to sleep. At first, he couldn't relax but the pain eased up and he drifted off to sleep.

Charlie was just about to enter the barn, when he saw a stranger ride up to the house and dismount. He knew Matt needed to rest so he walked up to the house. "Something I can do for you?" he asked the young man. "I have a note here for Sam or whoever is in charge," the man said. "I'm the one in charge at the moment," Charlie said. "Well, here then." The man pushed the paper towards Charlie, turned, mounted his horse and rode off at a gallop. Charlie opened the paper and cursed a few unsavory words. It was a ransom note for the return of Ralynn. He yelled at one of the boys over by the corral and motioned for him to come over. He waited for the cowboy to be next to him and told him to saddle his horse and be ready to ride, as soon as he spoke to Matt. He went into the house and found Matt lying in bed. He reached down to wake him; Matt woke instantly. "Charlie, what are you doing in here?" "I'm sorry to wake you, Matt, but we just received a ransom note for your sister." "Let me see it," he ordered. Charlie handed the note to him and waited. Matt, stunned by the demand of fifteen thousand dollars, repositioned himself and asked Charlie for pen and paper. "I have one of the boys ready to ride into Archer to send a telegram to Sam." "Good." Matt grabbed his leg, as tight as he could, to try to ease the unbearable pain going through his legs and feet. "I'm sorry, Charlie, will you write this note for me?" "Sure." "Tell Sam that we received a ransom note for Ralynn for fifteen thousand dollars, by noon Friday. Instructions will follow. "Who brought out the note?" "I didn't know him; a young man." "Isn't that funny, Charlie?" "What, Matt?" "That my sister goes missing in Emery, yet we receive the note here in Archer. Make sure to mention that to Sam." "Got it. I'll send this now. Matt are you okay?" "No, I'm not. My legs are on fire; just won't go away." "I'll have Dan stop and ask the Doc to come out." "Thanks, Charlie, now get to it." Charlie rushed out the door, but stopped in the kitchen long enough to jot down a few extra words on the telegram. He explained to Dan the urgency and to make sure to stop and get Doc after the telegram was sent. Dan mounted his horse, Charlie gave him the note, and hollered "Hurry!" as Dan took off. Charlie was concerned about Matt. He was having severe pain in his legs that didn't work. This was something new to him, he'd never seen anything like this and didn't know what to do to help Matt. He went back inside and told Matt that Dan was on his way and would be bringing the doctor back with him. "Thanks, again, Charlie," Matt said and laid back down. Charlie left him to finish up his chores for the day and did Matt's as well.

* * * * *

Luke and Seth had gone over the maps of the town of Emery and the county of Clayborne, while waiting for Clay Johnson to arrive. They wanted to talk with him privately, before talking to the men. They had discussed a plan, but wanted to get Clay's outlook on all of it first, since he knew the hills the best. Pouring himself another cup of very hot coffee, Seth told Luke about all the places they had already searched and where they could search next. He took a sip of his coffee and burnt the tip of his tongue. "Guess I shouldn't drink hot coffee when I'm frustrated; that burnt." Luke was so absorbed in looking over the maps that he didn't even hear the sheriff. He wanted to know this county like the back of his hand; he didn't want to get lost or turned around out there. His mind switched to Ralynn. Was she hurt or frightened? Does she know who grabbed her? What do these people have to gain by kidnapping her? All these questions and no answers. How long had she been missing now? He counted the hours; it has been over ninety-six hours since anyone has seen her. Luke's mind jumped back to the present when the door opened. They were expecting Clay, but it was Sam, instead, holding a piece of paper in his hand. He looked worried and scared at the same time. "What is it, Sam?" Sam walked over to Luke, handed him the paper, sat down, and rested his head in his hands. Luke read the note and sat down as well. The note read:

Sam received a ransom note for Ralynn's return, demanding fifteen thousand dollars by noon on Friday.

Instructions will follow. Charlie By the way, Matt's not well, in a lot of pain. He needs Martha.

"Sam, have you told Martha yet?" "No, I intercepted the telegram just before I came in the door. She won't want to go, but that boy needs her. I know Matt would not send for her, so Charlie must be really concerned." Luke agreed. "What do you want to do, Sam?" "I want to get Martha on her way, then I can concentrate on Rae." "I understand, Sam. Take care of what you need to do and then I'll fill you in. We're still waiting for Mr. Johnson to arrive and go over the maps, so we can make a plan. Go see Martha." "Thirty minutes and I'll be back," he said and rushed out the door.

Sam and Sonny were loading the rig, as Martha was getting ready to head home. She'd been so upset with Ralynn's disappearance, that she hadn't even considered Matt having complications from his injury. She had to get home and let the men search for Ralynn. Matt needed her there and that's where she was going. Sam was waiting for her at the rig to help her up; Sonny was already on the wagon seat, anxiously waiting. She came out of the hotel and stood in front of Sam. He wrapped his arms around her and hugged her tightly. He whispered that he loved her, kissed her on the cheek, and helped her up into the rig. Sonny flicked the reins and they were headed towards P3 Ranch.

Sam headed for the sheriff's office just as Clay Johnson made his appearance and they walked in together. "Sorry, it took so long, Sheriff, had a filly to deliver. Mom and daughter are doing fine." "Clay, this is Sam Frye and Luke Conrad of the P3 Ranch. "Good to know you," Clay said, as he shook their hands. "Now that we all are here, let's get down to business. There's a young lady that needs our help," Luke said, determination in his voice. "Clay, I'm told you know this area better than anyone. Tell us about the terrain around here. Luke pointed to the map they've been looking at. We believe there is a ranch somewhere in these hills. Have you run across any places like that up in these hills?" The sheriff asked. "No, I haven't, but, then again, I haven't been to the east of that area, yet, that was to be my next hiking destination." "Okay, then show me where you have been on the map here." Clay looked at the map and pointed out everywhere he had hiked in the mountains. "This is the area we have already searched in the last four days and we found no signs of homesteads or ranches. "How can a person hide a huge ranch so completely?" Sam asked. "Do we have a name for this ranch?" Clay asked. The sheriff looked at Luke, turned towards his desk, sat down his coffee cup and answered the question. "You've heard of Gerard Michaels ranch, right?" "Sure, I've heard of it, but have never seen it. It's supposed to be massive. Is that who we are looking for?" Clay waited for an answer. Luke explained to Clay about everything that they had been going through in Archer and how Gerard came to be their prime suspect in all of it. Now that Ralynn had gone missing and a ransom note had come to light, they were pretty certain it was Gerard that was holding her hostage. "So, now we need to find this place before noon on Friday. That's when the ransom is due." "Let me have a look here," Clay said as he sat down and studied the map. "I know there's nothing in this area. It's just stones and rocks up through there. There's a stream that runs through here, and this area is flat, with a few homesteaders along the way. Our best bet, I'd say, would be to follow the water up the hills and mountains. Surely, he would have built the ranch with water close by. I can't see Gerard hauling water very far." "How far up does that stream go?" Sam asked. "Not sure, but it has to start somewhere," Clay replied. "It's a longshot, but it's all we have right now," Luke said, in a discouraged voice. The door opened and a young boy came in and handed the sheriff a telegram. Sheriff Stevens opened it. "Luke, this is the answer we've been waiting for. He handed Luke the paper. Luke read it and handed it to Sam. "Seems Mr. Michaels has a bit of a history of crime, although no one can prove anything back East.

Rustling, theft, and even murder are just a few things he's been arrested for. So, we are on the right track, I'd say," Sheriff Seth Stevens said. "Luke, do you think he's harmed her?" Sam asked. "I don't know, Sam, I wasn't around him at the road branding, so I can't tell you what he'd do. My gut usually picks up on things like that, but I have nothing this time." Luke replied. "What about the cowboys that's always hanging around Gerard's office; does anyone know any of them?" Luke looked around the office and they were all shaking their heads, no.

Sheriff Stevens opened the back door and hollered for Virgil. Once Virgil was inside the office, Sheriff Stevens asked him, "Have you seen any of those cowboys that hangout at Gerard's office lately? Do you know any of them?" Virgil responded, "Yeah, I know a couple of them, but I haven't seen them. Come to think of it, that's strange because they are always hanging around his office or doing errands for him. Matter of fact, I haven't seen anyone around there in about four days. You know something, I haven't even seen Gerard in his favorite eating place for days." Luke looked at Virgil and the sheriff. "Luke, somethings going on in that mind of yours, what is it?" Sam asked. "Has anyone checked Gerard's office or the surrounding area?" "No, we haven't. Didn't have a reason to until now. Virgil, take a few men and check that out. If you find anything out of the ordinary, let us know right away." The sheriff ordered.

Virgil took two men from the P3 Ranch to assist him. First, they searched outside, around the building and then through the wooded area behind the office. Nothing was found. Virgil, then broke a window to get inside. The office and waiting room were almost spotless and they were just about to give up when one of the cowboys found a piece of material caught in the door that led outside. "Hey, Virgil, look at this!" Virgil came in from the other room. "What? Did you find something?" "Yeah, look here. I recognize this, it's from one of Ralynn's dresses." "Let's get this to the sheriff." "Hey, look over here!" The other cowboy shouted. They walked over to see what he was talking about. "This is Ralynn's bag and the store bag for the Tool Shop. She was getting this for Matt." "Okay, where did you find these?" "Behind the file cabinet. They weren't too good at hiding evidence. Probably never expected the office to be searched. I'd bet Gerard never knew about one of his flunkies stashing it." "Bring them along. The sheriff now has reason to arrest Michaels." Virgil and the two cowboys left Gerard's office and headed straight to the sheriff's office.

The men at the office and the P3 boys were filling their canteens and packing their saddlebags. No one knew how long they would be gone, so they were stocking up with a week's worth of rations. Arriving at the office, the two cowboys went to get ready, and Virgil went inside. He laid the evidence on the table on top of the maps. "One of your boys said this material matched a dress of Ralynn's; found it caught in the door that leads outside. The bags were found stashed behind Gerard's file cabinet." "That's hers alright," Sam said. Luke's thoughts went to Ralynn; his heart breaking and his anger rising. He had to find her soon; he can't go through life without her. Sheriff Stevens spoke up. "This is all we need for evidence now. Let's go find him!" Luke and Sam were out the door first and the rest followed. A plan was in place and now to follow through.

Matt was still having severe pain in his legs, excruciating at times, that he could do nothing but bounce up and down trying to ease the pain. At the same time, he would rub his stomach hard. The Doc had been by and gave him some morphine to take, as needed, for the pain. So far it eased the pain for a time, but would come back worse than before. He was miserable and had Charlie take over outside and feed Darby and Bullet, then turn them out in the corral, unless it was raining. Charlie, a big man, all five foot ten inches, told Matt it was no problem. Matt had just laid down on the bed, in his parent's room, and started to fall asleep, when he heard noises coming from the kitchen. He sat up, transferred to his wheelchair, and rolled to the doorway of the kitchen. Sonny was laying packages on the table. "Hey, Sonny, where did you come from? Anyone with you?" "Came from Emery and I'm not alone." At that moment, Martha came inside. "Martha!" he exclaimed. He rolled towards her and into her arms. "I'm so glad to see you. Is Sam and Ralynn with you?" "No, darlin, they aren't. They were getting ready to search when Sam sent me home. We were told that you were having some severe pain in your legs, so I came home to be with you. I was just in the way there and you needed me. So, tell me what is going on." "I just don't know, the pain comes and goes, but when I have it, I can't seem to function. I try to rub my legs trying to make it go away, but it doesn't. It's always below my knees and in my toes; it always feels like my legs are on fire or a sharp stabbing pain like a knife stabbing me." "When was Doc here last?" "About three of four days ago. I think Charlie sent for him, but he hasn't said anything. Doc gave me some morphine to take as needed." "I think I'll send one of the boys to get him. I want to find out what he thinks about this pain." Just at that moment, the pain hit him so hard that he bent over and started rubbing his legs, then sat up and started bouncing in his chair. He then began rubbing his stomach hard and fast. It lasted a good ten minutes until it eased up. "I need to lay down, maybe if I sleep it will go away. Wake me when Doc gets here, please. It's good to have you home." "It's good to be home. I'll wake you when he gets here. Do you need any help?" "No, thanks Martha; I got this." He rolled back to his parent's room and she just stood there; tears running down her cheeks. She was worried for both kids. They were like her own children, and her mothering instincts took over as well as her tears.

* * * * *

Ralynn was scared and miserable. Gerard kept to his word and she was never allowed out of the room. She was fed very little and not allowed to speak to anyone. The room had been changed. All the fine things that were in the room, before she refused to marry Gerard, were now gone.

Now, all she had was a mattress to sleep on that laid on the floor, the vanity and chair, and a small table to set her food on when he felt like feeding her. There were no more fancy meals and desserts, all she got was broth in a bowl and a slice of bread; three times a day if she was lucky. She was only allowed one bath a week and her reading material was boring. She usually just looked through them and set them aside. Every two days, Gerard would send a couple more books, otherwise, she sat in the chair and looked out the window. One day Gerard saw her looking out the window; today the window was covered on the outside, so she could no longer see out. She felt so alone. What was he planning for her? Was he going to kill her? So many thoughts were running through her head; it was making her crazy. This all has to do with a dead bull. He must be crazy thinking P3 would pay fifteen thousand for her. They didn't have that kind of cash. He's, probably, trying to take over the ranch about now. Her thoughts kept running, at least she had her mind for company. There was a knock at her door and then the key turned the knob, and the door opened. The maid came in with her evening meal. She sat down to eat and she picked up the slice of bread; underneath it was a piece of paper. It read:

Men are coming for you, stay strong.

That was it; nothing more. She felt a wave of relief and a weight had been lifted off her shoulders. She didn't know who was coming, but she hoped Luke would be with them. If anyone can find her; it will be Sam or Luke.

Gerard called the maid into his office. "Yes, Mr. Michaels, you called for me?" "Yes, sit down, Marge." He said, pointing to the chair in front of his desk. "How's our beautiful guest doing?" "She's skinny and weak. You don't give her enough to eat." "Well, fix her a good meal tonight and give her this." Gerard handed her a small box and a note. "Yes, Mr. Michaels, I'll do that." "Let her have a bath, take one of those gowns to her, and tell her to put it on and fix her hair. I'll be coming to see her later." "Yes, Mr. Michaels," Marge said. "You can go now, Marge." She left the room and went up to see Ralynn. She knocked on the door and the guard unlocked it.

She went inside.

Ralynn stood up from her chair and walked over to the table. "Miss Ralynn, I'm supposed to give you this and get you water for a bath. "I'll have one of the men bring up the tub and some hot water in a minute. I'm to bring you one of the gowns; which one do you prefer to wear tonight?" "Why is all this happening? What has changed?" "I don't know, except I know he will be coming to see you later so, you need to bathe, fix your hair, and put on the gown." "I guess I don't have a choice. Bring the green one I guess." "Okay, Miss Ralynn. I'll be back in a few minutes," she said and rushed out the door. She opened the note and read it aloud,

Miss Ralynn, tonight I'm giving you the pleasures of a
wealthy life. Accept my proposal and I will let you out of
the room. I'll be there later, after dinner. Gerard.

She opened the box and found the ring that she had thrown across the room. Someone may be coming, but when. She sat down on the chair by the boarded-up window and just stared at the wall. She began thinking that she needed a plan. Maybe, she should accept his proposal so she would have more freedom. She'd cancel the engagement when she gets rescued, whenever that may be. The water was brought in and the green gown and accessories were placed on her bed. When the tub was full, she stepped in and submerged herself in the water; it felt like heaven, she thought. She poured in some lavender oil and began washing her hair using the goat soap that was provided. She then took the goat soap, lathered the wash cloth, and began washing her body. She hummed while she was bathing; she felt clean, again. She soaked until the water began to turn cold, stepped out of the tub, and dried off with a large towel. She put on her under-garments and then the gown. She was sitting at her vanity, messing with her hair, when Marge, the maid, came in with some face paint to make her eyes, cheeks, and lips bring out her beautiful features. Marge helped button up her gown, fix her hair into a French Twist, and attached small yellow and white flowers and ribbons in it. One of the guards came in with another cowboy and emptied the tub and carried it out. Another maid, one she'd never seen before, came in and put a cloth over the table and set a vase of roses and baby's breath in the center of it. Then she set two candles, one on each side of the flowers, and lit them before she left the room. "You look beautiful, Miss Ralynn." Marge handed her the matching shoes. She was putting the shoes on when another cowboy entered the room with another box and handed it to her, not saying a word, and left the room. She knew what it was before she opened it; the diamond necklace that she also had flung across the room. She opened it and allowed Marge to fasten it around her neck. "Beautiful," Marge said again. "Thank you," Ralynn replied. "Miss Ralynn, it's not my place to ask, but are you going to do it?" "It?" she asked. "Marry Mr.

Michaels." "I don't see if I have a choice. It's either marry him or live in this room until he decides what to do with me." "I'm so sorry you are going through all this. I wish I could help you." "You are just by being a friend." "I'll be back with your dinner in about an hour."

Marge gave her a hug and left the room. When the door shut, she heard the key locking the door. Her thoughts ran wild, asking herself if she would always be a prisoner in this place?

* * * * *

Luke, Sam, Sheriff Stevens, Clay, and Virgil were riding up in the hills behind Gerard's office. They kept moving East as they went up. They had been searching for two hours and had not found one trace of tracks or trails, but they kept going. Clay and Luke were in the lead and both were puzzled that there were no signs of any one traveling through the area. "There's got to be a trail around here somewhere," Luke said. "I'll move farther East and look for any signs," Luke said. "I'll go up," Clay said. Luke and Clay parted, leaving Sam, Sheriff Stevens, and Virgil to stay on the path they were following.

An hour later, Clay discovered broken branches, telling him someone had passed through this way recently. He followed the broken branches and came to a heavy traveled trail going up and East. He fired one shot in the air. Luke was there within minutes. "I found the trail, Luke." Clay showed him the broken branches and the trail that continued East and North. "I'd say we're on the right track now," Clay said. "I agree. Let's get the others over here and follow this trail, hopefully it will lead us to Ralynn," Luke said, with a bit of hope in his voice. They had to wait for the others to join them, but Luke could hardly stand it. He wanted to go, wanted to get Ralynn, wanted to hold her in his arms, kiss her lips, and never let her go, again. She owned his heart and no other woman would do.

The men arrived and they were on their way up the mountain. It was a tough ride; brush, low branches, briars, thorns, and rocks. If they weren't careful, they could end up with cuts and scratches to their legs, arms, and faces. They had to keep their heads low to avoid the trees with thorns, making it hard to move ahead too quickly. Just as quickly, as in the blink of an eye, the terrine turned to rock. There were no tracks to follow, so Luke, Sam, and Clay dismounted and started walking around checking every crack and crevice in the wall of rock facing them. Luke's gut was telling him the GM Ranch was in this area, but where? Sam yelled, "Hey, I found something, over here. Luke and Clay went running to where Sam's voice was coming from. "Where are you, Sam?" Luke yelled back. Sam stepped out from behind the rock. "Look at this, there's a gap here between the rocks. You couldn't see it without going through here. See the rocks overturned here." Sam was pointing at the rocks floor. "Wait here, I'll get my horse and go through first. I'll fire once when I'm through," Luke said, as he ran to Comanche and jumped into the saddle, then gave him a nudge with his spurs. They headed into the path and quickly disappeared into the rocks. The rest of the men dismounted and walked around looking for anything that may lead them to Ralynn.

Luke rode through the pass pretty easily. Once through the first rocks, the path widened enough for a wagon to go through. Even though the trail widened, there was no way to get a wagon through the pass on the other side. They must carry things through on horseback and have a wagon waiting on the other side, Luke thought to himself. He pulled his colt out of his holster and fired one shot in the air, signaling for the others to come through. As he waited, he looked around the area; lots of trees, fresh green grass, and rock walls surrounding him. "It's no wonder not many know about this pass," he said aloud. The others started coming through the pass one at a time. Clay and Sam came through first and the rest followed. "Okay, boys, let's find this trail." "Luke! It's over here," a cowboy yelled. They headed in his direction, and sure enough, there was the trail, as clear as day. "Move out!" Sam hollered.

* * * * *

Back at P3 Ranch, Charlie was helping Martha with Matt. He'd become feverish overnight and his pain was increasing. Charlie sent for the Doc and was hoping he could come quickly. Matt was screaming with pain every time it struck him. Martha kept wiping him down with cool well water. Matt would grab her arm when the pain hit, squeezing so hard she was beginning to bruise. She had Charlie remove Matt's shirt; he gasped so loud that Martha turned from the bowl of water she was soaking rags in, and rushed over to the bedside. Her hands flew to her mouth to keep from screaming, herself. Matt's stomach was blood red and raw. He had rubbed himself so hard when the pain hit him, that the friction from his hand burnt his skin, like a road rash from being dragged by a horse. Martha went to the kitchen to get the can of grease she kept by the stove. She didn't know if it would help, but until Doc got there, that was all she had. Charlie sat at the head of the bed and held Matt's shoulders, while she washed the wound and applied the grease. Charlie held tight as Matt started screaming and fighting to get her to stop. He knocked the can out of her hands, slapping her in the struggle. Charlie grabbed his hands and put them above his head. Martha picked up the can of grease and continued. Finally, she was able to wrap the bandages around him so to stay in place. She moved off the bed and Charlie let go of his hands. He laid back and started crying, "Martha, it hurts so bad," he said through his tears.

Tears formed in her eyes as she watched this boy suffer in pain. She felt so helpless. Charlie leaned down and told her he was going to check on things outside, then he would come back and sit with Matt while she took a much-needed break. She didn't see the tears in his eyes as he left the room or hear his sobs once he was outside. She nodded and continued wiping Matthew's brow. "Doc, where are you?" she whispered.

Charlie headed out to the barn to bring Darby and Bullet in from the corral. He could tell that Darby sensed something was wrong. Matt hasn't been able to feed or spend time with them for over a week now. Charlie whistled, Darby and Bullet came running in the barn and straight into their stall. He fed them some grain and two flakes of hay, closed their gate, and left the barn. He headed towards the bunkhouse, running into the cowboys coming in from the range. They were washing the dust and grime off that they had accumulated during the day. He went inside and waited for them to come in. Once they were inside the bunkhouse, he whistled to get their attention. "Boys, as you all know, Matt is having a rough time. It's more serious than just pain in his legs. He is now running a fever, which could mean an infection, and his pain is so great that he has rubbed his stomach raw from trying to ease the pain. The reason I'm telling you this is because I need some volunteers to sit with him in shifts. Martha's exhausted and needs some rest or she'll collapse on us here, pretty quickly. So, who can I count on?" Each one of the cowboys raised their hand. "I can cook a few meals," one cowboy said. "I know how to do laundry," another spoke up. Everyone laughed. "I can go get supplies." "I'll take care of his chores and his mare and colt." "I can help with that, as well." "I'll sit with Matt in shifts." "Me too," another said. "Thanks, boys, it will surely help her out. If we all pull together, we can make this work. Mark, make a schedule with a list of all the jobs and have the boys put their names or marks beside what they will do and when. Make sure there are only two of you volunteering at the same time. We still have a ranch to run and we're short-handed as it is.

Hopefully, we'll have Sam back with Ralynn and the boys soon."

CHAPTER 24

Gerard was passing time by pacing back and forth in his office. Dinner had been over for an hour and he still had not been to see Ralynn. She would soon tire of waiting; he was sure. He was sure she would refuse him again and he wasn't ready to hear her rejection. He straightened his coat and tie and decided to get it over with. He headed upstairs, stood at her door for a moment, then had the guard unlock the door. He knocked first before going into the room.

Ralynn was standing at the table when he entered the room. His first glance of her took his breath away. He took her in with his eyes; the green gown fit her curves perfectly, the color brought out the hazel in her eyes, and her auburn hair shone like a halo around her. "How beautiful!" He exclaimed. Here, before him stood his dream woman; he had to have her, and it was now or never. "Miss Ralynn, you look just wonderful." "Hello, Mr. Michaels, the maid said you wanted to see me. I, also, read your note and it said the same, except I thought you would be here earlier; I am pretty tired." She was becoming nervous and wasn't sure she could carry out her plan. "I, also, got the ring and necklace; as you see I'm wearing them." "Yes, I see that.

What exactly does that mean?" he asked. "Well, I was sure you could figure that out without me telling you." "Do I dare believe that you are saying yes?" "I've thought about what you said and I decided, sure why not. There is one exception." "And that is?" "You know that I'm not in love with you, but maybe in time that will change. So, I do not want to be pressured into any romantic ideas you may have. If you can agree to that, then I guess we are engaged." Gerard stood there speechless. He couldn't believe she said yes. "Well?" "Yes, I will agree to that, but don't be surprised if I spoil you with gifts and things." "Fine." He walked to her and took her by her arms, pulling her into his arms. She tensed and struggled a bit to get him to release her; she wished she could vomit all over him right then. He, finally, stepped back and just looked at her. "Now, what?" She was looking at him, trying to get his attention off of her body. "Oh, well, we plan the wedding. We'll have it here, of course, and as elaborate as you want it. Just tell me what you want and I will have it for you." "Exactly where is here?" "You are at my ranch." "Well, I want my family here with me on my wedding day." "I don't know about that. I don't like having people here, knowing where I live and all." "Well, I won't get married without them; I expect no less." "We will be married, one way or the other." "What does that mean?" She asked, getting more upset by the minute. "You'll do as I say, or else." "Or else! I do as I please so don't think you'll have all the say in our relationship. I will be your wife but you will not order me around like you do everyone else. Please leave my room before I start throwing things." "Really, like what?" He was laughing, when, all the sudden, a book came flying across the room and hit him in the arm. He stopped. "Okay, I'm leaving." He walked out the door and it was locked once more. She took a deep breath and hoped she could carry on with her plan, long enough until someone came to rescue her.

* * * * *

Luke and Sam were leading the posse and Clay was up the trail scouting, trying to find the hide out of Gerard Michaels. According to what they had learned; he lived in town during the week, but on weekends he just disappeared and no one knew where. There were always two or three cowboys around him while he was in town. No one knew why he felt he needed bodyguards, but even at the hotel, he had a couple with him; guarding the door to his room, and one downstairs watching everyone that entered the hotel. This week, however, there was no Gerard and none of his flunkies anywhere around town. That's why they knew he had Ralynn out at his ranch; if only they could find it. Just then, Clay heard something; a faint noise that he couldn't quite make out. He dismounted and muffled his horse with his hand, so he could listen more closely. There it was again; a sound so faint that he had to clear his mind and focus. He listened. Once more the sound came and this time, he realized what it was; cattle. It was cattle bawling. He stepped up on his horse and headed back to Luke and Sam. Luke saw Clay coming and nudged Sam. He was coming fast, so he must have found something. Clay stopped in front of them and was trying to catch his breath. "I found a herd of cattle just over the ridge," he said, pointing at the ridge. "Did you see the ranch or a house of any kind?" "No, I didn't even see the cattle, just heard them." The sound was faint. I wanted to get you guys before I went any further up the trail." "Okay, boys, let's go. We want to find this place before dark." Luke ordered. Clay took the lead and the rest followed. It was around three o'clock pm leaving them only a few hours to find that herd of cattle. It was dark by the time they found the herd, so they decided to make a cold camp, no fire, no coffee, only water and jerky, for the night.

* * * * *

Back at P3, the boys were all pitching in to help with Matt. Martha was grateful. She was about to collapse with exhaustion before they started helping her. Thanks to Charlie for arranging to have the boys help, she thought. She was preparing the noon meal for all the boys today.

Charlie had called them all in, except for a few riding the fence lines. She was preparing a simple meal of beef stew and cornbread. She already had the beef cooking on the stove; now she was dicing up the carrots, potatoes, and green onions. As soon as she finished the vegetables, she would make the five batches of cornbread. Putting more kindling in the stove to raise the oven temperature, she placed all the vegetables in the pot of beef. She stirred it, then placed a lid over it. She had a few minutes before she needed to start the cornbread, so she went to check on Matt.

Matt was sitting up in bed, talking to the cowboy that was sitting with him. They must have just told a joke because they were laughing hysterically. Martha walked in and the laughter faded. "How are you feeling today, Matt?" "Hi, Martha, I'm not bad today, I'm still having pain, but I can deal with it. It's when the fire and burning hits my legs and toes that I barely stand it." "Did you take some morphine this morning?" "No, it hasn't been that bad." She walked over and put her hand on his forehead. "You're not running a fever today, so that's good. Why don't you let Steve take you outside to see your mare and colt? Charlie says they are missing you. They aren't eating all their grain and hay lately. Maybe that will lift their spirits. Steve will be with you if your pain returns or you have any problems," she said. "Which there won't be," Steve said. "Well, I have lunch to finish, so you two enjoy your outing." She started to leave the room, then turned around and looked at Steve with a very serious expression. "If his pain returns, you get him back in here, you hear?" "Yes, ma'am."

Matt and Steve made it to the barn and before they entered, Darby started snorting and pawing the ground. Bullet was running the corral fence wanting to get to him. "They must know you're here," Steve said. "Sure, sounds like it. It's only been three weeks since I've been able to be outside." They entered the barn and Matt rolled over to the corral gate to let them into their stall. Darby was whinnying and Bullet was running around his mom. "Come Darby, come Bullet," Matt said. Darby walked in the barn and instead of going straight to her stall, she went straight to Matt and started nuzzling him and Bullet was trying to do the same. Steve had the stall gate open and Matt rolled into the stall with both of them following. They were all over him, rubbing their noses on his neck and face, while Matt stroked their heads and necks. "Wow! I think they have missed you, Matt," Steve laughed. "I missed them too," Matt said. "Bullet has really grown these past weeks, how many hands high do you think he is now, Steve?" "Oh, I don't know, maybe ten or eleven hands." "Let's check." "Move over, Darby, just for a minute. I want to see how tall your colt is." Darby moved over and allowed him to roll up close to Bullet. "Stop, for a minute, boy, let Steve measure you." Steve walked over and placed his right hand flat against Bullet's hoof and then his left above it in the same way, walking his hands all the way up to Bullet's shoulder at the base of his neck. "Eleven hands high," Steve said. "He's going to be a tall one for sure. I think the Stud we used was seventeen hands, and Darby is fourteen hands." "I agree with you on that, Matt." Darby came up and nudged her colt away so she could get next to her Master. She placed her head on Matt's shoulder and just stood there. Matt rubbed her neck and hugged her. "I hear you've missed me?" She raised her head and moved it up and down, as if to say yes. Bullet was doing the same. "How about Steve getting a flake of hay; will you eat for me, girl?" Once again, both of them began nodding their heads. Steve placed the hay in the manger, while Matt hugged them both, then he rolled out of the stall and locked the gate.

They both whinnied as he left the barn. Charlie told him later that they had cleaned up all the grain and hay from his visit and were eating again this evening. Before they went back inside, Matt watched some of the cowboys breaking a Mustang they had rounded up earlier with twenty others. One cowboy was on a Sorrel while the others counted six, seven, eight, and off he came, hitting the ground hard. They caught her and held her for him to try again. He stepped up in the saddle, seated himself, and the count was on; two, three, four, five, six, and off he came again.

This time hitting the ground hard enough to hear his arm crack. The boys helped him up and out of the corral into the bunkhouse. The cowboy was mad as a hornet, holding his arm all the way. On the way to bunkhouse, Matt heard him say, "Where's Sam when you need him?" "On an important mission, trying to save my sister, that's where," he yelled. The cowboy looked back at Matt. "I apologize, Matt, I'm stupid with pain. Didn't mean no disrespect. I'm frustrated with that mare." "It's okay, I'm touchy myself. Hey, when you feel better, come find me and maybe I can give you some tips on how to break that mare. I learned a lot from Juan on the drive, before I got hurt." "I'll do that, thanks, Matt," the cowboy said. Steve turned his chair around and they headed back into the house.

Martha had lunch ready and the kitchen set up where the cowboys could walk through and fill their plates, then they would go outside to the tables and eat. Matt, Steve, and Charlie ate at the kitchen table with Martha. After the meal, Matt asked Martha if there had been any news from Sam. She looked at Matt, directly, and said, "Nothing lately. Last word I got was they knew who has her, they just hadn't found her yet." "Who has her, Martha, did they say?" "Gerard Michaels." "From the GM Ranch! The ones we just drove his cattle to Emery?" Matt yelled, his anger rising by the minute. "Yes, same one," Charlie said. "Is he the one behind the stampede and me getting shot?" "That, I don't know. We'll find that out when they catch him." "I wish I could be there when they catch him," he said angrily, under his breath. "Thanks for lunch, Martha. I think I'll rest for a while; I'm not feeling so good right now. Steve, you can take a break and get back to doing whatever you need to. I think I'll try to sleep some." He rolled away from the table and into his parent's room, shutting the door. "I'll check on him in about an hour, Martha," Steve said, as he left the table and went outside.

Matt rolled over to the bedside and transferred from his chair. He laid his head down on the pillow and cried for his sister. He missed her so much and prayed she was alright. Surely, Luke and Sam will find her soon.

* * * * *

Luke, Sam, and Clay, along with the others, had started at dawn and had traveled, approximately, twenty miles, seeing nothing but cattle. While they were riding alongside the herd, Luke started checking the brands on the cattle. He found the SW brand, the Rocking R brand, the P3 brand and other brands he didn't know. He found few with the GM brand. Now, he knew for sure that Gerard was behind the rustling and everything that happened on the drive; including shooting Matt. Now he has Ralynn. "He will pay dearly for what he has done," he said to himself. "You say something, Luke?" Sam asked. "Just talking to myself. I was thinking how Gerard will pay for his evil deeds." "Yeah, I was wondering that, myself. I'm sure my thoughts are the same as yours along that line; I just hope he hasn't hurt her." "If he has, I'll kill him with my own two hands!" "Let's not lose focus, Luke. Let's get Rae back first, then you can have him to do with as you please." "Thanks Sam. I'm angry and frustrated. I'm in love with her, Sam, and she doesn't even know it." Sam smiled, "Does she feel the same?" "I don't know. Every time I've tried to talk to her, she was either a touch-me-not or the Boss. She won't let me near her," he explained. "Oh, I've seen her look at you and watch you. I know there's something there. I can see it in her eyes. Just be patient, Luke, she'll come around," Sam advised him. "I hope so." Clay rode up to them and said he was going on ahead to see what to expect and rode off. Luke and the rest followed at a slower pace. They needed to find this place and plan a strategy before barging onto the ranch, although he assumed they had been on it for quite some time. That would only cause harm for Ralynn and he was not willing to risk her getting hurt.

Another twenty miles and nothing but cattle everywhere. "My oh my," Sam said. "What's that Sam?" "It's no wonder that Gerard always has lots of money on him. He's made a fortune stealing our cattle and selling them. He's only been here, in this area, for two years. How can he have stolen so many cattle in that amount of time?" "Well, Sam, look at the big picture here.

You told me, yourself, that you have lost cattle, but you, also, said you figured that the coyotes and wolves probably got some of them. Now, think how many you've lost. I'd bet Gerard's behind those lost cattle as well." "Putting it that way makes a lot of sense, definitely explains the numbers lost," Sam replied. "After this is all over, we'll have to get the ranchers together and sort all these cattle and get them back to their rightful owners," Luke said. "Heck, that will be fun compared to this," Sam laughed.

Clay returned, riding up beside Luke. "I found the house, if you can call it that. You won't believe it when you see it; three stories high and magnificent," he told them. "How many ranch hands did you see?" "I saw seven walking around, two posted at the front door, and two men at the gate where they entered." "That's eleven, I wonder how many are inside?" "It's heavily guarded. I'd say there's more that I couldn't see. It's a huge place," Clay said. "How far up is it from here?" "About ten miles up. There is a place where we can stop and make plans to infiltrate the ranch. I think I know where the lady is being held. On the left side of the house, on the third level, there is a window that is boarded up. I don't think Gerard would have a broken window and not fix it immediately. I'm assuming that it is boarded up to keep a certain lady from seeing out. The house is too grand to have that showing for too long." "Okay then, let's ride and get a plan in place to get Rae out of there and get her home," Sam ordered. With Clay leading, they all followed at a fast pace. The horses were tired but when ordered into action they all obeyed the command. They rode the ten miles and the ranch came into view. "Wow! Now that's a mansion, not a house," Sam said. "How are we going to get in there?" "With skill and expertise," Luke said. "Exactly what are your skills and expertise, Luke?" "I'm half Apache, Sam, I can go right up to that gate. They won't recognize me with war paint and long hair." "What about the rest of us?" Clay asked. "I figure we'll attack at night, they won't be expecting us, because Gerard doesn't think anyone could find that pass, otherwise, he'd have guards posted there and they would have ambushed us as we came through, one by one." "Okay, then what do you have in mind?" "Let's see, we have twenty-seven men with us, plus us three; thirty altogether. We will place eight men each on three sides of the house and the rest will come with us." "What are we going to do?" Clay asked. "We get the boys situated around the house as close as they can get. I will go up to the gate and you and Sam will be walking closely alongside my horse and before I get their attention, I want you two on each side of the gate. The other three will come in at the last minute to help you and Sam take out the guards. Then, once the gate is open, rush in and take out the two guards inside and the rest of you will ride right up to the door and take those guards out. I'm going to bust in the door and find Ralynn. Clay, you said on the left side, third level?" "Yeah." "Once inside, I'm heading straight up the stairs. Sam, you and Clay search for Gerard and the others are to keep anyone from leaving the house. The rest of you, once you hear my yell, will search for and capture anyone around the house and outbuildings, put them all in one place and put a guard on them, then come into the house and do the same. Unfortunately, you will all be on your own. We want Gerard alive, if possible, and his men.

If there are women and children, put them in a safe place and we'll let them go when this is over. Any questions or suggestions? Now's the time to speak up." No one said a word. "Okay, then we'll go at midnight. Get some rest, it's going to be a long night." Another cold camp, but no one complained. They all settled down; some slept and others not so much.

CHAPTER 25

Gerard was beside himself, Miss Ralynn Parker, owner of P3 Ranch, had said yes to his proposal and now all he could think about was getting her ranch. He was certain the boy, Matthew, would go along with whatever his sister said. It was just before dinner and he was patiently waiting for his bride-to-be. He was so anxious that he could hardly stand it. He figured that if he wined and dined her and gave to her, her most precious desires, that she wouldn't even think of the ranch or her brother. Once they were married, then he'd start the take-over of the P3 Ranch. He heard the rustle of her gown as she descended the stairs and rushed to meet her at the bottom. A few steps to go; she held out her hand to him, he took it and led her to the dining room. He seated her and, then, himself. He called the servants to be served. Marge came in with their salads and placed one in front of each of them. A few minutes later, she returned with the main course; roast beef, with a side of mashed potatoes, green beans with chunks of ham and onions mixed in, and homemade bread with sweet butter. They ate in silence. She was enjoying her meal, when he gave her some news of home. "Miss Ralynn, I received word today that your brother is doing well with no complications from his injury." "How did you find that out?" "I sent one of my men into Archer to ask around. Martha is home as well and is doing fine. I hear that she and Sam Frye are to be married soon, is that true?" "Yes," she said. All of the sudden, she became homesick and her food no longer appealed to her. "I'd like to be excused, please." "Aren't you feeling well, darling?" "No, I'm not. I'd like to lie down." "No problem. I'll let you rest; I won't be coming by your room then." "Thank you, Gerard, I would appreciate that." She rose from the table and headed up the stairs to her room. Once inside, she threw herself on the bed and cried herself to sleep.

* * * * *

It was eleven forty-five in the evening, leaving only fifteen minutes for the men to get into position. Luke became Bear Claw with just a bit of paint on his face and his hair loose from its leather strapping with feathers entwined in it. Sam looked at Luke in amazement; such a difference with just a couple of changes. Clay and the others were in disbelief, as well. "It's not that big of a change." He looked at them as they stared in his direction. "It is if you have never seen that side of you before," Sam commented. "Okay. Boys, it's time to end this game of Gerard's tonight," Luke told them. Sam called out to the three going with him and Clay and ordered the rest to get prepared to get into position. Luke had painted Comanche, as well, with paint and feathers. He left his saddle behind in the brush and was going to ride in with only the blanket; trying to be as authentic as possible. He mounted and the others followed. They only had to ride a half of a mile and then dismounted, except for Luke. Clay and Sam stepped up to Comanche and sucked themselves in as close as they could so as not to be seen. In the dark they were invisible. The other three waited for Luke's war cry before taking action. Luke rode to the gate and was talking to the guards, keeping them occupied. As soon as they opened the gate, Luke yelled his war cry. Sam and Clay stepped out and took out the guards outside, then rushed inside and took those two out. The other three rode right up to the door of the mansion and took out those guards. Luke dismounted, carrying a shotgun; he shot twice blasting holes in the hardware on the door. He kicked it open and Sam and Clay came rushing in behind him. Luke raced up the stairs to the third floor; finding two guards guarding one room. He knew that was the room Ralynn was being kept in. Looking his way, the two guards, thinking they were being attacked by Indians, were trying to get their guns drawn out of their holsters, but were so scared they couldn't get them out fast enough. With a war cry and a knife, he got one of the men right in the heart; the other guard finally got his gun out, but wasn't quick enough; a bullet caught him in the stomach. Luke rushed to the door and blasted the lock. He opened the door and there she was; he froze. She was as beautiful as always, sitting there with a book in her hand. The book fell to the floor as she jumped up and ran into his arms. He held her tight as she cried. He pulled away, tilted her chin and kissed her on the lips; she returned the kiss. Another tender moment between them.

Gunfire erupted and brought Luke to his senses. "Come on," he demanded. He took her hand and led her down the stairs. They were almost to the bottom of the steps when Gerard started yelling loudly, "Take your hands off my bride!" At that moment, Sam came rushing into the room behind Gerard and hit him with the butt of his colt pistol, leaving Gerard to fall to the ground. Sam pulled a couple pieces of rope from his belt loop and tied Gerard's hands behind his back. Sam, then, rushed over to Ralynn, grabbed her and twirled her around. "Thank God, we found you. Are you alright? Did he or the others hurt you in any way?" He released her and she answered, "Yes, Sam, I'm okay and no they did not hurt me, except for keeping me locked up and fed little at times," she replied. "It's so good to see you guys." "Bride?" Luke asked, surprised. "What?" "He called you, his bride." "Oh, yes, he proposed and I refused. Then he locked me in that room with little to eat and darkness. A week later he proposed again and I agreed just to get out of that room and have something to eat and have a bath. He wanted to marry right away, but I kept putting him off by telling him I wanted my family with me on my wedding day. I was trying to buy time, hoping with all my heart, you two would find me." "We almost didn't find this place, but Sam found the passage that led us here through the mountain," Luke told her. "Hey, Luke, we have Gerard and his men; ready to ride?" A cowboy asked.

"Sure thing, we are on our way out. Is there anything here that you need to grab?" "What day is it? How long have I been here? Do I need a coat?" "We'll talk about all of that on the way and no, you don't need a coat, I have one in my saddlebags. Let's get you on the trail. I know several people that would like to see you and know you are okay." Leaving several cowboys behind to take care of the rest of the people, they left the mansion, mounted their horses, and headed towards Archer.

Gerard was hanging over the back of a horse, head down and hurting. He looked around, but all he could see was the ground. "Let me off this horse!" he yelled. "Do you think we should?" Someone asked, then there was laughter all around him. "Stop this beast and let me off!" He demanded. "Your days of bossing people around are over old man," another one said. "You'll regret this!" He screamed. The horse stopped and someone had a hold of his pants, pulling him off the horse. He fell to the ground. Trying to stand up, he kept seeing the world pass by him by at lightning speed. Every time he would try to stand, his knees would buckle and down to the ground he would go. "Get up, old man, I've got places to be," a cowboy said. "You'll never get away with this, besides Ralynn can't testify against me, she's my wife!" He screamed. "Oh, no she isn't, you forget that you haven't been married?" "And won't ever be," she informed him. "I would never have married you, Gerard. I just agreed to so I could get out of that room and eat some real food. You didn't break me at all!" "You said you loved me!" he whined. "No, I said I thought highly of you, but I lied. After what you have cost me and my family, you honestly believe I would forgive you? I think not! I will testify against you," she said proudly.

"I'll not forget this. You'll regret what you said to me today." "I doubt that very much," she said, as she rode off to join Sam and Luke. "Everything okay, Rae?" "Yes, that man is crazy. He doesn't even know he's been beat." "He'll know soon enough, we'll be in Emery tomorrow, he'll know then when everyone finds out what he has done." Sam commented. "I'll be glad to get back home. How's Martha?" "About the way you'd expect a mother to be when one of her children is missing." "I'm so sorry, I didn't mean for all this to happen," she told Sam, with a saddened voice. "Don't go putting the blame on yourself, Rae. Gerard would have shown his hand sooner or later; just glad it was sooner and Matt and Luke figured it out." "Just wasn't me, Sam, it was a joint effort." Luke stated. "Yes, I believe it was," Sam replied.

* * * * *

Later that evening, when everyone but the guards were sleeping, Gerard and his goons plotted a plan to escape. Right before daybreak, they would grab the horses and ride out of camp. One of his men had got himself loose and cut the rest free. They quietly saddled the horses to ride and took the rest with them, running them far from camp. It would take several hours for their captors to round them all up and get them back to camp. Gerard thought it was a genius plan, or so he thought. Little did he know that all P3 horses were loyal and trained to come when whistled for. It wasn't long before Luke and the others had their horses back. Luke left Ralynn in Sam's care and took all but four cowboys, which he left with Sam, in case Gerard circled back around for Ralynn, and headed after Gerard and his men. Gerard didn't bother covering his tracks, so they could easily follow them, until they came to rocky terrain. It was then that Luke and Clay took the lead. They had been riding for about three hours when Clay found upturned rocks through another pass, this one larger than the last one. Moving forward, they came to a main road. "So, this is how they moved the cattle in and out," Luke stated. They headed South East and came right up to the town of Emery's County line. "Surely, he isn't stupid enough to ride into Emery in broad daylight," Luke said. "Think about it for a minute, Luke. No one but us here knows what he's done. No one will suspect a thing; just that he's going to his office," Sheriff Stevens said. "It's too easy, Sheriff. Boys, be on the lookout for side roads or possible turn offs. Watch for flat grass and broken branches." They rode on and before they realized it, they were in the town of Emery. Hopefully, Sam had already brought Ralynn into Emery, but since he didn't specify it, he didn't know if he would. He may take her straight home. Since Gerard was on the loose, she was not safe. The sheriff rode on to his office, found one of his deputies and quizzed him about any and all people that had come into town. He informed the sheriff that Sam had come into town with four riders and a woman and were at the hotel. There was no one else that he saw. Sheriff Stevens went to find Luke, but didn't have to go far. Luke and the boys were sitting right in front of his office. He informed Luke about Sam, but no one had seen Gerard or any of his boys. "Well, they had to turn off the trail somewhere and come in a back way, if they were in town." "That seems to be the case," Sheriff Stevens said. "Boys, rest your horses or get another one, and grab a bite, we ride in an hour. We've got to find him."

Luke stepped down off Comanche and handed his reins to another cowboy. He headed for the hotel. He checked the book, at the desk, to see what room Sam had checked in to. He knocked on Sam's door and was greeted by one of P3's cowboys. "Come on in, Luke." "Did you catch him?" Ralynn asked. He didn't see her sitting there. "No, we didn't. He pulled a quick one on us and led us right to main street. He just disappeared." "Sam, I want you and these boys to take Ralynn and go home. Have you given a statement to the sheriff's deputy?" "Not yet. We'll do that on our way out of town," Sam said. "Yes, please do that. I'll be sending a telegram to P3 and to the Governor as soon as I leave you. Then, the boys and I are riding out again to find Gerard and his men, hopefully they aren't smart enough to split up. Make sure there are two of you on guard at all times. There's no telling what this crazy man might do now." They all agreed to do just that. "Ralynn, may I speak to you for a moment, privately?" "Come on boys, let's check on our horses," Sam said.

While Luke was with Ralynn, the sheriff and Clay sat down in the office and wrote out the charges against Gerard and his men. "I'll see if Luke has any more to add when he gets here," Sheriff Seth Stevens said. "I'm going to check in at my office. If it's busy, I'll stay and work, but if you really need me just holler," Clay said. "Okay, Clay. Thanks a lot for your help." "No problem, remember just holler." Clay left the sheriff's office and went to see if any animals needed help. The sheriff sat down and looked over the paper reading it aloud, cattle rustling, kidnapping, attempted kidnapping, murder, and who knows what else. He thought about the cowboy that Gerard had killed in the process of his escape. He hit him so hard that the blow knocked him to the ground causing the cowboy's head to hit a rock that killed him. Luke had said nothing about whether the cow-boy had a family or not: he would have to find out.

Luke sat across from Ralynn in the hotel room. He was definitely nervous, turning his Stetson in his hands. "You wanted to speak to me?" "Yes, I did." "Okay, then speak up." "You know what I am now and what I do, I was wondering if you had any feelings for me, because I do for you. You have stolen my heart, Ralynn, and if you have no feelings for me, I'd like it back."

She was shocked. "You are very blunt and to the point, Luke." "Well, I have no time to waste. I've got to find Gerard as soon as possible. So?" "Luke, I've never been in love before, so these feelings that I have for you are very new to me. I'm not sure how I feel, too much has happened and I can't seem to think straight. If love is what I'm feeling, then I want to see where it goes." "I can accept that," he said. "You'll need to give me time to get my focus back and I need to see Matt and Martha. I want to go home," she said with tears in her eyes. "Okay, Ralynn, I'll give you your space." He stood up and walked over to her, placed his hand under her chin, and lifted her lips towards him. He leaned in and kissed her slowly and she returned it, wrapping her arms around his neck. He stepped back, looked at her, and knew if he didn't stop, now, he couldn't be held responsible for what might happen. He turned and walked to the door, then stopped. "Did Gerard give any reason for his actions?" "Yes, it's over a registered bull that my Pa bought, sight unseen. Apparently, the bull died in transport and Pa refused to pay for it.

Gerard had been threatening him, so he had his goons mess with my Pa's rig causing my parents to go over that ridge and die. He's so angry that he swore he'd make us pay. Since he couldn't get the money from Pa, he killed them and came after P3 and us, any way he could." "Okay, thanks, I'll be seeing you sometime." He walked out of the room and closed the door. She was a bit stunned by their conversation. She knew she had feelings for Luke, but what waited for her at home? She had no idea, but something inside was telling her that Gerard had lied to her about her brother and Martha. She knew something wasn't right because Sam had avoided a straight answer. She was needed at home and not thinking about how she felt about Luke. Luke left the hotel and went to the telegraph office. He sent two telegrams. The first one read:

Charlie, Martha, and Matt, Ralynn rescued, Gerard on the loose. Sam is bringing her home, be there in three days. Luke

The second one read:

Governor, Solved the crime. Suspect on the loose. Charges filed. Will be in touch. Lucus

* * * * *

Back at P3, all was not well. Matt had been having severe pain attacks for the past two days. Martha, Charlie, and the boys never left him alone. They were all there to help him cope. About the time for Martha to set dinner on the table, Charlie came in with a telegram. He read it to her. "That's great news. I guess we'll get the details when they get home. Charlie is the messenger still outside?" "I think so, he was talking to some of the boys." "Catch him and have him send Doc out." "Is Matt worse?" "Yes, please catch him," she said worriedly. Charlie rushed out the door and caught the boy before he left. "Yes, sir, I'll head there now." "Thanks," Charlie said as the boy took off in a gallop.

He went back inside the house finding Martha with the telegram in her hand, sitting at the kitchen table, reading it. "That's good news, right?" He sat down across from her and asked what was wrong. "Nothing and everything." "You mind explaining that please." "My girl's coming home safe and sound. I'm so happy, yet I'm so sad about Matthew. He just seems to get worse every time that pain hits. I don't know what to do to help him," she whispered so Matt wouldn't hear. "I think the first thing is to tell him his sister is safe and coming home. She'll be here in two days," he told her. "Yes, I'll do that now."

She walked into Matt's room. He was sitting up in bed, holding his legs; trying not to rub his stomach. "Matt, is the pain bad again?" "Yes." He answered her; his lips quivering. "I have some good news that will cheer you up. They found your sister and rescued her. She and Sam will be home in two days." "They found her! Is she okay? Did they hurt her?" he asked excitedly. "She's fine, just worn out. I don't know if they hurt her, Luke didn't say. I hope not. We'll see when they get here. I sent for the Doc; I want to know what he has to say about this monster of pain you are having."

Doc arrived an hour later and went straight to Matt's room. He examined him and gave him another two bottles of morphine. Matt handed them to Martha. "Put them up in the kitchen for me, please. I don't want to become addicted to that. I'll only take it when I can't handle the pain." "That's good because it is addicting. I'm glad you feel that way. Most of my patients take it for every little pain and then can't stop. Take two tablespoons when your pain is severe. Send for me if you need me." "Doc, do you know what is causing this pain?" "Yes, I believe I do but I want to explain it to Matt first, then I'll come in the kitchen and explain to you and Charlie." "Okay, we'll see you in a few minutes," she said and left the room.

Doc tried to explain to Matt what was causing his pain, but his pain became severe again and this time he was there to watch Matt. It started easing up and Matt wanted to rest, so he left Matt to rest and went to talk to Martha and Charlie. Martha was fixing coffee and brought two cups to the table; one for each of them. She went back to the stove and poured one for herself and joined them at the table. Doc sat down and sipped his coffee. "That's some good coffee, Martha," he said. "Thank you, my mama taught me when I was thirteen." "She taught you well." "Let me explain what I believe is causing Matt's pain. I tried to explain it to him, but he was hurting and I let him rest, so I'll explain what I know to you both. After Matt's first episode, I did some reading and also sent a telegram to some colleagues of mine asking their opinion on this matter. What we have concluded and have agreed on is this. Matt has a rare condition; it's called, SEVERE CHRONIC DIFFERENTIAL PAIN. There is no cure for it or medicine to make it stop. It is something Matt is going to learn how to deal with it for the rest of his life. The best we can do is give him the morphine, but no more than two tablespoons at one time, he can have less, but no more. He was smart, asking you, Martha, to put it out of his reach." "So, what causes this pain in legs and feet that don't work." Charlie asked. Doc scratched his head and then continued. "From what we, as doctors, understand, the bullet that hit Matt went in his left side and out the right. It severed most of his spinal cord, but has left a few nerves dangling. We think he has two or three left intact and they are sending sparks to his brain to move his legs but when the brain tries to send the message to his legs, it hits scar tissue and shoots back to the brain as pain. We do not know enough about the brain to do anything, maybe someday, but not at this time. All we can do is give the morphine to him and let him find a way to overcome it.

He will always have pain. One other thing is to keep him occupied: spending time outside with the boys, or with his mare and colt, anything to take his mind off the pain. Allow him to try to do whatever he wants by himself. I will tell you, that he will have good days and bad days and to let him find his own way to deal with it. That's all I know. We will just have to be patient with him, but by all means, do not baby him; it will make things worse for him. Treat him like you always have, he just can't do everything he did before." Doc finished his coffee and stood to leave. "Come get me if you need me, anytime." Then he left. "Did you understand all that he said," Charlie asked Martha. "Most of it. It's telling Matt that this pain will continue the rest of his life and that will be a challenge he'll need to face and overcome.. He's not going to take it well." "That's a lot for him to deal with, especially at his age."

CHAPTER 26

Two days later, Ralynn and Sam drove their team and wagon through Archer, WY. There is only one more hour before they are home. Ralynn was getting anxious to get home and see Matt and Martha. It had been a long and rough month. She couldn't wait to hug Martha, being that she's the only mother she has now, and Sam being a second father. With everything going on they never had the chance to discuss the future. Right now, though, it's time to get their wedding back on track. All of the sudden, there it was, the P3 Ranch. It looked heavenly to Ralynn; so good to be home; she shed tears. Sam drove the team and wagon through the ranch's gate and right up to the house. He put the brakes on the team and stepped down from the wagon, then helped Ralynn down. Charlie and the boys welcomed them home. "Martha must not know you're home yet. She's probably with Matt," Charlie said. "How's he doing? Sam asked. "He's had a rough time. We've all been helping Martha with him. His pain is something he'll have to learn to live with, the Doc said." "Well, let's go see them," Sam commanded. "I've missed my soon-to-be-bride." "We'll sneak in the kitchen, then," Ralynn said. They crept around the side of the house, ducking under the windows and being careful not to step on Martha's beautiful wild flowers and Blue Bonnets. They reached the door and stepped inside. No one was in the kitchen, so they quietly headed for Matt's room. The door to his room was open and they heard Matt asking Martha if Sam and Ralynn had made it home yet? Martha said, "No, not yet." Sam and Ralynn looked at each other and decided that now was the perfect moment. Sam moved to the doorway, as did Ralynn. They just stood there watching them. Martha was pulling the cover up over Matt when his eyes became teary. "Matt, honey, what's wrong?" Matt pointed towards the doorway. Martha turned, saw Sam and Ralynn, and screamed. "Sam! Ralynn!" She went to Ralynn, checked her over, turning her around, and then hugged her so tight, she couldn't breathe. "Hey! What about me, don't I get a hug?" Sam asked teasingly. "Oh, Sam, it's good to have you back." She hugged him and he kissed her until she turned red from embarrassment. Ralynn went to Matt's bedside and when she leaned towards him, he reached up and grabbed her, pulling her off her feet and onto the bed. He hugged her tight and wouldn't let her go. "I was so worried I would never see you again, Sis. It was a lonely feeling," he said, tears running down his face . "I know that feeling, I didn't think I'd ever get back home. I prayed and prayed that someone would find me, I cried every day. I'm so glad to be here and so thankful." They hugged again, as if, saying no one will tear us apart again.

At dinner that evening, Ralynn told them what happened. How she found her Pa's note in the ranch's financial book and how she confronted Gerard about it. She continued telling them what she went through and how Gerard was determined to take P3 away from them. This was my own fault, thinking I could confront Gerard and make him tell me it was a lie, which he did, but made it easier for him to kidnap me. I'm sorry for all the worry I brought on you all," tears collecting in her eyes again; seems to happen a lot lately. 'Rae, it's not your fault. You made a mistake by going alone. You should have told me about it and we could have made a plan to confront him." "I didn't want anyone to think badly of Pa; I knew something was wrong when I read gambling debt. I just had to find out, and when we went to Emery, it seemed like the best time. I thought I could clear it up without it getting anyone else involved." "Well, the next time you question something, come to me or Martha and we will help you figure it out." "I will, I promise." She looked at them with love in her eyes. "So, where are we with the wedding plans?" she asked. "Well, we haven't had much of a chance to do much with all the chaos going on," Martha said. "Then, I think it's time to get those plans back on track. It's only a couple weeks away." "I've been thinking about holding it off for a while until things calm down, but Sam says he won't hear of it." "That's right, I won't hear of it," Sam spoke up. "We are getting married in two weeks, rain or shine." "Yes, sir, two weeks!" Ralynn chuckled.

"Let's get these dishes done, and see where we are in the planning. Martha, did you get all you needed when in Emery? I apologize I wasn't much help." "You're home safe, that's all that matters, and yes, I got what I needed and your things as well." "Thank you, I didn't know if anyone would find them." She cleaned the table and washed the dishes. Martha came back into the kitchen with her arms loaded and set it all on the table. She took out the fabric swatches for Ralynn's dress and for the men's ties. She gave Ralynn their list of people to invite and Ralynn started making out the invitations to those that, otherwise, would not get the invite from word of mouth. She'd have one of the cowboys take them into town tomorrow. Martha had drawn a picture for her showing the kind of cake she wanted; Ralynn studied it. "This should be fun." she told Martha. She was thinking that she would make it as close to her sketch as possible. She looked up from the drawing and gasped. "Oh, Martha, that is beautiful." "I thought it would be perfect for your Maid of Honor dress." "I don't want to steal your show, Martha," she said jokingly. "I chose it because it will bring out the color of your eyes and it is your favorite color." "This is your day, not mine." "Your day will be here soon enough," Martha said. "Besides, you haven't seen my dress; it's my own design and one of a kind." "I can't wait to see it." Ralynn said. "Do you have a pattern or design for my dress?" "I have both. I need to get your measurements. We'll do that after breakfast in the morning when the men are busy and we have time alone." "Okay. Can I help with anything, now?" "Why don't we work on the flowers for the cake and I'll teach you how to make the roses with icing, I know you have problems making those." "That's great. I'll get the stuff ready to make the icing. Is it too early to make them?" "No, they need to harden and it will be best if they set for a few days." "I'll get the pans you'll need for the cake." Martha walked out of the kitchen and returned with three different size cake pans. "I'm so excited for you, Martha. I hope one day I'll find the right man to love me like Sam does you." "You will and it will happen sooner than you think." She looked at Martha with questioning eyes. "Do you know something I don't?" she asked. "It's possible. Just keep your eyes and heart open and you'll find that love you are looking for." Luke came to mind instantly. Could it be him?

* * * * *

Luke and Clay had been on Gerard's trail for three days. It seemed funny the way the tracks went East then doubled back, then doubled back again, went North and then South. "Where does he think he's going?" Clay asked. It's almost like we're going in circles." One cowboy said.

They were heading south when Luke stopped all of the sudden. "You know, you're right. We are going in circles. I can't recall, but were you all on the drive with me?" "Yes, we were." "Okay. Does any of this area seem familiar? Think about those that were taken and where we found them." The boys looked around for a few minutes, then one said, "I remember that crooked tree." "Me too, that means that cabin we found them is not too far away from here." Another cowboy spoke up, "That's right, it's east of that tree." Clay spoke up next, "Why don't we spit up into threes. You, Luke and I will go straight East, you three go Northeast, and the rest go Southeast. Maybe, one of us will find the cabin." "I believe they never thought of any one coming here to find them. Now that we have, we'll have them cornered," Luke said. "Okay," Clay said. "Let's move out." Luke ordered. They rode for three hours and found nothing. "What was that?" the cowboy asked. "Listen, in the distance." Luke and Clay silenced their horses and listened. Hearing nothing, they looked at the cowboy. There it was again, a warning shot coming from the South. "They found something," the cowboy said. "Let's get over there." They rode southwest for about six miles and ran into three of the cowboys. "It's about two miles south of here. There are four horses outside, saddled, and two guards pacing back and forth in front of the cabin and two more horses in a lean to in back of the cabin. We only saw the two guards; the rest must be inside." "Gerard's in there, Hank recognized his horse and gear."

"We'll stop for the night, here and have a cold camp. We need to come up with a plan that's quickly enforced so they have no time to get their guns. We can work on that while we wait for the others to show up." Luke and the rest dismounted, unsaddled their horses, and watered them from the creek nearby. Then they fed them some grain and then tied them out, got jerky from their saddlebags and sat by the fire and ate. Everyone was relaxed, as much as they could be, when the rest of the boys showed up. They all gathered around the campfire and discussed what would be the best way to attack at sunrise.

* * * * *

Ralynn was spending a lot of her time with her brother. The cowboys still helped Matt outside to see Darby and Bullet, and do some things with the boys. They fixed up a dummy calf out of a bale of straw and made a funny head with a bucket that they painted a face on it, for Matt to practice his roping skills. He was getting pretty good at it and all the cowboys would cheer him on whenever the rope fell over the pretend calf's head. He had mentioned to Sam that he wanted to ride Darby, but Sam said not until the Doc released him to go riding. His pain was a constant twenty-four seven occurrence, but it was manageable most of the time, even without Morphine. He had good days and bad days and he dealt with them as best he could. He learned to bathe and dress himself and get around by himself. Martha was even teaching him how to make biscuits, bread, and cookies.

Ralynn would read to Matt when he was having a bad day or they would play cards or checkers. She kept coming up with things to occupy his mind so he would not think about his pain. His best therapy was Darby and Bullet; there was such a bond between them when those three got together. One day Matt was having a really bad day and he wasn't able to get outside to see them. Sam sneaked Bullet in the house to see Matt, but when Martha found out she told Sam that he was lucky that she didn't have a frying pan in her hand. She was furious! Everybody else thought it was hilarious.

The wedding preparations were almost complete, with the big day only a week away. The happy couple spent their evenings together in the grape arbor sitting on their special bench. Ralynn had begun her preparations for the wedding cake. It was too soon to bake the cake, so she decided to make the wildflowers and vines that will go on the cake with the red, white, and yellow roses that she and Martha made a couple of days ago. The wildflowers and vines didn't have to dry as long as the roses, but they needed at least forty-eight hours to dry, so she would make them tonight. Martha had her dress close to finished; she thought it was beautiful at the last fitting, but Martha still had to add the lace and wouldn't let her see it until it was completely done.

Outside, Sam took back his foreman position, number 1 Top Hand, and Charlie went back to being number 2 Top Hand. The ranch was still not back to normal; eight cowboys short and everyone was pulling extra hours and chores, but there were no complaints. The ranch was running like a well oiled wagon wheel, but things were about to change before long if Ralynn and Matt have their way; a wedding surprise.

CHAPTER 27

By midnight, the boys had come up with a plan of attack against Gerard and his men. Luke assured them that it wasn't foolproof, nothing is, but as long as they move quickly, and catch them off guard, everything should fall into place. They settled down to get some shut-eye for a couple hours before the attack against Gerard and his men. It was a restless night for Luke; he kept running things through his mind. This has to work; I cannot go back to Ralynn without Gerard being caught and in jail. Ralynn and Matt needed this to end, as well as the others at the P3 Ranch. Luke settled some and pulled his Stetson down over his eyes to take a few winks before the next challenge/adventure began.

It was late, but Gerard was feeling uneasy. So far, they had avoided capture and he was grateful for that. He was still upset over Ralynn lying to him, he should have seen what she was doing. She'd played him well and his well-laid plans were failing again. "Why can't anything go my way, just once," he said angrily, feeling sorry for himself. He paced back and forth across the cabin's floor, while the others slept. He had already convinced himself that there was no posse anywhere near them, so they would leave for Mexico, the minute the sun came up.

Luke woke about an hour before sunrise, made coffee, and sat by the fire to drink it. The plan should work well if they can catch Gerard and his men quickly enough. The plan was to get on top of the cabin and plug or cover the chimney, then let the smoke do the trick. When the smoke gets thick enough, those inside will run out the door, but to be on the safe side, there would be men posted on each side where there is a window, in case they tried to come out that way. Then, they would capture them one by one. It was a simple plan and most effective most times. The others started stirring around the camp and getting ready for, hopefully, the last chase after Gerard and his men. Most were ready to go within fifteen minutes and Luke was one of them.

He was anxious to get the whole ordeal over with. He wanted Ralynn and to hold her again, but they still had to inform the other ranchers about their cattle and he had to meet with the Governor about him wanting to retire soon. His hopes that Ralynn would be happy about it too. Clay walked up to Luke and asked if he was ready because the rest were ready to get moving. Luke put her in the back of his mind, once again. "Yes, let's do this." Luke said, as he leaned over and slapped Clay on the back. They rode towards the cabin at an easy going pace, so as not to alert Gerard and his men. They rode upon the cabin thirty minutes later, dismounted, and secured their horses. Speaking in a low voice, Clay began sending the men to their positions.

Luke was to climb upon the roof and close off the chimney's air flow. When confirmation came that everyone was in their positions, Luke climbed on the roof and Clay was at the front door.

Once the chimney was covered, Luke climbed back down and stood opposite of Clay at the door. The smoke started rolling out the windows and door, like a puffy cloud of feathers. Then the door opened, quickly, Luke caught Gerard and Clay put the other four on the ground, as they came out coughing and gagging. The other two were caught by the cowboys out back in the lean-to.

Gerard, lying on the ground, hands tied behind him, began throwing a temper tantrum. "Why is this always happening to me? Nothing ever goes right! All I wanted was to be important and rich. Is that so bad?" "Come to think of it, yes, especially when you murder, steal, and hurt people and animals," Clay answered. "You don't know anything about me. You can't judge me!" Gerard said. "Whatever, you say, Boss man. It will be a judge and jury that will lead to your demise, not mine. Now get up and move it! You have a lot to pay for." Clay ordered.

There was no getting out of this now, Luke, Clay, and the men delivered Gerard and his men straight to Sheriff Stevens' office, walked him inside, and Luke locked the cell door then closed the door into the Sheriff's office. Gerard was still whining like a puppy when he shut the door. "Man, does he ever shut up?" The Sheriff asked. "No, not really." Clay answered. "Boys, if you don't need me anymore, I'm going to check in at my office. Some of us do have regular jobs." "Thank you, Clay, we would have still been out there if not for you knowing the area so well. Your time and expertise were and is much appreciated," Luke stretched out his hand and shook Clay's. "Well, if you need me again, you know where I will be." "Yes, we do. Hopefully, it won't be this type of job anytime soon." the sheriff said. "See ya, boys." Clay said with a wave of his hand and exited the door.

"Okay, Luke, what now? Are we trying Gerard here or in Cheyenne?" Seth asked. "I'll be sending a telegram to the Governor and I'll get back to you. I'll be staying at the hotel if you need me." Luke answered. "Okay, I'll be seeing you." "You sure will," Luke said.

* * * * *

Matt just finished his exam with Doc and was putting his shirt back on, when Doc came back into the exam room. "Well, Matt, except for the pain and paralysis, everything seems to be fine. Your wounds are almost healed. How is your pain these days? Any worse?" "I'd say I'm dealing and coping with it, but I still have those attacks when it seems like my legs and feet are on fire and like a knife is stabbing me. It's mostly in my left leg. It's not so bad on the right. I take my Morphine, but I have Martha keep it in the kitchen so I don't rely on it much. I don't want to become addicted to it." "Yes, you mentioned that earlier. I'm glad you feel that way and it's good that Martha is giving you only what you need. How's your mental state, Matt? Are you better at controlling your anger?" "I'm working on it and it is a lot better than it was." "Well, then I'll see you in a month, but do not hesitate to call on me if you need me. You are going to have pain for the rest of your life, but you can manage it. Like I said, have someone come and get me if you need me, anytime," Doc said.

He left the Doc's office and rolled down the street to their wagon. Ralynn was picking up supplies and a few last-minute things for Sam and Martha's wedding. She walked out to the General Store just as he rolled up. "You about ready, Sis?" "Just a few more things to carry out then I'll be ready." "I can help with the smaller packages, Sis." "Okay, come on." She piled Matt's lap full of small bags and he rolled back out to the wagon; waiting for her to come out with the rest. He sat there about five minutes before she came out; then loaded the wagon with the remainder of the packages she and Matt had. She helped him up into the wagon and then put his chair in the back. She climbed up and sat beside him, picked up the reins, released the wagon brakes, and they headed home.

"Hey, Sis, can we talk?" "Of course, we can talk about anything." "First of all, I'm sorry you didn't have a vote on Ma and Pa's room. It was just easier for Martha to tend to me when I first started having these severe pains. I hope you are okay with it." "It's fine, little brother, you need the room more than I do anyway. Was it awkward, at first, staying in there?" "It was at first, but then it began to feel comforting because the scent of Ma and Pa would relax me." "I'm glad it helps you." "Now for the second thing I wanted to talk to you about is your feelings on needing to be with and care for me. I appreciate all you do for me, but you need a life of your own as well. Don't you want to marry some day and have kids?" "I have a lot to do right here on P3 and I know no one that wants a *Boss* of a ranch for a wife. It doesn't matter to me if I marry or not." "You're not serious!" "I am." "What about Luke?" "What about him, haven't seen him in months and the wedding is just two days away. He was to be Sam's Best Man, and we've heard nothing from him." "He's crazy about you, Sis, don't you know that. You push him away all the time." "I don't either." "Yes, you do. When have you ever just sit down and talked to him?" "I don't have time." "Sis, you need to make time. Enjoy yourself and have some fun. I think the wedding will be good for all of us; visiting with everyone and all the festivities. Just do me a favor and try to have fun for a change, loosen up, and laugh. "Okay, Matthew, I'll try to do that."

She was thinking about what Matt had said to her earlier. She never gave marriage too much thought because her dream had always been to follow in her Pa's footsteps. Her ma had tried to get her involved with the things like sewing, knitting, cooking and all the things that ladies do; she could do them all but she was her Pa's daughter. Every year she would receive a new (in fashion) gown that her Ma made with her own two hands and a party, inviting all the neighbors and townsfolk. The one thing she always remembered was her parents telling her that they wanted more for her than just ranching. They offered to send her East to a school for young ladies, but she always refused. She felt that she could learn all she needed to know here on the ranch. It was the same when it came to men. They wanted her to meet doctors and lawyers and businessmen that would support her and a family, so she wouldn't have to work hard and she could age gracefully. She would have all the luxuries as a wife of a wealthy husband. She never cared about men or so she thought. A certain man, Luke Conrad, had been on her mind, or at least in the back of her mind, for weeks, but she never said anything to him, unless it was to criticize or order him around. She never gave him a genuine smile or flirted with him. He was just another cowboy, a hired hand, to her, or was he? She didn't know what had come over her; why he had taken over her thoughts. She knew nothing about love, except the love her parents shared with each other and what she saw develop between Sam and Martha. Lucus Conrad had her mind confused and her stomach in knots; was that love she was feeling for him, she didn't know. Maybe she could talk to Martha later when they worked on the last of the wedding plans. Dinner came and went, Martha and Ralynn laid out the last of the things for the wedding that needed to be finished on the table. Martha was putting the last touches on the ties for the men when Ralynn spoke up, "Martha, how did you know you were in love with Sam? I mean how did you feel? Was it like a lightning bolt struck you or was it slow and gradual?" Martha looked up from her stitching and giggled. "Now why would you be asking me questions like that?"

"I'm just curious." "Oh, and it has nothing to do with a tall, dark, and handsome man named Luke." "No." Her voice was a bit higher than normal, but definitely in denial. "Okay then, for me I saw Sam as the most handsome man I'd ever seen. I couldn't take my eyes off of him. He was so nice the day I came here and he has always treated me like a lady. As the years passed, I grew more in love with him. It's not something a person can put their finger on. It's a mixture of respect, communication, loyalty, and compromises, likes and dislikes, and the overwhelming feeling that you could live without him, but you cannot see your life without him in it, and you don't want to. I've been here at P3 for over twenty years and in that time, I've never even looked at another man like I look at Sam. We wasted a lot of years because we didn't know how the other one felt. For some reason, now is our time. We finally told each other how we felt and here we are; getting married in a couple of days. I feel so blessed." "But what about children, don't you two want some of your own?" "Sweetie, you and Matt have been my children all these years. I've watched you both grow up and accomplish all kinds of things. I've been happy and Sam feels the same. Our love for each other has kept us going, hoping one day we'd find each other and we did." She placed her hand over Ralynn's gentle and caressingly. "Why all the questions, my girl, are you changing your mind about marriage and children?" "I didn't say that, I was just asking." "Ralynn, I'll be up front with you. You are soon to turn twenty years old and you are at the age that you are ripe for marriage and having little ones and if that's what you want then don't be afraid to go after it, but if it's not that is okay too. Only you can decide what is right for your life and make it happen, although I do know of a certain man that has eyes only for you, my dear." She laughed as she watched Ralynn's cheeks grow pink and her reaction to what she had said. "If he cared even a little, then where is he? He's supposed to be Sam's Best Man and he isn't here! He just up and left without a word to anyone!" She spoke with anger in her voice and actions; throwing the papers in her hands on the table and stomping over to the counter. "Oh, now I see. You do have reasons for asking these questions." "So, I have feelings I don't know what to think of or what I'm supposed to do with them." "What kind of feeling, Sweetie?" "I don't know. I get angry when I'm around him, I don't want him to see me as a weak woman; I can do everything those men do. He confuses me when he looks at me with those dark eyes of his and I don't know what he is thinking. My stomach churns and feels all tied up in knots when he's around. I watch him out the window and my skin starts to tingle. It's like I want him to hold me and kiss me, but I'm so scared that he'll not feel the same way. It's just like at the hotel, after I was rescued, he told me he had feelings for me and when I told him I didn't know how I felt and I just wanted to go home; he walked out. I haven't seen or heard from him since. So, what am I supposed to think and feel about all of this?" She was trying hard to keep her eyes dry. "Sweetie, why are you trying to keep your feelings all tied up inside yourself? That's why you're all in knots and confused. If you didn't, at least, care for him it wouldn't matter, but you do have feelings for him and you seem to think that makes you less of a woman, which is far from the truth." "What do you mean?" Martha put her things on the table and went to Ralynn and put her arms around her. She looked directly in her eyes and said, "Oh, Sweetie, you're having these feelings because you are in love with him and don't even realize it. Did you ever consider the possibility that two together make each other stronger, that you're no longer alone and that you have someone to share all the ups and downs with and a chance at true happiness and love and maybe even your own children someday:``"No, I've never thought about any of that. I just always wanted to be a rancher like Pa was." "As you grow you have dreams, but as times change sometimes dreams change and what you wanted as a child isn't what you want as an adult." "I still want to run this ranch, Martha, that hasn't changed at all. I just don't know what to do with this other stuff. Maybe he won't ever come back and that will be that." She said firmly. "Oh, Sweetie, you don't really mean that." Martha was watching her closely.

"Yes, I do!" She said curtly. "Now what do we have left to do for your big day?" Martha knew her well enough to change the subject and not say anymore. "Well, I think we've got it all accomplished; now we just throw it together." They both laughed out loud and continued with their projects.

CHAPTER 28

Luke returned the day before the wedding. As he rode in, he could see all the activity of preparing for the wedding day. He thought about stopping by the house to see Ralynn, but decided against it. She wanted space and that is what he had given her. It was now up to her to let him know whether to stay or go. If she didn't make any kind of move; he'd be going home to Sedona, AZ after the wedding. He knew he couldn't stay here and work with her and not want her. He would want to hold and kiss her but would know it would never be. He just couldn't stay. He rode on to the barn, dismounted, and took Comanche to his stall. He unsaddled him, gave him some hay and began currying and brushing him down. When he finished, he put the curry comb and brush in the tack room and headed out to find Sam, hoping he wasn't in the house. He got lucky; Sam was in the bunkhouse trying to do something with a small box. "Need some help?" "Luke! You startled me. When did you get back?" "Just now. I took time to put Comanche up in his stall. I didn't see Twisted Mister in the barn?" "No, he's out with Darby and Bullet. Matt put him out there this morning. They're getting along fine." "That's good. I wanted to put Comanche up before coming to look for you. I have some news and I wanted to see you and tell you first. Didn't want to upset the women or Matt with it." "I see so you haven't seen Rae yet?" "No, I'm not sure that would have been a smart idea after the last time we spoke." "Put your finger here." Sam said. Luke placed his finger on the box so Sam could tie the bow. He set the box on the table. "Want some coffee?" "Sure." Sam went to the stove and poured two cups of coffee and set one down in front of Luke. Sam took a sip of his hot, black, and strong coffee and waited for Luke to start. "Sam, I apologize for leaving and not telling anyone, but I couldn't sleep with Gerard sitting in jail and knowing how tricky he was. I couldn't let him escape again. I left to help escort him to Cheyenne for trial. After the Governor heard of his escape, he wanted him transported to Cheyenne immediately and me to oversee it.

So, I left during the night, and got him there in two days. The Governor wasn't going to play games with him, so the trial was the day after I got him there." "He got sentenced didn't he?" "Yes, he did. The Judge was not easy on him. He was sentenced to life in prison at the Federal Prison in Uma, Wyoming." "I'm glad, he deserved it and more." Sam said. "That's not all.

After they sentenced him, he was escorted back to the County Jail until the next day, when they would start the trip to Uma. During the late evening, Gerard pulled one of his out-of-my-mind episodes and lured the deputy, which knew nothing of Gerard's tricks, into his cell to check on him, Gerard overtook him, grabbed his gun from its holster, hit the deputy, hard, in the back of the head, leaving him to bleed out, and ran. He was across the street and on a horse before the deputy got to the door and hollered for help; he died later. Sheriff Seth and I had just stepped outside from having a late dinner when we saw Gerard run by at a fast gallop. The sheriff got off one shot but missed him. We jumped on our horses and took out after him. My mind couldn't help but wonder how lucky this criminal is? Escaping twice and having a chance at us not catching him. We rode for a couple or three hours and could no longer see his tracks. We stopped and rested our horses for a few hours then we were after him again. We rode for an hour before we realized how stupid this man, really was; he was headed back to his mansion." "You cannot be serious," Sam just laughed and slapped his right leg with his right hand. "Oh, I'm so serious! We got to the place where we camped that night before the raid; Do you remember?" "Yes, I do." "We stopped and watched for a while, but he never came out so we got closer. His horse was tethered to the rail in front of the house and the door was standing open. We figured there must be something valuable that he needed before he could continue to run. After fifteen minutes, we decided to go in. Apparently, he was not expecting to have visitors, because when he saw us, he just stood there with his hands full of money. When the sheriff told him he was under arrest again and pulled out his cuffs; Gerard went nuts. He threw the money in the sheriff's face and threw a chair at me and ran out the door. We went after him and yelled for him to stop. He jumped on his horse and laughed at us; the sheriff aimed at him; Gerard was just sitting on the horse facing us. When the shot was fired, Gerard turned his horse and the bullet hit him in the back and right through the heart; he was dead instantly."

"Luke, I'm curious. Did he say anything before the trial?" "Yes, he said a lot and then nothing. On the way to Cheyenne, he kept talking about his wife and how she would break him out and how he had plans laid to take over P3 Ranch and a few others in the area. He said he had power over them and no one could touch him." "You mean he was still calling Rae his wife? What kind of power was he talking about?" "Yeah, he believes they were actually married. I don't know what kind of power he was talking about, but I plan to help Sheriff Stevens go through his mansion. He did say something about information, but he had begun talking nonsense and I quit listening, until he said one too many things about Ralynn. I stopped Comanche, stepped off, pulled him off his horse and told him that he should always check the brand to make sure he wasn't messing with another man's stock, then I literally beat him within an inch of his life, put him back on his horse and we continued on. He didn't say much after that and I was glad because he was getting on my nerves. So, my gut tells me that even with Gerard dead, there may still be some big play-ers out there tied to him in the rustling game. He had to be dealing with people who knew what he was doing with the brands all differ-ent. I don't think Gerard would have taken the time to rebrand them all that he sold, as fast as he was making money." Sam just looked at him and he just shrugged his shoulders. "Well, I, for one, am glad you beat his ass. If I had been with you, you would have had to beat me to him. Luke, you said you didn't think this is over. Are you expecting trouble here?" "No, not really. His men are all being tried in Emery and I don't think Gerard ever told them anything until he was ready to carry it out; he didn't trust any of them." "I think it's a good idea that you go with Sheriff Stevens to search that mansion.

It will save everybody a lot of trouble if you can find anything. It may have been only in his head." Sam said, scratching his head. Luke stood up from the table and started pacing the floor. Sam watched him for a few minutes, then asked, "Okay, Luke, spill the beans. You definitely have something on your mind, what is it?" "Well, Sam, I'm retiring from the agency at the end of the month. I told Ralynn I had feelings for her at the hotel, before we left to chase Gerard, and she said she wanted to go home and she needed space to think about it. I have given her that space, but I really don't know if she has even thought about it. I've left it up to her. If she doesn't talk to me or let me know anything before the wedding or shortly after, I'll be heading back to Cheyenne to finish out the month with the Governor, then back home to Arizona. I'm telling you now in case I don't get a chance to later." You're still going to be my Best Man, aren't you?" "Yes, of course. Please keep this part quiet until after I'm gone, if it turns out that way." "Sure thing. Oh, let's not mention what Gerard said about Rae and the information. It's best left between us for now."

The men went up to the house to check on dinner. Martha was in the kitchen and Ralynn was in the library. Sam and Luke sat at the kitchen table and talked about the happenings on the ranch and guy things. "I think everything is about ready for tomorrow, don't you agree Sweetheart?" Martha turned around and said, "I guess you being a man, you would think that. For a woman, there is still lots to do. Want to lend a hand?" Sam hesitated. Luke spoke up right then, "I believe I'll go see Matt, now." He stood up and left the table. Martha was still looking at Sam with questioning eyes. "Okay, dear, what do you want me to do?" "Well, you could take the trash out and burn it, and …….." Luke got out of the kitchen before Martha put him to work. As he was on his way to see Matt, he passed the large oak doors, which were open, and saw Ralynn at the desk; he didn't stop. She had to make the first move so he kept going. He reached Matt's door and knocked. "Come in," Matt said. Luke opened the door and walked in. "Luke, it's good to see you. Didn't know if you were going to make the wedding." "Wouldn't miss it." "Where have you been these past few weeks? I didn't even know you had left till the next day." "I was busy, I'll explain things at dinner when everyone is together. So, how you been doing, Matt?" "Oh, I'm doing okay. I have good days, like today, but the bad days can be hard to handle." "What do you mean?" "No one has told you?" "I guess not," Luke said. "Well, I've been having severe episodes of pain in my legs and feet. Doc says my paralysis is permanent and I'll have this pain forever. It gets bad at times; really bad that it's hard to function.

Morphine helps but only a little." "I'm sorry to hear that, Matt; anything I can do to help?" "Since you asked, yes there is. You can play some poker with me. I'm bored out of my skull." "Sure, got a deck of cards?" "I certainly do." They talked and played poker, Matt winning three out of five games. Sam knocked on the door, opened it, and told them Martha had dinner ready. Everyone met in the kitchen, then they took their seats at the table. "This smells really good, Martha." Luke said. "Well, if Sam will say Grace, then you can have all you want, Luke," Martha said. Sam led the prayer, then closed by saying "Amen." Ralynn was giving him the cold shoulder, so he decided right there that he would leave shortly after the wedding; no use putting it off. It was hard to do; but he put her to the back of his mind, enjoyed the meal and visited with the others.

Sam and Luke left the table and went to sit on the front porch to catch up on things. Luke repeated his story to the ladies and Matt at the dinner table, except the part about possible danger. He did, however, believe that Ralynn would have some kind of reaction to the news of Gerard's death, but she offered no response or reaction; she just snubbed him like before. To him, she was the same as telling him she wanted nothing to do with him; she proved that tonight. He may as well take back his heart, if at all possible, and forget Miss Ralynn Parker for good.

* * * * *

"What in the world is wrong with you, girl?" Martha demanded. "What do you mean?" Ralynn acted surprised, like she knew nothing about what Martha was talking about. "Oh, please, do not try to fool me. You were acting like Luke wasn't even here and even when he told us about that mean man, you said nothing. You know darn well he was trying to ease your mind by telling you that you were now safe and didn't have to be afraid any longer," Martha said sternly. "I knew no such thing." "Okay, Ralynn, you're going to push him away for good and it will be no one's fault but your own," "I'm not doing any pushing." She said, acting proud. "You don't think so?" "No, if he wants to be with me, he should have said something." She said, as a matter of fact. "Ralynn, you never listened to a word I said to you earlier. Maybe, you should think on that. I have a big day tomorrow and I need some rest. Goodnight. Dear." Martha left her in the kitchen and went to her room. She still had some finishing touches she needed to put on the wedding cake, then she was calling it a night as well. There were only a couple things left to do with the cake, in the morning, before setting it up for the reception. She went up to her room and was changing for bed, when she thought of what Martha had said. Why was Martha so upset with her? All she did was let Luke tell his story. She didn't need to say anything, besides, he didn't seem to mind. She sat at her vanity and brushed her hair, tied it back with a ribbon, and climbed in bed; she slept.

After the ladies had called it a night, Luke and Matt went over to the bunkhouse with Sam. Some of the neighbors, seven families that had traveled miles, came early to help with setting up the food and things for the wedding. They would spend the night and then leave after the festivities were over. Sam and Matt checked to see if they needed anything before calling it a night. Everyone seemed content, so they continued to the bunkhouse. Sam, a bit confused, asked, "Matt, it's late, why are you coming out here." "Oh, Luke said he had got something for me and I wanted to get it before I went to sleep." Sam looked at Luke. "I just picked up one of those dime magazines for him." Seeming satisfied with their answers, Sam opened the door and he was met with yells of congratulations and a beer placed in his hand. All his cowboys and the neighbors had come together to give him a bachelor party. "Are you surprised, Sam? Matt asked. "Yes, I am. I never expected this." Charlie walked over, "We thought you could use some guy time before your big day." He patted Sam on the back and walked away. Sam visited with the guys, telling stories and jokes, and then Sonny and Tom walked over with something under a blanket. Tom presented Sam the gift, "Sam, we have all came to love you just like a brother and we wanted to give you something special for your wedding so here it is; open it." Sam was overtaken with emotion, but kept it under control as he took the blanket off. It was the most beautiful saddle he'd ever seen; it even had his initials on it. He was speechless. Sonny, a little confused that Sam said nothing, said, "Don't you like it, Sam?" "Oh, yes. It's a beauty.

You guys didn't have to do this, but I thank you for it. I can't wait to use it." Charlie spoke up, "It'll be a week or more before that happens." They all started laughing; Sam, too. They carried on for a couple of hours, then Luke called for it to come to an end. "Hey, Ya'll, it's time to call it a night. Sam needs his rest for tomorrow." They all agreed and started to disburse. Luke asked Matt if he needed help getting to the house. Matt said no, and headed that way.

CHAPTER 29

The Wedding Day:

Martha woke up feeling excited, clear to the bones. It was her wedding day and she couldn't wait to be married to Sam. Mrs. Sam Frye, it sounded heavenly. She got out of bed, put on her regular work clothes, brushed her hair, and left her room to go to the kitchen to fix breakfast.

The wedding wasn't until two o'clock in the afternoon, so she had plenty of time to get breakfast over with and prepare the food she wanted at the reception. As she approached the kitchen, she heard several voices and a lot of racket. She stepped into the kitchen, only to find several of her friends, cooking and laughing. "Martha! Come on in and sit down. We have your breakfast ready." She was stunned. "Come on. You are being pampered today." Ralynn walked over to her and gave her a big hug. "Now, eat!" Martha shook her head and sat down. She looked around the room to see who all was there; Jenny, Kate, Josephine, Ellen, Sarah, Mabel, and Sissy. It was all her neighbors and friends. She wasn't hungry, but she ate some of the food; she didn't want to disappoint anyone. She took her plate to the sink and started to wash the dishes, when she was pulled away by Ellen. "No work for you today, Bride to be." "I have things to do. I have food to prepare and I have to oversee the decorations outside," she said. "No, you don't, Martha, everything is taken care of. Ralynn has already prepared the food, it's in the oven now. Luke and Matt are overseeing things outside, and we need you to come to the Living room, now." "What's in the Living room, did I forget the flowers or something?" "Just come with me," Ellen said. She led Martha to the Living room, and when she got to the doorway; she gasped and her hands flew to her mouth. "SURPRISE!" Everyone yelled. "What in the world?" The room was decorated in wild flowers and ribbons on everything. "Welcome to your Bridal Shower" They all said. "Oh, my gosh, I never expected this." "Well, sit here and we'll get started. The ladies had prepared tea cakes and a fruity drink for the occasion. They served everyone then began pulling packages out from behind the sofa. Ralynn stepped up first and handed her present to Martha. "Well, open it; don't be shy.: she said. She opened up the gift; her eyes widened, and a tear ran down her face. "Oh, just what I needed; a new pattern, material, sewing pins, and some lace. "Thank you, Sweetie." "You're very welcome." The other ladies gave her their gifts and she, along with the others, were laughing and having a good time.

Ralynn stood up, picked up all the gifts and took them to Martha's room. She went to the storage room and brought out the cake and set it on the kitchen table. All she had left to do was stack the layers and the cake would be done. She stepped outside and got Sam's attention. He came running. "Sam, she's still in the living room, can you take the tub to her room and fill it now?" "I'll keep her busy while you get that ready. "Sure enough, Rae. I got it." Sam stepped inside the storage room and brought the tub out and took it to Martha's room. He had already had the water heating so it took no time to carry it in. He then found Luke and they carried in the hot water for her bath. When they were done, Luke got Ralynn's attention letting her know it was ready. She nodded back. She walked over to Martha, "We need to go to your room now. I need to do your hair." Martha stood up, with tears running down her cheeks, thanked her friends for the surprise bridal shower and left with Ralynn. Ralynn led the way to her room and opened the door. She let Martha step inside first and then she handed Martha clean towels, wash cloth, new bar of soap, and she left the room, closing the door behind her. She became overwhelmed and emotional. It was her wedding day and she was going to enjoy it all. She locked her door, stripped off her clothes and stepped in the tub. "Oh, this feels sooooo good!" She washed her hair and wrapped it in a towel then proceeded with her bath. She guessed thirty minutes had passed; she was enjoying the soak so much she didn't want to get out, but she knew she had to.

She climbed out, dried herself off, put on her robe and unlocked her door. She opened it and hollered for Ralynn. Ralynn came at once to Martha's door. "Do you need something, Martha?"

"Yes, I do. I need you to go get your robe and come back here and take a bath. The water is still warm. You need some pampering yourself." "I have things to do." Everything will be fine without you for thirty minutes." "Okay, I'll be right back." "I'll be in the kitchen until you're done." She walked into the kitchen and found her friends busy cooking. When they saw her, they all started talking to her and asking questions. She sat at the table with a cup of tea and listened to all the gossip from town.

Forty minutes later, Ralynn came into the kitchen in her robe. She poured herself a cup of tea and sat at the table by Martha. She listened to all the news from town and, of course, the gossip. When she finished her tea, she said to Martha, "It really time to do your hair, Martha." "Okay, let me take a look outside first." "I'll go with you." They stepped out the back door and saw that the tables and chairs had all been set up and the band that Sam wanted was here. The arbor was decorated in flowers, ribbons and bows, and the cake was set up with flowers all around it. "The cake is beautiful, Sweetie." "Thank you. I tried to get it as close to your drawing as I could."

"You did a great job." Seeing that everything had been taken care of, they stepped back inside and went to her room.

Ralynn took the towel from her hair and brushed it out. "How do you want to wear it today?" "I think I want it up but with some strands hanging down." "Something like the way Ma fixed mine last year?" "Yes, can you do that?" "I think so. Do you have the pins within reach?" "Yes, they're right here." She opened a drawer in her vanity and laid them out for her. Ralynn started with the top and poofed it up by teasing it with a comb, then wrapped it around her hand, put it on top of her head and pinned it in place. She left two strands of hair hanging loose to frame Martha's face. Next, she combed out the back and made it into a French twist and pinned it in place. It took some time to do it, but it was done except for adding the tiny Baby's Breath and ribbons. Martha inspected it and was pleased. Ralynn added the flowers and ribbons and curled the strands with her finger. It was beautiful. Martha got up and walked over to her closet. She pulled out a green gown, and laid it on the bed. Ralynn was busy brushing her hair and didn't see it. "Okay, take a seat. I'll fix yours now." "You, don't have to do that. I was just going to pull it back and tie it with a ribbon." "No, I'm fixing it, so sit still." She brushed her hair out then teased it a bit on top. She pulled it back, pinned it and tied a ribbon in it. Next, she let the back fall to her waist and placed a small twig of Baby's Breath in the ribbon, "It's beautiful, Martha." "Thanks, I think so too. Now let's get you dressed." "I have to run up to my room to get my stockings and shoes first." "Okay, go get them." Ralynn took off and went up the back stairs so no one would see her. She was almost to her room when she ran into Luke coming out of Matt's room. "I'm sorry, what are you doing up here?" "I was getting something for Matt. You look beautiful." "Thanks. I'm in a hurry so talk later?" "Sure thing." Luke said and headed down the stairs. She grabbed her shoes and stockings and headed back to Martha's room. She knocked on the door then went inside. She squealed, "Oh, Martha, it is gorgeous!" Looking at her dress for the first time. "Now, let's get you dressed so I can do the same." "I can't wait to see your dress." "You'll see it soon enough; you'll have to help me with the buttons." "Okay, let's do this. I know it's your "Big Day," but I'm so excited, ' she exclaimed. "Me too," Martha added.

* * * * *

The men were getting ready for the big moment. Sam was having a terrible time getting his tie right; he couldn't steady his hands to tie it. Luke walked over and helped him. "What's wrong, Sam, you nervous?" "I guess I am, I didn't know I would be this way. I figured it would be like any other party we've had." "Well, it is and then it isn't. It's a party but adding a wedding in." Luke said. "I've never done this before, what if I forget my lines, or I faint when it's time to say "I do," or I get cold feet?" Sam began pacing the floor; he was beside himself. Matt and Luke were doubled over in laughter. "You two think this is funny, huh? Just wait until your time. I'll laugh so hard and then you'll know how it feels." He sat down, but got right back up and began pacing again, "What time is it?" "Luke pulled out his watch and told him it was fifteen passed one o'clock. "It's not funny!" Sam turned his back to them. "Sam, you'll be laughing at yourself, later. I should have mentioned this earlier, but the opportunity never came up. I'm giving you and Martha and all-expense paid trip to Cheyenne for a week. Charlie, Matt, and I will oversee the ranch so you two can enjoy each other." "You're doing what?" "You heard what I said." "I don't know what to say," Sam said, with tears in his eyes and a smile on his lips.. "You could say thanks." "Yes, thank you. We just planned one night away in Archer.

Martha will be shocked." "You and Martha deserve it." Matt rolled over by Sam, "I didn't want to give this to you around all the boys last night, so here," putting it in Sam's hands. He rolled back and watched Sam open it. "Did you make this, Matt?" "Yes, it's a riding whip. I figured you needed one." "This is great. Thank you, son." "You're welcome." "Think the ladies are ready to get this over with?" Sam asked. "I bet they are as anxious as we are. Let's go see," Luke said.

* * * * *

Back in Martha's room, Ralynn was staring at the dress Martha made for her. It was the color of Spring grass made from satin with a low neckline, puffy shoulders, short sleeves with white accent bows of ribbon. The bodice will fit snug around her midsection with a white satin sash tied in a bow at the back. From the waist down, the green satin flowed to the floor and on the front were three bows of white satin, just below the waist, with pastel-colored ribbons flowing down from them. "Oh, Martha, it's so beautiful. You shouldn't have spent so much time on this dress for me. I don't need to look beautiful on your "Big Day." "Sweetie, you will be turning twenty years old in three weeks and your Ma made you a dress every year. This is the pattern she had picked out for you this year, I just tweaked it a little. I figured giving it to you a little early wouldn't hurt and besides, you needed a gown for my wedding. Ralynn turned and gave her a teddy bear hug so tight that Martha couldn't breathe. "Thank you, Martha, I know Ma would have approved." "You're welcome, Sweetie. Now, let's get this on you, so you can help me with mine," she ordered. Ralynn stepped in the dress, pulled it up, put her arms in the sleeves, and Martha adjusted the bodice, then buttoned it and tied the sash around her waist; finishing with tying the bow in back. She stepped back and admired Ralynn. "It suits you well; makes your eyes pop." "Okay, now it's my turn. We have thirty minutes, so let's hurry." She walked to her closet and brought out her dress, covered in paper, and began uncovering it. As she pulled the remaining paper off, Ralynn gasped. "Oh, Martha, it's gorgeous! I've never seen anything like it!" she exclaimed. "It is, isn't it?" Martha laid it on the bed and unbuttoned the back of the dress, picked it up, and stepped into it. Ralynn helped her with the adjustments and buttoned up the back. She stood admiring Martha in her gown. Her wedding dress was made of white satin and lace trimmed in pastel ribbons. It was sleeveless and low-cut in front, trimmed with lace with pastel ribbon woven in. The bodice, covered with tiny white pearls, was snug-fitting and at the waist was a yellow sash that tied in the back, and from the bow flowed ribbons the color of wild flowers. From the waist down the gown flowed to the floor, beautifully after she added the three hoops under the gown with a four foot long train following behind her. The lower half of the gown and the train was sprinkled with more tiny white pearls, and her feet were covered in white satin slippers with little yellow bows. "Ralynn, help me with my veil, please." Her veil was white netting gathered at the top with a comb that Ralynn put in the back of her hair; the netting blended in with the dress and fell past her waist to the train; covered in white pearls as well. "You are stunning! Poor Sam will probably fall to his feet or faint." "Don't say that! I would like to get married today." She and Martha laughed. There was a knock on the door. "Who is it?" "It's Jenny. Everyone is ready and waiting for the bride to make her appearance. Are you two ready?" "Yes, we're coming now. You can open the door, Jenny."

She opened the door and was ahh-struck. "You both are gorgeous! Martha, your gown is amazing; can't wait to see Sam's face."

"Lead the way, Jenny." They had just started through the kitchen and the door opened. Ralynn turned and pushed Martha back a little so she wasn't in view of whoever it was. It was Luke looking for Ralynn. "We are just about ready to come out, is there something I can do for you?" "Oh, it's not for me, it's for Sam. He wanted to give this to Martha before now, but he forgot it. He wanted her to open it before the wedding." "Well, I'll take it and get it to her. We will be out in five minutes," Jenny informed him. Luke turned and walked out the door. Jenny handed the box to Martha; she opened it. It was a pair of pearl earrings and a pearl necklace. "Oh my, they're gorgeous!" Martha wondered how Sam knew about the pearls, her favorite gem. Ralynn helped her put them on and once again they headed outside; this time they made it.

Once outside, out of everyone's view, Ralynn stepped off the last step. The band started playing and a cowboy sang, "Amazing Grace," and she knew it was her cue to walk down the aisle, to the bench in the arbor, where Sam, Luke, and the Preacher stood. Luke was watching Sam and when he looked up, all of the sudden, his knees became weak. There was the love of his life walking towards him. Her auburn hair was pinned up on top and the back fell loose with ribbons wove through it and a bow at the back. The green dress made her hazel eyes pop and was beautiful lying next to her skin. She was an angel sent to torture him; how could ever live without her? As she neared them, she veered off to the left and turned facing the path she had just walked.

Matt was sitting at the bottom of the steps waiting to escort Martha down the aisle. When she came down the steps, Matt's heart melted and tears streamed from his eyes. "Martha, you are a sight to see, a beauty so beautiful. I'm so proud and honored to roll by your side down the aisle and give you away." "It's me who is honored, Matthew." She leaned down and kissed him on the cheek; making sure her lip stain didn't rub off on him. He held out his arm and she took it. All at once, Jenny said, "Wait! Your flowers." She ran into the kitchen, grabbed her bouquet of wildflowers, red roses, and Baby's Breath, and rushed out to give it to Martha. The cowboy began singing, "Together Forever" as they continued forward. When he reached the chorus, Martha and Matt started down the aisle. Sam looked at his bride to be and took a step backwards. Luke placed a hand on his back to steady him. Sam felt like he couldn't breathe. He was stunned, almost gasping for air.. He looked at his bride, she was always beautiful in his eyes, but today she glowed. He could see no one else but her. When she came to stand beside him; he leaned over and kissed her on the cheek; he couldn't help himself.

The Preacher stepped forward and whispered he had to wait a while longer then asked them to take each other's hands. Martha handed her bouquet to Ralynn and turned and took Sam's hands. The Preacher began: "We are here today to unite Sam Frye and Martha Simms in Holy Matrimony. Who giveth this woman to be wed?" "We do." Ralynn and Matt said at the same time. "What we are joining here today, let no man put asunder." He paused for a moment then continued. "Martha, repeat after me." "I, Martha, take thee, Sam, to be my lawfully wedded husband, to have and to hold, for better, for worse, for richer or poorer, in sickness and in health, to love and obey, till death do us part." Martha repeated the vows then placed a gold band on Sam's left hand ring finger. Then, Sam was asked to do the same. After completing his vows, he placed a ring on her left-hand ring finger. "I now pronounce you husband and wife. Sam, now you may kiss your bride." Sam looked Martha in the eyes then focused on her luscious pink lips.

He took her by the waist, pulled her close, pressed his lips against hers; then he bent her backwards as the kiss continued. Everyone cheered, some whistled, and the cowboys hooted and hollered. It was Sam and Martha's longest moment between them; a moment that will remain with them forever. When Sam finally came up for air, the Preacher said, "I, now, introduce to you, Mr. and Mrs. Sam Frye." Sam turned to the Preacher and asked him if he could stand aside; he reached down and uncovered their bench. Martha looked at the bench where she had shared so many moments with Sam. It was painted white with letters of green and gold. It read, "OUR MOMENTS BETWEEN." Martha's eyes filled with tears and Sam kissed them away. "Thank you, my husband," she whispered. "Anything for you, my wife." Martha looked up at him; "I'm so happy," she said. "Me too, dear." Everyone clapped and hollered as Sam escorted his wife towards the house. They stopped by the back porch and waited for Ralynn and Luke to stand with them.

Luke stepped to the center of the aisle and held out his arm; waiting for Ralynn to take it. She walked over and reluctantly took his arm. When she touched him, it took her breath away, her skin tingled all over her body, and her heart felt like a bolt of lightning had hit her. She glanced at him and at that moment she knew she wanted him; she knew she was in love; but how was she to tell him? How was she to open her heart and tell him that she loved him and didn't want to live without him? She knew her time was up and if she didn't do something he would be gone from her life forever. How can she get him alone? She started thinking of a plan; one that she could initiate quickly. They approached Sam and Martha and they all hugged and took a deep breath, now that the hard part was over.

As the guest dispersed after congratulating the couple, Sam and Martha went back into the arbor and sat on their bench. Ralynn watched them for a moment before disturbing them. Would she have a love like that with Luke? She wondered. She walked up to them, "Martha, I'm going in to change my gown, I don't want to spill anything on it." "Oh, no you can't just yet. I've requested to have the band play before we eat, so that we can have our first dance and then one with you and Luke. Sam, can you have them to start in about ten minutes? We'll have our dance then you and I can both change. Besides, we need each other to unbutton these beauties." "Okay, I guess Sam will tell Luke?" "I suppose he will. Have you spoken to him?" "Not yet, I'm working on it." "Well, don't wait too long. I have it from a trusted source that if you don't do something soon, he'll be going back to Arizona." "I guess I'll have to step it up then." Sam joined them and took Martha's hand. "Excuse us, Rae, but I have a dance with my wife waiting." He winked at her and led his wife to the dance floor. She watched them as they stepped on the dance floor and began dancing to a slow waltz. Something touched her arm and her skin tingled. She looked over and saw Luke standing there. "I guess we're supposed to join them when this song is over?" "Yes." "Okay, may I escort you to the dance floor?" "Yes, you may."

She took his arm and he led the way. While they waited for the song to end; she heard the guests talking about how beautiful the wedding was and the gowns were just gorgeous. She couldn't wait to tell Martha. She glanced at Luke and he was watching the couple on the dance floor. "Luke, I would like to talk to you later, alone if possible. Do you think you can step away from all this for a few minutes?" "I believe I can find time after the meal; would that work for you?" "Yes, just come and find me when you're ready. Thanks, Luke." "No problem. I think this is us." He led her onto the dance floor and took her in his arms. He held her close and they waltzed together. Luke could feel her heartbeat next to his and his arms tightened around her. "Luke, I can't breathe," she whispered to him. "I'm sorry, you just feel good in my arms." He loosened his hold and looked at her. "I can't wait to be alone with you," he said tenderly. He watched her cheeks turn a rosy pink. She looked so beautiful.

After the dancing was over for the bride and groom, Martha and Ralynn went into the house to her room and helped each other out of their gowns. "Martha, you should have heard all the talk about how beautiful everything was. Oh, and about our gowns, you did an amazing job. Just imagine you could open a shop and make gowns and such. I'm so happy for you." "Thanks, my dear, but I have my hands full here. We can't linger, we still have the meal and the cake to cut and more dancing; and of course, I want to be with my husband. Doesn't that sound wonderful? My husband." She twirled around and laughed. Ralynn laughed with her. When they came downstairs, Martha in a yellow dress and Ralynn in a pink one, they went straight outside.

Martha went to Sam's side and Ralynn went in search of Matt. They had a much thought and talked about gift to give the new couple. She, also, looked for Luke, but he was nowhere to be seen. She found Matt with the cowboys and got his attention. He nodded and rolled her way. Charlie went to the arbor and asked Sam and Martha to follow him. They walked with him to the front of the house and up the steps. Charlie hollered a loud, "Howwwdy!" to get everyone's attention. When the crowd quieted, he introduced Mr. and Mrs. Frye. There were whistles and clapping. Sam spoke up, "Martha and I want to thank you for coming to share in our new adventure and we hope you are having a fine time. Enjoy yourselves and have fun," Jenny stood up, "It's time to cut the cake." "Wait!" Matt said. "We, my sister and I, have something we would like to say to the newlyweds." He rolled up and took front and center. Ralynn noticed Luke had reappeared, but she turned her attention to Matt and went to stand beside him. "Sam and Martha, today we witnessed our friend's unity and we are so happy for them. So we sat down and discussed what we thought would make them even happier than they are right now.

Once we talked for a while, we finally came up with the perfect two-part gift, we hope." Sam and Martha looked at each other, confused. "So, if Sam and Martha would join us here, we'd like to have you accept our gift to you both, with all our love." They joined them and Ralynn handed them the paper she had been holding. She and Matt moved back while they opened and read what was on the paper. Sam had tears in his eyes and Martha was crying a waterfall. Sam composed himself and read it aloud.

> *Sam and Martha,*
>
> *Gift # 1: You both have lived with us on the ranch for over twenty years and we would like you to continue living here, so what we have done is talked to a lawyer and had a paper drawn up for you to pick out one hundred acres and five hundred head of cattle to start you off right getting your own ranch started, but until you do, we want you both to live here with us in the house.*

He choked up a bit but continued reading.

> *Gift # 2: We lost our parents this year and you both stepped in and brought us through some rough times. So, we want to ask you both to be our substitute parents. We will need your help and guidance along the way and we could think of no other than the both of you to fill that empty place in our hearts. For as long as we remember you two have been second parents to us and we would*

like to make it more official by asking you both to be our legal guardians. We hope you will accept our gifts.

With all our love,'

Matthew and Ralynn Parker

There was silence. Not a sound was heard. Matt and Ralynn were waiting patiently for their answer. Sam and Martha composed themselves and in unison said, "We accept!" Matt looked at his sister then said, "Well, which one or both?" Matt asked. "Both!" Matt rolled over and shook Sam's hand and hugged Martha. Ralynn just hugged them both, hard. "Let's cut the cake!" Someone hollered. "Yes, let's do that," Martha said. "Before we do that, I'd like to make a toast to the newlyweds." Luke said. "May God and love always be in your hearts and may you have many years together." He lifted his glass and everyone followed suit. The crowd applauded.

Sam thanked Luke and he and Martha cut the beautiful cake that Ralynn had made for them. Martha looked over at Ralynn and smiled a sheepish smile. Martha was expecting a white cake, but Ralynn had made the bottom layer chocolate; Sam's favorite. Ralynn stood there, smiled and said, "Surprise!" shrugging her shoulders in a child-like way.

The day had turned out to be beautiful with clear skies of blue and the temperature was in the seventies. The newlyweds ate and danced the night away. Sam told Martha what Luke had given them and they decided to wait a week before taking their honeymoon in Cheyenne. They would keep their night in Archer, then come back and prepare for their trip. They wanted to leave knowing that everything would be okay while they were gone. This was their family and they had never left them alone before without at least one of them being there. It would be difficult to leave but they were going to enjoy more than just moments between them. This was a new life and adventure for them and they were going to start it right.

Luke was waiting for Ralynn so they could talk. She had asked if they could talk alone during the festivities and he agreed to meet later. His hopes were high and he finally felt his life was falling into place. He wanted her opinion on his retirement but mostly he wanted to know if she was going to be a part of his life. Every time he went to look for her, she was visiting or cleaning up after the party. He tried one last time. He walked in the kitchen and was able to get her attention but she just nodded and went back to what she was doing. I guess she thought he would wait forever. He loved her with all his heart, but that didn't seem to register in her mind. He'd finally had enough. It was time to go; he was done. He walked over to the bunkhouse to get his gear, some of the cowboys were still celebrating, and tried to get him in on a game of poker, but he refused. He just gathered his things and left, not saying a word to anyone. He went to the barn and packed his gear on Twisted Mister, then saddled Comanche and walked out of the barn leading both horses. He stood there for a moment longer watching and waiting for her to come to him, but she didn't, so he mounted Comanche, said goodbye with a wave of his hand and rode towards Cheyenne to finish the month working with the Governor, then he was going home.

CHAPTER 30

Three months later:

It was a hot August day and Ralynn was miserable. It was her own fault; she never listened to anyone because she knew what she wanted; or so she thought. She now understood what Martha had been trying to get her to understand. But it's too late now; she has lost Luke forever. The last time she had seen him was on Sam and Martha's wedding day. She remembered asking him for time alone to talk later but she had been busy with all the friends and neighbors that were staying one more night, which was unexpected, and didn't get away till real late, so she ended up going to bed and thought she would talk to him that next morning; he was gone. No one knew when he left or where he had gone. When the newlyweds got home from their honeymoon, Sam told her that he did tell him that if you kept ignoring him that he would be leaving and maybe going back to Arizona, but it wasn't absolute. That's all he knew. They didn't see him in Cheyenne, so they had no idea. "I, myself, was sorry to see him go; he was a lot of help around here; a good man," Sam said. "Why all the questions about Luke now, it's been three months?" "I don't know. I have to get out of the house for a while. Baylee, come!" she commanded. She and Baylee walked around the house and stopped to check what was left of the garden. She had picked tomatoes and squash yesterday and it was close to the end of the pole beans. Martha and her had canned all summer long and had enough food put up for the winter months. Harvest would soon be over and they could relax now until next year. She walked into the house and grabbed a basket. She picked the beans, cut a mess of lettuce, and picked the remaining onions and peppers. She found one ripe watermelon and thought that would be good for after dinner.

She took everything inside, set the basket on the counter, took out the onions and peppers and set them on the counter. She then put the lettuce to soak in cool water and took the basket of beans and another bowl with her; outside on the front porch to break them; Baylee followed. While breaking the beans, her mind wondered, once again, to Luke. Sam, Martha, and Matt had warned her about her actions towards him, but she paid them no mind. She was too pig-headed to listen to what they were telling her. Now, she would never see him again and she had lost all sense of happiness and joy in her life. She wished she had listened to her heart instead of her mind. Why was she so stubborn? She just wanted to know where he was, what he was doing, and if she could ever change his mind. She knew, deep down, that he was the love of her life and they were meant to be together; she would never be happy without him. If only she could see him again.

The sweet scent of fresh bread came through the window which meant that Martha had just taken it out of the oven. It smelled so good; Baylee thought so too, he was drooling in his sleep. She finished with breaking the beans and was going to go back inside when she looked over at the barn and saw Matt exercising Darby, and Bullet was running around the corral; kicking up the dust. It was amazing the bond between these two horses and her brother. She had never seen anything like it. Darby seemed to sense when Matt was in pain and Bullet was learning from his mama. Matt was circling Darby and he would have her go in the opposite direction. He did this with her every day before he rode. Sam had figured out a way to keep Matt's legs supported, so he could ride; and he rode Darby every day, only in the corral. Matt loved it. He'd ride Darby with Bullet right alongside and some days Sam would supervise as he rode out in the grassy area behind the barn and Bullet would run free. He had tall legs and when out of the corral; he would run fast; faster than the other horses. He had convinced Sam to let him ride in the Fourth of July race next year; with training from Sam and the other cowboys. Sam talked to all of the cowboys and they agreed that it would be a great winter project to train Matt. Matt was excited about the training; he was bursting at the seams. Matt had asked Sam about building another outbuilding for an inside arena; like an inside corral. Sam decided that was a good project to start on as soon as the last harvest of hay was over.

She was thrilled for Matt. He had come a long way with learning how to handle his pain. He had made so much progress the past three months; keeping his mind busy and off of the pain. He had mastered roping calves, and riding Darby; now he needed to have a need for speed. Bullet wasn't at the age to ride just yet, but he would be soon, so Matt would exercise Bullet by getting him used to a riding whip and a riding saddle. He would desensitize him so he wasn't afraid of them. Bullet was still small enough that he could work with him from his chair. Sam, or one of the cowboys, would be with him when he was working with Bullet just in case there was a problem that he couldn't handle. Matt was so involved with his project that the pain had become a rare issue. She knew he'd never be without some kind of pain, but as long as it was not of the debilitating kind; it was a good day for him. She was so proud of her little brother; she had to learn to stop calling him that, because he was on his way to becoming a man. She hoped one day he'd find someone to love him and have a happy life.

She looked at the bowls in her hands and continued on her way into the house. "You coming, Baylee?" Baylee was busy watching Matt and the horses that he acted like he didn't hear her. She watched him for a minute. "Okay, boy, you can come in later. Go see your buddy." Baylee ran to the corral and sat down close to the fence. Bullet looked at Baylee and walked over to him. They rubbed their noses together and then started running races back and forth along the corral fence. She watched them and thought it was wonderful that they were best friends; they were family.

She walked into the kitchen and washed the beans. She went to the cellar and found a slab of ham. She took it to the counter and began slicing off a chunk and then diced it in small pieces; she did the same to an onion. She took out a Dutch oven and added some bacon grease, heated it and added the ham and onions. She sautéed them until the onions were caramelized, then added the beans. She stirred them until the beans were coated and added water just to cover them. She stirred them, once more, before placing a lid on top; just cracked enough to let out the heat. She went to the pantry and found several small new potatoes, washed them and added them to the beans. Now. all it had to do was cook until done. Martha was working on her pies, blackberry and squash, so she went to the pantry, again this time bringing out some fresh lemons for lemonade. She juiced the lemons and prepared the drink for dinner. It was at least two hours before dinner, so she walked out to the garden and picked a couple of tomatoes and cucumbers. She took the lettuce she had picked earlier, and finished washing it. She laid it out on a flour sack towel to dry, washed the tomatoes and cucumbers, and laid them next to the lettuce. "Martha, do we still have carrots?" "Why, yes, they are in the cellar, in the gray basket, over by the far wall." "Okay, I think I'll add some to the salad." She went to the cellar and found the carrots, picked up two of them and headed back to the kitchen. She washed them and laid them on the counter with the rest. "Is it time to start the chicken?" Yes, I already have it cut up and seasoned. Just heat the oil and it will be ready to put the chicken in. Sweetie, if you don't mind, you can cook the chicken for me; I need to finish mending Matt's shirt, I told him I'd have it done by dinner." "No problem, I'll get it going in a few minutes."

"What's little brother up to these days, anyway? He took the buggy out every night this past week." "All I know is that he's been spending a lot of time over at the Eastwood Ranch; they have a pretty, young daughter." "You mean he's courting her?" She was totally surprised. "I guess you could say that." "I had no idea; he usually tells me everything." "Sometimes, Sweetie, a man likes his privacy too. Men and women like a lot of the same things, but they also do the same things only in different ways. Same as with emotions, men and women can be facing the same challenges of everyday life yet handle them totally different from each other.

Everyone likes their business, whether social or private, to be in their control, but emotions cannot always be controlled. That is something you are learning now." "I guess I am," she said. A few hours later, at the dinner table, Sam was telling his story of when he first saw Martha with Mr. and Mrs. Parker. He was just twenty-one years old and full of himself. The day that Sheriff Tobe Mason brought her out to see if she wanted the housekeeping job, he just about tripped over his own two feet when he went to get her bags out of the wagon, but the sheriff beat him to it.

He was so tongue-tied with a dry mouth; he couldn't even say hello. I thought she was an angel with her long dark hair, big brown eyes, and her smile just melted me. I fell in love with her at that very moment and have been ever since. Over the years, we'd talk a little, and of course, worked together on things, but I never told her how I felt. I was just too embarrassed to show my feelings, so I loved her from afar all those years. Then, a few months ago, I finally told her how I've felt all these years and I found out that she felt the same way and here we are. All those years and moments in between; we are now married and happy." "What made you finally tell her how you felt?" Ralynn asked. "It was our moment in time. It was just time for us to come together; call it fate, I guess." There was a knock at the front door. "Who would be coming by this time of day? I hope it's good news," Sam said. He stood up, left the table, and went to answer the door. He opened the door and gave a wild yell, "Whoopi!" The ladies just looked at each other. All the sudden, as big as day, there he stood; Lucus Conrad had returned.

Ralynn couldn't believe her eyes. There stood the man she loved, only he didn't know it. He was dressed in black jeans, a black leather vest over a white western shirt, black boots and a black Stetson; the most handsome man she had ever seen. "Hello, Mr. Conrad, it's good to see you back. I wanted to thank you for the gift of the honeymoon; we had a wonderful time," Martha said. "It's good to be back and you are very welcome. You both deserved some time away." Ralynn went over to the counter and brought him a cup and poured coffee in it; then refilled the others. She set the coffee pot on a pot holder and took her seat. "Come on in, Luke, and take a seat. Have a cup of coffee," Sam said. They seated themselves and sipped their coffee. "Well, Mr. Conrad, it's been a while since we last saw you. What have you been up to all this time?" "First, I want to apologize for leaving so abruptly; there were things that came up. While the festivities were going on, a rider came here and gave me a telegram from the Governor. He needed me right away, so I had to go. I waited as late as I could and everyone was busy with the clean-up; I went ahead and left. I had to be there in two days so I couldn't wait any longer." "We weren't sure what had happened; I assumed you went home," Sam said. "No, not yet, but I will be here soon. I'm retiring from the agency; I feel like I've given them all they need from me, so I'm thinking of settling down; possibly buy a small ranch somewhere in the area around Archer. The agency is always on the lookout for trained horses, so I figured I could raise a few cattle and horses and start my ranch from there. I could hire a few cowboys and go after some of those wild mustangs up in the mountains, train them and sell them to the agency for a good price. What do you think, Sam, do you think I could build a ranch like that?" "I'm sure you could, Luke. You know that the GM Ranch is still up for sale?" "Oh, that's quite the place. What would I do with a place like that?" Martha smiled and said, "You could live there or you could turn it into an out-of-the-way, tourist Bed and Breakfast or something like that. I hear it has a huge horse training facility and barns just for horses." "Yes, it's immaculate. I'd have to give that some thought. It is a good idea, though." He sat there; thinking. "Do you think people would really come?" "I think they would come just to see the house alone. I know I'd like to see it." Martha looked over at Ralynn realizing what she had just said. "Oh, Sweetie, I am sorry. I didn't think." "Oh, Martha, that's not necessary. It was the man that did those things to me, not the house. It really is a beautiful sight." Luke looked at her wondering what she was thinking. "What do you think, Ralynn, do you think something like that would work?"

She sat there and said nothing. Luke was at his wit's end with her. He started to say something when she spoke. "It wouldn't take much to set something up. It's already furnished in most rooms, but you would have to hire people to run it if you're still planning to have a ranch and horse business." Luke was surprised she spoke, so he kept the conversation going. "Would you know what it would take to get the place ready? I don't mean money, that's not an issue. I mean the business and people side." "I'm sure I could find out if you want me to. I have a friend, Tara, that runs her own business, she could tell me the business side of it and the rest we could figure out as we go." "I'd really appreciate any help you could supply and find out for me." "I'll have Matt go with me, he's pretty good with the carriage these days." "How is Matt doing these days?" "He has himself a girl; sees her every day. Pretty young thing she is." Sam said. "Matt has a girl, well, that's great. I'm glad he's doing better." "He's doing good. He keeps his mind busy and that helps him deal with the pain. You know, he'd be a big help to you running a business like that. He's a people person and I'd bet he would have all those rooms filled in one day." "I think you have an idea there, honey. Matt would be good at something like that," Martha said. "He sure has the personality for it. I'll go to the bank tomorrow. Ralynn, do you think you and Matt could help me with it?" "I don't see where that would be a problem, do you Ralynn?" Sam questioned. "I suppose I could help, but I can't answer for Matt. He's got his mind on training for the Fourth of July race next year; he's training Bullet." "Really!" "Yeah, me and the boys have been working with him. Did you see our new addition when you rode up?" "The barn? Yes, I saw it as I rode in. What are you planning on doing with it?" "Matt's turning it into a training arena, like he saw in a magazine." Wow! That's great. I'll have to check that out," Luke said. "He may not have time; sounds like he has his plate full." "Won't hurt to ask him," Ralynn said. "No, it wouldn't hurt to ask." Luke was watching Ralynn and didn't see Martha nudge Sam. "Sweetheart, it's time we called it a night; see you two in the morning." They got up from the table and went to their room.

CHAPTER 31

Matt was feeling good as he drove the team of horses home. He had spent a good evening with his lady friend and now he was thinking about Bullet and his training. He'd been making progress with Bullet and was pleased with his own training. Doc was pleased with his progress as well. Matt neared the gates of P3 and turned the horses accordingly. He drove them into the barn and stopped them so Frank could unhitch them and put them in their stalls. Once Matt got his chair out of the wagon, he transferred into his chair, not an easy task for someone with working legs, let alone for someone without working legs. As he headed for the door of the barn, he noticed Luke's horse, Twisted Mister, in the stall. "Cool, Luke's home!" He hurried towards the house; thinking that maybe now, his sister will come out of the shell she has put around her, and actually talk to Luke this time. He rolled up the ramp and entered the kitchen. There he found Luke and Ralynn sharing a moment between them. Not to interrupt them, he went the back way to his room. He'd come back in a few minutes. He wanted to talk to Luke before he left again, which he has done quite often lately.

Luke and Ralynn had discussed their new venture and they decided to wait until he spoke to the bank before making any plans. Then Luke changed the subject. "Ralynn, I need to say some things to you and I want you to listen carefully. When I was here before we had a few moments between us and those moments were good for me. The last time we actually spoke, you said you needed space and I have given that to you. I told you that I needed you to tell me how you felt about me and us. When I was here for the wedding, you snubbed and ignored me again and I couldn't stay here and be around you. So, when I got that telegram and I knew I had to leave, I waited as long as I could for you because you said you wanted to talk but you never came out of the house. I came up to the house once more to see if you were ready to come out but you were busy with your friends and when I did get your attention, you looked at me, then went back to what you were doing. You did the same again and ignored me. I was at my wit's end. I mounted Comanche and led Twisted Mister off the ranch, and swore to myself that I'd never come back. I figured you had made up your mind, and that was the end of it. You gave us no chance to even try to see if we could have something special between us; more than just small moments." "But you did come back," she said. "I had to try one more time. I told you that I had to go home and take care of business, so here is my last plea to you. I know you have feelings for me, that one kiss told me that. I told you that you had stolen my heart. I'm going home for about two weeks but it will take four weeks to make the trip there and back. When I come back, I want an answer from you; No excuses! I'll go to the bank tomorrow and check on the GM Ranch and if I get lucky and the price is right, then I'll purchase it and we can go from there when I return. But, if your answer is" NO," then I'll leave here and never bother you again. Think hard on this. I believe we were meant to be in each other's lives so I'm willing to try one more time. I'll let you know when I'll be leaving, Ralynn. I love you and I hope you can clear your mind and listen to your heart." He stood up and leaned towards her and kissed her on the cheek. "I'm going to the bunkhouse now. I need some much-needed sleep. I'll see you in the morning; good night." He looked at her one more time, then left for the bunkhouse. She just sat there, confused as usual.

Matt had been ready to enter the kitchen when he heard Luke's plea to his sister; he stopped. He waited until Luke walked out before he entered. "Ralynn, what is wrong with you, why don't you let go of whatever it is holding you back? The man is clearly in love with you or he wouldn't have come back for you. So, what are you going to do about it?" "I talked to him," she replied. "Yes, you talked to him, but said nothing." "What! You were listening the whole time?" She questioned him with a bit of anger in her voice. "I was going to talk to Luke. I didn't know you two would be in an actual conversation, if you could call it that." "Oh, whatever, Matt, just leave me alone, I'm going to bed," she said curtly; she left the room. Matt just shook his head, "What's it going to take to get through to that sister of mine?" He asked himself.

The next morning, she was late coming down for breakfast, it was very unusual for her. Martha already had it cooked, served, and sitting on the table. Sam, Martha, and Matt were at the table discussing what Matt had told them about last evening. Sam was scratching his chin, "I don't know what's got into her lately. She's been in a bad mood for months; now she'll be worse, probably." "Don't jump to conclusions, Dear," Martha said to Sam. "She's young and confused right now. She's only ever wanted to be a rancher like her Pa; these feelings she is facing and feeling are new to her. She doesn't understand that her heart is different from her mind. I believe that fear of the unknown has her insides all torn up." "So, how do we help her? You know Luke is leaving for a month and wants an answer when he returns. Are we just going to sit by and let her lose the best thing for her?" Matt asked. "I'm not sure, son," Sam replied.

At that time, she walked into the kitchen. "Good morning," she said. They all greeted her anS watched as she went to the stove and poured herself a cup of coffee; then took her seat at the table. "Are you okay, Sweetie? You're usually not late coming down in the mornings." "I'm fine," was all she would say. "You look tired, Rae, did you not sleep well?" "No." "Something on your mind, Rae? "Oh, I'm just restless, I guess. Think I'll take a ride today; haven't done that for a while. Maybe, it will help clear my mind some." "Want some company, Sis?" Matt asked. "I'm not such good company, but you're welcome to come if you want," "Great, I'll get Darby ready." He was so excited; he rolled out the door and towards the barn and quickly. "I think it's fine that you want to ride, Sweetie, but don't forget our plans for today." "What plans?" Sam asked. We are going to start our Fall deep cleaning early this year." "Why the rush?" Sam asked. "We just wanted to get it out-of-way; we're only doing one room a day, so it won't be interfering with our chores or your meals, besides by the time we get the upstairs finished, it will be cleaning time. Now do you understand, my nosey husband?" she laughed. "Besides, we are taking the large room and making it ours, instead of the guest room." That sounds like a lot of work; you will need help." "I'm glad you mentioned that. Yes, we will need help with the mattresses and furniture." "I'll go see if Luke can help." "Is he still here?" Ralynn asked. "I believe he is, why is he leaving again?" "Said he had business in his hometown; be gone a month, he said." "So, you talked to him?" Sam inquired. "A little, he more than me." She replied. "I don't know about you, Rae. When are you going to get your head on straight? It wouldn't surprise me if he ever comes back." Sam stated. "Why won't you just leave me alone? I'll be back in an hour." She stormed out the door. "What did I say?" He asked Martha. "Too much, Dear, too much." Martha answered.

Luke was in the barn helping Matt get situated on Darby. He had already put in place the braces that Sam made for Matt to secure his legs, and was helping Matt get them secure against Darby's sides. Matt already had on his back brace that Doc had made to support his back while riding.

Matt was adjusting his seating and was ready to go. Luke walked away and returned with her mount; saddled and anxious to go. He handed her the reins. "Thank you." "You're welcome, have a great ride." "Oh, by the way, Sam would like to talk to you before you leave," she told him. "Thanks, I'll go look for him." "He was still in the kitchen when I came out." She mounted and they left the barn and went out the P3 gate to the open country.

"Well, at least you are talking to him." "Matt, don't start please. I've heard all I want to hear about that man. My problem is my emotions that I don't understand; they confuse me. I don't want to be a failure at something I don't know about or be a disappointment to Luke. "What are you thinking that you don't understand, Sis? Don't you think I was scared when I started courting Stacey? I had no experience, I was awkward and clumsy, but I kept trying. Want to know what kept me trying? It was Ma and Pa; watching them share their love with us and each other these past sixteen years. You cannot practice this, Sis, you go by how your heart feels, not your head." "Martha said the same thing to me the other day." "It must be true then," he said. "Give it a try, Sis, the only thing you have to lose is your heart, or at least a part of it. Maybe even Luke if you don't do something." They rode for a while in silence, and then turned back towards home. "We're burning daylight, Sis, and we both have things to do." "Yes, I told Martha that I would be back in an hour." "Let's gallop then; I need the practice." "Are you sure you're ready? What if something happ......." she let the rest of the words trail off. "Nothing will happen and if it does, it's my responsibility." They gave the command to go faster; Darby hesitated. Matt tried once more and then she moved into a gallop and towards home they rode. Within ten minutes, they were back at the barn. Frank took Darby's halter and led her into the barn. He helped Matt out of the braces and back into his chair. After putting Darby back in her stall, he went and got Ralynn's horse and took care of him. Matt came out of the barn and they headed towards the house.

Inside the house, Martha was supervising the moving of two bedrooms, telling Sam and Luke what goes where. Matt wanted some lemonade but there wasn't any made. Ralynn stopped, "Hey, Little Brother, go in the pantry and get me six lemons out of the basket on the shelf, and I'll make you some lemonade." "Cool! I'll get them right away." She knew there were enough lemons left, from this year's harvest, to have lemonade all winter if they were lucky. She squeezed the lemons dry, added some sugar and water, then poured five glasses; putting them on a tray with some fresh baked cookies she had made last night. She left a glass for Matt on the counter and headed upstairs. She made it to the top of the stairs and stopped so fast, she almost dropped the tray. "My goodness, what is going on up here? I thought we were only doing one room a day, not the whole upstairs?" She looked at Martha with questioning eyes as she handed her a glass and a cookie. Then she went to Sam and then Luke. "Thanks," they all said. "Where did the cookies come from, I didn't see them anywhere," Martha asked. "I couldn't sleep last night so I came downstairs and made cookies. I put them in the pantry, so Matt wouldn't eat them all. So, what are we doing up here?" "Well, after I got to thinking about it, I figured that we may as well get Matt's things moved downstairs so he could make it his own room; bring the things of your parents, that you two don't want now, up here and put in the attic for storage, and Sam and I will take Matt's old room since it's larger and keep the guest room as is. Is that okay with you, Sweetie?" "I think it's a great idea. I'm sure my little brother would like to have his things close. He's downstairs in his room if you want to make sure, but I'm pretty sure he'll say yes." "Yes, Sam, go down and talk to Matt, I don't want to move his stuff without asking first." Martha told him. "Martha and I will get the small things packed away that you don't need." Ralynn spoke up. "Sure thing, Luke come with me; we'll get some things and bring them up from their parent's room. May as well make a day of it. I need to holler at Charlie before anything else." The men went downstairs and the ladies started packing up the things no longer needed at this time. "I apologize, Sweetie, I should have asked you and Matthew first. I wasn't thinking." "No apology necessary. Besides, it's your home too, and when or if I get married, it will belong to you and Matt, I suppose. I doubt my husband would want to live here." Martha thought she was hearing things; a look of shock came over her. "Is there something happening that I don't know about and should?" "No, well, maybe, Luke gave me an ultimatum last night; I make up my mind while he's gone and have a clear and decisive answer when he returns, or else he will leave forever and I'll never see him again." "Then I guess you have an important decision to make." Martha said as she placed some items into a trunk. "Yes, I do. I believe I know what I want, just have to be sure it's right for me and him." "The men will be back up here in a few minutes, so let's hurry with this." "Sure, they will, unless they get busy with Charlie outside." She laughed as Martha gave her a disgruntled look.

＊ ＊ ＊ ＊ ＊

Matt was sitting in bed while Sam and Luke were packing up the small things of his parents. Sam asked him if there was anything he did not want brought down from his room. He answered, "I'd like to have everything and do you think I could have my bed brought down too? It's a bit softer than this one. Sam, can you come over here for a second?" "Sure, son, what's up?" "I need to tell you where I hid my stash and have you bring it to me." "Okay, I'll get it." He told him where to find his stash and a few other things he had hid away. They finally had the dresser cleaned out and moved it in the kitchen until they could move it upstairs to one of the guest rooms. "We should have done this for Matthew a long-time ago," Sam said, regretfully. "A lot has happened since he was injured, Sam, he understood. I'm sure he didn't want to bother you about it," Luke said. "Well, we're doing it now, that's all that matters." "Hey, Sam, don't forget to get my rock collection, please. It's on the top shelf by the window," Matt hollered. "Sure thing, Matt, I'll get it."

CHAPTER 32

The ladies were just about finished cleaning the floor by the time the guys returned. "Give it a few minutes before putting anything in there; let it dry." Martha put the bucket and rags in the hallway and was looking at the mess in front of her. "My goodness, I didn't think we'd end up moving three rooms today. Well, let's get on with it." "Luke and I have already made room for some of Matt's things downstairs, so we can work on that." "I'll go pack up Matt's clothes and then it will be just the furniture to move," Ralynn said. "Sam, do we have enough boxes and trunks to store my parent's things?" "I'm sure we'll make due. Once we empty the boxes from Matt's room, we'll have plenty, I think." "Oh, Matt wants his own bed, so where are we going to put the other bed?" Sam asked Martha and Ralynn. "Well, we have two guest rooms and the one we just cleaned was your room. Let me go check something with Matt. I'll be right back." She ran down the stairs. She walked into Matt's room. "Hey, Matt, I need to talk to you really quick." "Okay, Sis, what's up?" "Sam said you want your own bed brought down here. Is that right?" "Yeah, it's softer than Ma and Pa's." "Well, I was wondering if you thought it would be okay to give Sam and Martha their bedroom suite, since they don't have one." "I think that's a great idea. I'll get in my chair and when Sam and Luke come back down, they can take the bed and the other dresser out." "You go tell them," "Okay, get ready."

Ralynn ran back upstairs, stopping to catch her breath. "Matt and I talked and we want you two to have Ma and Pa's bedroom suite. It will fit nicely in your new bedroom." Sam and Martha looked at each other. "Rae, are you sure you don't want to store it and have it for later?" "Sam, it's a bed and a couple of dressers and a vanity. I can get a new one if I ever need to and so can Matt. It may have belonged to our parents, but it's not our parents. I think they would be happy to have you have it. We can put your bed in the guest room." "Oh, Sweetie, I don't know what to say. You and Matt have given us so much already." "We're family and that is what counts, and you are welcome from both of us. Matt's waiting for you to bring his stuff and he'll work on his room; he's out of bed and putting some of the things in boxes. You know he wants to be involved too." Ralynn went into Matt's old room and began packing up his stuff to take down to his room. "Oh, Sam, I didn't even think of asking Matt if he wanted to help. I feel awful." "I think Matt understands; he knows we are all adjusting," Sam reassured her. "Matt's a smart kid, he's almost a man. He understands more than we think. He'll be fine. Just remember to include him a little more; he'll let you know what he can and can't do," Luke said. "Okay, let's get this bed taken apart and get it downstairs." "We have to get the other one up here, but I think we can set it in the kitchen while we get Matt's room done first." "That will work. Let's go."

Ralynn packed up all of Matt's clothes and cleaned out the two chests of drawers in the room. Sam took down Matt's chair and desk first and then came back for his trunk and Luke carried down several boxes. When they got his old room emptied, the ladies cleaned the walls, windows and floor, then they went downstairs to help get their parent's things out and put them in the kitchen. Once empty, they washed the walls, windows and floor, then started moving Matt's things in. The guys put the bed in first and then the rest of the furniture. Matt told them that he could put his things away and if he needed help, he would holler. So, they started taking the bedroom suite up to Sam and Martha's new room. It took them about three hours to get everything back in its place and organized. By the time they finished they were all exhausted and went down to see how Matt was coming along. Sam and Luke went to check on Matt while the ladies made some fresh lemonade and started dinner. Matt had pretty much had all his clothes put in his chests of drawers, but the ones he wanted hung up, he couldn't reach the rod in the closet. He was working on that when Sam and Luke came in. "Matt, how you doing? Getting things like you want it?" "Yeah, but I have a problem. Is there a way we can move this rod down so I can reach it?" Luke walked over and looked the problem over. "Matt are there things you want hung up that you don't need, like suits and coats?" "Well, yes. Why?" "Let's see if Sam agrees with this. How about we keep the high rod where it's at and put another one where you can reach it. That way you can store your things on the high rod and what you do use on the lower one. What do you think?" "I like the idea. Sam?" "I believe that is a great idea.

We just need to make things where you can get to them easier. What else are you having problems with?" "Well, I hate to be a bother, but I had several shelves for my collections and I have none in here." "You know I didn't really look at your old room, let me go check with Martha on something. I'll be right back unless they have dinner ready first. I'm a bit hungry after all that work." He laughed as he walked out of the room. "Hey, Luke, how about a game of poker after dinner?" "Just me and you or are there others joining us." "Can you run and ask Sonny and Charlie if they'll play?" "Sure, be right back." Luke left the room and went to the bunkhouse to see if he could get some players. Sam and Martha went up to their room and looked at Matt's shelves. "I don't think we need these in here. Maybe just one," Martha said. "Okay, I'll take these down and put them up in his room. I can make him some new ones if you want to keep these." "No, take them to Matt. If we ever need more, we'll worry about it then." "Good, now go fix dinner, your husband is hungry." "I'm on my way to the kitchen. It will be ready in about twenty minutes."

The ladies decided on something easy and quick; it would be chicken salad on homemade bread with pickled beets, cucumbers and onions in vinegar, and a lettuce salad with homemade dressing. Martha was preparing the chicken salad; shredded chicken, chopped celery, onion greens, sliced grapes. Ralynn was preparing the lettuce salad; lettuce, carrots, tomatoes, and vinaigrette dressing. Then she sliced the bread and set the table. Twenty minutes later they had the meal ready and as the guys came into the kitchen, Martha had just finished making some sweet tea and was filling the glasses. Ralynn carried them over and set them in front of the guys. Martha brought hers and Ralynn's to the table and they joined the men to eat. Sam led them in saying Grace. Then he said, "I was thinking I could eat a horse, but looking at the food, I guess I'll have to adjust my belly to eating chicken salad, instead. Everyone started laughing.

Martha spoke up, "We were too tired to fix anything big." "I'm sorry Martha, I was just joking with all of you." The laughing quieted; they ate.

Clean-up was quick and easy; everyone went their own way. Sam and Martha went to their new room to work in there, Matt was enjoying having his own things around him, Ralynn had settled at the table with her mending, and Luke was standing at the back door waiting for Charlie and Sonny to come play poker. He walked back into the kitchen and watched her for a moment before speaking. He was determined to spend some time with her. "Would you take a walk with me?" She set aside her mending, "Yes, let me get my shawl." She got up and went to her room, returning with her shawl. Luke hollered at Matt saying that he would be back in thirty minutes. He turned back to Ralynn. "I haven't told you how beautiful you are today." "Seriously! I'm in my old clothes, I have circles under my eyes, and my hair is a mess, and you think I'm beautiful?" "Yes, I do, actually, that's when you are most beautiful. You're always beautiful, Ralynn, but when it's natural, it's most alluring." "Thank you. When are you leaving, Luke?" "I was going today, until Sam asked for my help, which was fine, because I got to spend the day with you. Like I said, I'll be gone for about four weeks; a week going down, two weeks to conclude my business, and a week back." He watched her reaction and thought he saw sadness in her eyes. "Will you miss me?" She hesitated, "Yes, I will miss you." "That's good to know." "Luke, I've been thinking about what you said, and......." He didn't let her finish. "I don't want an answer from you now, wait until I return. I'll have a reason to come back." "Luke, listen to me, please! I admit I do have feelings for you and they are deep in my heart, but I need to know something from you, before I make a final decision." "What's that?" "I need to know for sure, without a doubt, that it's me you want, because of how you feel inside your heart and not because of an urge you have or because of the ranch." "What a question." He was taken by surprise. He hesitated; trying to think, exactly, how to answer this question of hers. "Don't make fun of me, just answer the question." She was getting frustrated with him. "Ralynn, I told you weeks ago that you stole my heart, even though we've shared only moments between us. "Yes, I'm sure." "Okay, then I'll have your answer for you when you return." They walked in silence through the arbor and stopped at the steps leading into the house. "I'll come see you before I leave." "Come for breakfast, please?" "Okay, I'll see you in the morning. Ralynn, may I kiss you?" "Yes," she said in a whisper. He lifted her chin, lowered his head, and placed his warm lips on her soft ones. She tasted of sweet tea. He wrapped his arms around her, as she wrapped hers around his neck. He licked her lips with his tongue and she opened her mouth. He slid his tongue inside her mouth; it tickled her tongue, and she quickly pulled away and gasped. "Did I hurt you, Babe?" He asked, curiously. "No, it just surprised me. I've never been kissed before. Kiss me again," she said, eagerly. He did just that. He took her in his arms again and kissed her long and tenderly. Neither one was sure how long it lasted; both of them breathless once they parted. "Goodnight, Honey." He opened the door for her. "See you in the morning, Luck," she said before closing the door and locking it. Luke just stood there, then the door opened and Charlie let him inside; they were ready to play poker and Matt was waiting patiently.

The next morning, Luke came in with Sam, and they sat at the table. Ralynn smiled at him as he passed by her; Martha noticed. Once Sam led them in Grace, they all began to eat. Luke told them that he would be leaving today, and be gone, at least, four weeks; due to business obligations that needed his attention. He would try to get back sooner, if possible. Ralynn sat and listened; making no comment. "Do you really have to go, Luke?" "Yes, Matt, I have to take care of things at home. Matt, I haven't said anything to you, because I didn't want to get your hopes up. I plan on moving up here and I have to close my place and put it up for sale. So, yes, I need to go." "Okay, that's cool, as long as you're coming back." "I don't suppose anyone has filled you in on my plans, have they?" "Nope. What are they?" "Well, I talked to the bank, a few days ago; I bought the GM Ranch, which, of course, the name will change, but I'm thinking of turning it into a tourist attraction, where people can tour the house and also, stay there overnight. Maybe, have some activities there, as well, like rodeos, livestock auctions, even horse training, but as I told these guys, I'll need help to do it. I'll need help from all of you, especially, from you and Ralynn. Everyone here believes you would be great at marketing and customer service, so to speak." "I sure would! Stacy's Pa does a lot of horse trading and such. I'm sure he would help spread the word with his customers." Matt sounded so excited. "Think about how to market the place and all, while I'm gone." He stood up and thanked the ladies for his meal, then said, "I need to be on my way. I want to get as many miles rode as I can today." "Well, I guess we'll see you when you return. Be careful and have a safe ride home," Sam said. "Thanks Sam." He said his goodbyes and headed for the door. "I'll walk you out," Ralynn spoke up. Sam, Martha, and Matt, looked at each other in disbelief. Luke held the door and allowed Ralynn to go ahead of him. Once outside, she reached for his hand and placed her small hand in his larger one. Luke smiled. He had already packed and saddled Twisted Mister and Commanch and was ready to go. When they reached his horse, she looked up into Luke's eyes. "Luke, I'll miss you. Please stay safe and come back to me." She dropped her eyes, as if she were shy. "You watch for me, okay?" He lifted her chin and planted a kiss on her sweet lips.

The kiss lingered for a few moments; he pulled away, and stepped up into his saddle. He and Comanche turned and were on their way to Sedona. Ralynn stood there and watched until she could no longer see them; tears ran down her face.

The month passed slowly and Ralynn was counting the days Luke would return; thirty days had already passed and he had yet to return. She was preparing the garden for winter and spring crops, when she looked up and there he stood, watching her. She dropped everything in her hands and ran to him; right into his arms. They kissed. He pulled back; looking at her. "Am I to take it you have made your decision?" "Yes, I have, can you not tell?" "Is that what that was?"

He said laughingly. "Really? Do I have to explain it to you or show you?" "Just showing me will be fine." She wrapped her arms around his neck and kissed him with so much passion; he almost lost his footing. He picked her up and swung her around, not wanting to let her go. "Put me down, Luke." Her voice shrieked. "Why? I don't want to let you go." "We need to go see Sam and Martha and especially, Matt. He would kill me if I kept you to myself." "Well, we don't want that, I'd like to keep you for a while." "Oh?" He let her go and got down on one knee. She looked confused, until he said, "Ralynn Parker, will you marry me?" She covered her mouth with her hand. She knew she was in shock. She hoped one day this would happen, but she didn't think it would be so soon after his return. She took a deep breath, "Yes, I will marry you." He took her left hand and placed a diamond on her ring finger; the diamond sported a cushion cut with rounded edges, fifty-eight facets, and had great fire when the light hit it, in a rainbow of colors. She just stared at it for the longest moment in total amazement, and then she spoke. "Luke, it's beautiful. How did you know I would say yes?" "It was a feeling in my gut that ran clear up into my heart; I knew you loved me." "Can we go tell them?" "Yes, we can." He kissed her once more before going inside.

They went to see Matt first. He was on his bed with a bunch of papers around him. They knocked on the door and he said, "Come in." He looked up, "Luke, you're home." "Yes, you could say that." "Hey, I've got a lot of information for you about your ranch." "That's good, Matt. Let's talk about that later. We have some news; do you know where Sam and Martha are?" "They were up in their room working on something. Want me to call them?" "Yes, but when they get here don't tell them I'm here yet." "Okay." "Sam, Martha, could you come down here for a minute?" They waited, then Sam answered, "Sure, be right down." Luke stood behind the door and Ralynn sat on the bed with Matt. They walked into Matt's room with a curious look on their faces. "Something wrong, Matt?" "No, just needed you to come in here." Luke stepped out from behind the door. "Surprise," he said laughing. "Luke, you finally made it back. I know someone was counting the days." He smiled as he looked Ralynn's way. "Oh, really?" She turned two shades of red and covered her face with her hands. "Oh! Oh! Look at her hand, Sam." Martha ordered. Sam didn't notice it right away then he looked at her and Luke. "Let me see your hand, Sis, what is she talking about?" She put her left hand out for Matt to see. "Does this mean I'm going to have a brother?" "I believe it does." Sam commented. "If you all would quiet down, I'll tell you. Luke asked me to marry him and I said, yes." "That's wonderful," Martha said. The three congratulated them with hugs and kisses; everyone was happy.

CHAPTER 33

One Year Later:

Ralynn stood in front of the full-length mirror, at Luke's ranch, and stared at the woman facing her. She couldn't believe it was her wedding day. She was marrying Luke and she was so happy. After his return and their engagement, life seemed normal. Luke went to work with Sam and on his time off, he worked at their ranch. He hired people, with Matt's help, to work inside the house and outside as well. He supervised his crew working on the stables, preparing to bring the herd of horses he bought from Stacy's Pa, home. The inside arena was in great shape and didn't need any renovations, but the horse barn needed more stalls and a larger tack room. He decided to build another horse barn for the riding horses that visitors would be riding. The original barn, they were working on now, would stable the horses that he would be training.

There was a livestock barn that needed little work; he wanted to add more feeding space and a larger open shelter area. He purchased a herd of cattle from P3 and he would be moving them over in a month or so. She had been supervising the house workers and Matt and Stacy was doing the marketing and already had a few reservations set for when they opened. It was a lot of work, but it was good work. When Luke was at the ranch, she and Martha worked on the preparations for her wedding, mainly her wedding gown and guest list. They didn't have to plan much for decorating, since the house was beautiful already; just added some red and white roses in planters all around and at the place where they would be standing to get married. Luke was surprised that she wanted to be married at the ranch, but she explained that it was their ranch, The Crooked River Ranch, and would be filled with happy memories from now on; so, he agreed.

She was admiring her gown that she and Martha had made; satin white material designed with a sweetheart bodice, covered in rhinestones, and strapless. The skirt started at the waistline, covered with a spring green sash that tied in back into a large bow with tails that fell to the floor. The satin was covered in netting with rhinestones, sprinkled sparingly all over the gown. Martha startled her when she walked in carrying a small box. "Oh! You startled me." "I'm sorry Sweetie. Luke sent me in here with this, for you. He said to open immediately." She took the box and opened it. There in her hands was a diamond necklace with matching earrings. The diamond pendant was exactly the same size and shape as her engagement ring. "Martha put it on for me." She put on the earrings and looked in the mirror. "Sweetie, you look like you're in heaven." "I feel that way, Martha. I've never been so happy. The gown is beautiful, if I haven't told you yet. Thank you for making it for me." "You, my Dear, did a lot in making it as well. I would have never got all those rhinestones on there by myself; and Matt did too. Are you about ready? Where's your veil?" "It's over there on the bed. Would you help me with it, I was having trouble getting it centered, without messing up my hair?" "You sure you don't want me to fix your hair?" "Well, I was going to wear it down, but I think it would look better up with the veil. Can you do it quickly?" "Quickly! Psst, I don't think so. Luke will wait a few minutes longer." Martha took the brush and brushed through her hair, then set it down, picked up the comb and separated the top of her hair, and pulled it back on both sides, securing it with pins.

She picked up the back of her hair, separated into two strands and braided it, incorporating the top strands. When that was done, she secured the ends with green ribbon. She then wound each side with the opposite strand and secured them with pins. Martha looked at it and asked, "What do you think?" "I like it." Martha started to get the veil, then stopped and went over to the bouquet of flowers on Ralynn's dresser and picked out a stem of Baby's Breath and a white rose. She came back to Ralynn and placed it in the lower braid; then picked up the veil and centered it on top of her hair and secured it with pins. It was a double layer veil connected to a rhinestone tiara, adorned with rhinestones that matched her gown. Martha straightened it and let it fall down her back, where it blended in with the gown's six-foot train. "Gorgeous!" Martha said. "What about your boots, do have them?" "Already on." She raised the front of her gown and showed her the white cowboy boots that she had adorned with more rhinestones. Martha smiled, and shook her head. "Something wrong with them?" "No, I was just thinking that if these were all diamonds, how it would be the most expensive gown ever." "Only, we know it's not, but we'll let everyone else think it is." The both laughed out loud when her two bridesmaids came in carrying her bridal bouquet of red and white Roses, with white Baby's Breath, and hanging greenery and red and white ribbons. "Ralynn, you are gorgeous. Here's your bouquet," Tara, her best friend said. "I agree." Stacy, Matt's girlfriend, added. "Are you ready? It's time; Luke and the guys just came in and are up front already." "She's ready. If we don't get her going, she's going to get a big head." Martha laughed as did the bridesmaids. Tara and Stacy arranged her veil and took their places in front of her. Sam motioned the guitarist to start playing, and for them to start their walk down the aisle. The music started; Stacy led the way.

Sam, Matt, and Tara's husband, Tony, were watching Luke pace back and forth across the dining room floor; it had been sectioned off with curtains for the men to get ready in. "Why, Luke, I didn't know you were the nervous type, with all that work as an agent." Matt said laughing. "This isn't a crime case, Matt, it's a different kind of nervousness." Luke replied. "Not laughing so much now that you're getting married, huh?" Sam stated. Luke's face was a bit pale and rosy cheeked at the same time. The guys were laughing out loud when the Preacher came to the curtain opening and said, "Gentlemen, it is time to take your places." They all composed themselves and Luke led the way, following the Preacher's path. Sam was Luke's Best Man, but he stayed behind to escort Rae down the aisle. He felt so honored to stand in for her Pa. He was patiently waiting when the Preacher nodded at him to tell the girls it was time. He didn't even get to the staircase when they appeared at the top. He looked at Rae as she waited her turn to descend the stairs. What beautiful memories he had. She has always been his girl; like she was his own, and since her parents had passed, she had become his daughter and Matt his son. He and Martha wanted to do something special for her on this special day, so they did. She would receive it soon. Stacy reached the landing first, then Tara and Martha; She was almost to Sam when he stood up straight and tall and put his arm out to receive hers and guide her down the aisle.

The Quartet that Luke hired began playing "Together Forever." When she reached the landing, she placed her hand in the crook of Sam's arm and they proceeded into the Grand Ballroom.

Luke was standing up front with the Preacher, Matt and Tony; dressed in a black suit coat, black vest covering a white shirt with a green ribbon bolo, that matched her gown, and black jeans and boots. He was also sporting a new black Stetson with a gold band that she insisted he wore. She looked at him with adoring eyes through her veil. She wondered if he was as anxious as she was; since he was tapping his foot to the music. She and Sam were just about ready to walk down the aisle when the bridesmaids and Martha made a detour from where they were supposed to stand. They walked over to an easel that was covered and pulled the covering off, then took their original positions.   She made a loud gasping sound and tightened her hold on Sam's arm; tears running down her cheeks. "Your parents are here with you today, Rae. A gift from me and Martha," Sam whispered in her ear. "Thank you, Sam," she said looking at the portrait of her parents. "Ready?" "Just a moment Sam, let me compose myself." She wiped her cheeks and eyes dry with Sam's kerchief and then nodded and took her first step towards her new life.

Luke thought he had seen every beautiful side of her, but he hadn't. Today, she was extremely beautiful and glowing. There could be no other woman on earth that could outshine his bride. He watched as she came towards him; stopped, Sam lifted her veil, kissed her on the cheek, then replaced her veil. He then led her to stand between Martha and Luke; facing the Preacher; Sam took his place the opposite side of Luke. He looked at her, knowing he was the luckiest man alive. The Preacher started and told them to take each other's hands; she handed her bouquet to Martha and turned back towards Luke, taking his hands. He then asked, "Who giveth this woman away?" Sam stepped out of line, and said, "Her Ma and Pa, and Martha and I do." He stepped back in line. "And I do too," Matt hollered: everyone chuckled. The Preacher proceeded. "Before we begin with the vows, Mr. Conrad would like to say something to his bride. "Luke, you have the floor," he said as he stepped back. "Ralynn, at the beginning of our relationship, we didn't quite get along." Laughter erupted from the crowd. "But I fell in with you. Our first year was filled with so much chaos and danger that I was determined to make this world safe for you. It took a while, but we finally admitted our feelings to ourselves and to each other. It amazed me that we actually survived that first year, but we had our moments between the chaos and danger; our love continued to grow. I just wanted to say, I love you with all my heart; which you stole at the very beginning." As he looked at her, the tears fell like a flowing creek; he reached in his pocket and handed her his kerchief. "I knew I would need this today," he whispered. She took it; dried her eyes, and hung onto it, because she knew she would probably need it again.

The Preacher continued with the vows, and she and Luke repeated them. Sam handed him the ring and she lifted her left hand. Luke slid the glove off her hand and placed a golden band with two small diamonds, in the center, on her left ring finger next to her engagement ring. She looked at him with so much love that his heart was pounding. She then placed a gold band on his left ring finger. The Preacher said, "What we have joined together let no man put asunder." Jenny walked up front and the orchestra began playing the song she and Martha wrote just for this day, "Together Forever," she began singing. "*Together Forever our vows we have made. A new life beginning from this very day. I love you my Darling, close by me please stay. And now together let us pray. Dear Lord, up-on us thy bless-ings be-stow, as from this day forward together we go. Teach us to be grateful - come ev-er what may - facing with courage each dawning of day. Sharing and trusting along life's road As to-gether For-ev-er we go. (Amen) To-gether For-ever our vows we have made - A new life begin-*

ning From this very day. I love you my, Darling, close by me please stay. As to-gether For-ev-er we stay. Together Forever."

"Luke, you may now kiss your bride." He reached over quickly and planted his lips solidly on hers and kissed her like they were the only two in the world; then he lifted her up and swung her around. The Preacher quieted the crowd and said, "May I present to you, Mr. and Mrs. Luke Conrad." The crowd cheered and whistled. She had given Luke the responsibility of getting a band and allowed him to choose the music, except for the first song of the ceremony, so she had no idea about what he picked. When time came for them to exit the ballroom, the Quartet began playing a snappy two-step. Luke pulled her close, wrapping his arm around her waist and taking her right hand in his. Instead of walking out, he started doing the two-step with her all the way out of the room. The crowd cheered, as they laughed all the way.

They stood in the hall greeting each guest as they left the ball-room, while the hired help moved all the planters of flowers into the Great Room where the reception was to be held. When the last guest had been greeted, the wedding party hesitated and visited with each other, allowing the guest to get seated and comfortable. Matt rolled over to his sister, "That was an amazing gift Sam and Martha gave you." "Yes, it was. Didn't you know about it?" "No, I'm sorry I didn't think about it." "I'll loan it to you on your wedding day," she said. "Thanks Sis." He reached out his arms and she leaned to give him a huge bear hug and a kiss on his cheek. "I love you, Sis." "I love you, too." Ten minutes had passed and Sam said it was time to go. Tara and Tony entered first and stepped to the left side of the door, Matt and Stacy entered and went to the right side. Sam and Martha entered; Sam went right and Martha went left. The couple looked at each other wondering what was going on. They stepped into the Great Room; Sam held out his arm to her, while Martha took Luke's arm. They led the couple to the front of the room and seated them at the head table. The wedding party commenced and took their positions. Luke and Ralynn were looking around the room when the cake, that Martha was so secretive about, was rolled into the room. They were amazed. She looked at Martha and another tear ran down her cheek.

Martha just smiled back at her. The cake was four-foot high covered in white icing and trimmed in her favorite color, spring green. The top layer held the throw-away bouquet of red and white rosebuds, it was separated by four three-inch pillars to the next layer, which was chocolate, and held a box tied with multi-colored ribbons that flowed to the third layer, which was separated by four five-inch pillars. This layer was white, holding a bouquet of red and white roses which spilled over the sides with greenery. "Oh, Martha, it's beautiful, the most beautiful cake I've ever seen." "A true vision," Luke added. "It better be, it weighs seventy-five pounds when put together," Sam said. "Wow!" Luke commented. "Now, we'll see if it's edible," Sam joked.

Martha slapped his hand gently, "We eat our meal first, Dear."

One of the ladies, helping in the kitchen, came to Luke and asked if it was time to serve the meal; it would be ready to serve in ten minutes. He told her to come get his attention when it was ready by raising her hand over her head and making a figure eight in the air, then he would inform everyone it was time to eat. She smiled at him and said, "Sure thing, I'll do that." She left and hurried back to the kitchen. Less than ten minutes later, she reappeared and signaled Luke. He nodded, then stood and informed the guests that the food was ready. He and his Bride started the procession to the food table. Everyone ate and visited a while, then Sam announced that Matt and Stacy wanted to try out a couple of games they had come up with for the guests at the ranch when it opened. The guests were all in. After they finished the games, Matt raised his glass to make a toast. "To my sister and Luke, I wish you the best of everything in life and love." Everyone shouted, "Here! Here!" The band Matt hired started to play and Sam introduced the Bride and Groom's first dance. Luke two-stepped and twirled his bride around the dance floor through the whole song; then returned to their seats as the guests filled the dance floor. They opened their gifts and while the guests were dancing and enjoying themselves; they slipped out and went to their bedroom to change into their traveling clothes for their trip to Sedona, AZ for their honeymoon. Luke wanted to show her the country and his home place, which she thinks he sold; a surprise for her. Once in the room, she asked if they could leave the next morning because she was exhausted. He agreed and left the room; leaving her standing there alone. Luke came back a few minutes later and told her that Sam and the rest of the wedding party would see the guests out when the party was over. He, also, told her that the cook he hired would serve them breakfast in bed and then they would be on their way. She kissed him thoroughly, then asked for his help in getting her gown off. He was happy to oblige her.

CHAPTER 34

The next morning, the newlyweds were brought out of their slumber by a knock on their door. Luke stepped into his jeans and answered the door. The cook stood there with a tray in her hand, "Mr. Luke, you did say seven am for your meal?" "Yes, I did. Go ahead and set it over on the table. Thank you, Mrs. Harper." She set the tray down and left the room. Luke closed the door and walked over to the table to see what was for breakfast, grabbed a piece of bacon, then slowly got back in bed. He looked at his wife; he couldn't believe how lucky he was. With a sly smile on his face, he waved the piece of bacon under her nose. Her nose twitched, her head turned and her eyes opened. She looked at him and smiled; a smile so big that he could feel her happiness. He leaned over and kissed her tenderly; she kissed him back with a passion that he felt running through his veins. He pulled back, "Now, let's not start anything, we have a long trip ahead of us. Time to eat and play later," he said laughing. "Okay, I'm getting up. What's for breakfast?" "We were supposed to eat in bed, but come over here to see what was prepared." She climbed out of bed, put on her robe, and went to the table. Before she could sit down, he grabbed her and set her on his lap. "Who said not to start anything?" She teased him and scrambled out of his lap and sat in her own chair. Before them were scrambled eggs, bacon, homemade biscuits and blackberry jam; it looked delicious. They ate in silence; Luke got dressed, told his wife that they would be leaving within the hour, and left the room. She sat there in dreamworld for a few minutes; reminiscing about the previous evening. She was so happy; wanted to shout it to the world, but decided she had better get dressed and get their bags downstairs. It was a good thing they packed yesterday; it wouldn't be such a rush today. This way they could stop by P3 on their way to Arizona.

With the wagon loaded, they headed for the P3 Ranch, arriving right at lunch-time. They couldn't refuse the invitation to join them, so she helped Martha prepare the meal and then they sat down to eat; Matt wasn't at the table. "I assume my little brother is out with Stacy again?" Sam and Martha looked at each other; they didn't want to tell Ralynn the truth, but if they didn't, she would never forgive them. "Something has happened. Tell me!" She asked them with a demanding tone in her voice. Sam took a deep breath, "Rae, Matt's in his room. Last night he had a severe attack of pain when we got back from the wedding. It was so bad; he couldn't even take Stacy home. He'll be mad we told you, but we thought you needed to know." "We just hated to tell you on your honeymoon." Martha added. Luke spoke up, "Got a room for us tonight?" "You always have a room here, you know that, Luke," Sam said. "I'm going to go see him." "Rae, not now. He just fell asleep a couple hours ago; let him rest some first." Luke placed his hand over hers to calm her down. "I'm sorry to ruin your guy's honeymoon," Martha said, looking so tired. Luke spoke up, "Family first, always. We can go another time.

Everything will still be there." "I'll make us some coffee; thanks for staying," Martha said. She was just about to Matt's door when she heard him cry out in pain. She opened the door to find him doubled over and squeezing his legs and bouncing to try to end the pain. She went to his bed; sat beside him and wrapped her arms around him tightly. Minutes passed before the pain subsided and he laid back down. She picked up the pillows he had knocked off the bed; fluffed them and placed them under his head. His breathing was a bit erratic; he was trying to calm himself. When he opened his eyes, he looked at her, "Sis, what are you doing here? You're supposed to be on your honeymoon. "No, I need to be here, you need me, I'm here to help, what can I do?" "Will you read to me?" "Sure, what do you want me to read?" "Do you remember the book Pa had started reading to us before they left?" "Oh, yes, Moby Dick." "Yes, that one, please." "Is Luke with you?" She nodded yes. "On your way to the library would you ask him to come see me?" "I'll do that. Be right back." She walked out of the room and found her husband with Sam in the kitchen. She sat beside him waiting for their conversation to end. "Something wrong, Honey?" "Matt's pain is really bad. He wants me to read to him so I'm headed to the library, but he wants to see you now." "Is his pain worse than before?" "I believe it is. I've never seen him suffer like this before." He gave her a hug and a kiss on the forehead. "I'll go now."

When she returned to Matt's room, Luke had him laughing just a little. She walked in and sat on the edge of the bed by her brother. Luke saw the book in her hand. "Moby Dick; a good book." "Pa was reading it to us before he left. I wanted to hear it again." "Well, you two enjoy it; I'm going to talk to Sam." "See you later, Luke," Matt said through clenched teeth. At that moment, Matt let out a scream that was so alarming; it sounded like a sick animal. She sat down beside him wrapping her arms around him and just holding him. Her cheek brushed across his forehead; he was hot. After fifteen minutes, or so, the pain eased. Ralynn took the pitcher off Matt's dresser and left the room. Outside his door, she leaned against the wall and slid to the floor; tears filled her eyes and ran down her cheeks. It was almost unbearable. She knew she had to be strong for her brother and he must not see her cry. She pushed herself up, wiped her eyes, and turned back to his room. "Matt, would Morphine work? "Yes, but ask Martha when she last gave me some. I don't want to take too much." "I'll be back in just a few minutes." "Thanks, Sis." She walked into the kitchen, stopped by the table, where Luke and Sam were sitting; she leaned over and kissed her husband. "How's he doing," Sam asked. "Not so good.

His screams are so deafening; I almost lost it. Martha, he wanted to know if he could have more Morphine yet. I think that we should get the doctor out here as quick as we can; Matt's running a high temperature. I've got to get some cool water and get back in there." "I'll get some fresh water from the well," Luke said. He grabbed a bucket and went out the door. "Martha, I think he has some kind of infection inside him along with the pain; causing his pain to worsen," Ralynn informed them. "Sam walked over to Martha, "I'm going outside to see if one of the boys will ride into town, if not, I'll go myself."

While waiting for Luke to bring in water from the well, she gathered the wash cloths to use to get Matt's temperature down. Luke came in and filled the pitcher and carried it to Matt's room for her. She poured water into the basin she had placed there before, and then placed the cloths in the water. "Anything I can do?" "No, Darlin, just be available if we need you." "Okay, I'll be in the kitchen. If I go out, I'll let you know." She nodded and continued cooling Matt's head as best she could. She put a cool cloth on his forehead, and as soon as it warmed, she replaced it with another cool one. She repeated this for hours, at least, it seemed that way, while waiting for Doc to get there. She didn't feel like she was doing him any good and let out a big sigh. "Thanks, Sis, that feels good." "You're welcome. Sam went for the doctor; they should be here soon." "Why, he cannot help me." "Matthew, you're running a high fever and that tells me you have an infection. I can't help with that, but I can try to keep you comfortable." "I wish I knew what that felt like. I'm never comfortable." "I know, I wish there was more I could do." "Just you being here helps a lot."

Doc arrived around four in the afternoon and went straight to Matt's room. He cleared everyone out and closed the door. He examined Matt thoroughly, and asked him several questions about his pain and if the pain is different than before. Matt told him the pain in his legs were severe; more than usual, but he was also having pain in his side and back just above his waist. Doc then asked him if he was emptying his bladder four times a day, like he prescribed. Matt said he thought he was. Then Doc asked him if he had a strange odor when he was using the catheter. Matt thought for a minute. "You know Doc, there is an odor. I just didn't think about it much." "Well, Matt. I'm pretty certain that you have a UTI." "What's that?" Urinary Tract Infection, that's where you have an infection in your urinary tract. It's common with those who have to use catheters. I'll need to go back to town and make you some antibiotics to help get rid of that." "Okay, Doc, thanks." Doc walked into the kitchen to speak to Ralynn. "I'm glad you are all here. I examined Matthew and he has a severe case of urinary tract infection." "How did he get that?" Sam asked. "Sometimes it's caused by the catheters. That's why they have to be sterilized. Any germs that get on them can cause the infection. After he uses them, they need to be washed and sterilized in hot water for about ten minutes. That's the only way to stop him from getting infections. Matts had this a while; it's just now rearing its ugly head. It's very painful and with the pain he already has, he never noticed the pain was in his side and lower back as well. Make sure he washes his hands before and after he uses the catheters; that will help as well. I need to go back to town and mix up an antibiotic for him so we can get rid of it. I'll return as soon as I can." "Okay, Doc, see you shortly," Sam said. "Oh, while I'm gone, he needs to stay in bed and keep him warm. If he needs to use his catheter, get a bucket and have him do it in bed. The more he's up the pain will get worse. He needs to stay in bed for at least a week and rest his body as much as he can. You can give him a double dose of Morphine in an hour. I'll be back," He walked out the door and headed into town.

Sam went into Matt's room to see how he was doing. How are you feeling, son?" "Not so good, Sam. My lower back, stomach and side are in such pain. I can deal with my legs most of the time, but this is different. Doc said I can get infections from using the catheters and all. Is Doc coming back?" "Yes, he'll be back in a couple of hours. Need some Morphine now?" "Yes, please, I thought Sis was getting it for me?" "I'll check on that right now." Sam left the room and found the newlyweds sitting at the kitchen table talking.

Ralynn was talking to Luke when Sam walked into the room. "Matt could use some Morphine now. He said you were getting it for him." "Oh, I lost track of time, I'll do that now." She went to the cabinet, took out the medicine, and picked up a spoon, and went to Matt. "I'm so sorry, Matt, I lost track time. Doc said we had to wait an hour before giving you more. Here." Matt opened his mouth for the nasty tasting medicine, and then gulped down some water. "Thanks, Sis. I think I want to sleep now, please close the door." She walked out of the room; shutting the door behind her. She entered the kitchen, catching the last of Sam and Luke's conversation. "Think if I sneaked Bullet into his room; it might help?" "Martha would kill you, Sam." Luke stated. "Nah! She loves me too much." Martha entered the room at that moment and asked, "What's so funny?" Luke sat there and shrugged his shoulders, Ralynn was putting the medicine away, so that just left Sam to answer. "Aww, Honey, I was just thinking that Bullet pulled Matt through last time." "You mean you are thinking of bringing that colt into the house again?" "Well, yes, I was." "Okay, you're responsible for cleaning the floor and whatever else," she said. "Yes, Honey!"

Sam headed out the door and Luke followed. "You do realize that Bullet is not small anymore, don't you?" "Yes, I know that, Luke, but I'll do anything to help that young man in there, and if I mess up the house, so be it! Sam said, directly. "I understand, Sam, I'd do the same." "I think you already did." "What's that?" "You're giving up your honeymoon, aren't you?" "Not giving it up, just delaying it for a while, besides my wife wouldn't enjoy herself if she knew Matt was sick and she wasn't here, and neither would I." "You're right there. One thing I should tell you now that you're married, don't corner that girl, she's smart and determined. When she's made up her mind, it's difficult to change it. Remember how she got kidnapped?" "She's not always that way, is she?" "No, but she does have her moments, just better and easier to let her have her way; if something doesn't work out, then she'll learn a valuable lesson." "Well, I can be that way, too; I guess that's something we both will have to work on."

Sam led Bullet into the house with Luke right behind. Sam let go of the lead rope and Bullet walked right up to the bed and started nuzzling Matt's cheek. Matt stirred a little, then his eyes popped open. "Bullet!" How did you get in here? Martha's going to have your hide and Sam's too." He threw his arms around Bullet's neck and just loved on him; Bullet returned his love.

Matt raised his head and saw Sam and Luke standing across the room. "Sam, Martha is going to skin you alive." "Nah, she loves me, besides she gave me permission this time." "Really?" "Yes, really. I do, however, have to clean the floor and any messes that might happen." "Okay," Matt said, and went back to loving on Bullet. He was glad he called him Bullet, instead of Silver, because his coat was turning a chestnut color, before he had even turned eighteen months old. The color of his mane is blonde and he stood, approximately, fourteen hands high now, and still growing. He was so glad that the colt has such an awesome personality and was easy to work with. He was certain that they could win the race next year, and he was sure going to work and train himself and Bullet to win. He was whispering in Bullet's ear, "I'm sorry I'm sick, boy, we could be training right now. Bullet whinnied as if agreeing with him. Matt scooted up in bed and asked Luke to adjust his pillows for him. He was still clinging to Bullet; he could feel his love go right through him. Just at the moment, Baylee came running into the room and jumped right upon the bed; making himself a place smack dab in between Matt and Bullet. He started licking Matt's and Bullet's noses, which caused Matt to laugh out so loud that it brought everyone running to see what was going on in his room. When they all arrived at Matt's door, they were amazed at what they were witnessing.

Matt was sitting up in bed with Baylee in front of him and Bullet at his side. His head was hanging low, which allowed his face to be licked by Baylee and his neck nuzzled by Bullet. He was laughing out loud. Everyone joined in. There was a knock at the front door and Ralynn answered it. There before her stood Doc; he walked in, headed straight for Matt's room, hesitated, and said, "What is going on in there?" "Go on in Doc and see for yourself." She followed him to Matt's room. Doc stopped in his tracks. "Oh, my, there's a horse in the house, Sam. A real live horse!" "Yes, Doc, there is a real live horse in the house. The best medicine for him, Doc, don't you think? Sometimes all it takes is love, Doc." "Yes, I can see it is doing wonders for him. Well, let's get him better so he can visit him outside. I'm sure Martha would prefer it that way, wouldn't she?" Martha laughed, "She sure would, but if it helps, we'll deal with it." Sam let the animals stay a while longer and offered Doc some coffee. They sat at the kitchen table and visited while Matt wound down his visit with Bullet and Baylee. Luke offered to take Bullet back to the barn and Sam, Martha stayed at the table, while Ralynn went to see Matt with Doc. "Matt, how's the pain now, son?" "It's eased up some since Sis gave me the Morphine, and I believe seeing Bullet and Baylee helped me get my mind off of it." "I'm sure it did and you were having a time; nice to hear you laugh again, but we have to treat this infection so you can get back out to see that beauty in the barn. I'm surprised Martha or your sister let Sam get away with it." "Sam has a way with the ladies, Doc." "Does he, now?" He laughed as he took a bottle of medicine from his bag and showed it to Matt and Ralynn. "Now, this is the antibiotic that I mixed up for you; take one tablespoon, three times a day and no skipping. Take this for ten consecutive days. You'll start to feel better in about three or four days, but you continue to take it. We want to get that infection all the way out of your body." "Yes, Doc." Matt opened his mouth as Doc gave him his first dose. "Well, it doesn't taste too bad," Matt said. "That's good to know; now, don't rush this, Matthew, or else you'll be right back in the same situation again, and you need to completely heal from this," Doc said. "Okay, Doc, I'll do as you say. I can have visitors outside of family can't I, Doc?" "I'd prefer you wait for at least three days. I need you to sleep and get complete rest, this will make you sleepy; let me know if you see any blood in your urine, if you do see blood, have someone let me know; I'll need to increase the dosage. After three days you can have Stacy over as often as you want." He laughed as he finished Matt's treatment, then left the room. "Sis, can you blow out the lamp and close the door; I'm sleepy." "Sure, little brother, goodnight." She closed the door and went to find her husband. Doc was talking to the family in the kitchen and explaining the dosage of the antibiotic and that Matt was to have three full days of complete rest, then he could have visitors outside of the family. "No problem, Doc, we'll take care of him," Sam said. "I'll be back in ten days to two weeks, unless you need me. Goodnight." Sam saw him to the door, Doc crawled up into his buggy and left. "Is Matt still up?" Luke asked, messing with a deck of cards. "No, he wanted to sleep. I think Baylee and Bullet wore him out; he was having a good time with them. They have such a cool relationship," Ralynn said. "We need more days of his laughter around here," Sam stated.

The next few days were rough for everyone. Matt cried out in pain several times and the Morphine helped, but it never completely took the pain away. Sam helped watch for blood in Matt's urine; so far so good. "Hey, Sam, how many days have passed since Doc was here?" "Three, I believe. Why?" "Doc said I could get up and have company. I'd really like to see Stacy, Darby and Bullet." "Want me to send one of the cowboys to let Stacy know?" "I sure would appreciate it, Sam." "Is there anything else I can get for you?" "Do we have any extra milk?" "We should have, but I'll ask the wife to be sure. Frozen pudding sure sounds great, don't you think?" "It does. I'll even go to the neighbors to get milk if I have to." Sam went into the kitchen to see about the milk and Martha laughed when he told her about his and Matt's conversation. "See you in an hour or so," she said. "Why?" "You promised to get some milk.

We don't have enough here for frozen pudding." "Oh. I'll be back." He stepped outside, went and got his horse, mounted him, found Sonny and sent him on his way to deliver Stacy the message, and he went the opposite way to get milk; he just hoped he wouldn't have to milk the cow, but he did.

Sam got to the neighbor's house that had the milk cow. They told him he could have all he wanted, but he would have to milk the cow himself. He thanked them; then went to work milking the cow. His hands were too big to milk a cow, that's why it was easier for women and children to milk cows; their hands were smaller. He struggled to keep his hands around the teats, because her udder was tight and full. He started slowly, but he finally got the job done. He took the bucket of milk to the neighbor's house; the woman strained it and filled his container full.

Sam rode back to P3; arriving close within the hour that Martha expected him. She was smiling when he came in through the back door. "Here's the milk, Honey." "Did you have to milk Poppy, dear?" "Yes, but I got the container full this time." "Well, that's grand. I'll start the pudding; will you get some ice from the ice house for me?" "Sure, Honey, anything for my family."

A few hours later, dinner was served and then dessert. Martha took a bowlful into Matt. "I heard you wanted some of my frozen pudding?" Matt sat straight up in bed. "Yes, I do. Did you make some?" "I did, just for you." "Thanks, Martha, I love you." "I love you, too, Matt." She started to leave and then said, "Holler if you want more." Then, she walked out of the room. The next few days,

Matt, seemed to get better; Sam watched daily for any traces of blood and thankfully found none. He thanked God in a silent prayer. Matt could see visitors now and couldn't wait to see Stacy. He hoped she could come by.

Stacy came by the next day and Matt's spirits perked up, enormously. She came by every day and sat with him or went with him out to see Darby and Bullet. Baylee kept close to Matt, whether he was inside or out, as if protecting him. He and Stacy were sitting close on the front porch one afternoon, he leaned over to kiss her and Baylee started barking and jumping around like he wanted to scare her away. It took a few minutes for Matt to get him calmed down. He explained to Baylee that Stacy wasn't hurting him, she was giving him love and he didn't have to worry or be jealous of Stacy. Finally, Baylee found a cool spot on the porch, laid down, and went to sleep.

One the sixth day, Matt was out in the barn training with Bullet and Darby. If no one saw his legs, no one would know that Matt wasn't' the pillar of health. Luke and Ralynn were staying the duration of the ten days to make sure they were there when Doc came by. Ralynn was helping Martha around the house and Luke was working the ranch with Sam. If everything looked good after Doc's visit, they would go back home to their ranch, The Crooked Creek Ranch, if not, they would stay for a while longer. Luke would go back to the ranch to check on things and then return to the P3 in the evening; he wasn't about to spend a night away from his beautiful wife.

The days passed by quickly, and Matt was getting stronger every day. Doc gave him a clean bill of health and each one breathed a deep sigh of relief. He was beside himself and happy to get back to training Bullet; he was ready to ride. Doc discouraged him; wait a week before riding, build up your strength a bit more. He could ride Darby, since she was a gentle ride, but Bullet was a colt and very excitable, he wasn't ready for Matt to be jolted around just yet. He wanted him to heal completely and have his strength back to its fullest potential. He, also, told Matt that he needed to pay closer attention to his body and not force it into changes so quickly. Doc sat down with him, telling him that, although, he cannot walk and he can't feel his legs, doesn't mean that he couldn't get hurt, such as when he took out trash and burnt it, he needed to pay attention where his legs were, because the simplest bump up against the hot trash barrel could easily give him a third-degree burn and he wouldn't even feel it. He had to be careful. "Okay, Doc, I will; I promise."

Ralynn had been listening to the conversation and decided that it was time to go home to her and Luke's ranch. At dinner that evening, she and Luke let everyone know of their plans. "Well, I'd say it's about time, Sis. I was wondering how long Luke was going to continue sharing you with me." "Oh, brother of mine, he would have allowed me to stay as long as needed. He may not have liked it, but he loves me and you." "That's right, Matt, I'm always here if you need me or even if you just want to visit, just say the word," Luke explained. "Thanks, Luke, but it's time for you both to go home. I'm releasing you from any responsibilities and obligations, so go home!" "Are you sure?" "Luke asked. "Yes, I'm sure. It's time to start your lives together, so yes, go home." "Okay, then, it's settled; we go home tomorrow morning." "That's as it should be," Martha said. Sam agreed.

EPILOGUE

Six Months Later:

Themarker The Grand Opening for the Crooked Creek Ranch had turned out to be a glorious day. Ralynn and Luke had been busy hiring people for needed jobs, ordering supplies, and preparing for events, like the rodeo today. Matt and Stacy were hard at work promoting and marketing the ranch. It took four months to get everything ready and in working order to start moving the horses Luke had bought, into the corrals and barns. He had started training horses about two months ago and he felt he had purchased some of the finest horses around; some he would sell after they were fully trained and others, he would leave a bit rank for the rodeos. She had the monster of a house, in order and gleaming. She was excited to show off the place; all bad memories gone. She was checking off things that had been accomplished on her list when she felt the need to throw up and ran to the water closet; and did just that. She hadn't been sick, but lately, she found herself with an upset stomach more than not. She cleaned herself up and returned to her chores. Guests would be arriving soon and everything had to be perfect. Matt and Stacy were behind the courtesy counter to welcome their guests and Stacy had seen her return to the entry hall. Stacy walked over to her, "Ralynn, are you alright?" "Yes, I'm fine, just the jitters I suppose." "How long has this been going on?" "Oh, off and on for about two months. It's just nerves. I'm fine now." "You know I have two married sisters, right?" "I've seen the signs and girl, you are pregnant. I'd bet on it." "I couldn't be, we've only been married six months." "What does that matter?" "I don't know. I just never thought of being a mom." "What about your monthly, how long has it been since your last one?" Stacey asked. "I don't remember, a couple of months . I just thought it was my nerves and all. It has been chaotic around her," she replied. "Well, I'd bet my best horse on the fact that you are." "Does Luke suspect anything?" "If he does, he hasn't said a word." "Should I tell him today, of all days?"

"I would, he'd be the happiest man on earth." "I saw him walking out to the horse barn just a few minutes ago." She handed Stacy her notebook and went to find her husband. She found him at the corral gates looking over his rodeo herd of horses and bulls; both corrals were full. She stepped behind him and wrapped her arms around him. "A penny for your thoughts?" She said, leaning around him to kiss his cheek. "Just thinking how far we have come in such a short time." "Yes, it has been quite a ride." "Yes, it has darling." "Are you happy Babe?" She asked him, teasingly. "Yes, very much so. I don't think I could be any happier." He pulled her around in front of him and kissed her, deeply. When he lifted his head, he saw a glimmer in her eyes and a glow around her. "You're so beautiful, my wife." "Why, thank you, my husband, but I think I can make you even happier." "I don't know how," he said, looking at her curiously. She was just about to tell him her news, when the pounding of hooves were coming upon them. Luke turned around to see Sam and Martha in the carriage, and the cowboys of P3 Ranch coming up the road. "Luke, I need to talk to you." "In a minute, Honey, I have to tell these boys what their positions are in the rodeo line-up." He walked away, leaving a frustrated Ralynn standing at the gates, alone. Sam pulled the carriage to a stop and helped Martha down. She walked over to Ralynn and saw the disappointed look on her face. "What's wrong Sweetie? This is a great day; you should be ecstatic." "I am, Martha, but I really needed to talk to Luke." "He's just busy, he'll be around all day." "Martha, I'm pregnant." "What!" Martha screamed and hugged her so tightly, she found it hard to breath. "You're squeezing me too tight." "Oh, I'm so happy for you," she said. "You know what that means, don't you, Martha?" "Yes, you're going to be a mother." "Yes, that and the fact the you and Sam are going to be grandparents." "Oh, that is even more wonderful. Wait until Sam hears the news." "Do not tell Sam, yet. He gets excited and will let it slip. I haven't told Luke. I was getting ready to when you all arrived." "Well, don't you think you should?" "He's busy." "So, what, go interrupt him and give him the news, otherwise, you'll be miserable all day." Just then, her stomach turned over and she looked at Martha with her hand over her mouth. "Come with me around the corner here. Now, let it out." She bent over and threw up; Martha holding back her hair. Martha went over to the carriage and retrieved a container of water and a kerchief. She washed Ralynn's face and gave her a drink. "What would I do without you. I think I should call you mom from now on." "That's something we'll talk about later, right now, find your husband and give him the news, if you don't and he sees you throwing up, he'll worry all day." "Okay. Matt and Stacy are at the entry counter just inside the house, if you'd like to go in. I'll be up in a few minutes.

Ralynn searched the horse barn and couldn't find her husband, so, she went back out and looked around the corrals. She spotted him over by the bull pen, talking to the cowboys. One of the boys saw her and tapped Luke on the shoulder to get his attention. "I think your wife needs you, Luke." Luke turned around and saw her standing there just watching him. "I'll be back boys." He went into the barn, walked through, and came out the other side to stand beside his wife. "Something wrong, Honey?" "No, but I need to talk to you, it's important." "Sure, what's up?" "Remember when I said earlier that I could make you happier than you are now?" "Yes, you were teasing me. We don't have time for that, now, you little tease." "Oh, stop! It's not that. I wanted to tell you that you're going to have to work harder than you thought." "Really?" "Yes, because we are going to have another mouth to feed." "What did you do; get another stray or something?" "Seriously, Luke. I'll just say it; I'm pregnant." "Oh, is that all? Okay, Honey, I have to get back to work, the guest will arrive any minute." He kissed her and went into the barn. He was walking through and stopped dead in his tracks; she's pregnant. He turned and ran out of the barn, saw her standing there with that glow around her he had seen earlier. "A baby?" He took a few steps forward and wrapped his arms around her, then took his right hand and laid it on her tummy. "Are you sure?" "I am. This is good news, right? I wasn't planning on having a family this soon." "Yes, this is great! We're having a baby!" He shouted aloud for everyone to hear. He shouted again. That time it caught Sam's attention and he came running. He reached the couple, speechless, then he shook Luke's hand and congratulated them. He, then picked up Rae and swung her around, laughing. "So, you think you'll like being a grandpa?" she asked him. "Oh, Rae, I'll be the best grandpa ever." He put her down and hugged her. "Well, it's time to get this party started," Luke said. Sam walked away and started greeting guests.

Luke stood there with her for a while, just looking at her and rubbing her tummy. "I love you, Luke." "I love you, too. Look at all of this, he waved his arm towards their surroundings, and now a baby; it all happened because of the beginning of a few moments between us."

DEDICATION

This book I dedicate " IN THE MEMORY OF MARY L WAGGONER-CHITWOOD," to my mother. She believed I could, someday, write this novel. The song, *"Together Forever,"* was written by: Mary L. Waggoner, for my own wedding. I love and miss you mom.

Also to Mike Heltzel and Shelley Walker for inspiration and support.

SYNOPSIS

Before modernization began, the West was still wild in the mid 1800's, and families faced all kinds of hardships, rustlers, kidnappings, theft, killings, and etc. While still working with and against the changing weather, wild animals and Indians. It was no different for the Parker family of the P3 Ranch in Archer, Wy. It was a year like no other, but they faced each challenge head on. Lives changed dramatically for this family, but amid all the chaos, friendships grew, love blossomed, and miracles happened.

Brother and sister, Matthew and Ralynn Parker, grew up fast this particular year and became adults with responsibilities before their time. Will they survive the evils that await them and the decisions they need to make? Will a stranger appear in their lives and make a difference by helping them or causing them more harm?